Books by Shelley Katz

ALLIGATOR
THE LUCIFER CHILD
THE SHADOW PRESIDENT

THE
SHADOW PRESIDENT

Shelley Katz

A DELL BOOK

Published by
Dell Publishing Co., Inc.
1 Dag Hammarskjold Plaza
New York, New York 10017

To my sister, Lesa

ISBN: 0-440-17875-4

Printed in the United States of America
First printing—February 1982

THE
SHADOW PRESIDENT

INTRODUCTION

Even at six o'clock in the morning Los Angeles lay like some great, stunned beast in the grips of a heat wave that had broken all records. For ten days straight, thick, poisonous smog blanketed the city while a white-hot sun beat down mercilessly. Everything that wasn't melting was parched and brown, as dried out as the tanned hide of a Beverly Hills housewife.

Held in the grip of temperatures hovering around the 110-degree mark, the elegant wooded areas of Beverly Hills burst into flames; while below, the residents of Hollywood started fights with one another.

Since the onset of the heat wave the Los Angeles Police Department had noted a marked increase in homicide and assault. In contrast, there was an equally sharp drop in rape. This was no weather for exertion.

As alarm clocks went off all over the city, the temperatures were already well into the nineties. Those unlucky enough not to be able to escape to the mountains or seashore opened heavy eyes, smacked sleep-dried mouths, and padded their way to cold showers, angrily cursing. A weather that was taken for granted had suddenly rebelled.

As the heavy-panting city slowly awakened, the Beverly Continental Hotel was alive with activity. Secret Service men were all over the sprawling modern building, crouching on the roof like insects. The crackle of shortwave radios disturbed the airless morning, and the clipped words of those used to giving and getting orders seemed out of place in the tropical stillness.

On the top floor, in the air-conditioned presidential suite that for once deserved its name, President Robert M. Lacey and his wife, Elaine, still slept.

Even sleeping, Lacey looked presidential. His features were strong and rugged, nose a bit too prominent, brow a bit too ridged, uncompromising features that promised honesty and power.

There were those who said it was the way Lacey looked, more than anything else, that had won him the presidency when he was just a dark-horse senator from Illinois with an embarrassing habit of honesty.

No one was saying that anymore.

Lacey was a man with a dream. He believed in America; he believed in its strength, its potential, its destiny. Once again words like "honor," "pride," "morality," and "hard work" were being used.

Lacey's speeches were elegant, his gestures brilliant, but it was the force of his dream that captured the people. As he spoke, the creeping cynicism and bitterness that had held America for so many years vanished. He reminded the country that it was young and vital, that it had strength and purpose. He rekindled the dream.

Almost immediately after his election Lacey made a clean sweep of the White House, turning out the hacks and replacing them with men of conviction and purpose. Suddenly government was flooded with the young and the able. New ideas flowed easily and quickly up the chain of command to a President who was eager to listen. The press was embraced as a partner rather than an adversary; the electorate, treated with respect rather than callousness. America was beginning to turn around both domestically and internationally, for the first time without resorting to war.

Not that Lacey didn't make mistakes. He did, though he had that rare ability to own up to them without tarnishing his luster. Not that Lacey was all-powerful. The growing stranglehold of industry on government was perhaps the most important plank of his platform, and in four years he had done little to correct that. It wasn't that Lacey wasn't very human. He had a bad temper, and everyone knew about it. He had fits of depression when he became morbidly philosophical. And America knew about that, too.

But Lacey was the best of America. He was the kind of man who had braved the Atlantic Ocean and stalked the vast plains of early America, carving order out of chaos. He was the kind of man who had hunkered into the small on-the-come cities and made them his own.

And now he was about to make the announcement that he would run for a second term. Though Lacey was no god, he was the closest America had to such a being. Even his enemies had to concede it would take a catastrophe to deprive him of reelection.

As sunlight tipped through a crack in the closed curtains, Elaine Lacey stirred and looked across the rumpled bedclothes at the uncompromising face she knew better than her own.

Had reflection been possible so early in the morning, Elaine might have thought about the thirty years of happiness she'd had with him. Even counting the wrenching death of their only child and the long nights without Lacey while he was in some city she couldn't keep track of, Elaine would have lain there in the early morning half-light with the warmth of her husband only inches away and rated her life as rich and whole and real.

But six o'clock in the morning was not a time for reflection. And in a few hours it would be too late.

While President Lacey slept peacefully under his wife's loving, if slightly numb, gaze, J. J. Foyle was wide awake. He sat on the edge of his unmade bed, sipping tepid instant coffee, staring at early-morning television with red-rimmed eyes.

On the screen a gray, lanky geology teacher was droning on about the Mesozoic Era. Foyle leaned forward, straining to understand a vocabulary and concepts his brain had never been meant to grasp. For a moment he felt as if he understood what was being said, but just as quickly everything shifted like a cloud, and he was staring blankly again.

Angrily he shut off the television and grabbed a small black notebook from the crippled old nightstand beside his bed. He hesitated before opening it, running his thick, dirty thumbnail along the fake leather grain of the cover.

He wouldn't let himself open it yet. First he would savor what he knew was inside. He could visualize his scrawled blotty handwriting, setting out in minute detail the preparations he'd made. Who would have believed that J. J. Foyle, a man who had been kicked around more in his short life than a ten-year-old's football, would be capable of such painstaking care?

The thin young man smiled, and his intense little knot of a face resolved into almost boyish happiness. Then slowly he opened his precious notebook.

They would be pleased with the preparations he had made. They would all say to one another it had been well worth the money to take on that man Foyle. Yes, in just a few short hours they would be very pleased.

Whoever they were.

At exactly six thirty Senator E. Bud Fuller entered the Beverly Continental Hotel and was directed to a special bank of elevators. As Fuller entered the only elevator allowed up to the top floor, he smiled at the Secret Service man. Though as a senator and a member of the Lacey Brain Trust, Fuller, with his thick mop of prematurely white hair and tanned, youthful body, was well known all over Washington, he received no response. Fuller had been around Washington long enough not to be surprised. The legion of mirror-glassed men who surrounded the President seemed to pride themselves on living up to the blank-faced Secret Service image, as if some Xerox machine at the Pentagon had gone berserk.

When Fuller had first arrived in Washington, many years ago, he'd been told the Secret Service men wore short haircuts and mirror glasses for a reason. But he knew that was only part of the story. Men wore uniforms, especially in Washington. During the Kennedy era it had been dark, well-cut suits from a good East Coast shop. When Nixon was around, the White House could have been the central office of IBM. And now that Lacey was in, he'd transformed even the most confirmed of the D.C. dandies into the kind of guy who bought suits with two pairs of pants.

Fuller snickered to himself. Lacey could make even a five-hundred-dollar jacket look as if it were ready for the Salvation Army truck. If Elaine ever let that man into a clothing shop alone, he'd come out with the only sharkskin suit in existence. Fuller smiled broadly and ran his fingers through his thick mop of hair. It was part of Lacey's charm.

But as the elevator arrived at the top floor, Fuller's smile faded. He could feel his eyelid begin to twitch, and his body felt taut like a stretched-out rubber band.

Fuller had been with Lacey since the beginning. He'd picked him out of all the eager young faces that crowded into the Senate every few years. Men like Lacey came along rarely, sometimes never, in a man's career. And once you saw them, there was no mistaking their potential. When you were confronted with a man like Lacey, there were only two choices: You could hate him or love him. Fuller had chosen love.

No two men had ever been closer, as both friends and colleagues. With unwavering devotion, for over ten years, Fuller had helped Lacey forge his career; he helped him grow and flourish as a senator; he helped him gain the nomination and win as President. And from behind the scenes, as a member of the Lacey Brain Trust, he helped him create the century's most remarkable administration.

Today was to be the crowning achievement of Lacey's

14

career. Today he would announce the new Salt agreement with the Russians and confirm that he would be running for a second term. Yet Fuller knew all too well that the seams were starting to show. Things were beginning to unravel. And as Fuller entered the Lacey suite, where the four other members of the Brain Trust were waiting, he wondered tensely if they'd be able to stop it before it was too late.

They were all there, the best and the brightest, Paisley, Keiler, Colton, and Nadler. Together with Senator Fuller, they constituted the Lacey Brain Trust, the five most elegant minds in Washington. They were sitting around the living room of the ornate gold and rose Presidential Suite, waiting for Lacey to call them into the other room, making what seemed to be just idle conversation. But in fact, the air crackled with tension. Only Elaine Lacey didn't seem to notice it. She was sitting in the corner of the room, pouring coffee. In her burnished pink morning robe, she looked like a delicate Victorian lady, a creature from another era.

"Jed McKuen's in town," Representative Louis Paisley said as Fuller walked in. Paisley was small and weaselly-looking, with slicked-back blond hair and a finished smile, legacy of the tens of thousands of dollars spent to educate him. Though he was in his early thirties, his eyes were very old, beyond pity or anger, beyond any hunger at all, except maybe survival.

Fuller smiled tensely. "Jed's one of those guys who figure just because they're breathing and still occupy an office, they aren't dead."

Paisley laughed. "It's certainly hard to believe he

15

doesn't understand. Not with a stack of unanswered phone messages higher than the Trade Towers."

John Thomas Colton, a thin, wispy gray-haired man with the rumpled air of a college professor, was staring into his coffee cup. He was the oldest of Lacey's Brain Trust and by far the most successful. As chairman of the board of Rock Island Oil and head of the Colton family banking and industrial interests, he had a personal fortune tipped way over the millions into the astral region of billions. Yet among the brash young Lacey men, he was always soft-spoken, almost differential.

"Jed asked me to tell Lacey he must see him right away," Colton muttered into his coffee cup. "After all, he is assistant attorney general. He has the right to see the President."

Paisley waved Colton's words away with his hand, like a disturbing gnat.

General Nadler, a young baby-faced man with a mind like a computer, and Justice Samuel Keiler, a stalklike man with one of the greatest legal minds to come out of the South, turned away. They were sitting this one out.

But Colton wasn't finished. "I think he wants to talk to Lacey about the two Russian scientists."

Paisley cut him off. "You know exactly what the hell he wants to talk to Lacey about. And those Russian scientists aren't the half of it." Paisley was sitting forward, fixing Colton with his cool, ironical gaze.

Fuller glanced over at Elaine, wondering if she was listening to what they were saying, hoping that she was not.

But Elaine obviously was listening, and it was Fuller

16

she fixed with her porcelain gaze. "I don't understand. Why won't Lacey see Jed?"

Fuller's eyes retreated to his coffee cup, and he ran his fingers through his brush of white hair. "It's not that Lacey won't see him."

"Well, it certainly sounded like it. Jed's been with us since the beginning. What has he done?"

Fuller glanced around at the others, but they were all avoiding his eyes. It was his problem.

"It isn't what he's done," Fuller answered after a while. "It's just that he isn't exactly a friend, if you know what I mean."

"Since when have we gone in for that friend–enemy business?" Elaine asked, surprised.

Fuller looked away, embarrassed. How could he possibly explain to Elaine what was happening? He was having trouble understanding it himself.

Fuller was still trying to frame an answer when suddenly the door to the bedroom burst open.

"Get your asses in here!" Lacey called out heartily. "I've got one hell of a busy day ahead of me."

Jed McKuen, the man whom Lacey's Brain Trust was just discussing, climbed into his rented Pinto and turned toward Beverly Hills. His angular face was tight and determined; his hands clutched at the wheel, full of pent-up tension. He felt like a fool. Leaving Washington in order to see your boss whose office was only a few blocks away from yours was hardly a logical plan. But it had been well over a month since he'd been able to see Lacey. His Brain Trust had taken care of that. Perhaps with the press crawling all over the place,

Jed would be able to embarrass Lacey into seeing him. At least it was worth a try.

The garish billboards and neon signs strung along Sunset Boulevard like a cheap necklace seemed to intensify Jed's black mood. The tall, lean, almost Lincolnesque man, with dark black eyes that burned deep from his face, glared out at the rough-and-tumble, hustling America with a revulsion that had made him a monumentally effective consumer advocate by the age of twenty-five.

In the early years, when Lacey was a senator from Illinois, he had supported Jed both publicly and privately. He believed strongly that big business had a grip on America which was becoming a stranglehold. He too knew that more members of Congress owed their elections to the boardrooms of oil companies than to the electorate. And when Lacey was elected President, he backed up his support by making Jed assistant attorney general with the special assignment of discovering the role of industry in government.

At thirty-two it had been a hell of a coup for Jed. But personally he remembered locking himself into his apartment and shaking with fear for three solid days. It was an enormous job, overwhelming, and he believed too much in America and Lacey to think a punk from Oregon with an overactive sense of justice could fill it.

Later he'd come to realize that Washington was filled with young punks from all over, some a lot less experienced and smart than he. Besides, Lacey believed in him, and Lacey didn't make mistakes about people. Lacey didn't make mistakes about anything. At least that was how it had seemed.

Those early days had been exciting. Lacey had organized a headhunting unequaled since Kennedy raped the universities of their finest. He'd gathered the best brains in the country to the seat of government. Everyone wanted to become a part of the Lacey administration. Lacey had a dream, and he was going to let the whole country share in it. The feeling had been open, honest, freewheeling.

Until the past year. That was when everything began to close down. Slowly doors slammed all over the White House; there were knots of men in the corridors, and the open, honest Lacey administration was beginning to erode.

As Jed swung his car south toward Wilshire Boulevard, he felt his heart pounding in his chest. He felt like John Dean crawling into the President's office to tell him there was a cancer on the presidency. And he felt scared, too.

Nothing was as it had been. The special investigation of big business's role in Congress was being balked. The strange claim of Russia that America had stolen two of its laser specialists and smuggled them into the United States was rushed through his office while he was away for the weekend. But worse, there were growing rumors about Lacey and the Delano girl. Rumors he was ordered not to investigate.

He supposed he knew why now.

The noise in the boiler room of the Beverly Continental was deafening. J. J. Foyle waited in line at the door as the employees were searched by the Secret Service. Foyle's thin face was knotted tightly; his short, thin fingers flexed nervously. Even though he had nothing incriminating on him, fear was making a meal of his insides. He was positive he would succeed, but he knew he could fail.

After submitting to the search, Foyle punched in, then walked through the gray inner workings of the hotel, the roar of machinery all around him. He opened his locker, slipped into his gray-green coveralls, and neatly folded his street clothes.

The overhead pipe was only a foot away. In his mind he could see the .38 wrapped tightly in plastic, held to the inside with strong surgical tape. He would have given anything to open up the pipe and check that the gun was still there. It was possible that the Secret Service had gone over the place with X rays, found the gun, and now was waiting for Foyle to make his move.

He rummaged around the bottom of his locker and found his suit and tie. He touched the shoulder pad with the press pass sewn inside and felt its edges under his fingers. He looked at the shoulder pad closely. There were no signs that anyone had torn any of the threads or resewn it. If they'd found the gun, they would have found the pass. He was in the clear.

"Got a hot date tonight?" Foyle whirled around, still clutching his suit jacket. Sid Feinstein, the head janitor, was looking at Foyle's suit jacket, an ironical smile on his gray, lined face. He was leaning against the pipe where Foyle had hidden the gun.

Foyle felt himself shiver and hoped Feinstein hadn't noticed. "Yeah. A date."

Quickly he slammed the locker shut, trying to appear as relaxed as possible, but his muscles were tightening, and the skin on his face felt two sizes too small.

Feinstein seemed to watch him too long, his lined old face twisted into that ironical smile. Then he laughed.

"Well, tell her you swept the floor a President walked on. Maybe you'll get into her pants." He nudged Foyle playfully, then headed back into the bowels of the hotel.

Just one floor above the basement, President Lacey, flanked by a flying wedge of Secret Service men, swung through the glass doors of the Beverly Continental and hit the dragon-hot breath of Los Angeles.

Two Secret Service men watched from the limousine that stood waiting. Their bodies were alert, ready to spring, like stalking animals. If anything were going to happen to the President, it would be in the next six hours with its motorcades, factory visits, and handshaking.

When Lacey and his wife were seated comfortably in the limousine, the order to move out was given, and slowly the long line of cars slipped down the circular driveway to begin the long, grueling day.

Jed McKuen arrived at the hotel a moment too late, and all he could do was watch the black cars as they entered the traffic on Wilshire Boulevard and sped off into the smoggy Los Angeles morning.

As Lacey and his wife were waving at the crowds through the bulletproof car windows and Foyle was pushing his broom, the ballroom of the Beverly Continental sprang into activity.

The huge snakelike cables that would carry Lacey's address to every corner of America, as well as to the world via satellite, were brought in. Workmen pulled them along the floor, where they pooled into snake pits. Planks were set up to make a stage at the back of the room. A podium was put at the front of the stage, and two chairs were placed on either side.

At ten o'clock a tall wooden wall was thrown up between the stage and the rest of the room. From the moment the enclosure was erected, no one was allowed to enter the stage area.

Feinstein, who'd been head janitor of the Continental for close to twenty years, stopped in surprise when he saw the wall. He'd seen kings, shahs, and presidents pass through that ballroom, but never had he seen such security. Still, it meant less space for his men to clean, so to Feinstein the enclosure was welcome.

To George Howard, the manager of the Continental, the wall was just something else to make him nervous. Having a President staying at your hotel was a mixed blessing at best. And while all the security around Lacey should have been reassuring, it served as a constant reminder that something terrible could happen.

Howard reached into his jacket, slipped another Valium into his mouth, and swallowed it without water, then returned to the lobby to find someone to yell at.

At noon Feinstein heard a great deal of noise coming from behind the barrier. There was a brilliant flash of light, as if a big sheet of glass were reflecting sunlight. Then just as suddenly it was gone, and there were no further noises or flashes of light.

At five o'clock a hint of a breeze drifted through Los Angeles. All over the city, people paused, raising their faces and arms to the air. But almost immediately the breeze calmed, and once again everything was stillness. As if the world were waiting for something to happen.

Lacey's limousine slid back to the hotel, only two

hours off schedule. Sandwiched between Secret Service men, Lacey and Elaine pushed back to their suite, the press snapping at their heels like hungry animals.

Usually Lacey would have stopped, no matter how tired, and made a few remarks, even if it were only a private joke to one of the reporters. Today he didn't. As Jed McKuen stood in the lobby, fending off his own plague of reporters, he wondered if the reason was that he'd spotted him waiting.

The minute Lacey and Elaine hit the suite, they made a mad dash for the bathrooms. Among the various prerequisites for the presidency, strong kidneys ranked high on the list.

Lacey slammed the bathroom door and locked it, then turned on the cold water. Once again the terrible nausea overcame him, and he grabbed the sink with both hands. Salt flowed into his mouth, and his body began to shake. A freezing sweat stood out on his forehead. It was the illness again. With shaking hands he reached into his pocket and pulled out the tiny yellow pills his doctor had prescribed as a relief rather than a cure for the illness. There was no cure for radiation sickness, except perhaps time.

He caught sight of himself in the mirror and stopped. His face was cut with lines so deep they looked like scars. His dark brown eyes were wide and staring. He thought he had never seen such fear and anguish on a face in his whole life.

Suddenly Lacey was crying. Shoulders hunched, he covered his face with his hands. "Oh, God, I want to die," he whispered softly. "I just want to die."

Then slowly the nausea receded and Lacey straightened up. The deep lines in his face relaxed, and the fear was gone from his eyes. There were many kinds of death. Sometimes it could even be the beginning.

Alexei and Boris, as they'd been nicknamed by the few Americans who knew of their existence, sipped wretched instant tea out of styrofoam cups and stared out at the strange parade of traffic on Wilshire Boulevard. So far America was only a silent scene glimpsed through glass windows or seen briefly as it swept by their swiftly moving limousine. Later, of course, there would be the promised citizenship, the new papers, the dacha in the country, the facilities to continue their work.

Ever since they'd been abducted from Russia, two supposedly unimportant laser scientists who wouldn't have thought they had a prayer of getting into the United States, they'd been treated like visiting dignitaries. There had been sumptuous hotel suites, long black limousines, and, even more important, the most modern, efficient laboratory they'd ever seen. What they had expected, however, was the relatively simple pleasure of walking in the clear fresh air and the company of other human beings. And this they had not received. But they'd been promised that after tonight they would have that, too. Once the laser was set up. Once it was used and quickly removed, the world of America would open up to them.

Vaguely they wondered if they would be considered heroes. But mostly they drank their tepid drinks and thought of the pleasure that would be theirs soon, walking in the brilliant sunlight, their collars open to the soft, cooling breezes, a pleasant evening with newfound friends.

24

Unaware that in a few short hours they would be dead.

Most of the day shift had left the basement when Foyle returned to his locker. He dressed slowly, waiting until the night shift was at work; then quickly he opened the overhead pipe with a wrench and fished inside until he found the plastic-covered revolver.

He slipped it into his pocket and ducked into the men's room. There were four stalls; Foyle chose the third one as the least often used. He stripped off several pieces of surgical tape, hung the plastic-covered revolver in the tank of the toilet. Though no one else was in the room, he flushed the toilet, then carefully washed his hands.

Foyle walked back through the basement, punched his card, and placed it in the rack that indicated he would be working overtime.

"Have a nice evening," said the Secret Service man guarding the door as Foyle passed.

Foyle felt his heart jump for no reason. But of course, there was a reason, or at least soon there would be. "Some nice evening," he answered. "I'm working another shift after dinner."

A few pedestrians passed Foyle as he headed to a small restaurant around the corner. He had to hold himself back from taking them by the shoulders and shaking them. Look at me, he thought. Don't pretend you don't know who I am. I'm J. J. Foyle. I'm the man who'll murder President Lacey.

By six thirty the ballroom was crazy with activity. Crewmen rushed through the room, testing sound and camera equipment. There was the constant loud crackle of walkie-talkies as the Secret Service tried to hear one another over the noise. Reporters, smelling of tobacco, liquor, and garlic, were beginning to crowd in. They laughed and shouted across the room; already beads of sweat were beginning to mar their makeup.

The security guards around the wooden wall indicated to several of the hotel workmen that it could now come down. The crash of wood joined the rest of the din.

The noise and the last-minute rush reached even the most jaded reporters. Though it was highly unlikely that Lacey's speech would contain any news that wasn't anticipated, there was something about this gearing up that always thrilled and excited those attached to it. As the room filled, the elect, whose business it was to send an event into the homes of the world, began to feel a pride and importance in what they were doing. Unpaid bills, unfaithful lovers, and recalcitrant livers faded in importance.

If by this announcement Lacey became the hero of the hour, the press at least were the bards who recorded it for posterity.

When Foyle got back to the hotel, his stomach was a tight knot. He submitted to the body search, punched in, then headed for his locker. His throat was so tight he doubted that he could speak.

Suddenly Feinstein came out of the laundry room, where he'd been chatting and drinking coffee. He saw Foyle walking down the corridor and called out in surprise, "Hey, Foyle, I thought you had a hot date to-night."

Foyle stopped. Everything inside him lurched with fear. "I got stood up."

Feinstein was walking toward him, shaking his head. "Jeez, sorry about that. But what the hell you doing back here? This ain't no home for wayward boys, you know."

"I signed up for overtime."

"Unh-unh. No more overtime. You got enough already. I have Grievance on my back for giving you as much as I have."

Foyle felt his knees buckling. "Just this once. I promise it won't happen again."

"No deal. I got enough problems with the union as it is."

Foyle looked up and down the corridor desperately. He felt as if he were about to cry. "Please," he said. It was all he managed to get out.

Feinstein looked at Foyle, that strange, lonely shadow of a man who worked quietly in the basement, talking to no one, and felt sorry for him. He wondered how often a guy like him even got a date. And then to have it broken just like that. It was easy for a guy who had a wife at home. Fat though Sally was, at least she was something warm in the darkness.

"Okay," he said finally. "But I want you out of here by ten. You understand?"

"Don't worry," Foyle answered. "I won't be working any later."

Lacey stood by the window of his hotel suite, staring at the Rolls-Royces and Mercedeses on the street be-

27

low. He could imagine the slim, tanned bodies inside the cars, listening to quadraphonic rock and roll, thinking about a quick dip in the swimming pool before dinner. So many tanned bodies. So many swimming pools. The American dream gone mad. It was impossible for a boy from Pekin, Illinois, to understand such inhuman perfection.

"I wonder if anyone dies in California," Lacey said without turning from the window.

Elaine was sitting on the couch, sipping a glass of wine. "Absolutely not," she answered. "I hear they get zoned out on their fortieth birthday."

"Yeah." Lacey sounded tired. "I'll never understand how I carried this cockeyed city, you know? I mean, what could a bunch of suntanned tennis players see in me?"

Elaine smiled. Lacey was feeling his usual pre-speech jitters. It was amazing to her that a man who gave so many speeches still got nervous. "Are you worried you won't carry it this time?"

Lacey laughed, and there was a bitterness in his laugh that surprised Elaine. Lacey was many things, but bitter wasn't one of them. "Are you okay, Lacey?"

Elaine got up from the couch, walked over to him, and put her arms around his waist. Lacey didn't turn around. His body was rigid with tension, and Elaine could feel a muscle ticking nervously in his belly.

"What's going on with Jed McKuen?" she asked nonchalantly as she took a place by the window.

"What do you mean?" Lacey snapped.

"Why won't anyone talk to him? I asked Fuller, and he gave me some crazy answer that sounded pure

28

Nixon. Nadler and Paisley played dumb. Which isn't easy for those two foxes."

"Can we talk about it later?" There was an impatience in Lacey's voice that Elaine found almost as strange as the earlier bitterness. "I want you to go down to the ballroom early." Lacey added quickly, "Fuller and I have to say a few words to each other before the speech."

Elaine nodded, feeling the sting of his tone. For some time she had felt changes in Lacey. It was as if a barrier had gone up between them, a barrier she couldn't understand, couldn't even define.

Lacey smiled and put his arms around her tightly. Elaine could feel the tiny flutter of his heart against her cheek. It was so fragile, so like a little animal, that once again she was reminded of the vulnerability of human life. And with that thought came the memory of Brian, their nineteen-year-old son who had headed out for a night on the town and come back a twisted, broken mass she could only imagine in nightmares. She wondered if Lacey thought about Brian often. She supposed he did, though he rarely mentioned his name. Perhaps it was that which caused the barrier. But something inside told her it wasn't Brian's death that was bothering Lacey. It was something quite different. And very powerful. She didn't know what it was, but she felt if she tried hard enough, she could reach out and touch it. Elaine stopped herself automatically, as if she knew that whatever it was was too frightening, too terrible, and she didn't want to know about it at all.

Lacey and Elaine held close to one another for a moment longer; then a knock on the door interrupted them. And as Fuller entered, Elaine left with one of the Secret Service men.

Foyle sat in the third toilet stall. With the aid of a hand mirror, he clipped his long, greasy hair into almost military shortness. On his lap was the suit, his press pass already pinned to the lapel. All he would have to do was retrieve his revolver and he would be ready.

Suddenly fear gripped Foyle. Everything around him seemed to be moving; dizziness made him cling to the toilet bowl, as if he would fall off the earth. He forced himself to stand. His legs felt like Cream of Wheat, and he was gulping for air. He had come so far, so very far. It seemed typical of his whole life that it would end here, in the third stall of a crapper. Clamping onto the walls, he kept himself up, but the swimming fear held him for what seemed like an eternity.

Finally he forced himself to change into his suit. He opened the toilet tank and pulled out his gun. Then he took two strips of adhesive, placed each end along his groin, and covered the center of the adhesive with toilet tissue. He slipped his gun in and it was held like a holster.

Foyle flushed the toilet. Now that the gun sat in his groin, cold and hard, he felt much better.

As Elaine entered the ballroom, several members of the press smiled and waved to her. Elaine was a popular First Lady, just as Lacey was a popular President. Soft and feminine but with a sense of wit and style, she had that rare, indefinable quality that some people called being a lady. And the press loved her for it.

30

Elaine was given a seat to the right of center, and she sat in the line of empty chairs, feeling uncomfortable. Her sitting on the platform all alone was more than just a break with tradition, it was damned silly. Finally Fuller, Paisley, and Keiler joined her, and she felt less exposed.

As Elaine was waiting in the line of folding chairs, Foyle was being stopped by one of the Secret Service men checking press passes.

"You're awful late to be just showing up," the man said, mirror glasses glinting in the bright lights.

Foyle could feel the gun pressed tight to his groin. It no longer was cool and soothing but hot like fire. The men who had hired him had promised he'd be on the press list. But what if they'd forgotten or couldn't get him on?

"I haven't missed the speech, have I?" Foyle's voice sounded frantic.

"Naw. You've got two minutes till he goes on the air."

Foyle tried to keep his voice from shaking. "Traffic out there is terrible."

But the guard was no longer listening, and already the chain was being opened for Foyle to pass through.

The heat and the noise inside the ballroom were overwhelming. As Foyle pushed forward, he caught sight of the pale, delicate Mrs. Lacey sitting with her hands folded in her lap. Until then it hadn't occurred to him that Lacey wasn't just the President, he was a man with family and friends, he was a human being. Foyle watched the woman with fascination. Silently he apologized to the pale, delicate woman sitting only a few feet from him. Then he forgot all about her.

31

Over five minutes had passed since Elaine entered the ballroom, and she was beginning to get jittery. The rest of the day came creeping back on her, the tension of Lacey, the evasiveness of the Trust. Suddenly she felt that something important was going on. Nothing had seemed right all day, and yet she'd spun along, avoiding all the signs, terrified to confront the fear that always was just under the surface. She could lose Lacey, just as she had lost her son.

For the past month Lacey had traveled with his own private physician, Dr. Greenaway. And while Lacey had said he was doing it to calm her obsessional fear of his having a heart attack, she wondered now if Lacey weren't himself frightened. She quickly glanced to the side of the stage and saw the tall, stooped Dr. Greenaway standing in the wings. It made her feel better to see him there. If something were wrong with Lacey, Greenaway wouldn't be standing around, surveying the huge room of press and Secret Service with a good-humored smile on his thin face.

Then she saw the man.

He was standing toward the front of the crowd, a small, insignificant man with a tight, knotted face. His fingers were working at something. It took her a few seconds to realize it was his fly. Even several feet away she could tell he was sweating profusely. And his eyes were like nothing she'd ever seen in her life.

Elaine whispered to Fuller, "Second row. Fourth man to the right of center. I'm scared."

Fuller didn't seem to hear her. He just sat, looking out into the room, a smile pasted across his face.

"Bud, please, I'm scared. There's a man."

Still Fuller didn't answer. He just sat trancelike, staring straight ahead.

Elaine wanted to scream. The man in the crowd was reaching for something. She could see it from where she sat, and it looked like a gun.

Foyle held the revolver tight in his hand, the jacket of his suit covering everything. The heat of the gun was so intense it seemed to burn the flesh from his hand. Then everyone began clapping, and Foyle knew that the moment he'd waited for so long had come.

Quickly Foyle pushed to the front row, careful that he didn't touch the ring of Secret Service. He tried to imagine which of them had been paid off, but they all looked the same to him. It didn't matter in the end. All that mattered was that the man create a diversion after the shooting. A few seconds. That was all he needed. But he needed those few seconds badly.

Suddenly the applause was deafening. Lacey was at the door, bustling onto the stage with energetic steps, his strong, rugged face smiling.

Foyle started counting to thirty slowly. His hand felt numb; his whole body was shaking, and he could feel sweat trickling down his chest as if a thousand flies were crawling all over him.

Lacey paused at the back of the stage for what seemed like an impossible length of time, while the press applauded. Elaine was watching Lacey, but she kept glancing at the man. He'd moved up to the front row, and his hand was under his jacket. She felt as if she were locked in one of those terrible chase dreams where you fall and can't get up, where you can't even scream.

Lacey started forward. Foyle lifted his gun, silently

counting. All at once the awkward silencer caught in his jacket lining, and he panicked, trying to pull it out with force. Then he ordered himself to relax and slipped the gun free.

Again Lacey paused. It was as if he were trying to make himself a perfect target.

Foyle was no longer aware of what he was doing. By the time he reached thirty he was all instinct.

The bullet cracked. Loudly. The silencer failing.

Suddenly there was red everywhere. Spattering outward.

A scream. Then more screams.

Lacey was collapsing inward. He was slipping to the ground. Slowly. Almost like slow motion.

Everyone was held trancelike, screaming without understanding what was being seen. Elaine was blind, her voice silent. All she was aware of was the terrible red.

Only the Secret Service was alert and clear. The two men in front of Foyle lurched forward, grabbed his arm, threw the gun across the room, and forced him to the floor, while the rest of the Secret Service had formed a thick line of muscle and were shoving the screaming crowd out of the ballroom.

Elaine was trying to push to the back of the stage, but Fuller was holding her. Her mouth was open as if she were screaming, but there was only a hissing of breath as she clawed at Fuller to get to her husband.

Paisley and Keiler joined Fuller. They held Elaine tightly, saying things to her that she didn't hear.

Lacey was a limp pile of clothes on the ground. Two Secret Service men stood over the body. Other than that Lacey was alone. Even his doctor was being shoved away.

Within one minute almost everyone was gone from the ballroom. As Elaine was pushed from the room, she thought she heard an ambulance. But it was only the sound of her own scream.

Then there was total silence. Two Secret Service men surrounded the crushed body on the stage. In the center of the room Foyle lay handcuffed under the gaze of two other Secret Service men. He was crying softly, and a terrible stench came from him. He must have dirtied his pants in terror.

The hundreds of cameras and microphones stood deserted, like mute spectators, but many of them were still working, and all across the world people watched the silent room of death.

As the people huddled around their televisions, the all-to-familiar bulletins began to roll in.

"At exactly eight forty-five President Robert M. Lacey was rushed to UCLA hospital. He was pronounced dead on arrival. Every attempt was made to resuscitate the President, but even if they had been successful, the brain damage would have been massive and irreversible."

Endless diagrams were produced by an endless stream of doctors. "The bullet entered the right anterior portion of the skull, shattering it, forcing the parietal bone up into the scalp, fracturing the occipital bone along its lateral half. . . ."

At exactly 9:47 that evening, Vice President Chesapeake was sworn in at his family home in Roanoke, Virginia, where he had been watching the presidential address with his wife, daughter, and son-in-law. Immediately he announced that all of Lacey's administra-

35

tion and policies would be carried forward intact. Privately he added, For the next six months anyway. Elsa Chesapeake stayed by her husband's side that whole long night and the next day. But in her mind she was shifting furniture and planning new color schemes.

J. J. Foyle was characterized by those who knew him as a misfit, a loner. Feinstein shook his head solemnly. "He acted strange that day, all right. I knew he was up to something." And less than a week later it was all academic. Foyle died in his sleep of a massive coronary.

America was plunged into mourning. Once again the horror of the assassinations of the sixties was reenacted, the grim cortege, the streets lined with the frightened and the confused, the all-night vigil of the bereaved. Not since the death of Kennedy had the American people suffered such a loss. And this time it seemed worse, much worse. It would be a long time before America would be able to get over this death, maybe never. There was a terrible hopelessness and anger in the crowds as they watched their President torn from them. Before the souvenir men wove his image into garish rugs or struck his profile into gold coins, there was only the grief and outrage, the purity of mourning.

For days the front page of every newspaper in America carried pictures of Elaine. While all of America was allowed to cry at Lacey's death, only she was denied that right. She stood erect, pale, a frozen look of valor on her face. But everything inside her was collapsing. Guilt burned deep scars that would never heal. She'd seen all the signs.

She'd seen them and done nothing.

36

Chapter One

Jack Beal moved from rock to rock, his head filled with the roar of the rushing waterfall, his young, slim body moving finely underneath him.

It felt unearthly to be moving fast and smooth through the arid mountains, the bright, sharp sun above, burning his mind clean of all thoughts except his next step and a general sort of cosmic wonder. Gone, at least for a while, was the heart-contracting realization that this time he'd messed up his life but good.

It was late June, and the icy, rushing water was everywhere, catching the sun and reflecting it back into the air in dancing prisms, making damp rocks gleam black and gold. Every now and then a lizard slithered through the parched desert rocks down to the water. Occasionally a mountain goat appeared on one of the crests towering above him. Other than that he was all alone. Or at least that was what he thought.

SHELLEY KATZ

As Beal crossed the waterfall, skimming from boulder to boulder, it amazed him that he hadn't lost his touch. It had been close to five years since he'd been backpacking, and those five years hadn't exactly been filled with abstinence and clean living. On top of that his backpack weighed close to fifty pounds. Beal didn't care. He liked to be prepared for any emergency. Although he hadn't used his backpack in months, he kept it ready in his car trunk in case of germ warfare or nuclear holocaust.

Besides the tennis shoes and ripped long underwear he used for climbing, there was the usual cooking and camping equipment, a tape recorder and several boxes of tapes—what if you felt like Beethoven and all you had was Ronstadt?—a set of books on graphoanalysis which he'd been trying to learn for the past three years, two novels half read, his juggling balls, five harmonicas, including a large chromatic one, two knives, a camera, a barometer, a first-aid box, steel fishing wire, rope, safety pins, and a needle and thread.

This was typical Beal. Ever since he could remember, he'd been alert to all emergencies. As a boy he'd lain awake for hours planning against imagined tragedies. What if his father took the old Pontiac across the freeway into the oncoming traffic? Suppose an earthquake caught him while he was at Dodger Stadium?

Years ago, when Beal had been fifteen, he had scrambled up to the fifth canyon and found his own secret cave. Over the next few years he had gone back there every chance he got, carrying supplies, burying them deep into the ground. Just in case.

He was headed for that cave now, though he doubt-

40

ed any of his secret preparations would still be there. Time marches on.

Even for Beal. Beal was twenty-seven, closing in fast on thirty. There were the beginnings of tiny tracings around his eyes and mouth. Slowly little parts of Beal were starting their brush with time. Scars, nicks, hair left in brushes and shower drains. Erosion. Mortality. Beal was starting that long, slow, but inexorable process of falling apart.

Not that it was noticeable to the world. His slim, muscular body was still young and smooth; his frail baby face and dimpled smile, engaging. His blond hair still curled childlike at the nape of his neck. Nevertheless, all the signs were there.

As Beal reached the upper half of the third canyon, the rocky ground changed into dry, pebbly dirt. Huge cacti fingered toward the sky, strange exotic blossoms stuck onto them, masking the fact that cactus needles packed a hell of a punch if you had the bad fortune to touch one of them.

The cactus field was relatively horizontal. If you paced yourself just right, it made a good rest before you hit the fourth canyon, which was no more than a pile of rocks stretching a good three thousand feet in the air to the even more difficult Passman's Ledge.

As the slope flattened, Beal could concentrate less on what he was doing, and he began to daydream. A look of total absorption crossed his thin, sensitive baby face. Daydreaming wasn't just a pastime to Beal; it was serious business, maybe even a way of life.

It had always been like that for Beal. His parents, delicatessen owners, worked twenty hours a day and lived the rest of their tight, cramped lives in the small rooms behind the store. They were always scared, always kowtowing to their customers, as if they were innately inferior to anyone who could afford pastrami at eight dollars a pound. You couldn't get more respectful than the gray, ghostlike Beals. Police, government, even neighbors seemed to hold a mystical authority. The Beals were the kind of people the Nazis marched off to the gas chambers without a protest. They would have probably even thanked the guards for the soap. It was a tight, rigid life that the Beals held out to their daydreaming son. And it amazed, infuriated, and even shamed them when he rejected it.

Beal paused. Ahead the fourth canyon yawned toward the sky, patchy sunlight illuminating the rugged uphill terrain, lighting Passman's Ledge, which was a dangerous, difficult climb even if you were fresh and rested, which Beal wasn't. His muscles ached; his feet were covered with blisters. He hurt, but the truth was he wanted himself to hurt.

He had come here to think. He had come here to try to make some kind of sense out of the Jack Beal who had the potential to succeed at just about anything he tried and had never done anything but drift.

He was in trouble, all right. His grass closet had cost close to two hundred dollars and had taken weeks of work. Beal had removed his clothes, placed them in boxes, then strung fluorescent lights across the ceiling, covered the walls with reflective aluminum foil, and laid plastic on the ground. He'd crammed as many planters as he could into the closet, then filled them with a mixture of steer manure and topsoil. Next, he'd planted the seeds carefully, exactly four inches apart, then flicked on the fluorescent lights and watched them dazzle brilliantly on the soil. Finally he'd watered his garden carefully and closed the door.

It was the water that got him, dripping down slowly into his landlord Krammer's living room, probably hitting him on his bald head while he soaked his feet in front of the television.

Beal had been in the Santa Cruz University practice rooms, beating himself to death over the *Goldberg Variations*. Of all of Bach, the *Goldberg Variations* were the hardest. There were three or four independent lines, each going in different directions. Beal had spent about a thousand hours trying to figure out how to manage that with just two hands. Of course he was kidding himself that he could become a concert pianist; deep inside he knew he was just finding another reason to be a perennial student.

Meanwhile, that damn closet was dripping and dripping. Beal could just imagine Krammer pounding at his door, his ripped undershirt straining around his heavy barrel chest, then, the fact that Beal wasn't home suddenly dawning on his dim brain. Beal could see him grabbing the passkey in his meaty fist, opening the door, and finding the source of the water in a closet of light, while all those tiny little seeds of California's finest were just germinating.

It wouldn't matter how much Beal swore that the grass was for his own use. No one would believe him, though in fact it was true; the grass really was for his personal use, that and, of course, his friends. For Beal didn't need the money. He had a number of enterprises to help him through college. Besides occasional stints in the kitchen of a local health food restaurant, he had a thriving computer dating service. In truth, the Jack Beal Computer Dating Service was really two laundry bags marked "Girls" and "Boys," and the only thing computerized about it was a few sheets of dummy printout given to him by Max, an insane flutist he jammed with, in exchange for a blonde, brunette, and redhead to be named later. But no one seemed to mind all that much, and as soon as the parents drove away at the beginning of the semester, Jack Beal moved in with his laundry bags and his promises of love for just five small bucks.

But Beal doubted the police would believe him. And he supposed the fact that he was a twenty-seven-year-old sophomore with a sometimes girl and only a few friends drifting in and out of his life would hardly qualify him as an upstanding citizen.

He wondered how much a person got for dealing these days. He supposed it was enough.

Krammer, dimwit landlord that he was, had still obviously been smart enough to know that whatever Beal was growing in that closet, it wasn't carrots, and he'd called the police.

If it hadn't been for Mrs. Conway, the old lady next door, Beal would be sitting in some jail cell right now. He'd just pulled up to the small wood frame apartment building when Mrs. Conway put her little wizened head out the window and whispered loudly, "Krammer found the closet and called the cops!"

Beal had stood dumbly in the darkness, Mrs. Conway gesticulating wildly at his window next door. "Cops," she hissed.

Beal hadn't waited around to check. He'd jumped into his car and headed off, he didn't know where. The next morning he was almost five hundred miles away, climbing into the rocky canyons he'd explored as a boy.

As Beal looked into the fifth canyon, a sharp chill passed through his body. Only a few yards ahead he could see the outcropping of his secret cave, a gnarled spruce tree guarding the entrance to it like a sentinel.

Beal started toward the cave, his heart pounding with anticipation and fear. He hadn't realized it until that moment, but somewhere in the back of his mind he thought that the cave held a magic power of predicting his future. It was simple. If he found something he had left before, anything, an old tin can, a book of matches, even a page from one of the ten books he'd carefully chosen to survive disaster with him, then Beal would make it, too. It was crazy. But omens did that kind of thing to you. They got under your skin.

The question was: Was it too late to change? It was too late for him and his ex-wife, Maggie. Much too late for that, though the memory of her shiny auburn hair and pale, upturned face had never lost its painful sharpness. He could still hear her soft southern WASP accent, pure dizzying aphrodisiac to a lower-class Jewish boy from L.A. But she'd walked from Beal's life five years ago, empty-handed, leaving him everything but what he wanted most, her. Yes, it was far too late for Maggie. It was possibly even too late to avoid going to jail.

Beal heaved his pack to the ground with a yelp of pain, then entered the rock-strewn cave. He was astounded by memories. Every rock and pebble, every discoloration and clump of grass were filled with past hopes and dreams.

He moved swiftly to the back wall and began to dig. Almost immediately his hand struck something solid. He clawed at the object excitedly but it was only a rock. His disappointment amazed him. Surely one rusted old tin can had nothing to do with the next fifty years of life. Tin can or not, what was there to stop Beal from starting fresh anyway, from absolving himself of all past sins and declaring today day one, the first day of his life?

And suddenly he realized there was nothing to stop him. He could go out and get himself a nine-to-fiver and work until the sun slanted across the horizon. He could sit under the shade of a tree or play his piano all night. Maybe there'd even be a woman with great legs and the soft, sweet breathing of a sleeping child in his lap. There was nothing to stop him. He'd call legal aid. Since it was his first offense, perhaps he could get off with a suspended sentence.

Just as he was reassuring himself, his hand hit something hard. It was a bent old C harmonica, clogged with dirt, probably useless, but definitely his.

Beal stood up, filled with excitement, and rushed back out of the cave. The pure, clear, shadowed mountains surrounded him, stunning him with wonder. He let out a hoot of happiness that built and built, releasing all sorrow and remorse, leaving him clean.

The silent alarms went off an hour later.

Photoelectric cells were set off. Within seconds they were relayed back to a central panel, and red lights went off all over the place.

Deep in the earth, in an abandoned gold mine that had served as the skeleton for what was now a three-story bunker, five men jumped up as one, threw on their clothes rapidly, grabbed rifles, and headed for the cage where two sleek Dobermans were barking loudly.

It took only two point three minutes for the men and their dogs to emerge to the surface. But even in that short space of time they were too late.

At first Beal thought he'd seen a mountain goat, movement was so unexpected in that barren land. But quickly he realized it was a man.

The pale, sunless body was tall and stooped, the face, knotted and angry-white, as hard and tight as the rocks that set it off. In the brief moment that Beal saw the man, he felt something terrible about that face, and deep inside, he registered something familiar about it, too.

Then Beal stopped registering anything. Because suddenly men were coming from everywhere. And they had rifles and big dogs.

There was the crack of a rifle.

Beal took off out of sheer instinct, feeling a stab of terror only after he was moving fast down the rocky trail. Somewhere in the back of his mind he decided they were a bunch of crazy, boozed-up hunters. It seemed impossible to find anyone up in those arid mountains, but he could think of no other explanation. Whatever they were, though, they were dangerous. They had shot at him.

Four men took the trail after Beal, moving down the path as if they'd been primed for it. The fifth man stationed himself on a high ledge. He stood, heavy and silent, his craggy face as pitted as the rocks around him, his underslung jaw giving an angry, questioning look. Slowly he lifted a pair of binoculars and searched the darkening landscape for the intruder.

He captured him in the lens, then pulled a walkie-talkie from his belt. "He's only a few hundred feet ahead. Don't use the dogs unless I tell you to."

Beal didn't dare look back and see how many men were behind him. It would slow him down. Yet the terrible sound of their steps and the barking of the dogs filled his ears, and the question of who and why revolved in his brain along with the pounding of his rushing blood and heavy breathing. His already tired legs felt like fifty-pound weights.

The trail narrowed, snaking along the ridge. Beal slowed instinctively. He tried to force his body to move faster, but the ground was suddenly powdering underneath his feet. Rocks were tumbling off the edge and crashing to the rushing water thousands of feet below, and he was sliding forward, legs wobbling on the unsteady ground.

The man with the angry, underslung jaw jerked down his binoculars. Dark evening shadows made it difficult to see what was happening below, but he had a pretty good idea that the intruder had still not been caught.

He clicked on his walkie-talkie. "What the hell's the matter?"

"Don't worry. We'll pick him up at Passman's Ledge."

"He's almost through the fourth. You should have had him by now."

"You try making the run with rifles and two damn angry dogs trying to break free."

"Well, make sure you get him at Passman's."

There was a hard laugh. "I wouldn't worry about that."

Beal's body was being torn apart. Huge cactus needles jabbed into him, poisoning his legs into welts, and his hands were ripped and bleeding from grasping the craggy mountain wall. Breath racked his chest, and his heart felt swollen as it pumped crazily. But still, he ran on. The sound of the dogs and the angry yells of the men behind him were like a whip to his back.

The trail widened, and the roar of the waterfall grew louder. Beal knew there would be a brief respite of stable, steady path before he crossed the waterfall. Then he would be at the lip of Passman's.

Passman's Ledge was a one-hundred-foot expanse of sheer, slick mountain wall. There was a ledge up there all right, but at best it was five inches wide; in some areas it was less than two, with few places to use your hands. Strung up between the fourth and the third canyon, it acted as a natural barrier to everyone but lizards, mountain goats, and only the most experienced climbers. One wrong move was likely to throw you over the edge, and the drop was one thousand feet. Enough to ensure a closed-coffin funeral.

As the roar of the waterfall grew louder, it blocked out the sound of the dogs, and for that Beal was truly grateful. Beal picked up speed, and for a moment he thought he was going to black out. Breath was hot in his lungs; searing pain radiated through his chest, making his body shake with suffering as he sucked in the desperately needed air. His throat began to close, as if he were going to retch his guts out.

Suddenly the water rose up in front of him, black and crashing, careering downward, filling Beal's head with its loud roar. The boulders became more humped, slicked down by the water that foamed all around them.

Beal crawled across the first boulder, gripping its smooth, frozen surface with torn fingers; he forced himself to the next boulder and the next, until he could no longer feel his hands and feet from the icy water. He thought he heard himself cry out from the numb pain, but he couldn't be sure. There was very little he could be sure of anymore.

The man with the binoculars had moved down into the fourth canyon. He stood on a rock that gave him a view of the entire area right down to Passman's Ledge. The deep shadows muddied everything, and for a long while all he could make out was the smudgy outline of his men and the two black dogs. But as he slowly turned the binoculars along the path toward Passman's, he caught a hint of movement along the waterfall.

His men were less than one hundred feet behind the flickering silhouette, the dogs straining against their leashes, barking angrily at the restraint. Giving the command to release the dogs was tempting, but his orders were to bring whoever breached security back alive. Unless, of course, things got out of control. No matter who the intruder was, he must not be allowed to get away.

The flickering image of Beal disappeared into the crumbling descent to Passman's, and the man lifted the walkie-talkie. "Split into two groups. Ames and Faraday take the upper trail."

"What upper trail?" returned Faraday. "That's sheer wall."

The man ignored this remark. In fact, he knew his men were glad for the excitement on a job that held little but canned TV and an occasional smuggled-in whore. "There's a spot about fifty feet along where you can get a clear shot down at Passman's. Shore off a good chunk of ledge. Isolate him up there. Then Sunday and Thruman can bring him back."

"Roger. He's slowing up but good now."

Beal's eyes were on the thin ribbon of Passman's Ledge. Darkness had flattened everything out, and though he knew there were holds on the hard, slick expanse in front of him, he couldn't see them.

He stopped. It was useless to push himself farther. If they didn't get him at Passman's Ledge, it would be because he'd lost his footing and fallen to his death. Maybe they didn't really mean to hurt him. Maybe they were just out to scare him, and if he stopped, they'd leave him alone. It made sense. At least a hell of a lot more sense than that they were trying to kill him.

The alternate trail along the mountain wall rose up like a thin black scar. Ames and Faraday shook their heads to one another as they started the climb. Clutching their rifles, the men moved quickly upward. Before, the chase had been pleasurable excitement and no one had pressed full out to capture the man. But now was the time to end the hunt. Down below, the dogs felt the tension and began to bark angrily.

Beal heard the furious barking of the dogs and

sprang back to life. The ledge was still wide enough to hold half of his foot, only his heels hung free and nicks and breaks along the mountain wall were shallow but deep enough for a hold. He began to move, crablike, kicking into the ledge, his hands grasping at the sheer, slick rock that rose up next to him.

Just behind Beal, Sunday and Thruman followed the lower trail, moving to the lip of Passman's. Thruman held the leashes tightly, trying to calm the dogs. Sunday leaped onto the ledge first, his small, agile body sliding sideways immediately, closing the gap at every step.

Beal could hear the men moving only feet behind him. Pain spread through his body in sickening waves until he was light-headed from it. His bursting lungs took in torrid breath in gasps that radiated burning pain all through his body. He heard himself whimpering. Nothing more, just whimpering.

The ledge narrowed into a crack and Beal kicked into the mountain scar, his toes curled like talons. He clawed at the sheer face but found only smoothness.

All at once there was a shower of loose dirt and rocks scattering from above, and it was then that Beal realized there were also men making the run on top of him.

Sunday and Thruman were moving fast along the lower ledge less than ten feet behind Beal. Ahead, they could see the break where the two men above would get off their shots. Thruman stopped, and the dogs pressed against him, anxious and disappointed. Only Sunday continued, sliding even faster than before. Though the smallest of the four, Sunday was by far the best equipped to handle the sheer mountain cliffs. Up until now that had counted for nothing. When he and the others wrestled and played attack games to while away the hours, Sunday always came in last. Perhaps he could have won had he played dirty. But they had their code. Here, however, Sunday's small feet and hands, his light body weight, gave him an advantage, and he scuttled forward swiftly, his small face set and determined.

The man in the fourth canyon clicked on his walkie-talkie. "Sunday! Stop! Let them break the trail."

But Sunday was skimming toward Beal, his feet sliding along the tiny scar of the mountain, his arm reaching out toward him.

Beal could hear the breath of the man pressing toward him. He could almost feel the heat from his body. Suddenly there was a brush against his shoulder. It was a hand. Beal cried out, forcing himself away, moving faster and faster as he hung from the sheer mountain. But the heavy breathing was right behind him, and again there was the brush of a hand.

Suddenly a loud rumbling cut the quiet. Dirt and rocks broke loose, crumbling over the edge. Sunday screamed, loudly, piercingly. Desperately he clawed at the rolling earth. Then all at once his scream became a terrible howl, and he was falling to the bottom of the canyon in a shower of rocks and dirt.

Beal closed his eyes to shut out the sight of the man as he plunged, screaming, into the rocky chasm. But he couldn't block out the sound.

Above Beal, the two men sped up. They were trained to expect death. As they reached the break, they swung their rifles free. Clinging like flies, they aimed through the break in the rocks and simultaneously got off two shots, which shattered the ledge, making a break in it over four feet wide.

Beal clawed at the smooth mountain walls with torn, bleeding fingernails, but he found only flatness. The handholds were gone. The four-foot gap was only inches ahead. There was no chance that Beal could make it across that gap.

Again there was the crack of the rifle. Rocks scattered through the air, and dirt showered down onto Beal's head. They had missed badly. If it was possible at this point for Beal to find comfort in a thought, the fact that they could miss would be on the top of his list.

Beal lowered his body weight and stood at the edge of the break, poised. Suddenly he released, springing sideways, his leg leading him forward over the gap until he was touching nothing but air. There was a terrible moment of weightlessness, and then he was coming down on the other side. His foot touched the ledge. His body leaned forward, seeking out the comfort of the wall, while his hands grasped desperately for a hold. But everything was off-balance, and he was grasping at smoothness without so much as a vein or a crease. His first foot began to spin backwards as his second foot hit; then it, too, slipped. It held to the edge at an impossible angle.

A shot rang out and showered Beal with dirt and rocks. He forced his body away from the wall, struggling to bring up his foot which hung over the edge, dragging him downward, like a weight that didn't belong to him. Slowly he brought it up over the chasm and toward the ledge, until it was level; then he kicked into the stone, trying to clutch it with his toes. His foot held, and he slid the other one forward.

The man watching from the fourth canyon lowered his binoculars angrily. His underslung jaw worked nervously, as if he were chewing at something. It was a botched job, and his anger at his men was multiplied by what he knew would be the consequences to himself. He snapped on the walkie-talkie. "Let go of the dogs!"

Again he lifted the binoculars. Without moonlight, the figures on the ledge were only black shadows. But as the two sleek dogs began to move, he could see their dark outlines springing with grace and agility. They sprinted toward Beal, two black holes in a black landscape. The way they moved was magnificent. Pure muscle sprinting at unimaginable speeds along the face of the mountain.

Beal was just inches from the end of Passman's Ledge when he saw the dogs. Even in the darkness he could make out their parted mouths and their fangs, foamy with spittle. The lead dog had just reached the gap and was pausing to spring. Behind it, the second dog waited impatiently for his turn.

Beal commanded his body to move, but it wouldn't. Pressed against the face of the mountain, he watched the lead dog as it went into its spring, but he was paralyzed; there were no more reserves for him to call on.

The lead dog split the air, its slick black body gleaming like coal. It leaped the gap in one liquid motion. The second dog impatiently leaped right behind it but it was moving too fast. It landed only seconds after the lead dog, and dirt scattered, flying downward.

There was a terrible howl and the lead dog was sliding,

its muscular legs clawing at the rubble that crumbled into a fine, powdery dirt, until the black paws were tearing only at thin air and the Doberman was sent plunging into the rocky canyon below.

The second dog held to the edge, watching its companion as it went howling into the blackness. The dog was motionless. Caught between fear and duty. Whining and growling, it turned its narrow head toward Beal.

Thruman yelled, "Get him! Now!"

The dog didn't move.

Again Thruman shouted, "Get him, damn you!"

The dog looked back in the direction of the shout, then tilted its head down toward the black canyon, where the twisted, broken body of its companion lay.

A moment later the men above Beal were on the move, their tall, lean, angular bodies slipping fast over the smooth mountain.

Beal started, as if waking from a dream. He slid crazily along the ledge, leaped back onto the path, and took the trail, half sliding, half running. The loose rocky earth rolled underneath him, scattering rocks and pebbles downward. He could hear them shatter as they hit bottom.

The unstable earth was like a river. Beal rode it, allowing the slipping rocks to pull him forward, skidding him into the third canyon.

Slowly he became aware that there were no sounds behind him. He refused to slow up enough to check, but as he ran, he listened. The sounds he heard were all his, the rasping of breath, the crumbling of falling rocks, the strange whine of fear and relief.

It was only later, with the crashing waterfall all around him, that he stopped.

The moon had risen, sitting on the crest of the mountain, huge and golden, larger than he had ever seen it in his life. Soft, silver light bathed the high ridges of the canyon, illuminating them like the regal façade of some foreign capital. He made a slow survey of the rocky ledges below him but saw nothing.

Beal leaned toward the icy water, scooping up a handful that burned his aching throat. His body was crushed with pain, and his legs wobbled and shook underneath him.

Beal didn't dare sink to the ground. Once down, he doubted that he would be able to get up. He stood watching as the moon rose out of the mountains to begin its nightly circuit. Then once again he began his descent, only this time more slowly.

But far up in the fourth canyon, outside Beal's secret cave, his backpack lay in the darkness. And that was how they found out who he was.

Chapter Two

Ten days before a meeting of the Trust a messenger would appear at each member's door with instructions laying out the exact time and place that a private jet would be waiting. Usually the messages were routine. Every three months at precisely 8:45 A.M., five different Cessnas would be at separate airfields, three just outside Washington, D.C., one in New York, and another in southern Illinois. The destination was a small private landing strip five miles outside Palm Springs, California. A helicopter would complete the trip from there.

The meeting would last close to ten hours, and an exhaustive amount of material would have to be covered in that very short space of time. In general, the meeting was divided into two parts—the first international, the second domestic. At the beginning of each meeting ten minutes were devoted to internal affairs, the actual running of the Trust. But for the most part these discussions were confined to general issues, with almost no details. Separation of duties and lack of accountability were perhaps the first rule of the Trust.

In terms of agenda, most of the concerns facing America for the next three months were discussed and a policy decided. Everything from oil depletion allowances to equal rights for women was reported on, debated, and eventually resolved. The primary concern was, as always, the good of the country as a whole. Regional bias was not to be tolerated; worldly considerations, like who financed whose campaign, who was owed a favor, or who deserved a rap across the wrist, did not belong at a meeting of the Trust. This was to be a deliberation by unbiased, impartial men. And rarely, if ever, did any member find trouble in shedding these concerns before he entered the Spartan meeting room in the mountains.

In general, these discussions were quick, brutally honest, and extremely intelligent. All of the men present were highly placed in America. There was little need for a great deal of information or explanation. They knew all the sides of the argument before they came.

After all the votes had been taken, generally about ten hours later, the helicopter returned. The members were exhausted and drained. And they would sleep most of the way home.

How each of them explained his day's absence from the world was left up to the individual. And for the most part, none of them had all that much trouble. Even important members of government, the Army, and industry had appointments with oral surgeons, sick aunts, or secret mistresses.

Nor did they have to worry about their secret meetings being revealed by the messengers. The five men had not changed since the beginning, testament to the care that was used in their selection as well as to the power of a great deal of money.

Everything about the Trust was geared to work smoothly. Each man with his own area of expertise, each man with his own area of responsibility. The Senate, the House, the judiciary, the Army, and big business. One man was in charge of supplying money for the Trust; another, in charge of the large group of "spooks" who protected it. Everything was kept separate and orderly. It was only the implementation of policies that presented a problem. And that was another matter entirely.

Though each member of the Trust carried back with him a sensible approach to America's problems, there was not a great deal that he could do about it. For while the great halls of Congress might ring with noble rhetoric, it was much more the ring of the cash register and the grind of the voting machines that ruled a legislator's vote, and no amount of logic or moral force could make him cast it otherwise.

It was for that reason that the Trust instituted a policy of blackmail. Next to the large Spartan meeting room was a computer. There wasn't a senator or representative, a judge or appointed official whose name hadn't been programmed into the computer, along with a listing of which corporations had contributed to his campaign. The comparison of a man's

60

voting record with a list of his contributors was, to say the least, enlightening.

Once again the five messengers would be sent out. Only this time the messages they were carrying were of quite a different nature. On the whole, it was relatively easy to blackmail a public official, especially if it wasn't for money but for their votes. Petitions and memorandums passed over their desks all the time. And if the petitions had a somewhat thinly veiled piece of damaging information about illegal campaign contributions, it would indeed catch the official's attention. The vote demanded was always for a sound piece of legislation, though often not pleasing to the special-interest groups that had contributed to his campaign.

So far just under one hundred messages of this type had been carried to the men of Washington, with an eighty percent success rate. The other twenty percent quickly learned to regret their decision. Within three days the damaging information was leaked to the newspapers.

Unfortunately, while the success rate of the blackmail scheme was extremely high, in the end it didn't work. Once a member of Congress bit the hand that was feeding him, his campaign contributions began to dry up. Gone were the television time and heavy canvassing so necessary for reelection. And pretty soon gone was the politician himself, replaced by a man who had not yet been blackmailed, a man who had the special-interest group's support. It was like cutting the limb from a salamander. Corruption was that deeply entrenched in the fabric of America.

Slowly several members of the Trust were beginning to realize what was needed was a shock, a jolting that would turn the country inside out. It would have to be a startling blow, one that no member of the Trust would want to make and yet one which would in the end prove necessary. This subject had been brought up before and voted down. But since the presidential convention was due to begin in less than a month, it would undoubtedly be brought up again at the next meeting.

It was called the State of Emergency Plan, and only two of them knew that no matter what the outcome of the debate, the plan was well on its way to becoming a reality.

On June 30, at nine o'clock in the morning, the five messengers set out for the members of the Trust. Their instructions on the private jets were the same as they had been for the past five years. But this time the destination of these planes would be different. Instead of a private strip just outside Palm Springs, the planes were to head for an arid strip of land in northwestern New Mexico. When the members of the Trust received their instructions, they would know exactly what that meant. Still, they would not call one another to speak about it. Despite their edginess, they would wait the ten days until their meeting. They were used to keeping their own counsel.

Chapter Three

Police Sergeant Fellini had a thick-featured face, pitted with acne scars like the surface of the moon. The craters served as a reminder of the huge welts and boils that had made him one of the loneliest kids in Brooklyn and sent him as a young adult to the sun of California and the pleasure of carrying a gun in the West, which was some pleasure for a fat, pockmarked kid from New York. They also acted as a reminder of the years of humiliation.

Beal was seated across from him, slouched down in his chair, a tough, punky smile plastered on his face. It was a façade that Fellini had learned from experience crumpled fast. The hard ones were the kind that whimpered and pleaded. Guys like that were taught to lie at their mothers' knees and you never broke their stories. Guys like Beal were a cakewalk.

Beal watched Fellini pretending to make notations on a report, stalling for time. It was an old police ploy: Keep a person waiting until he's so nervous he says something stupid. Unfortunately it was one that worked. Beal's heart was wailing like a rock and roll drummer, and cold sweat was standing out on his forehead.

It was his own fault. He'd turned himself in on the advice of legal aid. Of course, that was in Southern California. Now that he was back in Northern California, legal aid was nowhere to be seen. So far he'd spent almost six hours stewing his guts out in a crowded cell, keeping his nose closed and his back to the wall.

So much for legal aid. Still, the advice was probably good. After all, Beal didn't have a record. The courts were crowded. Summer was just around the corner. They'd be glad to be rid of him with a suspended sentence.

Beal felt a great wave of relief wash over him. He'd tell them the truth, not let them walk all over him, and he'd be back whipping himself over that Bach fugue in a couple of hours.

Fellini dropped his report and laid his meaty hands, fingers intertwined, over it. He smiled. "So, Mr. Beal, we've been hearing a great deal about you the past couple of hours."

"Krammer's an idiot. I wouldn't believe a word he says if I were you."

"Krammer?" If Fellini was playing coy, he was doing a very good job of it.

"My landlord. He's the one who called you about my closet."

Fellini sounded disinterested. "Oh, yeah, the closet."

"It was strictly for my own use. I mean, I suppose

I'd give some to a couple of friends. But I wasn't in business. And that's the truth."

Fellini was back reading that report again. There was a fly buzzing so close to his face that it must have taken a great act of will for him not to swat it. That, or whatever he was reading must have been plenty interesting.

"You can't hold me without letting me see a lawyer," Beal said after a while. He was trying to keep his voice even and calm, but he could hear the tension creeping into it. And he supposed Fellini could hear it, too.

Fellini looked up, the corners of his mouth drooped down into false solemnity. "Oh, no, Mr. Beal. That would be against the law. I wouldn't dream of not safeguarding your rights." Fellini leaned toward the squawk box on his desk with a grunt, then flipped it on. "Is the report from ballistics here yet?"

A man's voice answered. "They just called. They're sending it over."

Fellini glanced over at Beal and shook his head as if to include him in on the ironies of police work, then answered caustically. "I don't suppose they gave you sort of a little hint as to the outcome, did they?"

"Yeah. It matched."

"Good." Fellini beamed moonlike. "That's very good. Bring it in the moment it arrives."

Fellini clicked off, lifted a pencil, and began making notations in the margin of the report. He was smiling again.

Beal turned from that smile, trying to keep cool. Even when he was innocent, he disliked the police a whole lot. He supposed it had something to do with universal guilt. Like walking around when there were a lot of cripples in wheelchairs or hating your mother. But now that he was indeed guilty, his dislike intensified into loathing, which was not the best emotion to display at a time like this.

Beal looked around the puke-colored room, from the drab beveled glass to a couple of yellowing notices and a calendar from Ace Tool and Dye Inc., trying to beat down the anger that was rising in him.

Finally Beal could stand it no longer. "I want a lawyer," he said.

Fellini slapped his jowly face and shook his head in shock at his omission. Again he flicked on the intercom. "Mr. Beal is interested in obtaining legal advice. Come in here and he'll give you the number of his attorney."

Fellini clicked off the intercom and smiled hugely. "You see, everything's moving along smoothly."

The door opened, and a large black officer filled the opening. He looked at Beal as if he were a piece of furniture.

"Tell Officer Harrison the phone number and he'll call for you."

"I want to call for myself."

Fellini laughed. "There'll be plenty of time to talk to him when he arrives. Plenty of time."

"Now wait a minute. I know my rights." Beal folded his arms belligerently.

"Then you know you have the right to have an attorney present when I question you. But am I questioning you, Mr. Beal? Am I? Have you heard so

66

much as one question since you entered the room?" His voice was saccharine. "Now just give Officer Harrison the name and number of your attorney, and we'll rectify the omission." Again the smile. "Yes, sir, we certainly will."

Beal had heard how two policemen would be used in rotation. They called it Good Cop-Bad Cop. But obviously the Santa Cruz police force was shorthanded, and Fellini was playing all parts. Nerves started making a meal of Beal's insides. He could feel the sweat on the roll now.

Beal slid down even farther in his chair and crossed his arms, desperately trying to hold on to his dignity. He flashed a cocky smile at Fellini. "What's your lawyer's name?"

"I don't need one. I keep my nose clean."

"A massive undertaking," Beal muttered.

Fellini kept his cool, and in fact his smile widened. "Very unwise not to get legal help. Believe me, you're going to need it, Mr. Beal."

"Call me Jack. None of my friends do."

"Cute. But inappropriate. You've got a lot of trouble coming in your direction, and that kind of talk can only make matters worse."

The black cop was staring right through Beal. Fellini was still smiling. There was a clock ticking far off, and the sound of distant phones seemed very loud.

Beal smirked. "Did you know in California there's one lawyer for every three hundred eighteen people, and that includes children?"

"Fascinating."

"I don't happen to have a lawyer."

Fellini nodded to Harrison. "Call the Public Defender's Office."

Harrison left the room soundlessly, and Fellini watched after him, playing with the pockmarks on his face. Beal supposed he was the kind who tried to hit the mirror with his whiteheads. Then once again he was reading that report, penciling in notations, his face fixed in an enormous smile. He looked as if he were about to tuck into a big meal, and Beal was beginning to suspect that he was the entrée.

Beal's façade was crumbling. He could go to jail, and he knew what they did to you there. He didn't want to go to jail for one hour, one minute. He was getting scared.

Again the tall black officer entered, carrying the long-awaited report in his hand. Fellini snapped it up hungrily. Beal thought he detected saliva at the corners of his mouth.

"A public defender will be out in a couple of hours," the officer said as he gave Fellini the report.

But Fellini wasn't listening. He was scanning the pages with voracious eyes. He didn't even bother looking up. "Tell them we're transferring him to Santa Cruz County Jail. They can reach him there."

Fellini reluctantly left his report and turned his gaze on Beal. "The officer will see you to a holding cell."

Beal was trembling. "Wait a minute! Is that it?"

Fellini snorted. "Oh, no. That, Mr. Beal, is very far from it. But that is it for now."

Beal cowered back into the chair. "No. Wait. I want a chance to raise bail. You can't send me to Santa Cruz without giving me a chance to raise bail."

68

Fellini shook his head and made a great display of sighing wearily. Slowly he rose from his chair. "Now, now, Mr. Beal. We both know bail is out of the question."

"Like hell it is. I've got friends who'd raise it for me in a second. I know my rights."

Fellini glared at him calmly. "Mr. Beal, didn't you know? Murderers have no rights."

Beal didn't move. Everything was spinning and lurching underneath him. He heard his voice choke off with shock. "Murder? What are you talking about? I grew some jerk-off grass in a closet, for Christ's sake. That's all."

Fellini was watching him from across the wide expanse of desk, a sarcastic smile playing across his pitted face. "We have laws against killing women, Mr. Beal. Even old ones. You were seen leaving Mrs. Tania Conway's apartment by your landlord. In fact, it's safe to say you left a trail wider than a freeway."

Beal felt the world jerking out from underneath him. "Mrs. Conway is dead? I used to play cards with her. I liked her." There were tears in Beal's eyes. "She was a nice old lady. Who would want to kill her?" He stopped, shocked. "You think I killed her. You really think I would kill her?"

Fellini didn't bother to answer. The officer placed his thick black hand under Beal's armpit and began pulling him to the door.

Beal didn't even resist. He could barely stand. He just kept repeating, "I didn't murder anyone. I'm innocent."

But there wasn't another soul in the world who was listening.

Chapter Four

Jed McKuen felt a vibration at his thigh as his electronic beeper buzzed. He looked around to make sure no one was watching, then shut it off and scanned the crowded fund raiser for his wife, Betsy. Finally he spotted her on the other side of the room, tight in a huddle with several senators' wives. Standing nearby, all ears, was a lady reporter from *The Washington Post*. Jed was attorney general; his rough Lincolnesque face was handsome, his view iconoclastic. He made good press.

Jed knew that getting to Betsy without being waylaid by the ever-present fourth estate was going to be a lot harder than Washington's crossing of the Delaware. But he couldn't leave the party without an explanation. Their relationship was becoming shaky enough as it was.

As Jed pressed through the crowd, he saw Supreme Court Justice Samuel Keiler talking to E. Bud Fuller, president pro tem of the Senate, men Jed had known since the old Lacey years. Farther along were Representative Paisley and, at the bar, General Nadler. It could have been a meeting of the Lacey Brain Trust. But that was no surprise. The most powerful men in Washington today belonged to the old Lacey administration. It was only logical. Lacey had picked the most talented men around. And in a country that still almost fanatically mourned his death, being an old Lacey man counted for a lot.

As Jed passed, Justice Keiler reached out his long, bony hand and nabbed Jed's shoulder. "Hey, you gotta hear the latest Chesapeakism."

Senator Fuller leaned toward Jed, bathing him in Scotch and soda breath. Fuller was running his fingers through his thick white hair until it stood right up on end, and there was a malicious smile on his tanned face.

He liked tearing Chesapeake apart. Everyone did.

While all Presidents were considered fair game for gossip in Washington, Chesapeake was a blessing to the tired, overworked minions of government.

The President was a tough conservative saber rattler with little talent for back-room bargaining. Still, he was a hell of a public speaker, and that plus some decent advisers got him elected after Lacey's term ran out. It would undoubtedly get him nominated at the convention in Detroit this August 1. Despite the fact that his own party rarely supported him in Congress. Despite the fact that men in his own Cabinet seemed to respond to a will separate from his, a will that Chesapeake himself didn't seem to understand or suspect.

71

But Jed's grudge against Chesapeake was less the result of his saber-rattling conservatism or even his unsteady control of his party. Jed's grudge stemmed from the fact that almost five years before, Chesapeake had killed the investigation that he had been making for Lacey into the corruption of the legislature by big business.

Only weeks after Lacey was assassinated, Chesapeake had demanded the incomplete files, which Jed had refused to give him. It had been a long, angry battle, and finally Jed had tendered his resignation over it. Eventually Chesapeake backed down and even appointed Jed attorney general, though he would not allow him to continue the investigation. And the files, full of more explosive material than a neutron bomb, were held locked in Jed's office safe, never to see the light of day.

Or at least that was what Jed thought. Recently some of the secret information was beginning to turn up in blackmail notes. It was information that only he and Lacey should have known. Unless, of course, Lacey had confided in someone. If he had, it was very likely a fatal mistake.

It was not the first time Jed had made the connection between the assassination and the blackmail.

Senator Fuller was watching Jed with curiosity, seeing the faraway look in his eyes and the nervous shuffling from foot to foot. But faraway looks and nervous shuffling were fairly standard at fund raisers, and Fuller was anxious for a fresh ear to tell his latest Chesapeake story to.

Fuller smiled cruelly. "Last night I get this summons. So I go to the White House and there's Chesapeake in his dressing gown, that stern presidential visage peeking out over his blue silk jammies. Anyway, so I tell him, no way is he going to get that Russian trade bill through the Senate unless he makes some accommodations. Well, you know what he does?"

Jed was looking across the room at Betsy, his mind on getting to her, making his explanations, then leaving the party fast. By mistake he nodded.

Fuller looked crestfallen. "You do? Who told you?"

Jed came out of his fog. "Told me what?"

"Jesus, Jed," Fuller whined. "Anyway, what he said was nothing. I mean, the guy just stares at me blankly. So the way I figure it, Chesapeake is just dying for me to leave so he can call that asshole aide of his, Salmon, and ask him what trade bill with the Russians."

Keiler roared. "That ninny!"

Jed laughed falsely and took a gulp of his drink to hide the falseness.

"What's eating you, Jed?" Fuller was eyeing Jed closely.

Jed shrugged, then lied. "Family problems, you know."

If Senator Fuller didn't know, Justice Keiler certainly did. He put his long, lean arm on Jed's shoulder. "Take it from a man who's been there," he drawled in his most southern accent, a sure sign that he meant what he was saying. "Just ain't nothin' worth breakin' things up. Everythin' else will pass. It's what you got at home that really counts."

Jed looked at the lean, sallow, stalklike man who hadn't followed his own advice and nodded seriously. He was able to pull away just as Keiler began his usual tirade on alimony payments.

As Betsy saw Jed approaching, she excused herself from her companions and met him halfway. "Don't tell me. You have to leave, right?"

Jed searched her face for bitterness but found none. Of course, after almost eight years in Washington, smiling when her feet hurt her, laughing at inane and often tasteless jokes, even the sharp, smart Radcliffe-liberal Betsy had learned how to veil her face.

"I'll try to get back before the end of the party."

Betsy nodded and smiled gaily at him. With her passionate black eyes and upswept ebony hair, her gaiety seemed out of place. It was a sure sign to Jed that Betsy was putting up a front. Betsy was many things: solid, ironic, loving, clever. But gay, no.

"If you don't make it back in time, I'll just meet you at home," she told him.

"Again," Jed added.

"You said it. I didn't." Still the gay façade. It killed Jed to watch her struggling against the obvious thought.

He touched her thin, expressive nose tenderly. "You know how much I wish I could explain."

"Forget it." She turned to leave, then thought better of it. Her eyes were serious and even blacker than usual. "I trust you."

As Jed pushed out of the cocktail party and into the hot June afternoon, he realized his burning desire to explain everything to Betsy was only partially to relieve her mind. Mostly it was to relieve his own. It was terrifying to have a secret. It was terrifying to lead a double life. He didn't know how much longer he could bear the weight of carrying the world on his own inadequate shoulders.

Unfortunately he had no other choice. That was

the worst part about getting older, realizing that as stupid and inept as you were, you were still the best around. It sure knocked the hell out of hero worship, that was for sure. Unless maybe he was wrong. Maybe he was just on an ego trip and should dump the whole problem on Chesapeake's pudgy lap. But he knew that was impossible. Chesapeake was, as Keiler had said, a ninny. Or perhaps he wasn't a ninny and was smarter than anyone thought. Perhaps he was one of them.

There he was again, paranoid McKuen searching through the list of possibilities. Finding villains everywhere.

And yet the feeling that the country was rushing headlong to disaster was still there, pressing, urgent. It was as if an unseen hand were running the country, a shielded but powerful presence, using blackmail and assassination. To what end? It was a question Jed had been asking himself for a long time with no answer.

Jed entered a crummy bar on one of the pestilent streets that make up most of unofficial Washington, ordered a beer, then went to the men's room.

The beer remained untouched. Jed slipped out the back door and turned back into the growing rush-hour crowd.

A woman sat in the phone booth outside Woolworth's. She had a cigarette in her mouth, a full pack handy, and her hair was in rollers only partially covered by a babushka. She seemed to have settled down for the evening.

Jed stood close to the glass, letting the woman know that he wanted to use the phone. She studiously ignored him.

Jed looked up and down the street nervously,

though he knew he didn't have the slightest idea how to spot a tail anyway. He glanced at his watch. It had been over half an hour since he'd been buzzed.

The woman was still yakking. Jed placed himself directly in her field of vision. She turned away, and he moved with her.

He tapped loudly. The woman looked up; her eyes narrowed into two slits of fury. But she hung up the phone soon afterward. Outraged, she pushed past him, her terry-cloth slippers flapping angrily, her bumpy babushka askew with indignation.

Jed slipped into the phone booth and opened the phone book, pretending to be looking up a number.

He didn't have to wait long. The phone rang almost immediately, and he snapped it up.

"Hello. Is this 555-4645?" asked the voice on the other end. It had a slight Yiddish intonation.

"No, I'm sorry. This is 555-4646."

"Jesus Christ, what took you so long?" Sparrow asked querulously.

"I was at a fund raiser. When the buzzer vibrated, I just figured it was the junior senator from Nebraska's wife getting friendly."

"I've seen her. She's a real bag. Listen, I've got some info you might be interested in. You know that guy we think delivered the last blackmail note? Well, he turned up in Santa Cruz, California, poking around in some cockamamy murder indictment. So I checked it out, and sure enough our friend is passing out money around the Justice Department like Nixon was still in office. It looks like they're rigging a trial."

"I don't get it."

"So who does? I've slipped someone into the joint

76

to keep his eyes open, but so far he hasn't got anything."

"Maybe there's no connection."

"Maybe. But a hell of a lot of money is being spent to indict some kid for a murder that smells to high heaven."

"And you think he might be someone important?"

"I think we're at a dead end anyway, so what the hell. We might as well find out."

"How?"

A loud crunching noise came through the phone. Then little smacking noises. "What the hell are you eating?" Jed asked angrily.

"Antacids. I've got a bum stomach."

"Problems at home?"

"Men like me don't have homes."

The phone booth was heating up. Jed wiped the sweat from his forehead and said impatiently, "I asked you how you are planning to handle this, Sparrow."

Sparrow giggled softly, then chewed up another antacid. "Carefully, my friend. Very carefully."

Chapter Five

John Berger folded his *Washington Post* and placed it on the bench next to him, then relaxed back, his plain, nondescript face tilted to the sun.

West Potomac Park was relatively crowded for a weekday. Mothers watched their cranky children play in the dirt and develop heat rash. Lovers slid under blankets to hide impassioned hands. A group of middle-aged men tried to play soccer, but mostly they just ran around yelling and panting heavily. Several bicyclers with numbers on their backs pedaled past, scattering cinders. Across the soccer field Berger could see a blond man, wearing a business suit and tie, slowly walking toward him.

Suddenly the blond man stopped, took off his shoe, and emptied out a stone. He tried to replace his shoe, then gave up and, hopping on one leg, made his way over to the bench where Berger was sitting.

"Damn stones," said the blond man as he sat down and began to replace his shoe.

"The park's full of them," Berger answered with little interest. "You're new," he said after a while.

The blond man smiled coldly. "Life is full of little surprises. That's what keeps it interesting."

Berger watched suspiciously as the blond man finished lacing his shoe, then pulled a package of cigarettes from out of his breast pocket and lit one up. He breathed in the smoke deeply, then sat back against the bench, releasing smoke through his nose.

The blond man was young, though Berger suspected not as young as his handsome chiseled face would indicate. And there was something ageless about his eyes, cold dark eyes that reflected light like one-way glass and revealed nothing inside. It was the blond man's eyes that told Berger that things had changed. There was a cold professionalism and, Berger suspected, a resourcefulness to the blond man which had been lacking before, and Berger found himself approving of the change without even knowing what it would mean.

It had always surprised Berger that his whole job as messenger had been handled with so little finesse. Usually he would wait on the park bench for the tall scarecrowlike man who carried a newspaper stuffed with the messages and his money almost in plain sight. The man would stop to remove a pebble from his shoe as planned, hop over to the bench, and make the switch, right out in the open; then quickly he would leave. Most of the time he didn't even bother to go through the code words.

This had always burned Berger. There was a time

79

when drops were made with a little more invention, plans were varied, made more complex, elegant. Even if a person weren't scared of being caught, he still wanted to impress others with his skill.

Of course, Berger knew it was getting like that all over the country. Productivity was down; gone was the pride of workmanship that had made America a great power. Now if something worked okay, you did it any old way. Just slap a car together, shoot your way out of a bungled bank job. What the hell, as long as it worked.

But there was something about the blond man that told Berger he was different. In him you could feel the precision and strength of a quality operative.

The blond man finished his cigarette, then stepped on the butt and, to Berger's surprise, got up from the bench. For a moment Berger felt himself panicking. There had been no switch. Something had gone wrong.

It was the blond man's eyes that stopped him from speaking. There was a glance as cold and hard as a knife, a stiffening of the blond man's body, and Berger felt his heart tighten and the words choked off in his throat.

The blond man brushed off the seat of his pants, then quickly strode away, disappearing into the crowd of soccer players, completely fading from view, as if he had been a vision.

Berger sat immobile for a long time. Maybe the blond man had been a vision. Maybe Berger's fifteen years in the business were beginning to get to him. Those things happened. He'd seen it himself.

Berger shook off the thought and forced himself to pick up his newspaper and head home. It was only when he touched his newspaper that he noticed what had happened. It was heavier, much heavier, and a fraction of an inch of manila showed in the fold.

The blond man had made the drop without Berger's even knowing it. Not only had he made the drop, but from the weight of the envelope Berger surmised it must be an extremely large one. Usually he carried only one or two envelopes to the members of Congress or the Cabinet. This felt like ten times that amount.

A thrill went through Berger as he stood up from the bench and started to the soccer field. It was a thrill of excitement mixed with intense danger. Things had changed all right. And Berger was a part of it.

Chapter Six

Judge Kaplan was a man who had seen it all. In his eighteen years on the bench he'd watched the endless parade of life with first sympathy, then irritation, and now merely indifference.

He was just putting in his time. In a few short years he'd be eligible for retirement. He already had the lot picked out in Key West. There was even enough room for a small boat dock in the back. It was that, much more than any great belief in justice and the law, which made Judge Kaplan comb his silky white hair, don his judicial expression and robes, and walk into the courtroom each day.

Beal sat in the courtroom, staring straight ahead. He was wearing a suit. After a week of wearing prison clothes it felt strange and uncomfortable to him to be in anything else, and even though he'd been allowed to shave, he still could feel the prison on himself. Looking out at the clean, well-dressed people in the courtroom, he felt like a visitor from another planet.

Only a few feet away he could see the grand jury waiting for the judge to ask them their verdict. There were twenty-three of them, all sitting upright, their hands folded neatly in their laps like children on their best behavior. It occurred to Beal that they, too, felt like strangers.

Next to Beal, A. J. Kite, a fancy-pants lawyer slumming with the Public Defender's Office, was joking with the prosecuting attorney, a not entirely encouraging sign. Nor was it much of a surprise. Kite was the third attorney Beal had had. Each time Beal complained about his lawyer, he was replaced with someone even worse. Finally Beal stopped complaining. Though Kite was impossible, Beal was scared by who would be next.

Yesterday Kite had stirred himself and made a few points. But very few. Mostly he had sat around showing as much interest as a nineteen-year-old wife for her eighty-year-old husband when he was feeling frisky. Kite looked as if he were making mental laundry lists or playing handball or planning out his hot date for the night. Whatever he was doing, he wasn't in that courtroom.

After a week in the American judicial system Beal was getting used to indifference. All the first night Beal was in jail, he'd sat huddled in his cell, listening to the terrible night howls, the smell of urine and disinfectant burning his nostrils, yelling to the walls that he was innocent.

The next morning he'd spent his energy telling the same thing to his lawyer. With about the same results.

By the time Beal got down to Kite he was well aware that the evidence against him was overwhelming. The police had a body, a gun, fingerprints, powder traces, witnesses to swear that Beal had purchased the murder weapon, witnesses to swear that he was not a man of the highest caliber. There was no question that all of his lawyers would have preferred representing the other side.

When finally Beal took Kite as his lawyer, he had poured his heart out to the thickset man with the thinning East Coast Kennedy hair and ducklike waddle. He'd told Kite how he'd grown grass in his closet, how Mrs. Conway had warned him about the police and he'd taken off to the mountains to think.

"If I had murdered the old woman, I wouldn't have turned myself in," Beal said, almost pleading.

"Stranger things have happened," Kite answered, unmoved. "So tell me what happened after the mountains."

Beal shrugged. "I drove to Santa Cruz and turned myself in."

"Did you talk to anyone? Did you see anyone?"

Beal slumped. "No one. At least no one who would testify to it. You see, when I was up in the mountains, there were these men with high-powered rifles and Dobermans . . ."

Kite's eyebrows shot up to his receding forehead, and he cleared his throat. Beal supposed he didn't believe a word that he was saying. He couldn't blame him either.

"I'm telling the truth," Beal said desperately. "There were four or five of them, and they seemed to come out of nowhere."

"Most interesting." It was clear from Kite's face that he was not interested. "And after the mountains did you see or speak to anyone?"

"Just a few gas station attendants. I went to the police the moment I hit Santa Cruz."

"The murder happened two hours before you turned yourself in."

"I was still on the road."

"And you're positive you didn't talk to anyone? Some girls in a lunch counter, for example. Did you stop and tell anyone anything, say, about those men in the mountains?" He rolled his eyes to the ceiling, a mocking smile across his face.

Beal was silent a long while. He could hear the empty hollow hum, the sound of the prison steel and loneliness. Finally he said, "I loved her, you know."

Kite looked confused. "Who?"

"Mrs. Conway. I wouldn't have hurt her for a million dollars, let alone some lousy savings she didn't even have. I used to kid myself that I played cards with her to be nice. But the truth was I kind of liked sitting in her living room. Everything was so old. It even smelled old, and it reminded me of being a kid."

But Kite wasn't listening. He was gathering up his papers.

Beal could stand it no longer. He reached over and grabbed him by the lapels. "I'm innocent, God damn it. You're my lawyer. You're supposed to believe me."

Kite had merely pulled away from Beal and rung for the guard.

Beal had paced his cell the whole week. Everyone who entered was told he was innocent; anyone who even glanced at him got the whole story. Not that one of them believed him. Men who were up for murder one had a reputation for being somewhat lax with the truth.

After three days his mother and father had come. Beal never thought he'd be so happy to see his parents. But the terrible indifference of jail, the anonymity made him rush to the visitor's room excitedly.

His mother had walked in stiffly, her back rigid, her lips pressed thinly together. And Beal thought bitterly it was inevitable that a woman whose favorite part of the newspaper was the obituary column wouldn't miss out on this. His father had shuffled in behind her, looking neither right nor left but at a place on the floor.

It was his mother who took the microphone and watched him through the thick bulletproof glass.

Beal waited for her to say something. He didn't trust his own voice. He didn't know whether it was relief or fear, but something made him want to cry.

"Hi, Ma," Beal said finally. "I was beginning to think you weren't going to show up."

"Your father and I have come up here to tell you something." She stopped, looking at Beal through the thick glass as if he were a shark in an aquarium.

"I didn't do it, you know. Mrs. Conway was a friend of mine."

Mrs. Beal didn't seem even to hear him. "It was only right that we come and tell you ourselves. Your father and I have decided we must sit *shiva*."

Beal felt the blood rushing to his head. "What the hell are you talking about?" He thought he was going to faint.

"You're dead to us, Jack, from this day on. We'll

86

go home and say the prayers for the dead. From now on we have no son."

Beal looked over at his father and rapped sharply on the glass. "And you, too, Dad? Is that it? You don't care if your son is innocent or guilty? Just sit *shiva* and forget I ever existed?"

The thin, stooped man turned away, but there were tears in his eyes.

Beal screamed. "Well, then get the hell out of here. You're no parents of mine."

The guards were up and moving toward Beal.

"Get out," Beal yelled. "You're dead for me, too."

The guards were over to him, but he didn't struggle. He felt sick to his stomach; his head was pounding, and just for the moment he wanted to be dead.

There was a noise in the courtroom, and Beal was torn from the past. Judge Kaplan was scanning the room with his pink, newly shaven face pursed into a solemn frown. "Mr. Foreman, has the jury reached a decision?"

The foreman of the grand jury had a wandering eye and so was able to fix both Beal and his fellow members of the jury with his fishy stare. There was the faint trace of a smile on his thin Iowa-farmer lips. His sparse gray hair was neatly combed, as if he were attending a birthday party.

Beal watched the foreman, looking for signs. For example, the smile. Was he smiling because he was delighted to be freeing an innocent man, or was it because he was nailing a psychopath?

Or was it just pride? For once the little gray-haired man with the wandering eye had the destiny of another man in his bony old hands.

It had taken several hours to reach a decision. Now that was a good sign. He scanned the jury's faces. Obviously several of those faces had believed in his innocence. Maybe more. Perhaps they all believed him. Or perhaps they just all sat around eating tuna sandwiches.

"Yes, we have," answered the foreman.

There was a pause as the foreman surveyed the courtroom with his wandering eye. He was enjoying this, all right.

Beal thought he was going to faint. Everything was far away and hazy, and moving fast, like a roller coaster ride.

"Jack Beal is hereby indicted for the following crimes: Statute number . . ."

Beal heard the words but didn't understand them. Everything seemed so distant and cloudy. Even as the judge was remanding him to the Santa Cruz County Jail until he could be brought to trial, Beal stood stunned, watching the muted events as if they were on the TV screen.

It was impossible to believe that this was happening to him. It was imposible to believe that someone wouldn't come in yelling, "Surprise!" Then they'd all go out for a beer and have a good laugh about everything that had happened.

Beal closed his eyes, waiting for someone. But no one came.

Nor did they come as Beal stood in the courtyard, waiting for his turn to board the prison bus.

Mostly he was thinking about chickens and cows. It seemed that every time Beal took a ride in the country, it would be his luck to draw parallel with a truck carrying chickens or cows, crushed into cages, being carted off to a destiny Beal had every reason to believe they understood.

One time he'd drawn up to a stop sign and by mistake caught one large, sad brown cow eye staring at him. In that stare he'd seen an almost Christ-like resignation and forgiveness. The memory was so powerful he hadn't been able to eat meat for a long time after that. Or maybe it was only a week. Thus man forgets.

The prison bus waiting in the courtyard had many of the same properties as those cow and chicken trucks. There were the bars and the crowding. The destination seemed pretty much the same, too.

One of the guards stood next to the bus, checking the prisoners' names off on a large clipboard. As each man was swallowed by the dark barred bus, Beal felt a rope tightening around his neck. This was really happening. He was on trial for murder.

As Beal's name was called and he was shoved toward the large sardine can waiting to take him away, a police car screeched into the courtyard. An officer jumped out and made for the guard with the clipboard. He handed him a slip of paper. Beal stood waiting as the two of them nodded and talked. The guard pointed toward Beal.

The policeman, a tall, gangly man with a shock of red hair and the kind of skin that ran to boils, sauntered over to Beal. "You're coming with me." He reached out a freckled hand and caught Beal under the armpit.

Beal held back. "Wait a minute. I want to know where you're taking me."

"To a birthday party." The redhead with the inventive sense of the humor put his other hand on his holster to emphasize his point.

It certainly put his point over to Beal. He allowed the officer to nudge him along until they were standing by the man with the clipboard. Then Beal said loudly, "Wait, I'm supposed to be on this bus. That's what the judge says. You can't just take me anyplace you want without telling me. I want to know where I'm going. And why."

Beal could hear the chuckles from inside the bus. Several of the guards turned to one another and mimicked Beal.

But the man with the clipboard merely shrugged. "Don't make no difference to me."

"Well, it just might make a difference to me, you know? All I want is someone to tell me where I'm going. Okay?"

It was obviously not okay, however, and the redhead pressed deeply into a place in Beal's armpit that sent everything reeling. Beal felt himself going down, but he never reached the ground since the redhead was pulling him along to the police car, where a squat, beetlelike officer was waiting in the driver's seat.

Beal was just beginning to feel a bit better as the car started up with a roar and sped through the courtyard to the gate. He turned and saw the guard with the clipboard shrug and snicker as the police car sent gravel spinning behind it.

But that was the last thing he saw. Because suddenly there was a stabbing pain in his arm, and everything began whirling again, spinning faster and faster until it faded into black nothingness.

In the courtyard the prison bus started up. The driver shoved into gear and headed out the gate. As the driver stopped, waiting to feed into the rush-hour traffic, the bus's brakes screeched loudly. It would be several minutes before they failed completely. The man who had tampered with them had made sure of that.

Chapter Seven

The blond man stood on a grassy hill, his cold, knife-like eyes scanning a half mile to Detroit's Metropolitan Airport. It was close to 100 degrees, and the sun beat down mercilessly. Nevertheless, the blond man looked cool and refreshed. His Bermuda shorts and plaid button-down shirt were fresh and unstained; his face was smiling and pleasant as he leaned toward his surveyor's transit fitted with a special telescopic lens and fixed the Metropolitan runways in view.

There were four runways at Metropolitan Airport, with over 650 planes landing daily. But there was only one runway and one plane that would be of any interest.

The blond man shifted his sight over to the back hangars of the airport. There were five of them far enough away from the terminal. Two, in particular, were very isolated. There would be plenty of room around them for the giant Air Force One and the helicopter that would undoubtedly be waiting in readiness.

The problem for the blond man was where he'd put his men. Slowly he shifted the sight of his transit to the countryside around the airport. There were several houses surrounding the airfield. Unfortunately they were so far away they would present a certain amount of problems, even for the best of marksmen. To make matters worse, it was unlikely that with only three weeks to go, there'd be enough time to secure one for his men. The whole situation was just too complicated.

The blond man shrugged but still remained smiling. Slowly he packed up his surveying equipment, walked to his waiting car, and climbed into the driver's seat. He pulled a map out of the glove compartment and studied it. Tomorrow he would go to the seventy-five-acre Civic Center. He suspected that the presidential convention site would serve his purposes better.

Chapter Eight

A large, bloated, definitely throbbing head floated in a sea that was white. Slowly the head became aware that it was attached to a body, and that body hurt a great deal. The white sea began to resolve itself into walls, and the giant, distorted head into Beal. Then everything was on the move again, the white sea, the bobbing head. And the light slipped away.

When Beal opened his eyes, he was vaguely aware that some time had passed. He tried to sit up, but pain shot through his wrists and ankles, and after a few moments he realized that he was tied, hand and foot, to a large four-poster bed.

This time more carefully Beal lifted his throbbing head and looked around. It was a small white-walled bedroom dominated by the enormous four-poster bed, and everywhere there were feminine touches.

In the next room a TV blared, and he could hear the snickers and chortles of an *I Love Lucy* rerun.

Beal fell back on the bed. He was too sick to be scared, too sick even to cry out. His head felt as if it had been put through a Waring blender, and any noise, no matter how soft, would start those little blades up again.

Even if he had cried out, it would have done no good. He was trussed up like a roasting chicken, and it seemed probable that whoever was watching *I Love Lucy* in the other room had done it.

As if in answer to his unspoken question, the door opened and a tiny middle-aged man with balding hair plastered to his head looked in. He was wearing a slightly wrinkled, ill-fitting suit, a frayed tie, and an out-of-date shirt. There were a row of pens in his right-hand top pocket and a handkerchief in his left. He looked like an accountant.

The Accountant paused, then cautiously tiptoed to the bed, like a man who didn't want to disturb his sleeping child. He watched Beal in silence for several moments, then smiled and rubbed his little hands together. "Welcome back," he said with delight.

Beal tried to shrink back into the bed, but the ropes held him tightly, and all he could move was his head. "Where am I?" he asked shakily. He was starting to be well enough to feel scared.

The Accountant merely smiled. He opened a small wooden card chair, placed it at the side of Beal's bed, and sat down. As he came closer, Beal noticed a sprinkling of dandruff on the little man's shoulders. He smelled of tea with lemon.

The Accountant sat in silence for a long while. He looked like a man visiting his sick mother; then he nodded to himself several times. "You must be some

big man to have a whole trial rigged against you."
Predictably the Accountant had a Yiddish intonation.

Beal startled. Here, finally, was someone who believed what he'd been trying to tell his lawyer, the judge, everyone he met. In his excitement he tried to jerk up, but the ropes tore his wrists and ankles, and his excitement vanished.

"Where am I?" he asked shakily.

"Later." The Accountant's voice was calm and slightly condescending.

"How do you know about the trial?"

"I'm like God. I know everything." The Accountant paused, enjoying his remark; then he sat back in his chair, resting his feet on the edge of the bed, and looked into thin air.

"For example," he continued, "you are Jack Samuel Beal, born twenty-seven years ago of Abraham and Meta Beal at Mercy Hospital. It was a difficult labor, and Meta suffered complications that eventually led to her being cautioned by the doctors never to have another child. The *bris* was held at Uncle Joe's because Meta still wasn't feeling well enough to handle the catering and Aunt Sophie owed her a favor anyway. Little Beal weighed in at nine pounds four ounces and was named after Abraham's brother, who had died the previous year of a ruptured spleen."

Beal's heart was pounding fast and heavily, and he could feel the blood rushing through his body.

"Why are you doing this to me?"

"You're not in jail, are you? That's better than you had any right to expect. So, like they say to women about to be raped, just lie back and enjoy it." Once again the little man smiled at his own joke, nodding his head up and down several times. "Shall I go on?"

Beal closed his eyes. "Suit yourself."

The Accountant did. Once again he leaned back and looked off into space. "Little Beal's school record was, to say the least, checkered. He was thrown out of grammar school three times, all of them for truancy. In high school his behavior took a turn for the worse, and he racked up punishments for locking a kid in his gym locker, smoking dope in just about every nook and cranny of the entire school, and whipping off a quickie with a teacher's aide in the boiler room.

"However, since our young friend Beal was smart, he was accepted into Los Angeles City College, where his record was equally unspectacular. While taking a course in theater costuming—I believe they called it a Mickey Mouse subject back then—he met and eventually married one Margaret Ann Malone."

He shook his head and tsked loudly. "Malone, a Catholic no less. Well, anyway, this lasted exactly two years and a month."

"Stop it!" Beal screamed. He began struggling against the ropes, desperately trying to get at the little condescending man who was watching him like a moth wriggling on a pin.

The door flew open, and the tall redhead and squat beetle rushed in. They were no longer in police uniforms. The Accountant waved them away. "That's quite all right. Mr. Beal is just taking a trip down memory lane."

The redhead laughed. There was something very nasty about his laugh. Then the two of them retreated back to the television.

The Accountant turned back to Beal. "Now that we've just about completed the known portion of Mr. Beal's short career, minus his sudden call to the musical profession and a brief attempt to duplicate what is called a blue box by tones on the piano—a highly illegal enterprise, Mr. Beal—let's move to the unknown part."

Beal turned his head away from the little man and stared at the wall, confused, scared, and very angry.

"The question, as you so aptly put it, is: Why am I doing this to you? The answer is wrapped up in another greater question. And that is: Why was your trial rigged?"

Beal didn't answer. More than anything he wanted to hit the little man who smelled of tea and lemon. He wanted to smash his little sarcastic smile right off his face.

The Accountant patted his arm kindly. "Look, you're a nice Jewish kid, but believe me, I can be less understanding if I have to."

He waited for Beal to answer for a long while. Then he shook his head, making little tsking sounds, walked to the door, and opened it.

"Mr. Beal is having difficulty finding the words to express himself."

Beal heard a lot of foot shuffling, and when he looked up, the redhead and the beetle were back in the room, looking down at him.

The Accountant gave them plenty of room. "Take my advice. It really would be better if you cooperated."

Beal was just about as scared as he'd ever been in his life, but his pride, which had taken a pretty severe

98

beating recently, demanded that he ignore it. Beal was turning his head back to the wall when two strong hands grabbed it in a viselike grip and swiveled it back around. The hands belonged to the redhead, who was pushing Beal's cheeks so tightly he looked like a chipmunk.

The Accountant was watching Beal, his eyes cold and impassive. Gone were the grins and the nods. For the first time Beal realized he was a killer.

"Talk!"

"I don't know anything," Beal managed to say through the clamped hands.

"Soften the bozo up."

The redhead let go of Beal's head. A moment later his fist slammed down into his stomach. Beal screamed. Electric pain tore through him. Instinctively his hands and legs tried to protect his exposed body, but the ropes ate into his wrists and ankles, and he lay open and vulnerable.

Again the redhead smashed into Beal's stomach. His breath was forced from his lungs; searing pain split him in two. Beal's cry strangled off. He was gasping for air, but nothing inside him was responding, and the choking breathlessness grew in intensity until Beal could see nothing but a blinding light that was his pain.

His breath came back in painful stages. Gasps, then burning drafts. Eventually the bright light faded, and Beal saw the three men staring down at him. He managed to get out: "Please, please stop!"

"Good." The Accountant walked back to his chair and sat down. He waved the two men away. "You can go back to your reruns. I'll call you if I need you." Then he leaned forward anxiously. "Let's begin."

The pain in Beal's stomach was resolving itself into a bruised lump, and he could feel thirst. "Can I have some water?"

"Later. After we've talked for a while. Now, exactly why was that trial rigged against you?"

Beal's anger evaporated, and he was scared he was going to cry. "I don't know."

"Look, a great deal of time and money was being spent to get you indicted for a murder I'm beginning to see you wouldn't have the guts to commit. Why?"

It amazed Beal. There he was trussed up like a turkey, being pounded by a couple of goons, and he actually was offended because the head goon thought he didn't have the guts to commit a murder which, indeed, he hadn't committed. Sometimes he really astounded himself.

"I asked you why."

"I don't know. Honest. All I know was I went to confess growing grass in a closet and suddenly I was being held for murder. The next thing I know, I'm being grabbed and drugged by you. And I haven't a clue why. Not a clue."

"There must be a reason. Sometimes life is unexpected. But always there's a reason. Don't you find that, Mr. Beal?"

"Sometimes. Yes, sir, sometimes that's true. But you see, here is a case of my not knowing the reason. Honest. I don't know why." Beal's voice was becoming humble and pleading, and he hated himself for it.

"You're forcing me to call Albert and Simon."

"I'm not forcing you to do anything. I'm telling you the truth, God damn it!"

The Accountant got up from his chair with a world-weary sigh.

"No! Please don't call them!"

The little man slipped back into his chair. "Good. I hate to interrupt them. They're crazy about *I Love Lucy*. Personally I never liked it, not even when I was a boy." He smiled ironically. "Right now you find it difficult to imagine I ever was a boy?"

It was true. Beal couldn't picture the little bald man as anything but sitting behind a large ledger. So much for instincts.

"You were about to tell me why this is all happening to you."

"I swear I don't know."

The Accountant's eyes glittered coldly. "You're playing with me." He got up abruptly and went to the door.

Beal screamed, "No!" But the redhead and beetle were back in the room, standing over him. The redhead seemed to be surveying Beal for his tenderest parts. Beal could see he was a man who enjoyed his work immensely. He closed his eyes tightly against the sight of the men.

Brilliant pain tore at his chest, spreading outward until every inch of his body burned with it. He was screaming, and the sound of his own pain scared him even more, compounding his hysteria until he thought his heart was going to burst with it. He could hear himself pleading, "Please don't, oh, God, don't." But once again the shuddering pain flashed through his guts as a fist came down on him.

There was a blaze of brightness and then pitch black.

The Accountant was whistling "Night and Day" when Beal came to. The minute he opened his eyes, the little man reached toward the nightstand and picked up a glass of light brown liquid.

He put a straw in it, then leaned toward the bed and lifted Beal's head gently. "It's just milk and coffee," he said softly, then placed the straw between Beal's lips, making motherly clucking sounds as Beal sucked in the sweet, milky coffee.

After Beal finished, he replaced the glass on the table and sat back in his chair, crossing his legs primly. "Feel better?"

"No!" Beal's voice was a sob.

"Just tell me what I need to know and I promise we'll go away." His voice was sickeningly sweet with understanding.

"I told you before. I don't know anything."

"All right. Let's suppose for fun that you told me the truth. What do you know about a man named Harry Langdon?"

"I don't know anyone by that name."

"We can't play if you don't cooperate. Okay, we'll start with an easy one. James Chesapeake."

"The only Chesapeake I know is President of the United States. I wouldn't say we're exactly pals."

The Accountant sat forward excitedly. "But you do know him?"

"I was joking."

"Ha-ha."

"Look, I swear I don't know the President of the

102

United States. You can give me a lie detector test if you want to."

"About that question but not the others?"

"No. Please. All of the questions."

"Okay, okay. Let's go along with that one, too. Who do you know in the government?"

"My uncle was a postman."

"You really are a very foolish young man."

"I'm telling you the truth. I don't know anyone in the government. I don't even read the papers."

"All right, let's pass that one by, too." He paused, then glared directly at Beal. "What do you know about blackmail?"

"It's against the law."

"Believe me, my friend, this is a question to which I will receive an answer."

"I swear I've never blackmailed anyone. Are you kidding? Blackmail? Jesus, Jesus," he kept muttering to himself. "All I did was grow grass in a closet. Jesus. What's going on?"

The Accountant watched him coldly. "Do you know a man names James Luce and another named Kip McBride?"

"Never heard of them."

"They, my friend, are the heads of the FBI and CIA respectively."

"I told you. I don't read the papers."

"All right. Then who do you know at those bureaus?"

Beal tried to laugh. He was not successful. "No one. Really. At least I don't know if I know them, if you see what I mean."

"Clearly." The little man's eyes were glittering

again. He stood up, went to the door, and called his men.

"No, please, God help me. I don't know anything." Waves of nausea and fear were shaking Beal. He could feel tears, hot and burning, streaking his face. But he was beyond shame.

Then there was the pain again, horrifying, gripping pain, radiating through his body. He strained at the ropes, trying to protect himself, tearing at his own skin in his feeble attempt. Another punch and he thought he heard the sound of his ribs cracking and, over it, his terrible screams. The blazing brilliant light returned, and then, almost immediately after it, the blackness.

The little man stared down at Beal for some time. He reached into his pocket and unrolled an antacid. He crunched it loudly between his teeth, smacked it down, then turned to his two men and shrugged. "He knows nothing."

"Good morning." The Accountant's voice was cheery, as if he were greeting a secretary after spending a pleasant weekend with his wife and kids. "Simon's making coffee and eggs. I can't say I recommend them, but it's the best we could do on short notice."

Beal jerked up, shocked that it was morning and that he was alive to see it. It took awhile before he realized he wasn't tied anymore and he could move. Instinctively he cowered back against the wall.

The little man laughed. "Well, the eggs aren't that bad. We'll be at the table when you decide to come eat. You'd better, by the way. You'll be taking a long trip today, and you know airline food, all those horrible little packages of carbohydrates."

Beal pressed himself tighter to the wall, as if it could give him shelter. "What do you people want out of me?"

The Accountant stood in the middle of the room, looking very small and wrinkled. "If it's any help, I'm sorry."

"You're what?" Beal screamed. The fear was receding, and once again anger came up. "What the damn hell does that mean? You're sorry. You could have killed me."

Sparrow shrugged. "Anyway, I am. Now get cleaned up and come out for breakfast. And don't bother trying the windows. They're nailed shut." He started to the door, then stopped. "By the way, my name's Sparrow." Then he closed the door quietly behind him.

The minute Sparrow left, Beal tried to raise himself from the bed, but there wasn't any part of his body that wasn't screaming with pain. It took him close to a minute to get to the window. As the little man had told him, it was nailed shut.

Beal sullenly dragged himself into the dining room. Sparrow looked up from the table; there were smears of butter running down his chin. Though Beal had planned to refuse to eat, the smells reached out to his aching, empty stomach, and he slumped into the chair Sparrow pushed out for him.

"You see. All very homey, isn't it?"

Indeed, it was all very homey. The dining room was aglitter with copper pots and little mementos. On the wall a little pencil-sketched boy peed into a pencil-sketched river.

SHELLEY KATZ

Immediately the beetly squat man named Simon stood up and began spooning large clumps of eggs onto a plate, arranging several wedges of toast attractively along the side. He seemed to care genuinely about making a nice presentation. Simon waited as Beal took his first bite, as if expecting a compliment. He didn't get it.

Beal could feel Sparrow watching him with that condescending, peering gaze he remembered painfully from the night before.

Finally the little man asked, "Have you ever been to Morocco?" Beal didn't look up from his plate of eggs. "It's a very interesting place. I'm sure you'll enjoy it. Now, after breakfast, I'll be giving you your papers. You know, passport, driver's license, that kind of thing. Your name is John Peal. I usually find that it's better to make a new identity as close as possible to the old one. You're a student at UCLA on an extended vacation."

Beal threw down his fork. "I'm not going anywhere."

Sparrow was unmoved. "You know, my friend, you bring most of your troubles on yourself. Hostility. You definitely have a personality problem. You might look into getting some professional help."

Beal pushed back from the table, almost knocking it over. He was about to spring at the little man when the redhead reached one freckled, preternaturally fast hand over and grabbed him. He shoved Beal back into his chair with a clatter.

"That's all right, Albert. Jack is understandably upset."

Simon leaned toward Beal. On his dark, greasy,

106

round face was a look that contained vague traces of caring. "Listen to Sparrow. He's doing this for your own good." There seemed an almost pathetic need to make Beal understand that the little bald man deserved profound gratitude.

Sparrow reached into his breast pocket and threw an airline ticket and traveler's checks on the table.

"You'll take a plane to Casablanca and from there a train to Marrakech. There's a reservation under the name of John Peal at the Hotel Marrakech. I think you'll find it clean and cheerful, and it's quite close to the medina. By the way, stay away from the hashish there. Most of the dealers are police informants. At any rate, you will remain in Marrakech, occasionally dropping letters to your devoted family. Their addresses are in a phone book I'll give you. At all costs, do not contact anyone in your real family or any friends. It will be dangerous for them and fatal for you. At the end of the month someone will contact you with more money. Oh, before I forget, try to keep a record of your expenses. You have no idea how much easier it makes it for me if I can justify your expenses."

Beal turned to Simon. There was a glimmer of hope that he might help him, but it was quickly doused by the look of dull adoration on Simon's greasy little face as he listened to Sparrow speak.

"A word of caution," Sparrow continued, "don't try to slip off somewhere. You will be found. On that you can rely. You will be found."

Beal felt the whole world reeling around him. He clasped the side of the table as if trying to find something stable and sure. "You're wrong. I'm not going to be found. Because I'm not going."

Sparrow laughed. It was a cruel laugh, and his eyes began their glittering act, like two little blue-white ice cubes. "Oh, yes, you will, my recalcitrant friend. You will do exactly as I say. In case you haven't realized it yet, there are men who are out to kill you. Very competent men. As to why these men want to kill you, I don't know as yet. But believe me, I do plan to find out. Until that time I have been hired to protect you. Take my advice. If you don't do exactly as I say, I can assure you these men who are out to kill you are going to succeed." Then once again he broke into an amused smile. "Relax. Just think, a paid vacation in Morocco. You're going to have a ball."

The blond man stowed his clothes in the trunk of his car and locked it. He was wearing a khaki uniform with a small insignia that said "D & K Exterminators." He pulled his equipment out of the front seat and locked the door.

Ahead was the Civic Center, large, sprawling, open spaces studded with giant buildings that could accommodate conventions both large and small. It was a long walk from the parking lot to the largest building in the Civic Center, the Joe Louis Convention Arena. But the blond man didn't mind. It gave him a chance to look around.

The Convention Arena was a massive modern building, clean lines, efficient-looking, yet in its own way grand. Unfortunately the Convention Arena had rats. There had been a running controversy about those rats ever since the center was built. The city claimed the workmen had left them behind when they constructed the building. The construction company claimed the rats had nothing to do with them. After all, rats were no strangers to Detroit. Any city on a river was always plagued with rats, and Detroit was one of the dirtiest river ports in existence.

In fact, the rats generally kept pretty much to themselves, coming out only for special occasions like luncheon parties or afternoon teas. Nevertheless, with the presidential August 1 convention in just three weeks, the city was anxious that none of the conventioneers be sent squealing through the hall.

The blond man entered the Convention Arena and went directly to the third-floor office, where he sat, waiting patiently, while a secretary with soft brown eyes and spectacular legs bent to a filing cabinet. She pulled out a large folder labeled "Blueprints" and handed it to him, smiling.

The blond man smiled back, but his eyes were impassive. His mind was on the plans before him, running through them quickly, efficiently, like a computer.

In the morning he would return to southern Illinois, where under the brilliantly efficient military eye of his boss he would make his report. From what he could see, the Convention Arena would do very nicely. It would do very nicely indeed.

Chapter Nine

At precisely 10:42 every Friday, Harry Langdon took a small cloth sack out of the bottom drawer of his desk, walked down the long line of women's lingerie cutters, his hawklike eyes alertly watching for any sloppiness, and went to a nearby bank.

As he strode down the street, his hairy thick body held erect, his hooded pale blue eyes looking neither right nor left, he looked like a pink and white rhinoceros, stubborn, clumsy, and incredibly stupid. But in fact, there wasn't an inch of Hill Street that he hadn't seen. His eyes clicked like a camera, recording the position of every car and pedestrian, sensitive to light and shadow, on the lookout for danger. Danger was the one sure thing in Harry's line of work, where people's loyalties were bought and sold like ITT stock.

Harry Langdon had once had loyalties. Things like God and America were something pretty personal to him. It wasn't just that he got a thrill when he saw Old

Glory or any of that rot. A piece of rag had nothing to do with his America. His America was like a giant wave, rolling onward, gathering momentum and power until it was a wall of water, sparkling and clean, sweeping across the universe.

When he was twenty-five, he'd fought in Korea. He'd watched men, good men, die writhing belly up like gray-white fish. He'd seen the fresh young faces and felt their fear as they were carted off to some foreign land, where the faces of hate were all around them and death had no face at all but came as a brief whooshing sound. He'd watched the death and destruction with a profound sadness but never with bitterness. For he knew they were fighting for something wonderful.

He'd been captured himself and seen and felt unspeakable things during those terrible ten months. But every day he'd spent in prison camp, every punishment he'd undergone meant something. It counted. Even if he had died, it would have counted. Every man sacrificed left a monument behind him. They left America.

In the sixties Harry joined the CIA. He'd burned with indignation at the growing bunch of rebels who were trying to tear down everything he loved. That giant wave was rushing headlong toward a breaker. It was terrifying to watch America tearing itself apart. He felt like a martyr on the side of honor and idealism and right.

To pin Harry's loss of faith entirely on Richard Nixon would be an exaggeration. He was a catalyst more than anything. He made Harry doubt, and that was something Harry was not equipped to do.

The revelations about Kennedy, whom he'd loved

with the devotion of a brother; America's abandoning of its allies; the unrest of the sixties; the growing economic malaise—all had contributed to Harry's loss of faith.

Doubt and cynicism crept in and spread through him like a blot of ink, seeping into his marrow, until all the fervent love was gone. Harry had been betrayed.

After that Harry became hard-bitten. He trusted no one. Loyalties were something given to the highest bidder and could be revamped at the wave of a dollar bill. In this new real world Harry saw all around him, results were what counted. How they were obtained was of little consequence.

Harry thrived. He quit the CIA and became part of the large underground of spooks working for industry, politics, and the underworld. Eventually he ran a large network of other spooks. Over the next few years Harry was able to build a brilliant reputation as a brutal realist, a man who survived. In the pecking order it was Harry who did most of the pecking.

As a front Harry maintained a medium-sized lingerie factory in downtown Los Angeles. But Harry didn't know how to do things halfway. The Française Lingerie Company was one of the leanest, best-run middle-sized businesses in the country, according to *Business Week*. And with a typical lack of proportion, Harry could be just as burned at a brassiere pattern that used too much cloth as at an operative messing up an important hit.

Harry's schedule was rigid, precise, and incredibly demanding. Among his two businesses, a golf game in the low seventies, and a string of girl friends that ran mostly to tits and ass, Harry rarely had a moment to

112

think. The honor, the pride, and patriotism had vanished, and nothing had taken their place. Instinctively he knew if he ever slowed, he"d be swallowed by the deep pit of emptiness that was in his guts.

Harry entered the bank. Even if someone had followed him this far, which was highly unlikely, his quick exit and the subsequent circles and backtracking of the next few minutes would lose the follower completely.

Harry slipped into a phone booth at an Arco station and placed several calls, all of them to different numbers, allowing each of them to ring only once. On the fifth number a machine clicked in and transferred the call to a Washington, D.C., telephone booth very near the White House.

On the fourth ring someone picked up. The voice was angry. "I just received a report of a prison bus crash."

"That's right," Harry answered calmly.

The man screamed, "What the hell did you think you were doing?"

"Don't you remember? You told me that kid Beal could damage America with what he knows. You hired me to kill him."

"But, good Lord, man, there were twenty men on that bus."

"Nineteen."

There was a long pause. "What do you mean?"

"Our young friend was picked up by a police car just before he boarded the bus. Needless to say, the real police know nothing about it."

"Then who was it?"

"Could be concerned friends and relations. Could be someone's on to you. It's too early to tell."

There was a long hesitation as the man on the other end digested this and tried to come up with a solution. He was a man used to giving orders, and he hated coming to Harry for advice. Finally he relented. "So what do we do?"

"Cover the airports, train and bus stations. The usual."

The voice was scared. "But what if you don't find him?"

"We'll find him all right. It'll be expensive. But we'll find him."

"You better, you hear me, Harry? You better find him and fast."

"Don't worry. Just make sure I get the money and Uncle Harry will make all dead."

Harry replaced the receiver, then quickly retraced his steps, slipping back into the bank and filling his cloth sack with the cash he paid his workers. It was exactly 11:10 when he returned to his factory.

Senator E. Bud Fuller put down the receiver angrily and ran his fingers through his thick white hair. But it was mostly himself he was angry with. It was his job to safeguard the Trust. And at the moment he was afraid he wasn't doing it very well.

Then abruptly he patted his hair back into place, straightened his athletic shoulders and strode back to the limousine. He got ready to board the private plane.

Chapter Ten

Even today, as Fuller climbed out of the helicopter, with his worries about Harry and the agony of what he suspected about the Trust squeezing at his heart, he still found himself stopping and staring around in amazement. To anyone passing by, it was just a large rambling piece of ranchland in one of the driest corners of New Mexico. Built deep back on the land, just barely seen through the trees, was a large ranch-style house of good sand-colored brick. Cattle and sheep grazed the front acreage. Though it must have been a struggle grazing the rocky land, they looked reasonably well fed and healthy.

No one in the nearby town knew a great deal about the couple that owned the land except they'd inherited it five years ago from a distant cousin. He was a retired army colonel from Norwalk, and she wasn't very friendly. But while the large man with the complexion of raw hamburger and his birdlike wife lived their solitary life above, there was a whole world operating independently beneath them.

The ranch had been set up as an auxiliary plan, to be put in use only if the bunker deep in the arid California mountains became insecure, as it had. Yet it was as intricate and competent as a missile base.

In the basement of the house, an elevator had been constructed that could descend three levels into the ground. The first stop was a central clearing area. Here the sensitive detection devices that were strung along the ranch acreage terminated in a wall panel connected to a good-sized computer. Anything that moved within a four-mile radius was monitored by the computer, which alerted the guards.

Ten Dobermans were housed in a large cage across the hall. The door to the cage was operated by both the computer and manual switches. The dogs had been taught the smell of the eleven men living in the complex plus the other five members of the Trust. Any new smell was considered enemy, and the Dobermans were well trained to deal with enemy.

On the next level were barracks where the men who guarded the complex lived their sunless but highly lucrative life. There was a bunkhouse, military style, with a locker beside each bed. Down the hall was a large recreation room, stocked with every kind of electronic game, a minigym, a badminton court, and a fully stocked bar and snack bar. The men divided their guard duty into four-hour shifts, and they always worked in twos. At first there had been the concern that the extreme isolation would get to the men and that security might be breached. But in fact, nothing of the kind had happened. They were all mercenaries who understood discipline and liked it, the pay was spectacular, occasionally women were smuggled in to keep them occupied, and the possibility of a sunny, powerful future had been implied strongly. It seemed to be enough.

The last level was given over to two rooms, a large office with a floor-to-ceiling computer and a small, almost cell-like bedroom. While it would have been extremely easy to have made this level luxurious, even opulent, it was quite the opposite, barren, devoid of anything but the barest necessities, like the rocky, arid land above.

Fuller stepped into the house and passed through the living room. It was cluttered with chintz-covered chairs, fauna on glazed plaques, and lively mottoes painted on shellacked wood. The owners were eating their breakfast, but neither of them looked up as Fuller passed through to the basement. It was as if he were invisible.

Fuller stepped into the elevator and descended to the bottom floor. He supposed the rest of the Trust was there waiting for him. He didn't look forward to what lay ahead.

The Trust had changed. Everything had changed. In the beginning it had all seemed so clear. America was being run by industrialists. There was hardly a senator or congressman who hadn't been bought or pressured into submission. Government was just one big pork barrel with a bunch of hungry pigs running around selling themselves for campagin contributions.

Each man had his own area of responsibility; each man, his duties. The Senate, the House, the Supreme Court, the military, the moneyman. There wasn't an area where pressure couldn't be applied. Especially the pressure of blackmail.

But, of course, none of that had worked.

Fuller felt sure the State of Emergency Plan would be brought up again. He could hear the words echoing in his mind. "America must be brought to the brink of ruin before it can be straightened out." The word "ruin" had been spoken with as much emotion as if they were ordering in sandwiches.

During a state of emergency, even the Bill of Rights could be suspended. During a state of emergency anything could happen.

Fuller stopped, listening to the terrible barking of the dogs as they revolved around their cages. The State of Emergency Plan had been voted down last time. It might even be voted down again. Still, that didn't seem to relieve Fuller's anxiety. For in his heart he had a dark fear that no matter what the majority of the Trust decided, the plan was already in effect.

Only two days before, a bill extending the jurisdiction of the military in case of a state of emergency had been introduced into both the House and the Senate. There was every indication of its being rammed through. All at once. With no buildup. The amount of support had led Fuller to suspect that pressure for its passage had been applied and that it must have been tremendous. It terrified him to think where that pressure came from.

But deep down he knew. The pressure had been heavy, strong, profound.

At the end of the third basement's corridor, several guards stood outside the office door. They also did not seem to notice Fuller when he walked past them into the room.

As Fuller entered, he saw the six chairs for the Trust were set up along the sides of a wooden conference table. And Representative Paisley, Justice Keiler, General Nadler, and John Thomas Colton were already in place. Senator Fuller took the fifth seat; only one more chair remained to be filled.

Chapter Eleven

The medina, Marrakech's great monument to greed, is set in a bowl of red dust, separated from the rest of the sparkling white city by high walls and several thousand centuries of progress.

As the stark Moroccan sun lifted over the Atlas Mountains, filtering lined light into the intestinal, rush-covered back alleyways, the great marketplace sprang to life.

Iron gates crashed open. Crates of oranges, lemons, eggplants as tiny as fingers, peaches as big as a baby's head were pried open. Racks of jellabas, caftans, leather coats clattered as they were shoved forward for passersby to see.

Gritty charcoal fires were lit, and brochettes were strung with seductive beads of lamb, chicken, and fish that would send intense meaty smells through the serpentine streets. Spices and honey candy, thick with wasps, were piled into high mounds.

In one street oily black pelts were being thrown from ancient trucks. They slapped to the ground until they covered an entire street, glistening darkly.

A sea of chickens, their feet chained to one another, was piled high in the next street. A sudden rustling, and they all fluttered like a giant wave, then settled back to their half death.

Already starving children lurked around the food stalls, and rows of chanting blind beggars were staking out their claims.

Within fifteen minutes there wasn't an inch of dusty ground not covered with food, clothes, transistor radios, or stainless steel cookware. Merchants with the wiles of Harvard Business School graduates stood poised for the wheedling, crying, and bargaining. Supple eyes scanned the empty streets, waiting for prey. In just minutes those eyes would be transformed into pools of tears as their owners described how they must sacrifice this caftan or that camera in order to buy their baby girls crutches or their wives iron lungs.

Suddenly dark-robed buyers, smelling of strange perfumes, rushed in, combing the streets for bargains, howling in outrage. They, too, had wives in desperate need of iron lungs.

Everything was in motion, brilliant colors, intense smells, clashing sounds. Only the shriveled old men who squatted in dark doorways remained motionless, frozen like statues. They were stoned on hashish.

Beal stood in the medina, his eyes two startled points of light, his brain scrambled. He felt as if he'd just awakened after a two-hundred-year sleep to discover a new land he couldn't even begin to understand. Suddenly all the anger and fear of the past ten days vanished. He was in a madhouse, filled with madmen. He felt strangely at home.

Beal found a café in the courtyard of the medina and, by grunting and pointing, made a waiter understand he wanted coffee and a roll. On the chair next to him was a *Herald Tribune* left from the day before. He picked it up and riffled through the pages.

Inflation was on the rise again; the gross national product, on the decline. Everyone was gearing up for the presidential convention to take place in Detroit on August 1. Chesapeake announced that the awesome weight of today's issues was too heavy for him to pursue any active campaigning for renomination. Meanwhile, he made speeches daily. A new bill extending the power of the military in case of a state of emergency was expected to pass through Congress.

The coffee came. It was thick and muddy, bitter yet very sweet. Beal decided he liked it and ordered another.

He glanced down at the paper again. A congressman from Michigan was being accused of taking money from the oil industry. A judge was exposed as being on the dole of an aircraft company.

Nothing had changed. The world was in shit shape. Only now, for whatever reason, Beal had been plucked from it and dropped into outer space. He decided he was going to like that very much.

He ordered a third cup of coffee, much to the delight of the waiter, then began to skim the newspaper with an interest he'd never had before. It was like a report from another galaxy.

It was only when he reached the back page that he saw the small item datelined California describing a

prison bus crash en route from the Santa Cruz court-
house to the county jail. There were no survivors, but
bystanders said it looked as if its brakes had failed.

He sat where he was, sipping his coffee, but he could
feel the all-too-familiar panic rising inside him.

Finally he could stand it no longer. He got up and
walked back to his hotel, forcing himself to go slowly.
Even as he held onto the phone, waiting for someone
in the Paris office to check the casualty list, he was
able to tell himself it was just idle curiosity on his
part.

It was only when the reporter returned to the phone
that Beal began to shake uncontrollably. Jack Beal's
name was on the top of the list.

Chapter Twelve

David Burns watched the bored, pudgy, middle-aged belly dancer with equally bored, expressionless eyes. His elegant young body in its stylish clothes was sprawled on a brightly embroidered cushion, finding comfort in a position that none of the others at the table could even began to imitate.

Beal shifted on his cushion, exposing a new portion of his anatomy to the brutally hard floor. He sat among one of those loose-knit groups of tourists that form, dissolve, and re-form when a person is traveling alone and looking for dope. He had met David first. They were staying at the same hotel. Later they'd picked up Marianne, a brooding tall blond French student, and George, an equally brooding small dark American, who were staying at a ratty hotel in the medina. They smoked together, then decided to have dinner together.

David had been living in Morocco for six months,

and he'd made all the arrangements, talking constantly in that monotone nasal voice that seemed to mock everything, including his own existence.

David's disinterested sarcasm seemed to match Beal's mood nicely. It had been three days since Beal first learned he was dead, and he was getting used to it.

The first day he'd agonized over why this was happening to him. Certainly he was still alive, but there were a hell of a lot of others in that bus who weren't. That meant the little man with the killer eyes was a great deal more lethal than Beal had suspected. Or perhaps it was the men Sparrow had told him were out to kill him. In the end it didn't matter who had arranged it. Nineteen men were dead.

The next morning, as he stood at the hotel window, watching the first thin streak of dawn cut the horizon, he realized it didn't matter why. A shock of white birds tore the blackness, and suddenly Arab prayers were blasted on loudspeakers. The street was empty except for two mute robed figures, frozen in prayers addressed to the east. He was a passport-holding resident of limbo. Whatever had happened had happened. Of course, dope helped him along in this line of thought, and David's monotone whine and jaded eyes emphasized the point.

The middle-aged belly dancer rolled her jellylike hips toward the tables. Placed strategically in her cleavage was a sampling of various currencies. The only thing missing was a sign that said she also took Master-Card. She slithered over to the corner of the room and leaned toward a solitary diner. He looked up from his pigeon pie, which he ate neatly with a knife and fork, and saw the mountains of flesh rolling only inches from his plate. His precise brush mustache trembled with confusion. His eyes darted around the room nervously.

Then suddenly the little man realized with mortification but also relief that all that was expected of him was money. Reaching into his pocket, he pulled out a Moroccan one-hundred-franc note. He was about to ask for change when the still-undulating dancer snapped it up. The bill disappeared into the dimpled fleshy cleavage before the man had a chance to open his mouth.

Beal watched as the man agonized whether he should demand the money back and risk a commotion. Beal judged him to be an Englishman when he didn't.

The man returned to his meal, his back rigid, his movements more precise than before, his watery green eyes downcast. It was the look of pained resignation that reminded Beal so much of his father, and he watched him with a combination of pity, embarrassment, and anger.

It was a less than comfortable combination of emotions, and Beal laughed in response to it. "Poor guy probably just lost a day's salary and he didn't even cop a feel."

Marianne's eyes were devoid of sympathy.

She glanced at George, but he was hunched over the community bowl of couscous, trying to balance as much of the stew as he could on the small wedges of bread.

David snickered uninterestedly. "Believe me, that money will harm her more than our friend in the corner. Nothing cripples people more than getting something for nothing."

The fleshy hips rippled toward David. He peeled a one-hundred-franc note from a rather large wad and slipped it in the dimpled fleshy chasm, but his eyes showed little interest. "Another nail in the Arab coffin," he told them, smiling maliciously. "Tonight she'll take home her earnings and hungrily count them well into the night, delighted with her good fortune. Tomorrow she'll expect the same and not get it. So she'll eat too much and roll her hips too little in her fury. She'll be fired within the month."

"For someone so young, you certainly are cynical." Marianne looked to George for support. But George, well aware that it was David who would be paying the bill, ignored her glance. When you were traveling, reasonable lays were a dime a dozen. Free meals were not.

David shrugged. "I'm a prime example. I was given a trust fund of thirty thousand a year on my twenty-first birthday and I haven't done a productive thing since."

Marianne's head swiveled to David, her eyes glazed, her brain feverishly converting thirty thousand dollars into French francs. She smiled broadly when the accounting was finished and moved imperceptibly closer to David.

But David's eyes were on Beal. "And you, my silent friend, any trust funds, frozen assets, liquid cash?"

Beal shrugged and began working on the couscous, aware of David's bored, expressionless eyes probing him. "I sure didn't get any trust fund."

"But you have money."

"A little."

"More than a little."

127

Beal stiffened. "How do you know?"

"I saw you keeping your hand on your pocket as we walked down the street. You must have been protecting something. Neither Marianne nor George seemed to care if anyone tried to get into their pockets. Only you and I were so careful."

Marianne had turned her attention to Beal. She was a woman torn between two carrots. George didn't seem to notice or care. He was finishing off the couscous.

David's eyes were fixed on Beal. "When you travel alone for a long time, you learn to become observant. Heaven knows, there's very little else to amuse you." He leaned forward and lowered his voice. "For example, our little friend in the corner, the one who's a hundred francs lighter? He's following us."

Marianne and George turned quickly toward the man in the corner and were staring at him with undisguised interest. Beal noticed that neither he nor David had turned to look. David because he didn't care, and Beal because he cared very much. He tried telling himself that Sparrow had warned him he would be watched. He tried to calm himself by noting that if Sparrow had wanted to kill him, there had been plenty of opportunities.

He was less than successful. "Don't be stupid," he said to David with too much anger.

David was smirking. "Oh, is he yours?"

"I've never seen him before," George told them, though no one was listening.

Marianne was watching David and Beal, sensing everything, though understanding none of it.

David laughed, but his eyes were serious. "What-

128

ever, I suggest all hashish be passed to Marianne under the table. At a convenient moment, Marianne, excuse yourself and go to the bathroom."

Everyone nodded solemnly and began digging into pockets. Only Beal kept his eye on the corner and the wiry man who was eating his couscous with a knife and fork and watching the belly dancer with a baleful eye.

Chapter Thirteen

Jeremy Richards shuffled back from the restaurant to his small hotel on the rue Blanche. He looked like any one of a thousand provincial Britons who pass through Marrakech, carrying small sample cases to be filled with leathers or worked brasses, jewelry, or spices, like the traders who brought the exotic East to England, a troupe of wrinkle-suited, mustached little men described from Sir Francis Drake and Robert Clive.

Richards stopped at the hotel desk and asked a lush Arab girl to place a call to London for him; then he climbed the stairs.

He entered his room and carefully locked the door. After that he emptied his pockets systematically, laid out his pajamas, then went back to the door, opened it, and checked to see if people left their shoes outside to be polished. They did not.

Once again Richards closed the door, locked it, then shuffled to the bathroom. He removed a bottle of

Kaopectate from his toilet bag, unwrapped a spoon from a bit of plastic, and measured out two teaspoons. It wouldn't do to have everything start happening and him stranded on the toilet.

The girl at the desk rang the phone and told him the wait for calls to London was four hours. By that time it would be two o'clock in the morning. He canceled the call with relief, delighted for any excuse not to call home. His wife, Moira, would only launch into a litany of complaints about her burden in life and the eight daughters he'd stuck her with, while he gallivanted God knows where.

Richards laughed bitterly, staring at his little bony face with its thin mustache and watery green eyes. Gallivanting indeed!

He changed into his pajamas and said to himself, as he did at least once a day, that it hadn't been his fault they'd had eight children. He would have been glad to have taken precautions. What the bloody hell, they weren't even Catholics. But there was Moira, year after year, dropping another one like a cow, until the small bungalow in Putney was filled with squalling children and there wasn't a corner of the house for him. All the traveling he had to do had become a blessing.

Moira had been told he was an importer, dealing with the trendy shops in Chelsea and Kensington. She'd accepted it with very little interest. The only thing that seemed to count in her little world of dirty nappies was the money he brought in—never enough—her eight howling little girls, and, of course, how tired and overworked she was. He guessed she was overworked. Served her bloody well right for not taking precautions.

Richards took a Len Deighton thriller from his valise and crawled into bed. The night-light was broken, and the overhead light was dim with the bodies of dead moths and flies trapped in the smeary glass. He had to squint to read.

The truth was he wasn't understanding a word of what he was reading anyway. He wiped his hand across his tight little face with its thin mustache, trying to banish the tension. He felt a thin film of perspiration forming on his forehead. He might as well recognize it. He was nervous, perhaps even scared. And he couldn't put his finger on why.

He laid the book on his lap. Of course he knew why. Good old Len Deighton would have spotted it in a moment. He was losing it. He hadn't quite lost it yet. But the beginnings were there.

It was time to quit while he was still one of the best in the European market. Perhaps not number one, but certainly number three or four. When he'd been on that job in Paris and run into several others at the Crillon Grill, hadn't they all heard of him? Hadn't they invited him over to their table and picked up the check, a treacherous one at that? There had been an American at the table, named Harry Langdon, a thickset man who said he dealt in ladies' brassieres as a sideline. The bull-necked Harry had snorted into his icecold Scotch and told everyone that he held 'em up as well as mowed 'em down. He said he'd heard about Richards, and he'd spoken to him with respect and deference, unusual for an American. It was proved out when Harry called him yesterday. So Richards didn't have to doubt whether he'd lost his standing. The Americans didn't play around with amateurs or losers.

None of that erased the edgy feeling in the pit of his stomach. He could undoubtedly make it through this job, maybe the next, maybe even the one after that. But sooner or later he'd make a wrong move, a tiny slipup, and he'd end up like so many of the others.

A lot of mystery writers would have said that Richards couldn't retire, at least in a vertical position. But Richards knew that was rubbish. Half the private investigators and security men in London had some experience in the field.

It would be so easy. Already he had a very sizable Swiss account just waiting to be drawn upon. He could go to one of those hot-blooded islands where the girls had burnished skins and lovely tight breasts. He could sit, sipping drinks from coconuts at the local bar; he could take long rambles along clean white beaches and watch the sun setting over craggy rocks.

He closed his eyes and allowed the dream to play before his eyes. All he had to do was finish this job, then pack it in. Wasn't that what he'd been saving for all these years?

Richards's eyes opened. He knew he was going nowhere. In the end he couldn't walk out on a wife and eight daughters. It wasn't that they would miss him. In that house crowded with brassieres and sanitary napkins, he didn't count for much more than his paycheck. But there were some things that a man didn't do.

Richards climbed out of bed and switched off the overhead light. He'd worry about the future later. Right now, for the present, he had a simple job. He stopped himself. Sometimes simple jobs became complex. It never did to underestimate. It was always better to expect the worst, then be relieved when everything worked out.

Still, essentially, the job was clean and straightforward. And an opening into the American market, an extremely profitable one, no matter how shaky the dollar might be at the moment.

Richards slipped back under the covers and waited for sleep to overtake him. Tomorrow he'd follow the American boy carefully and wait for the opportunity to kill him.

The opportunity always came.

The blond man stood in front of the counter at Gauge Sales, looking down at the enormous display of weapons with a practiced eye. There were three choices. The AR-15 assault rifle was good. He'd used it several times and liked it. There was also nothing wrong with an Armalite, especially with a good scope like Bausch & Lomb or Zeiss. His eyes drifted over to the H&K sitting off by itself like a coy princess.

The H&K was FNFAL, each part made by one person on one machine, not mass-produced like most of them. It was heavier than the others. He had heard that they used thenolic for the stalk and grip instead of plastic, and that gave it the weight as well as its almost mystical resistance to damage. H&K made its own scope, a Zeiss, and you couldn't beat it. Of course, there was a difference in price, but money was no object. Accuracy was the key, and an H&K was as accurate as they made them.

"Can I help you?" the young pimply boy behind the counter asked as he moved over to the blond man. He was eyeing the man carefully. Though he didn't look like the type that shoplifted, you never could be too sure.

The blond man didn't move, his dark, impassive eyes fixed on the glass counter. "I'll take the H&K semi-automatic assault rifle and Zeiss scope," he said carefully. Then he turned his gaze on the boy and smiled pleasantly. "Three of them."

Chapter Fourteen

Beal was startled awake. It took him several moments to realize it was morning and someone was knocking on the door. It took him several more moments to feel the burning warmth of another body next to him.

It was a sluggish, voluptuous body, dark-skinned and smooth, smelling faintly of orange-blossom water and intimacy. Beal remembered vaguely that her name was Nicole and that he'd met her in the hotel bar. He remembered vividly that she'd taken him with the hunger and abandon of an unhappily married woman, pulling off his clothes and working over his body with her hot pink tongue until he begged her to stop. She didn't. But she'd awakened him several times during the night to pick up her share.

Again there was a knock at the door. Nicole shifted slowly; her warm round hand found its way to Beal's crotch. Her eyes opened and gazed at him hotly.

Beal managed to pull himself from her and padded

to the door. Propped against it was a chair, tilted back against the knob. Beal removed the chair and opened the door a cautious inch.

It was David. "If you're worried about the local Gestapo, forget it. They don't bother knocking around here."

David walked in. He was wearing British army walking shorts and a freshly ironed short-sleeved shirt. "I rented a car for the day. A Cadillac of an uncertain age. However, it has a convertible top and automatic transmission. It seemed to plead to me from across the lot. I suppose it was as lonely for the sound of an American voice as I am. At any rate, I thought you might like to go for a drive in the country."

Just then David caught sight of Nicole and blushed. "I'm sorry. I didn't mean to disturb you."

Beal laughed at his discomfort and scampered back to bed. Nicole was transferring her hot, sluggish eyes to David.

"I think that's an invitation," Beal said, winking. It was only when he saw David's face that he realized he'd made a mistake. It was an awkward moment.

David turned away and sat stiffly on a chair. "Well, you're right. I am a homosexual. But you're safe. I'm not the type that lurks in the men's room wearing a dirty raincoat. Even if I were, there's enough in this country to keep even the most active of us busy."

Beal was uncomfortable. "Hey, relax, man. I don't care."

David smiled thinly, embarrassed by his outburst, and Beal suddenly felt affection for the slim, bored young man.

Nicole had been watching the two men talk with

137

little understanding. Only instinct told her she was out of luck. She got out of bed and went to the bathroom to dress. Neither David nor Beal seemed to notice.

"Anyway, how about seeing the countryside?" David asked, relaxing in his chair.

"You got it."

"And also, how about a little truth?"

Beal was stopped. "What do you mean by that?"

"You're just extremely secretive, that's all."

Beal searched David's eyes but found nothing menacing in them. "I'll be damned if I become part of your collection."

David raised an ironic eyebrow. "Collection?"

"Absolutely. You drew out Marianne and George last night until you had them classified and pigeonholed. She was a gold digger and he was an unproductive mark. You allowed them to bare their souls to you."

David interrupted. "Pathetic little souls."

"You see what I mean? Then you chewed them up, sucking all the nourishment from them, and spat them out."

David placed a small nugget of hashish in a pipe. "My psychiatrist called it detachment. I have a detached personality. It sounds quite medical, don't you think? Like a detached retina."

Beal held out his hand for the pipe. "Is everything a joke to you?"

"Absolutely everything. Though I had to stop my cancer jokes. They just don't go over well. But in point of fact, I find cancer quite hilarious."

"Jesus!" Beal shook his head, then escaped to the softening of the hashish. It occurred to him that, given a

138

little more time in Morocco, he might become as cynical as David.

Nicole came out of the bathroom and walked to the door, her hot eyes extremely cold. It was clear she was not pleased.

Beal decided not to think about becoming cynical, and he put the thought away with all the other unpretty thoughts he'd shoved into the back closet of his mind.

Several hash pipes and a pitcher of strong coffee later, Beal and David were frying in the front seat of a flamingo pink rusted-out Cadillac, watching the exotic parade all around them.

The city of Marrakech slips into suburbs unexpectedly. Suddenly the jumble of white buildings is replaced by the thick red dirt that makes up the houses, streets, and air of Moroccan towns. Cars become scarce, but the traffic is even worse. The wide red streets are clogged with carts pulled by donkeys, camels, oxen, horses, anything that moves. Tiny mopeds, buzzing like mosquitoes, weave dangerously through the crowded streets, while dark-robed pedestrians dart and dodge through the traffic like daredevils.

The noise was astounding. There was the buzzing of the mopeds, the honking of cart horns, the braying of donkeys, the clatter of Arabic.

David was looking into the rearview mirror. "So, our English friend returns." He jammed on the gas. "Let's just run a little experiment. I'll turn off, and you watch for a battered white Fiat."

David suddenly changed lanes and abruptly turned left. He laughed excitedly. "Hey, this is fun."

Beal laughed, too, as they picked up speed and

headed toward the broad stark African flatlands. Then he turned back and saw the Fiat was right behind them.

"Maybe we'd better stop. He could get the wrong idea," Beal said nervously. If the man were one of Sparrow's, he might think Beal was trying to escape.

"What wrong idea?"

Beal searched for a lie. "What if it's the police?" It sounded fairly convincing to Beal as he said it.

David was unimpressed. He squealed with delight as he found a small winding street leading off to the right and slipped the car into it quickly. But the white Fiat screeched into the street behind them.

"I think you ought to slow down!" Beal said tensely. He was getting good and scared now.

David just pressed harder on the gas, scattering the robed figures that were walking slowly to the red dirt hovels they called home.

Beal grabbed David's arm. "What the hell's the matter with you?"

David laughed loudly and sped up. "Where's your sense of fun?" But his face was tight and anxious as he kept glancing in the rearview mirror. The Fiat was sticking to them.

David skidded back onto the main road and tried to slip the unwieldly car through the knot of traffic. A traffic light flashed ahead. David pounded his fist angrily on the dashboard. His other hand went to the door. "Damn it. We're going to have to run." He screeched the car to a stop and leaped out.

Beal remained where he was, unsure whether he was more frightened of the man in the white Fiat or David.

140

David crossed to Beal's side, threw open the door, and pulled him out. "Run, damn you!" he growled.

The white Fiat had also stopped. The thin, wiry Englishman was lifting something to the window.

Beal caught a glimpse of the movement just before David pulled him from the car. Crouching, they ran across the crowded street and toward a side street.

Horns and angry shouts followed them as they wove through the back streets. David had dropped his hold on Beal and was running just ahead, his eyes scouring the dirty buildings for a side street.

"Don't waste time looking back," David said. His voice was calm and professional.

The sound of David's voice chilled Beal as much as the sight of the Englishman lifting something to the window. Panic spread through his chest and closed off his throat. Suddenly he knew he was in as much danger from the effete American as he was from the Englishman. Perhaps more.

David found an alleyway and turned down it. He had run several hundred feet before he realized Beal wasn't behind him. "Asshole!" he hissed. His voice was knifelike. He turned and began to retrace his steps.

Beal was running down a parallel street, pushing through the dark winding passageway with its smell of kef and urine. Clusters of Arab women stood watching their dirty children playing in the dust. Old men squatted at the black holes that served as doorways, eating from cracked bowls.

Beal turned and saw the Englishman running after him. He picked up speed and shifted into a larger street. The Englishman appeared behind him only a few seconds later.

Robed men and women darted out of their way, laughing and jeering at the two white men running through their streets. Someone's been playing with someone's wife. Or perhaps it was a pickpocket. It didn't matter. Their reality was the camel.

Beal tried to run faster, but already his breath was coming in short, painful gasps and his legs were beginning to ache.

He spotted a tiny winding passageway leading off the street and ducked into it, running blindly, crazily. He was almost at the end of the alley when he saw it was a dead end.

The Englishman appeared at the top of the alley. Even his small silhouette blocked out most of the light. Beal looked around wildly, then began pounding on a large wooden door. The man wouldn't chance killing him if there were witnesses. Or would he? It was Morocco. Beal didn't know what the laws were in Morocco. Maybe there weren't any.

There was no answer to his knocking. Beal rushed to the next doorway and again began pounding. This time he shouted "Help!" loudly. Though they might not understand the word, his tone would make his meaning clear.

But his shouts just echoed through the empty street. Beal tried kicking at the door. With his luck it was the only solid object he'd encountered since he'd come to Morocco.

The Englishman slowed and pulled a revolver from under his jacket.

Beal pressed tight against the door, pounding with his fist and yelling. A few splinters and red dust rose from the door, but it didn't move. It was then he realized he was pounding on the door of a factory, and it was Saturday, the Arab day of rest.

A strange spitting sound split the air.

Beal pressed tighter to the door. Again the *pfft*, louder and closer. A piece of the red building was sheared off. The strange sound was a silenced bullet.

All at once there was the roar of a car. Loud, angry shouts broke the silence. The sound of footsteps clattered toward him.

Beal pressed tightly to the door, waiting for the inevitable.

A hand grabbed him, tightening around his arm, wrenching him from the doorway into the center of the alleyway.

It was David. "Bastard got away," he said mostly to himself. To Beal he motioned toward a dark green Opel at the end of the passageway. It was then Beal noticed he was holding a gun.

Beal allowed David to nudge him toward the car. He had stopped looking like an effete American tourist long ago. As Beal got close to the car, he spotted the bony redhead named Albert watching him from the driver's seat.

And in the back, peering out condescendingly, was Sparrow. "Hasn't anyone ever told you never to enter a dead end when you're being pursued?" He made some moist clucking sounds, then reached into his jacket pocket and peeled an antacid free. He popped it into his mouth and began crunching it into a chalky powder.

David shoved Beal into the back seat next to Sparrow, then hopped into the front. Albert started the car and began winding back to the main street. His bright red slash of a mouth was curled into a nasty smile. He looked like an evil Howdy Doody. "That clown Richards sure is losing it."

Sparrow wagged a gnarled finger at him. "Now, now, Albert. Never underestimate the opposition, especially Richards. He's done some very nice work."

Albert obviously did not like instructional fingers being waved at him. He grunted, then muttered angrily, "Well, he sure was a turkey this time."

"I don't think that it can be pinned entirely on Richards. He was badly informed. He expected no opposition. The next time he will."

Beal's eyes narrowed into two furious points of light. "I've got a news flash for all of you. There isn't going to be a next time."

Sparrow chuckled. "I certainly hope you're right."

Beal went for the door, but he'd hardly touched metal when Sparrow's wrinkled old hand grabbed his, found a place on his wrist, and squeezed.

Beal released his hold on the door with a loud cry of agony. There was no question that these men were up on their pressure points. He held his throbbing wrist tightly.

"I wouldn't try that again," Sparrow said calmly. "It's our job to protect you."

"Protect me? So far you've tortured me and murdered an entire bus load of prisoners. Some protection!"

Sparrow slapped his face in frustration. "A moron I've got. As if this job weren't hard enough, I get a schmuck. Look. So far I've saved your life twice. That

144

prison crash was staged to kill you. It was me who took you away from that bus. Right? Then, when they found out you weren't as dead as they wanted you to be, they sent Richards after you. Time number two, I saved your life."

Beal leaned back in his seat sullenly. "You expect me to believe that? You're all a bunch of liars. Including David, or whatever the hell his name is."

David leaned back. "It's David."

"Tremendous. A gem of truth amongst the bullshit. Well, anyway, as I was saying, even good old David over there has been handing me a string of lies, except maybe the bit about being a fag. That I believe!"

David's neck flushed, and Beal realized that in his own strange way he'd confided in Beal. Sparrow glanced at David quickly, and Beal could see the surprise and disapproval in his eyes. Sparrow covered it almost immediately.

"The truth, plain and simple, Mr. Hotshot, is that our lives are inextricably intertwined. Like it or not. I've been hired to protect you. And as much as I'd like to throw you to a destiny you seem to crave, I'll do just that. As for that night in the country, I explained I was sorry about that before. I had to find out what you knew."

"Oh, yeah? Well, what the hell did you find out, huh? You found out what I told you all along. I know nothing."

Sparrow shook his head. "Oh, no. We got some very valuable information that night. There is no question that you do know something. You just don't know what you know."

Sparrow paused, watching the road ahead. As they

passed road signs, he pointed in the direction of Casablanca. When they'd turned, he shifted his gaze back to Beal.

"Have you ever been to Athens? The food is a bit heavy, but the wine is quite good, I think."

Chapter Fifteen

Richards placed two calls, one to London and the other to Casablanca. With the usual eccentricity of utilities, his London call came through first.

"How are you managing, Moira?" He tried to sound cheerful.

As always Moira didn't notice the inflection of his voice. Her mind was on her own life. "Vanessa's gotten herself thrown out of school again."

"So let her stay out. She's fifteen. Won't hurt her to work."

"She needs a proper education." Implicit in this was: So that she doesn't end up like me, saddled with eight children and a gadabout loafer for a husband.

"Whatever you think best, my dear." Richards flipped open his gun and spilled the cartridges out onto the bed; then he clicked it closed, raised the emptied gun, and aimed at a lamp.

"When are you coming home?"

Richards pulled off an imaginary shot, then shifted the barrel to the top dresser drawer. "Soon. I've run into a bit of trouble here. Someone's been dipping into the till."

Moira's voice was a whine. "Why can't they get someone else to straighten things out? They can't be sending you all over the world. After all, you have a wife and children. It wasn't as if they paid you a proper wage to start with."

"I don't notice you or the girls wanting for anything." Richards pulled the trigger and pretended to demolish the bureau.

"That's because I'm bloody frugal. I have to be, with ten mouths to feed."

"Nine," said Richards as he moved the gun towards the mirror. "As you said, I'm never around."

Richards aimed and popped off an imaginary shot that blasted his reflection to kingdom come.

He smiled, then said hurriedly, "I've got to get off now. Expecting another call. Bye, love." He smacked a kiss and hung up the phone before Moira had a chance to answer.

The call from Casablanca came through less than a minute later. Richards snapped up the phone and barked, "Get to the Casablanca airport quickly. Keep your eye on the planes. I'll be there as soon as I can."

The man on the other end tried to ask what had gone wrong, but Richards had already hung up and was reloading his gun.

Chapter Sixteen

The sun was going full blast. A tall dark-skinned shepherd in white robes stood against the endless sky, flicking flies with his crook. In the distance a small village of mud houses baked in the brutal afternoon sun, as it had for centuries.

Beal stood watching the shepherd flicking flies, wondering what kind of life he led in that cluster of mud huts in the distance. Despite the filth, the heat, and the flies, it seemed not without its charm compared to Beal's.

Sparrow, in his wrinkled business suit and tie, looked exotic against the burning Moroccan landscape, a domestic animal in the midst of jungle. He walked toward a malnourished tree, looking for a patch of shade, then motioned for Beal to join him.

David stood by the Opel, eating a candy bar, while Albert peed against a rock, his eyes vacant and serene.

Beal resisted following Sparrow for a moment, then relented. He had very little choice in the end.

"This time I think we'd better take a different tack," Sparrow said amiably. "Since you know nothing about the blackmail, what do you know about the Lacey assassination?"

Beal's eyes broke from the horizon quickly, and he turned them on Sparrow. "Jesus Christ!"

Though all along he supposed whatever was going on had to be big, this was overwhelming. Slowly he slid to the ground next to Sparrow.

"Jesus. Just what everyone else knows. Lacey was killed by some creep called J. J. Foyle, who died of a heart attack a week later." He grabbed Sparrow's arm urgently. "Hey, you don't think I had anything to do with that, do you?"

"Directly? No. On the day Lacey was assassinated you were home with your wife, arguing. We checked that possibility out right away. We've done a lot of work in your behalf, you know."

"And indirectly?"

The question sat on the burning air. Sparrow reached into his pocket and pulled out several pieces of paper. "I've drawn up a list of everyone closely associated with the Lacey assassination. Tell me if any of them strike you as familiar." He handed Beal a sheet of paper covered with names.

Beal ran down the list quickly. The top names were familiar, but only because they were famous. The rest meant nothing to him. He handed the sheet back to Sparrow and shook his head.

Sparrow handed him another sheet of paper. "These were friends of Foyle's."

Beal studied the list more carefully. If there were a

150

connection, it was much more likely to be with Foyle. After several minutes he handed him back the paper.

Sparrow refolded it with a shrug. "Not surprising. I figured Foyle was a dead-end clue."

This stopped Beal. "Wait a minute. How the hell could you think the man who killed Lacey was a dead end?" He paused, trying to gather his thoughts. "Unless you're trying to tell me it wasn't Foyle who killed him."

"Believe me, I'm not trying to tell you anything."

Beal's mind was churning. "But that's what you meant all right. Now, if Foyle didn't kill Lacey or if he didn't do it alone, who did?"

"Who did, indeed?"

"I haven't a clue." Beal hesitated, shaking his head in amazement. "But you think I do have a clue. That's what you meant by saying I know something but I don't know what it is. That's why my trial was rigged; that's why someone's trying to kill me."

"It's gratifying that you're starting to believe me."

Beal's eyes were guarded. "Or this could all be a setup to find out what I know. Don't think I'll fall into that trap, okay? I'm not an idiot."

"I wouldn't touch that with a ten-foot pole."

Beal ignored him; he was thinking hard now, his mind shuffling through his friends and acquaintances, rejecting them quickly. "I can't think of any connection."

"Ah, but there is a connection. Be assured of that. The question is: Why now? Why after five years should they suddenly be coming after you?"

"Because I saw or heard something recently."

"Perhaps. Alternatively, maybe you mentioned something to someone recently. The possibilities are infinite."

Beal was thinking. Finally he said, "Just before I was put in jail, something weird did happen."

Sparrow sat up. "Ah, good."

"I was backpacking in the mountains, and suddenly these guys came out of nowhere, and they had guns and dogs. I think they were trying to kill me."

"And?"

"I ran and got away from them. I think one of them was killed during the chase."

"And?"

"And that's it." He paused, discouraged. "I don't guess that has anything to do with senators and Presidents, does it?"

Sparrow didn't answer for a while. "I don't see how it connects, but we'll check it out."

"They were in Briar Canyon. That's right near Palm Springs."

Sparrow nodded abstractedly but said nothing.

"So what do I do?" Beal asked impatiently.

"I told you. You go to Athens. I have a new identity in the car. In a few hours you'll be Mr. Evan Saunders, on your way to Athens for an extended vacation."

Beal slumped. "Aren't you even going to tell me what's going on?"

"No."

"You said before you're protecting me. At least tell me against who."

"Well, you met Mr. Richards earlier, I believe. He is being run by a gentleman named Harry Langdon, the owner of the Française Lingerie Company, a rather effective front for a top-notch spook lend-out corporation. Mr. Langdon, too, is being run by someone. But as to who, I don't know."

"Great. And who are you?"

"Well, just think of me as the polar opposite to Mr. Langdon. I, too, have my network. You know them as Albert, Simon, and David."

"All right. And who runs you?"

"Let's just say I work for a very suspicious man who has some very grave question about what's happening in America."

"And I have something to do with his very grave questions?"

"It's a complicated situation. You came to our attention because . . . let's call them the bad guys were after you. Beyond that I really don't know, all I can do is surmise. You could hold some kind of clue to the whole mystery. Or perhaps you don't. Whatever, it's worth keeping you safe. At least for a while."

"I'm overwhelmed."

"You're also alive. Try thinking about breathing for a while. It's one of those things you don't think about much until it's gone."

Sparrow stood up and dusted off the back of his pants. "By the way, this Evan Saunders is a brunette, so we'll have to change the color of your hair. David's volunteered to try using one of those temporary rinses out here so we won't have to waste time finding a room. But you'll have to keep it up yourself." He paused, then glanced over at Albert and David, who stood by the car, talking. "Tell me," he said softly. "Is it really true?"

Beal felt Sparrow's discomfort and enjoyed it. "Is what true?"

Sparrow was looking for a neutral place to put his eyes. Finally he fixed them on the ground. "About David. Is he really a *fegele?* You know, a queer?"

"What difference does it make?"

"No, no. No difference," Sparrow told the ground. "I just wondered."

Beal was tempted to tell him the truth. It would probably ruin David's career. It would give Beal great pleasure to ruin a lot more than his career, so it surprised him when he answered, "No. I was just talking. David's as straight as an arrow."

Sparrow looked relieved. "I'm glad. He's such a nice boy."

At the side of the road Albert unzipped himself again and was peeing against the front tire. Beal wondered what was going through David's mind as he turned away from Albert and stared out at the horizon.

"Oh, yeah," Beal said softly. "David's swell. So are you all. You're all a bunch of swell guys."

Chapter Seventeen

It was a hot, muggy day in Washington, and the air sat on the city like a fat woman, heavy, wheezing, and very smelly. It was the kind of weather that did nothing good for people's tempers, and even in the park there was a closed-in, heavy feeling. Though the crowds were bigger than ever, people seemed to be trying to stay away from one another. They sat or walked separately and apart, encased in their own little sections of sodden air.

John Berger sat on a park bench, fanning himself with his paper. He looked like just any other overheated Washingtonian as he stared into space despondently, but in fact he was alert and ready, watching a point in the distance carefully.

The blond man looked cool and comfortable as he sauntered through the park. He was wearing a beautifully cut business suit and sunglasses, and he looked like one of those Italian actors who lounge in sidewalk cafés or step gracefully out of bright red Ferraris.

Just as the blond man reached the edge of the soccer field, he stubbed his toe on a rock. Quickly he picked the rock from the ground and threw it away angrily; then he walked over to the bench and sat down.

"Damn stones," he said with a frown. He removed his shoe and began rubbing his toe.

Berger smiled to himself. "The park is full of them," he answered.

The blond man rubbed his foot and gazed reflectively into the distance. Finally he said, "Undoubtedly you were surprised at the amount of messages last time."

"It's not my business to be surprised," Berger answered tensely.

The blond man smiled coldly, but Berger could tell he was pleased. Once again he replaced his shoes, then took out a cigarette.

"You are good with an assault rifle. How good?"

Berger didn't lie. "It's been some time. I'm rusty." Berger stopped. His heart was beating excitedly. He didn't want to blow this opportunity.

"How rusty?"

Berger glanced at the blond man cagily. "That depends."

The blond man seemed to gain respect. "Of course. There's ten thousand in your pay packet this time."

Berger shrugged, trying to show little interest. "It would take a lot of practice."

"That's only a holding fee. The rest will come in two stages. Twenty just before, twenty just after."

Berger didn't move. He was hardly even breathing. "Five days," he croaked out. "I'd need five days."

The blond man nodded, then stomped out his cigarette, and without another word he was gone, stepping coolly through the crowds and into the glaring Washington day.

Berger was breathless. Next to him was the newspaper. Once again he hadn't seen the blond man even touch it, but he no longer wondered if he had.

Berger began fanning himself with the newspaper again and staring into space. From the corner of his eye he could see something between the folds of the newspaper. Cautiously he slipped the pages back and caught sight of twenty five-hundred-dollar bills.

Berger sat thinking for a long while, fanning himself with his newspaper, though, in fact, he felt a cold spike in the base of his spine. It was a chill of anticipation mixed with fear, a feeling more alive and real than any other in the world. Berger smiled. He had been right before. Whatever was happening was very big.

Chapter Eighteen

Beal's head itched from the hair dye, his horn-rimmed glasses repeatedly slipped down his nose, and the name Evan Saunders kept escaping him so that he had to sneak panicky looks at his passport every few minutes.

The plane to Athens had been delayed for two hours, making Sparrow jumpy as hell. David had stayed away from Beal, out of either anger or fear. Or perhaps he was just disappointed in him.

Finally, when the plane had been called, Sparrow, Albert, and David had stood at the barrier and waved good-bye, clustered together like friends watching a loved one leaving forever.

Beal pressed through the crowd of Americans with cameras and Germans with athletic equipment and found his seat. Sparrow had chosen one on the aisle, which Beal supposed made sense, though he doubted at ten thousand feet escape was much of a possibility.

A moment later a huge man carrying a tattered briefcase and several packages wrapped in plain brown paper leaned over him, trying to read the seat number. He could have been an Arab or a Greek with his greased-back black hair and sweat-stained shiny suit; the smell of violet aftershave mixed with sweat was overwhelming. He squinted at the number for what seemed like hours, until the stewardess came and confirmed Beal's darkest fears.

The man stowed his parcels in the overhead rack, banging Beal twice in the head and once in the arm, then tried to squeeze past him to his seat.

As the enormous man wedged himself into his seat, he removed a large handkerchief from his pants pocket and began to wipe the beads of sweat from his forehead.

Beal watched him from the corner of his eye. It seemed impossible that anyone in his right mind would use such an obvious leftover from a Sidney Greenstreet movie to get at Beal. He took some comfort from that thought, then ordered two double martinis from a blond stewardess with big breasts and a wonderfully vacuous smile.

The plane began its dash down the runway. Everything began to tilt as the earth quickly dropped underneath them. Beal closed his eyes, feeling the incredible power that was sweeping him up into the air and would totally control him for the next few hours. It felt like his life.

As Casablanca wobbled below them, the fat man leaned a jowl toward Beal. "Casablanca is my home. You like?"

Beal took a glossy airplane magazine from the

pocket in front of him and began flipping through its aimless pages. "I hate," he muttered darkly.

This was obviously not the answer the fat man expected. He pulled his tattered briefcase to his ample lap, took out a long sheet of computer printout, and began ticking off figures, intermittently clucking his tongue and nodding with satisfaction.

Beal read a long article about riverboating in Idaho and an essay on the life and lore of the Dover sole. He drank his martinis quickly, feeling nothing until the middle of the second drink, when suddenly the plane became a roller coaster, and Beal checked to make sure airlines still carried sickness bags. They did.

The airline meal only increased his nausea as it glittered and gleamed plastically at him.

It didn't seem to disturb the fat man at all, however. He tucked the tiny napkin deep into the folds of his chin and wasted his tray in just under a minute.

Beal looked down the aisle and saw the blond stewardess leaning toward one of the passengers. She was flashing that first-rate dumb-blond smile, her big blue eyes wide open and innocent. Beal imagined the sound of her warm damp thighs as they rubbed one another. He imagined the two tiny indentations just above the curve of what looked to be a spectacular ass. Then he felt the mammoth man's dark, beady eyes on him.

"You no like your cake?" The fat man had his beefy arm poised over Beal's untouched meal.

Beal handed him the entire tray. The fat man sighed with satisfaction and emptied it of everything but the utensils and a small packet of salt and pepper.

The buttocks were gone, and the aisle was clear. A bored child whined loudly. Beal closed his eyes, trying for a sleep he knew he didn't have a shot at. It occurred to him that the fat man could easily be a double feint. Someone that obvious could be overlooked. He remembered Sparrow's words: "Never underestimate the opposition." He opened his eyes.

The fat man was daintily wiping his mouth with a paper napkin. His hunger satisfied, he grew ebullient.

"So you not like my city Casablanca. That is probably because you don't go to the right places. Next time you let me show you." He reached into his shirt pocket, extracted one slightly greasy worn card from his billfold, and handed it to Beal.

The card had the name Hamad D. Fadu in ornate script, the cryptic words "Import/Export" underneath it. In the corner was a telephone and telex number.

"So you see, please to call anytime. My wife and I show you many, many things you never see. There are still places where the blind birds sing while you eat delicious food."

Despite his better judgment, Beal asked, "What's so special about blind birds?"

The fat man laughed at his ignorance. "Oh, it is very important. Very, very important. When they are young, the hot needles go right in the eye." Beal shuddered as the fat man made a quick stabbing motion with his hand. Undaunted, the man continued. "They sing better when blind. Perhaps they have nothing but the singing then. You think it is barbaric? Yes, perhaps. But then you have never heard them sing."

Beal was getting the sneaking suspicion that the outsized tub of lard was waxing philosophical. He tried to decide if that was a sign that he was or wasn't Hamad D. Fadu, Import/Export.

He pocketed the card. Perhaps one day he would go see the blind singing birds. Or perhaps he'd be dead. The latter seemed the more likely.

"I have been many times to America. Urbana, Illinois; Ames, Iowa; Spokane, Washington. I have seen many things unusual and sad. I have seen Fourth of July parade once. Fantastic with those . . . you know . . . *kaboom?*"

"Fireworks?"

"Exactly. So American."

"Fireworks are Chinese."

The fat man grew thoughtful. Perhaps he was storing this little bit of knowledge away for his next plane trip. "And this Fourth of July, is that also Chinese?"

Beal laughed despite the edgy lump of fear that had settled permanently in his stomach. "No, the Fourth of July is American."

The fat man brightened. "I like this very, very much. How long you stay in Athens? I myself don't stay long. Overnight only. Then I go to Toulon, Loughborough, and Cork. As you see, I travel a great, great deal. Too much. I have a girl in Athens, but I only see one day, maybe two in the months. She is very, very beautiful. Thighs like couscous and breasts like . . ." Again he paused, searching for the English word.

Beal let him fumble, hardly anxious to supply what he could assume was a repulsive adjective. "I thought you said you were married?" Beal asked, trying to steer the conversation from his girl friend's breasts.

The fat man smiled, and for the first time Beal understood the full meaning of the verb "to leer." "Certainly. Marriage is obligation, no?"

"No."

"Ach, you Americans. Always the kid."

"Yeah, we're a real bundle of laughs all right."

The huge man chortled amiably to illustrate the point. "Oh, what the hell," he said. "You come with me and my girlfriend tonight. We show you fun time."

The plane began its descent into Athens. It bobbed around in the clouds for a minute, and then suddenly Athens was spread below them, golden yellow and fractured, like a well-baked cake.

Beal was tempted to take Hamad up on his offer. Whichever side he was on, it might be better to keep an eye on him. The thought of all three hundred pounds of blubber leaping out at him from some dark corner was even more unsettling than the idea of a showdown.

The plane began its descent in earnest. Beal felt his face flatten as the pressure changed. Hamad was looking out the window with fascination. Beal suspected he was regretting his earlier invitation for the evening and was trying to figure out a way to retract it.

Beal was surprised to find that he was sorry. He almost began to believe Hamad D. Fadu, Import/Export, then gave up wondering and allowed himself to feel the roar of the plane as it touched down and boomed with power held back by the brakes.

Beal jumped up quickly so that Hamad could get to his parcels without slaughtering him in the process. Nevertheless, Hamad managed to scratch Beal across the face and elbow him twice.

As the passengers began moving, Hamad told him, "I stay at the Hotel Dionysus in the Nephali Street. It is very, very clean and very, very cheap." But Hamad's voice was absentminded, and he was craning his puffy neck to see over the line of passengers.

Customs looked like one of those pictures of evacuation on the Ho Chi Minh Trail. It took fifteen minutes before Beal was ushered into a small cubicle and body-searched by a straight-faced customs official. Beal supposed everyone coming from Morocco was searched, for obvious reasons.

Beal looked around for the fat man several times, but he was gone. He hadn't even had to clear customs. It certainly settled the question of whether he was on the up-and-up but left the question of which side he was on still in dispute.

Beal didn't get a chance to mull it over. Two large, stocky men were leaning against the wall of the escalator directly across from the sliding door from customs. One of them was reading a newspaper; the other was smoking a cigarette. Neither of them seemed to be paying any attention to the people filing through the door, and perhaps that was the tip-off.

Beal bolted, avoiding the escalator and rushing down the long corridor of shops. He pushed through the crowds, banging them with his suitcase. Everyone stood back, allowing him room. He looked like a man about to miss a plane.

As Beal followed along the curving corridor, he turned his head. The man who had been reading the newspaper was right behind him. The other one was probably waiting at the airport exit.

The corridor curved, and the line of shops gave way to offices. A group of stewardesses came out of one of the rooms, teasing and laughing with a tall dark-skinned pilot.

Then even the offices became scarce, and Beal thought with horror that the corridor could be a dead end. He sped up. In the quiet he could hear the man's footsteps behind him. Then all at once there were shops again and the crowds increased. They were running in circles.

As Beal took the circuit, he looked around desperately for an exit. He could feel that the man was right behind him, though in the noise he could no longer hear his footsteps.

Once again the shops stopped and the offices began. He passed the same group of stewardesses and heard the pilot yell something in a strange language. He didn't need a translater; the meaning was clear. It would be only moments before one of them called airport security.

The footsteps were just behind him now, and he could hear the man's heavy breathing even over his own gasping for air. If airport security caught up with Beal, what would they do to him? It was something he preferred not to find out.

This time, when the shops began, Beal hopped the up escalator and started pushing past the crowds, taking the stairs two at a time.

The man must have been taking them three at a time because he was gaining on him. Beal let go of his suitcase. It bumped twice, knocking people off-balance, then opened, scattering clothes and toilet articles all over the stairs.

Beal didn't pause to see if the man was stopped. He leaped off the escalator, found a door leading to a staircase, and slipped into it.

He paused for a moment, crushed in the darkness,

listening for the telltale sounds of someone following him. He heard them.

Beal threw his tired body down the stairs. Above him there was the click of a door opening, then the clatter of feet. He got out at the first landing and almost cried when he saw the long line of lighted shops. Again he jumped on the escalator, this time down. As he disappeared down the escalator, he caught a glimpse of Hamad kissing a tall, attractive woman. He had been telling the truth.

Beal took the escalator down as far as it went. In front of him was a huge reception area and then, leading off from it, the airport gates. All around him large windows glittered brightly from the electric Greek sunset outside. Everything was tinged red and bloody, even the air. It looked like the end of the world.

He ran down the long line of gates, looking for a door out to the field. He found one and rushed to it. It was locked.

Ahead, a janitor, juggling a large pail of soapy water and an unwieldy mop, stood at one of the doors, searching for his key. Beal steeled himself, then rushed him, knocking the little man and his pail to the floor. The mop skidded several feet down the hall before it clattered to a stop.

With shaking fingers Beal grabbed the bunch of keys and tried them in the door. On the third key the door opened.

The heavy smell of diesel fuel and summer heat smacked Beal in the face. A giant jumbo jet taxied toward him, and he saw the tiny pilot in his cockpit cursing angrily.

Beal didn't stop to watch anymore. In the distance,

beyond the dusty ground and smooth runways, he saw a meadow. Beal took off for it, feeling his heart pounding in his chest and the all-too-familiar aching of muscles.

He turned back and saw a group of orange-uniformed mechanics pointing in his direction and shouting. But he didn't see the man with the newspaper or anyone from airport security.

He sped up. The field wasn't far off. He could see a cluster of cypress trees and some red-roofed houses just beyond it. The roar of the airplanes had softened, and the air was less poisonous. Beal started to relax.

Suddenly noise like a great solid wall crashed all around him. Beal's insides hurt from it; his skin felt on fire. It took awhile for him to understand the roar, and by then it was too late to do much about it.

Huge and glinting red in the setting sun, a DC-10 was swooping down toward him, headed for the landing strip only inches away. Beal watched stunned as the mammoth jet cut toward him, sending hot fumes rushing out all around it.

Beal hit the ground and rolled. The fire and roar became unearthly. It was as if the whole world were in flames as the plane touched ground only a few feet away, then streaked toward the airport, brakes screaming.

Slowly Beal pulled himself up. Sirens were going off all over the place. It was one thing to go sprinting through an airport, but running headlong through the airfield was another matter entirely. He imagined every truck and cart in the whole airport would be searching for him now.

Beal broke for the meadow. His body was still heaving for breath, and his legs were throbbing, but it was hardly the time for a rest. It wasn't until ten minutes later, when

167

Beal spotted a small stream running through the dried-up earth, that he stopped.

It was quiet except for the racking of breath in Beal's lungs. He sank to the ground and lay facedown. Even the parched earth felt cool next to his skin. The sunset had become even more spectacular. The entire sky was lit with magenta and red fires. Far in the distance he saw a father and son, both carrying scythes, walking slowly from the wheat fields toward their stone house. Beal could see smoke rising from the chimney and assumed dinner would be waiting for them. He wanted to cry.

As the sky muted to blue-black with just traces of pink, Beal found a pomegranate tree and picked the ripest one. He emptied his pockets, looking for something to help him open it. Keys would have worked. But Beal had no keys on him. He considered that significant.

An hour later the cicadas started their loud night sounds, the distant cottage windows glowed golden and welcoming, and Beal realized he just couldn't run anymore. Jerk that he was, he was going home.

A soft, cool evening breeze rushed over him. A sliver of moon slipped over the horizon, and a billion stars dotted the sky.

Beal supposed in the end it was the only answer to his problem. If he had to die, at least he might get a chance to find out why.

That night at least one unused ticket form disappeared from every major airline office at the Athens airport. A little later the name of Evan Saunders was added to the passenger lists of planes leaving for Beirut,

Casablanca, Marseilles, Madrid, New York, Los Angeles, Tokyo, Rome, London, Djakarta, Edinburgh, and Brisbane. The flight to Brisbane was already filled, which Mr. Saunders found staggering, since he didn't have the slightest idea where Brisbane was. His reservations on all the other planes, however, were confirmed.

The fact was, if anyone were looking for Mr. Evan Saunders, as indeed they were, the passenger lists would have been of little comfort since he was leaving Athens at the rate of once every five minutes for most of the next morning. And at 9:35, he was leaving twice.

At exactly 9:15, Mr. Saunders sprinted from a men's washroom, where he had spent a fitful night, his head resting against a roll of toilet paper. And five minutes later he was sitting on a plane headed for Tokyo, where he would make his connection for Los Angeles.

Chapter Nineteen

John Thomas Colton had indigestion. Once a man reached sixty-five, indigestion became a regular occurrence; by seventy-five it was a constant companion.

As he strolled slowly through the fragrant darkening streets of Beverly Hills back to his hotel, he cursed the process of getting old, the inconvenience of it, the indignity of it. How many mornings did he awaken, the precarious state of his innards on his mind? When he was a young man, the iron-handed president of Rock Island Oil and undisputed ruler of his family fortune, he'd jumped out of bed thinking of business or golf or breakfast or warm round thighs. Now he'd pull his aching shell from the crisp white sheets ruminating on the rumblings and creakings of his bowels, the twitch of his colon, or the burning of his stomach.

Colton walked, a lone figure on the darkening evening streets, his wispy white hair and dignified but shrunken frame out of place among the tropical evening. Sprinklers whooshed circles of water onto the broad green lawns on either side of the street. Golden light shone from the large houses, and there were sounds of laughing children.

Being old meant many things, all of them bad. There was the faulty plumbing, the brittle, dried-out frame, but most of all, there was the desperate aloneness. Friends and family were dead, childhood buildings demolished, but even worse was the eroding of the old values. Colton knew every generation's old men thought that the world was going to hell in a hand basket, and yet, miracle of all miracles, the world just kept spinning along, onward and upward as a new generation of old men mourned its demise.

Yet Colton couldn't help thinking this time it was different. That's why he had come to California to see Bud Fuller.

They'd had dinner together in one of the dozen French restaurants in Beverly Hills and they'd talked. But the salmon had been overcooked, Fuller evasive, and now Colton was wondering if it wasn't all just because he was getting too old for this world.

Colton slowed up. His stomach was burning hot and heavy in his brittle rib cage, and he could feel perspiration on his forehead.

No, he was reasonably sure that it wasn't just his age. It was the Trust. Things were becoming distorted. What had once seemed a salvation for the country was going sour, as corrupt as the evils it sought to correct.

It had started at the meeting before last, the vague references to causing an upheaval, economic, racial, or political, to drive the country to the brink of ruin. It had been voted down, and surprisingly it had not been brought up at the meeting a week ago. But there had been the congressional vote extending the state of emergency, and even if there hadn't been, there was the feeling that the plan was already being set into effect.

When Colton brought it up over dinner, Fuller had been evasive, but Colton felt sure he suspected it, too. And if they suspected it yet did nothing, wasn't it the same as going along? Colton knew it was.

At seventy-five years old, about the last thing a man wanted was a fight. Just getting up in the morning was a struggle. But Colton had no choice. He knew he had to take the Trust on. Of course, they were going to put up a terrible struggle. They had indicated as much by their silence at their last meeting, when Colton had brought up the subject. Fuller's evasiveness tonight could mean little else.

But Colton held the purse strings. It was his family fortune, his hard-earned cash, that oiled the wheels. Cut off from its funds, the Trust would wither and die. They knew that. They would have no choice but to listen.

Colton stopped. His stomach was on fire, tight and white-hot like molten metal. His legs were weak and shaky; his head was empty with a terrible echoing. And he knew he must sit down.

Slowly he lowered himself to the pavement, loosening his tie, wiping his thin parchment-skinned hand across his damp forehead. He was sick, very sick. It wasn't just indigestion at all.

The pain spread, clutching at his chest with burning talons. His throat began to close, and everything seemed to be spinning and lurching underneath him.

The sounds of the lawn sprinklers and children receded, and all Colton was aware of was the pain and the choking breathlessness. Time was expanding and contracting.

He tried to scream, gathering all his energy up, then pushing his tortured body until his chest expanded and his lips parted. There was a brief soft hissing of air, and then Colton died on the street, alone, except for the car parked several yards away where the blond man sat, smoking a cigarette.

BOOK 2
MID-JULY

Chapter Twenty

It was the loneliness that was the killer.

Beal stood at the grimy window of the Two Palms
Motel, looking out at the heavy evening traffic on
Hollywood Boulevard.

Beal's feelings about Hollywood Boulevard had always been mixed. It was life at its rawest, desire
without explanation, hunger without decoration. When
Beal was feeling good about life, he could see the odd
mixture of whores, pimps, muggers, pederasts, and
tourists from Iowa as a colorful parade. The intense
smells of cheap hot dogs, pizza, incense and pot
screamed to him boldly, like a twenty-dollar hooker.
The constant shriek of police cars stunned the night air,
as if saying, This is real life; underneath all the rococo
trim of Beverly Hills you'll find this.

When Beal was feeling bad about the world, Hollywood Boulevard seemed his own private rot. The crumbling façades housing porno movies, head shops, and

motels featuring waterbeds blazed neon messages to him alone. You failure, they said. This is where you belong. This is all you deserve.

Beal turned from the grimy window. It was not one of his good days.

Nor was room 416 at the Two Palms designed to cheer him up. It was one of those musty, decaying rooms that smell of disinfectant even though they're filthy. The furnishings were limited: a chipped and scarred dresser with drawers that didn't fit; an eviscerated armchair; a cracked mirror. In the center of the room was a lumpy bed that had seen things in its long life Beal couldn't even bear to contemplate. In the corner were the skeletal remains of a television set, the innards undoubtedly for sale on the street below. The sound of Muzak came from a vent in the wall. Even when it was turned down as low as possible, Beal couldn't escape the sound of a whole battalion of strings massacring "I Wanna Hold Your Hand." Mutters and groans filtered through the wall from the next room. The husky voices of sex. Beal counted three of them, all masculine.

Beal had chosen the Two Palms not because it was cheap—he still had most of the thousand dollars Sparrow had given him for Athens—but rather for the anonymity that motels, big among the waterbed crowd, afforded.

Beal had arrived only two hours before, after three days of crossing the globe on stolen tickets. It had given him time to think out his plan of attack.

It was a simple plan, and that bothered him. Somehow something a little more complicated would have made Beal feel more in control. After getting a gun

178

and a disguise, he would have to go to the library and read everything he could about the Lacey assassination. Now this hardly gave him the feeling of a competent intelligence running his life. When Superman or Plasticman ran into trouble, he didn't exactly rush over to the libe for a good read.

Beal shook off the thought, but as the fear receded, intense loneliness quickly took over, and he found himself staring at the phone.

There was no one to call. Beal was a dead man, and he doubted there was a friend or relative who'd be delighted to discover otherwise. He wondered briefly if his father would care, then stopped himself. His father had made his decision at Beal's arraignment. In truth, he'd made it long ago.

It amazed Beal, but even after all these years this hurt him. When he was eighty years old, was he still going to be carrying on mental arguments with parents who were no more than rotting bones in the graveyard? What was with people that they nursed hurts and failures from their childhood well into senility?

As if in answer, a deep voice from the next room shouted, "Gimme some more rope." The rest was lost in heavy breathing. Then, once again, there was the quiet, and Beal found himself almost wishing that Sparrow and his men were there. He supposed there were times when company, any company, even that of jackals, was preferable to loneliness.

Beal's eyes drifted back to the telephone. He wondered briefly what pathetic kind of hopefulness made people keep battering at doors that were clearly closed. Then he lifted the receiver.

Beal's heart sank when he heard his mother's brittle

179

"Hello." For a moment he was tempted to hang up, but the fear and the loneliness crept back into his bones.

He tried to disguise his voice by deepening it. "May I speak to Mr. Beal?"

"He's not here. Who is it?" his mother's voice snapped across the distance. Beal could imagine her thin, shriveled body hunched over the phone.

"Do you have any idea where I can reach him?"

"Who is this?" Her voice was sharp with suspicion.

From one of those deep recesses of the mind Beal pulled out, "This is Academy Rug Cleaning. Mr. Beal set up an appointment for tomorrow."

Beal was congratulating himself on his quick thinking when he heard the line go dead.

He redialed quickly. When Mrs. Beal picked up, he started in right away. "Look, lady, I got an order form that reads Two Twenty-five West Cayoga, Mr. and Mrs. Abraham Beal."

"We don't want our rugs cleaned." His mother's voice was high-pitched and hysterical. Beal wondered if she suspected who it was.

"Hey, lady, I'm just trying—"

Suddenly she was screaming. "For God's sake, haven't I got enough trouble? My husband is in the hospital. He could be dying!" She was crying, and her voice came out cracked and breathless. "Please leave me alone!" she screamed, then hung up.

Only occasionally in Beal's childhood had he been able to see beyond his own anger into his mother's world. It was a vast world, empty and dark, with huge, shapeless shadows of fear hulking in the darkness, and he could see his mother cowering in the corner, shriveled and tight, praying that she would be overlooked. In those moments Beal had felt a profound sadness, guilt, and kinship for his mother. It was the kinship that threw him the most.

Beal tried to calm himself by remembering his mother's dramatics. He'd grown up with her lying in a darkened room, her forehead swathed in a damp cloth, her eyes closed in mute resignation. It had been years before he found out that menstruation wasn't a synonym for cancer. In all probability his father had something simple like piles or planter's warts or infected tonsils.

Nevertheless, he found himself only a moment later, heart pounding, running down the long list of hospitals in the phone book. He located his father on the fourth try.

When Abraham Beal picked up the phone and said, "Hello," Beal knew he really was ill. His voice was far away and faltering. Beal thought he'd never heard anyone sound so old.

Again Beal changed his voice. "Mr. Beal? This is a friend of your son's."

There was a long hesitation, then softly: "I have no son."

The words tore at Beal like a physical assault. Sense told him he should hang up the phone and forget all about it. But it was the aloneness, the terrible separation from love, friendship, comfort, warmth, anything even slightly human and real, that was driving Beal, and before he had a chance to stop himself, he was telling the truth.

"Dad, it's Jack." Beal's voice sounded shattered even

to himself. "I'm not dead, Dad. I can't explain now, but I wasn't killed in the bus crash. I'm alive."

"This is no joke for someone to play on an old man in the hospital."

"Please just tell me how you are."

"This is not funny!"

"For God's sake, I'm not trying to be funny!"

Mr. Beal was silent for a while. Then he hissed, "Who is this?"

"We'll argue about who I am later. Okay? Just tell me how you are."

Again there was a long silence, then: "I'm doing pretty good. The doctors all say, 'Mr. Beal, you must be as strong as an ox.' I was walkin' around today. Close to fifteen minutes. Even went to the toilet myself."

"What was wrong with you?"

"Ticker. Remember how I use to tell . . ." He stopped.

"So you believe me?"

Beal's father sighed weakly. "They told me you was dead."

"Dad, I want to come see you, but I can't just now."

"They called us from the prison and told us."

"I know, Dad. I know. Things are happening, things I can't tell you about. But I want to see you, and I will as soon as I can. Do you understand?"

"I understand nothing."

"Dad, I'm in trouble."

There was a long pause, then: "Always you are in trouble. Always." This time his voice sounded stronger, and Beal could hear echoes of his mother in every word.

"Not now, Dad."

"What's the matter, you don't want to hear the truth? Your mother looks so old. Ever since that day she hasn't been the same. You should see her, Jack. You made an old woman of her."

"Good. Terrific. I'm glad." Beal stopped himself. "Please, let's not do all that again. You're in the hospital, and I'm in desperate trouble, and for once in our lives let's try to say more than two words to one another without arguing."

Beal's father sighed. "It's good we should try. It's a terrible thing to say, but you get used to arguing."

Beal laughed, not because anything was especially funny but because it was so sad. "Yeah, I know. Half the time I didn't even hear what either of us was saying. It was just the same old garbage over and over. Sometimes I thought it would've saved a lot of energy if we'd have recorded one of our fights and just played it back whenever we were angry."

"I never meant it to be that way. I don't know. Lying on my back all day, I did some thinking." He laughed sadly. "What else is there to do but think? You know, Jack, when you're young, everyone tells you it all goes by in the wink of an eye, but who's to believe? Then suddenly, just like that, it's gone. And it's too late."

"Come on, Dad. Cut it out. You said you feel better."

"No, no, listen to me. For once listen to what I have to say. I've been doing some thinking. I know in a lot of ways you blame your ma for things, but she worked so hard, Jack, so hard. And neither of us made it any easier for her. You were a kid, so okay. But me? I

183

don't know, Jack, I was trying to keep our heads above water. It wasn't like I looked at another woman. It wasn't like that. But there was times when you and your ma was so angry at each other, and you both looked to me to help." His voice broke. "And I didn't stand by her and I didn't help you. I just wanted quiet. That's all. I just wanted quiet. But maybe I wasn't such a good father and husband. Maybe there was times I let you both down."

"You were fine, Dad. Really, you were swell. I mean, sure, we had our differences. But most families have differences." Beal was certain his father wouldn't believe what he was saying and was surprised when his father's voice sounded relieved.

"We had our good times, didn't we? Remember how we used to go on picnics, and your ma would make a roast chicken to take with you? You can have your fancy restaurants, Jack. Remember how that chicken used to taste?"

"Even with a ton of sand on it, there was nothing like that chicken."

"And lemonade, too. Remember how she'd make a whole jug of it? None of that packaged crap. No, sir. She'd squeeze all those lemons by hand. My God, how that tasted!"

"I remember."

"What went wrong, Jack? How could so many people meaning so good make everything so bad?"

Beal could see his father as he used to be, packing up the old Plymouth for a picnic, nervous that they were going to forget something, racked with anxiety that he would have to brave the freeway for close to two hours. And this was the highlight of his life. Beal felt an overwhelming sadness for the frail old man. Finally he said, "Dad, the trouble I'm in, it wasn't my fault. I swear I didn't cause any of it. Do you believe me?"

"Does it matter?"

"It matters a lot."

"Yes. I believe you."

Beal had trouble speaking for a long while. Finally he asked, "You still drive that old heap?"

"Now, Jack, that Plymouth is a hell of a car. I don't care what you say. I never spent a dime on it. And I picked it up for under three hundred, including taxes."

"That was ten years ago."

"Yeah, yeah, ten years ago they made cars, not the junk they make today. So who needs fancy paint jobs? That's just salesmanship. Now you listen to your father, Jack, don't go for that shiny paint job. It's what's under the hood that counts."

They had been having this discussion for years, and it felt great to Beal to be having it again. "Yeah. Well, maybe that's okay for Plymouths, but for women give me the shiny paint job anytime."

"No, Jack. It's even more important with women. Forget all the peroxide and red nails." He hesitated, unsure whether to ask, then finally continued. "You ever see Maggie?"

"No, Dad, never."

"She was a nice girl. You know, in the beginning I wasn't so happy because . . . well, you know . . . she was a *shiksa* and all, but she was a nice girl, Jack."

"Yeah, Dad. She was a real nice girl."

The old man sighed. "I feel tired now."

"I'll call back again. Maybe I can visit later."

"That's good." He did sound very tired.

"Dad, you can't tell anyone that you talked to me. Not even Ma. It's very important. You have to promise me that."

"I promise." There was a long hesitation. Then the old man's voice quavered. "I'm glad you're alive, son. I'm real glad you're alive."

Beal was crying now. "I'll come see you as soon as I can. I love you, Dad." But already his father had hung up, and the only answer was a mechanical hum.

Chapter Twenty-one

There were ten of them. Three women and seven men. Four of the men were assigned to cars with shortwave. The other six had the city divided into zones.

They came in all sizes, shapes, and ages. There was even a very old couple with a two-way radio secreted in the woman's compact.

Not one of them knew why they were combing the city for Beal. It didn't matter why. The money was excellent.

Roy Waller, a tall, bony, flaccid-featured black guy who was always being told he looked like Jimmy Walker, hit pay dirt the next morning.

The woman behind the desk at the Two Palms Motel hesitated when she looked at the picture Roy handed her. She was a large dark-skinned woman with sly eyes peeking from under a prehensile forehead, and she was watching Roy with a look that told him money was not going to be the key to get her talking.

Roy smiled his own sly smile and leaned over the counter. The woman was wearing bright pink pants that were so tight they made her ass look like a camel's back. The job had dividends.

Richards got the call from Roy just after ten in the morning. He was sitting on his bed in the Holiday Inn in Hollywood, waiting for a call to his wife in London to come through. With relief he canceled the call, fitted his .38 into his shoulder holster, and put on his suit jacket, looking around the room to make sure he'd forgotten nothing.

Richards was thinking about people and how predictable they were. When they were scared, they headed home, like salmon. Himself included. Maybe that was why he'd known what Beal would do right off while Sparrow and company were probably still beating the bushes in Europe.

He shut off the lights and locked the door, then walked slowly to the elevator. How many times had he driven down his street, knowing that he was going to be greeted with nine different-sized brassieres and indifference? He would slow his car as he drove up to his house, and always he was thinking, Why not turn around right now? Why not head anywhere but here? But of course, he wouldn't turn around. He'd stop at his house and park. Just like a salmon. If he'd been some factory worker at two pounds an hour, he could have understood his reluctance to venture out into the world of the unknown. But he was a paid assassin, a killer. It didn't make sense. Or perhaps it was that which made him a killer.

His car was in the parking lot, a wide dark green Grand Prix. When Richards had accepted Harry Langdon's offer to come to America and finish the job, he'd made him promise to outfit a car to his specifications. But · Richards had taken the car out earlier on a test drive and found it sluggish and unwieldy. He'd put in a call to the lingerie factory, but Harry hadn't seemed to care that Richards was angry. It was a clear indication who was boss.

As Richards pulled out of the garage and into the baking city, he was trying to block out the nagging doubt that had started only a few weeks ago and now had grown into a premonition.

While Richards was heading over to Two Palms, Beal was walking down Hollywood Boulevard toward the library. It had been a full morning. Already a Saturday night special bumped heavy and awkward in his pocket. He'd bought it in the parking lot of a liquor store, and while it wasn't quite as easy as buying a head of lettuce, it wasn't a lot harder either. Just a flash of cash and a sideways glance, and in ten minutes he'd been offered heroin, cocaine, grass, pills, a car, a TV, a diamond ring, twin boys of fifteen, a reasonably attractive woman of forty, and a carton of grenades.

Next he'd stopped at one of the sleazier clothes shops on Hollywood Boulevard and picked up a phosphorescent green suit, white panama hat, and enough chains for his neck to disable King Kong effectively.

The concept was simple. While Beal knew it would be impossible not to notice his clothes, it was hardly likely anyone would notice his face.

In actuality, on Hollywood Boulevard he looked like just another guy.

The library was on one of the side streets off Hollywood Boulevard that look like London after the blitz. Just as Beal rounded the corner, a small yellow VW screeched out of a parking lot and almost collided with the oncoming traffic.

There was a shock of brilliant auburn hair, a pale, freckled face peering over the steering wheel. And Beal knew instantly it could be only one person.

Maggie was looking his way, pale green eyes, childish upturned nose, pouting mouth turned toward him, stirring years of memory and pain.

Beal froze. His face was stinging as if he'd been slapped; his heart was pounding hard and tight.

The VW was stopped in the middle of the street. Already traffic was piling up behind it. Maggie's head was still tilted toward him.

Beal turned away and forced himself to head in the opposite direction. Hard thing to do, brutally hard not to go running back toward the little yellow car and the only woman in his life who had really meant anything to him.

Beal kept walking. He was pushing his feet forward, trying to ignore his mind, which was fighting him for every inch of the way. Maybe he was wrong, his devious mind reasoned. Maybe it wasn't Maggie. After all, she didn't have a corner on the auburn hair market, and there were plenty of lousy drivers in L.A. If he just turned around, he'd see exactly how ridiculous all this was, and that would make him feel a hell of a lot better.

He slowed and glanced back. But already the VW was moving down the street, pausing at a stop sign. And then it was gone.

Once again the street was just a bleak string of parking lots and iron fences, and Beal was standing on the pavement in the morning heat, on the run and alone.

Beal didn't move for a long while, wondering how Maggie was doing, who she was living with, and if she ever thought about him. Then he gave up wondering and entered the cool, impartial library.

Just ten minutes later Richards was leaning toward the door of room 416 in the Two Palms Motel, scanning the rotting wood with a magnifying glass. He smiled as he saw the blond hair Beal had obviously placed there, then took an envelope out of his pocket and placed the hair in it. He pushed the Do Not Disturb sign over to the side and slipped a credit card along the lock until it clicked free.

As Richards was about to enter, he glanced back. Roy Waller was standing lookout by the graffiti-scratched elevator, making Jimmy Walker faces, picking his nose, and in general looking disreputable, which made him blend in pretty well at the Two Palms. Roy goose-necked up and down the hall, then gave the all-clear sign.

Richards entered the room and went over it for a while. There was nothing of interest. It was just the room of a tired, scared kid who'd gotten himself into a heap of trouble. The furniture looked as if it had been moved, and Richards supposed he'd barricaded the door with it the night before. The pathetic uselessness of the gesture touched him. It was a bad bargain for the kid. But he guessed life was full of bad bargains.

He sat on the bed and dialed Harry, loosening his

tie and opening his collar. He suspected it was going to be a long wait for Beal.

The blond man was smiling. The real estate agent smiled back, then glanced at herself in the rearview mirror. She looked awful. She wished she hadn't had her hair dyed black; it made her look older. Still, all in all, she supposed there were plenty of days she'd looked worse.

On the whole she had to admit she was feeling good. Three cabin rentals in one day was not bad, especially in Colorado, where the summer season could be slack. Perhaps if the man were pleased with the cabins, it would be the beginning of a long, happy association. He'd certainly hinted as much. After all, not many companies rented cabins for the whole month of August just to reward their top salesmen.

She liked the care the blond man had taken in choosing the cabins, too. He'd spent a great deal of time going over the grounds to make sure they afforded privacy and quiet. He'd even asked that he be given duplicate keys so he could totally ready the cabins with food and supplies. It was the kind of thoughtfulness that must make the company he represented a fine place to work. She supposed a handsome-looking employee like that didn't hurt either.

Once again she glanced from the road and smiled at the tall, almost militarylike man sitting next to her. The blond man smiled back, his face pleasant and open, but his eyes were very dark and shut away.

Chapter Twenty-two

At five o'clock in the afternoon Beal still sat on a high, hard stool in front of a microfilm viewer. He had a small notebook open in front of him and was diligently taking notes, hunched over his pencil, exclaiming and muttering to himself, nodding excitedly, like those brownnoses he used to hate in school.

It was a gloomy room, government-green walls, colorless drawn shades, gray microfilm viewers. There were only two other people in the room, both of them pear-shaped men with terminal acne and goggle-thick glasses. The one closer to Beal was clicking a pencil against his teeth. In the intense quiet it sounded like a Krupa solo.

Beal sat back, rubbing his eyes. What he'd gotten was pretty meager, a few incongruities, a few contradictions. Only a raging paranoid could doubt that Foyle had assassinated Lacey. Beal flipped back through his notebook, reviewing his day's work.

First off, there was the trajectory of the bullet. Experts claimed the angle of the entering bullet was not entirely compatible with the position of Foyle in the room. Of course, there was an equally large group of experts who claimed the bullet had been deflected slightly by Lacey's hand. It was impossible to tell who was right, and it was equally impossible to see how that related to Beal.

He moved on. There were several strange facts surrounding the assassination. For one, the clearing of the ballroom by the Secret Service. There had been a lot of discussion in the press about this, mostly as a way of blaming the Secret Service for botching the job. All the controversy had quieted when it was learned the order to clear the area in case of injury to the President had been issued several weeks before. By the President himself.

Of course, it was possible that the order had come from someone else. After all, Lacey wasn't around to argue the fact, was he? But whatever the origin of the order, the upshot was only two men were left with Lacey when he was dying, Faraday and Sunday, both of them Secret Service, both of them with at least ten years on the job. With only these two men present and the rest of the area cleared, it would be easy for someone to pick up any clues that had been left. And if that were true, those men knew who really killed Lacey.

Beal circled the names. It was a clue that could be dangerous to follow up, but it was the one that presented possibilities.

Closely related to the clearing of the room was the barricading of the stage area for ten hours before the speech. Certainly it made sense that the Secret Service had to check for hidden bombs and people. But ten hours? One of the janitors reported he'd seen a flash of light coming from behind the barricade. Now, all of this sounded suspicious as hell. Only Beal couldn't begin to imagine what to be suspicious of. And once again it had absolutely no relevance to him.

Beal stretched. Inside his head, thoughts were whirling around like August flies. Fat, heavy, furtive, and just about to die. Next to him, the man with the drumming pencil was tapping at his teeth with a frenzy of clicks, working on both uppers and lowers, into a real Vegas finale. Beal was tempted to walk over and congratulate him. Here was a man who didn't have to spend a sunny afternoon in the library. With teeth like that, he could be packing them in at Caesars Palace.

Beal forced himself back to his notebook. There was the story of a black limousine that had been spotted leaving the back of the hotel only moments before Lacey was killed. It was possible that it was just a rock and roll star or some kid showing off to his mother from Des Moines that he'd made it in a city that was tearing his guts out. Still he circled the limousine story. If he kept drawing blanks with the other clues, he'd check out the rent-a-car companies.

He could try the hospital. Lacey had died before he reached UCLA. His private physician, Dr. Isaiah Greenaway, had been with the coroner when he issued the statement. Perhaps if he went to UCLA or talked to Dr. Greenaway, someone would be able to tell him what was going on. Anything was worth a try.

Beal had labeled one whole page "Motive," and written boldly across it were the words "Find out who stood to gain most by Lacey's death." The only person Beal could see who stood to gain was Chesapeake. Beal wondered if it were possible one man could kill another just to be President. It was not without historical precedent, if not in America, at least in most other countries, but it hardly seemed worth the trouble. He could see murdering to be emperor, maybe even king or pope. But President? All you got was a lousy eight years on the job.

Unless, of course, you changed the rules. Chesapeake was definitely worth looking into.

The entire next page was given over to rumors about Lacey's being involved with an underaged girl named Gina Delano. There had been vague whisperings that he had arranged the death of this girl and her mother in an auto accident. What if these rumors were true and the girl's father had arranged to kill Lacey?

It didn't hold together. The father, if there were such a person, might have a good reason to kill Lacey and even Beal if he knew something damaging, but it was doubtful he'd be powerful enough to rig a trial and send killers all over the world.

There was another set of rumors about two Russian laser scientists who supposedly had been abducted by America. Lacey had flatly denied that America had anything to do with their disappearance, but the pressure from the Kremlin persisted, and several columnists suggested that Lacey might be lying, though for what reason they couldn't begin to speculate.

Nor could Beal.

And that was it. There wasn't a familiar name, place, or event, nothing to connect the Lacey assassination with him. On the contrary, the splash of famous names made Beal even more aware how impossible it was that his everyday life would have anything to do with a worldwide event like the assassination of a President.

Beal turned away, discouraged. The guy with the magical teeth had stopped his drumming and was collecting his things to leave, taking his books and his monumental talent out into the indifferent world of Hollywood.

Beal glanced back at the microfilm screen and saw the front-page picture of Lacey's wife kneeling at the grave site, her pale, brave face, confused and solemn, frozen for eternity in her moment of agony. She reminded him of that calf he'd seen being carted off to market. And he turned from the sight of her. Beal wondered what kind of torment these last five years had been for her. Or was she remarried, playing golf and going on cruises with that nice couple from next door?

Beal understood exactly where his mind was going and shut his notebook loudly to blot out the memory of Maggie.

He returned the microfilm to a librarian, pocketed his notebook, then decided it would be better to hide it.

As he exited the library, he stopped at a thick clump of scrubby bushes along the side of the building, looking up and down the street to make sure no one was watching. The dismal street was empty except for a frail old couple several feet away. The shriveled man was leaning on a three-pronged cane, and next to him his wife, a tiny white-haired woman, cupped his elbow.

Beal couldn't take his eyes off them. He thought he'd never seen anything like the sweet, loving look on that old woman's face. Surely the man at her side was an added weight for her to carry, and yet the caring softness on her face was unmistakable.

Even after Beal had slipped his notebook in the bushes and walked past them, he found himself turning back. The old woman had paused and was glancing in her compact, patting her hair into place. It was an inconceivable gesture. Was it possible that after all those years she still cared how she looked for that shriveled little man by her side?

Beal found himself wondering if he'd ever find the kind of love that would survive old age.

At this point he was having trouble imagining he'd even make it to old age.

But as Beal turned away from the old couple and moved onto Hollywood Boulevard, the old woman's lips began to move. "He's heading east on Hollywood," she whispered into the microphone in her compact. "He dropped something in the bushes. We're on our way to retrieve it."

The darkening streets outside the Two Palms Motel set up long shadows, making every building a hiding place, every pedestrian a potential threat. Beal had bought a sausage pizza from a restaurant with red walls the color of the Apocalypse, then headed back to his motel, stopping every few feet to check into store windows and see if anyone was following him. He saw nothing.

When he got back to the Two Palms, he bypassed the elevator and took the stairs. At the fourth floor he stopped and carefully checked the halls, but everything was quiet.

Slowly Beal walked to his door. Juggling the pizza,

he pulled a small flashlight from his pocket and shone it on the door. The hair was in place. With relief Beal slipped his key in the lock and opened the door.

It was dark inside the room, and the curtains were drawn so that no light filtered in from the streetlamps outside. Beal tried to remember if he'd drawn the curtains. He could picture himself standing by the window last night and also in the morning. He had no memory of closing the curtains afterward.

It occurred to him that a maid had closed them. But he'd left a Do Not Disturb sign, and judging by the rest of the service at the Two Palms, Beal had no doubt that the maids were delighted to comply. If the curtains were closed, it was because he had closed them. Unless someone else had.

Beal's heart started pounding. He put down his pizza and sought the cold hardness of his revolver. He had shot a gun only a few times at police summer camp, and his performance had been undistinguished. Still, having it calmed him somewhat.

Without entering the room, Beal felt along the walls for the light switch. There was none. Beal knew that meant the switches were on the lights themselves and he was going to have to walk across the room in the darkness.

Again his heart started pounding.

He shone the feeble flashlight around the room, illuminating the grotesque furniture and the humped bed. There was a lamp close to the window. All it would take was five seconds, ten at the outside, to make it across the room; then he could flip on the light and barricade his door with furniture. Then he would be safe. At least for another night.

199

Beal was just edging himself over the threshold when the muted flashlight beam caught a long black shadow lying motionless on the floor like a pile of dirty clothes. Beal ran the light along the hunched outline, trying to imagine what he could have left on the floor.

But there was nothing he could imagine.

A slam. The door was shut. Beal started to whirl, but already someone was grabbing his wrist and tearing the gun from his fingers.

Beal pressed tight, holding onto the gun with more strength than he knew he had. Meanwhile, the rest of his body was working. Firming his grip on the ground, Beal bent his knees, and in one movement he kicked his front foot back, grabbed the hand that held him, and heaved the man over his shoulder, slapping him to the floor.

There was no scream. No words. Nothing but the sharp intake of breath and the sound of 150 pounds of flesh hitting hard floor.

Beal sprang over the body, holding his gun shakily, pointing it at the face in the darkness.

"For Christ's sake, I give up, you idiot!"

It was unlikely Beal ever enjoyed anything as much as the next few moments. Keeping his gun trained on Sparrow, Beal inched back to the lamp and pulled the chain.

Sparrow got up slowly, brushing himself off. In the dim light Beal could just barely make out a bright red mark across Sparrow's face and a line of blood trickling from his nose. Beal thought he'd never seen Sparrow look better.

Sparrow turned away quickly, wiping his nose with

his sleeve. The back of his neck was red with humiliation.

Beal watched him with pleasure for some time, then sauntered back to the door, his gun trained on Sparrow. "Are you hungry?" he asked with a smirk. "I've got a sausage and pepper pizza in the hall."

Sparrow waved his words away with his hand, trying for a sarcastic smile. "Crap like that'll kill you. Too much cholesterol."

"Yeah, well, if it's planning on killing me, it'll have to get in line."

Just as Beal reached the door and his waiting pizza, he saw the hunched shadow that had looked like a pile of dirty clothes in the darkness.

The lean black man was sprawled across the floor, arms and legs splayed into swastikas. There was the bright red stain of blood haloed around the man's head. Other than that, he could have been asleep.

"His name's Roy Waller," Sparrow said calmly. "I found him waiting here earlier."

Beal tried to ignore the sprawled body. He retrieved his pizza, pulled out a slice, and leaned against the wall, eating it, but the sight of the hunched black man clouded his mind. He was horrified, yet he couldn't take his eyes from him. It was as riveting as a car accident.

"I had a hell of a time with him, too," Sparrow continued as he walked to the armchair and made himself comfortable. "Roy was no amateur. He got his start with Vesco, and I know of at least two senators who've used him. As a matter of fact, I even used him once."

Sparrow was smiling. Already the red mark was fading from his face. And though Beal still held the gun and was pointing it at Sparrow, the power he'd felt before was fading fast, and his old friend's impotence and fear were back full force. He tried for a smirk.

"Real interesting, Sparrow, but I'd like to eat in peace. So please just pick up your cadaver and leave."

"You aren't curious what's going on?"

Beal laughed bitterly. "Dying of it."

Sparrow ignored him. "Unfortunately Roy had one fatal flaw and it was attached between his legs. It seemed he'd already won the heart of your lovely motel receptionist. She made a little surprise visit to him." Sparrow chuckled cruelly. "Sadly for him, I was right behind her with my trusty Walther Seven sixty-five m/m."

Beal stiffened. Like an idiot, he'd totally forgotten that Sparrow would be armed.

Sparrow caught Beal's concern and waved it away. "Relax. Walther is well out of reach. We're just having a pleasant little chat. You see, I've discovered something extremely interesting." Sparrow licked his lips excitedly. He was a man who enjoyed the hunt. "There seems to be a power struggle going on between Richards and Harry Langdon. It happens in any organization. But it's much less likely to happen in our line of work since the stakes are so high. Be that as it may, from what I can guess, Richards called in to Harry. By the way, it was Richards who caught the hair on the door. At any rate, Harry must have ordered Richards back and told Roy to take over. I happened to get a glimpse of Richards as he was leaving, and did he look furious! Here is a man not used to taking orders. Of course, all this is excellent for us."

Beal was still leaning against the wall, the slice of pizza clutched in his hand, but he was no longer eating. "They were waiting for me in Athens," he said after a while.

"So were we."

"That's reassuring."

"It should have been. Hamad is one of our best men."

"Sure. Of course. It figures it was Hamad."

"What the hell are you doing back here, Jack?"

"I missed hot dogs."

"I have a passport, identity papers . . ."

"No deal."

"We'll be more careful next time. I assure you, you'll be safe."

"I said no deal. I'm staying right here. I don't care if you tie me up and send me clear across the globe. I don't care if you lock me in a room with a twenty-four-hour guard, I'll sneak out and come back. I'm not running anymore."

Sparrow looked at Beal's intense face and knew this was true. "You're making a big mistake."

"No doubt. But at least I'm the one who's making it." Beal watched the little bald man, his eyes burning with anger. "You see, this little assignment of yours is my life. People want to kill me. Me! I'm the one who bleeds. I'm the one who dies. Up until now I've been thrown around like a ball in some crazy game all of you have cooked up. But that's over. This time I declare myself a player."

Sparrow almost levitated from his chair. "Player? For Christ's sake, you were having trouble making it as the ball."

203

"I'm still alive, aren't I?"

"A mere oversight on God's part. One that will soon be rectified, I assure you. Listen, kid, don't be a *shlemiel*. You know what a *shlemiel* is?"

Sparrow took Beal's silence as a yes. "Good. Then don't be one. We're pros. Look at that outfit you're wearing. Sure, for the man on the street maybe crazy clothes are a distraction. But men like us are trained to notice everything. Take a man's walk. You ever notice how a pimp walks? He doesn't hunker like you do. He slides down the street, head held high, shoulders back." Sparrow laughed nastily. "And that gun! When the going gets rough, how much good do you think a Saturday night special is going to do? Even if it fires, chances are fifty-fifty it'll go off in your own face. Junk! It's junk!"

Beal looked crumpled and tired. What Sparrow was telling him made sense. He was an amateur trying to fight professionals. His chances of success were nonexistent. And yet the other seemed even worse. He took a deep breath. "I'm afraid I'm going to be a *shlemiel*, but you see, I'm not going to run anymore."

"I know, damn it!" Sparrow found himself shouting. He stopped, looking around, surprised. When he continued, his voice was soft and there was almost a trace of sadness in it. "You're crazy. You're stupid. You take risks that expose me and my men, and you've opened up a whole can of worms for the person I work for. You're trouble. But you just won't quit."

"I did enough of that before."

"Well, you sure as hell picked a lousy time to start making a life change."

Beal shrugged and moved toward the door. His gun

was still trained on Sparrow, but he didn't fool himself that he'd use it.

"If I were you, I wouldn't take the stairs," Sparrow said as he watched Beal head for the door. "Wait for someone to use the elevator with you; then go right through the front lobby. There'll be too many people around for them to try anything."

"What makes you so sure someone's waiting for me? I didn't see anyone when I came in."

"You aren't supposed to see them. That's the beauty part. Look, they were staying well back because they figured Roy would take care of you. Once you leave, they'll see what happened. As near as I can tell, there are ten people after you. They even have some old couple about one hundred years apiece."

Beal felt like he was going to puke because if that sweet old woman who had been looking at her husband so lovingly was a fraud, then there wasn't anything in this world that was going to be good and sweet.

"I don't suppose you're going to tell me where you're going." Sparrow laughed, but there was a tinge of sadness in it. "I don't suppose you even know, do you?"

Beal didn't answer. He didn't have to.

"If you change your mind, call the John Tyler Dance Studio and ask for Mr. Shine." He sighed. "Go get my jacket on the bed. In the right-hand pocket you'll find the Walther and several magazines. Sorry there's no holster. It's an aversion of mine."

Beal hesitated for only a moment, then moved sideways to the bed and found the revolver.

"I'm assuming you know how to use a gun," Sparrow said. "Which, judging by past experience, is an act of faith. Just do me a favor and leave your popgun on the floor. I've got to get out of here, too."

Beal nodded and put the Saturday night special on the floor. He looked over at the little bald man sitting in the armchair across the room. Nothing was as it seemed. There was treachery in old people, kindness in killers. But that wasn't true. Sparrow was a pro and he could have been hired for either side; it was all the same to him. No one was particularly interested in Beal. Not Sparrow. Not any of them. He was just a pawn to them all.

As Beal backed to the door, Sparrow said, "You know, Jack, you're a fairly good scrapper. You floored me before. Not that I was trying. But I underestimated you. And maybe if you have any chance at all, it will be because everyone underestimates you. I don't know. Maybe pigs can fly and they just pretend they can't."

The three men from next door had opened their door, and Beal could hear them tripping into the hall. He opened the door and saw them, tall, lanky, all with clipped mustaches and short haircuts. He imagined he could even see the rope burns on their wrists.

Beal backed out of the room, flashing a big smile, and joined the group as they entered the elevator to begin their early-evening prowl of the boulevard.

Neon splashed the dark street. Traffic pounded. The sidewalks were packed with people, laughing and shouting. Silent bums limped in their Salvation Army sneakers, the lucky ones clutching brown paper sacks. An old woman pushed a supermarket basket filled with soiled newspapers. Another in orange toreador pants and a peasant blouse walked two neurotic little yapping dogs. While groups of teen-agers linked arms and played Red Rover with the oncoming pedestrians.

A summer night on Hollywood Boulevard.

Beal stood outside the Two Palms Motel, looking both ways, realizing with aching clarity that he had nowhere to go.

Finding another hotel room in the neighborhood was suicide. Finding a hotel room anywhere else wasn't much better. Movies were out; they closed them nowadays. There was a bus station a little farther on, but there were only two benches in it, and anyway, it would be one of the first places they'd look.

Beal felt tired and lonely and scared, most of all scared. It hadn't made any difference that he'd come back. He was on the run again. He might just as well be back in Morocco.

Beal started walking down Hollywood Boulevard, watching the heavy flow of traffic on the street. Almost any one of those cars could be after him. He searched the passing faces. It could be anyone in the crowd. For Christ's sake, they were using golden agers.

Out of the corner of his eye he thought he saw a small, slim man skimming along behind him. He quickened his pace. But the little man only moved faster. It looked like Richards.

Beal glanced back and thought he saw the man's hand go to his jacket. He tried to control himself from running. Running was exactly the wrong thing to do. It attracted attention. But panic was clutching at Beal's throat, and his heart was heavy and painful, and he couldn't hold himself back any longer.

Beal took off down the street, shoving through the

growing crowd. He knew Richards wasn't about to give up on him easily, especially if Sparrow was right about his ego's taking a severe beating recently. Ego beatings made people meaner than usual. So Richards wasn't going to give up until Beal was good and dead, and that made the panic even stronger in Beal, pushing him faster down the street.

Several people turned around to watch the young man in the bright green suit run down the crowded street, feeling quickly to see if their wallets were in place, then quickening their pace, hoping to catch a glimpse of the fun.

Beal tried to slow himself up. But keeping his head wasn't a possibility anymore, and he ran even faster, glancing back and catching sight of Richards pressing forward just behind him.

Two policemen looked up from hot dogs as he passed. In his bright green suit Beal looked like a prime candidate for the tank. They bolted down the last of their hotdogs, then, clutching their nightsticks, started down the street after him. Within seconds a cruising cop car spotted the running policemen. The siren flicked on, and the patrol car screeched forward.

Beal heard the siren and ducked down a side street. All around him were parking lots and darkness. A perfect place to get dead.

Beal stopped and pressed himself against a brick wall. His heart was contracting into a hard, painful knot, and he wanted to cry. Held by the darkness, fear pounding crazily in his ears, he didn't know whether to rush forward or go back. The street was empty, no cars, no people, only the parking lots and darkness. And suddenly it occurred to Beal that no one was following him. Only his own terror.

The roar of a helicopter broke the night. Intense light shot from the sky, flooding a nearby street with brilliance. The light revolved, scanning the area with a solid beam, moving toward Beal. It was the police.

Beal flattened himself against the wall, watching the giant dragonlike helicopter combing the area for him. The street was still. There were no shadowy figures, no sounds except his own.

Pressing himself against the darkness of the wall as the police light passed by, Beal knew for certain there had been no Richards skimming along behind him. It had been only his own fear pursuing him, making him run crazily through the streets. But now the police were hunting for him, too. It was his own fault. And Beal saw with frightening clarity that if the others didn't get him, he would probably get himself.

Chapter Twenty-three

Senator E. Bud Fuller had another fifteen minutes to wait for the call, so he paced around his chrome and glass Los Angeles office, his thick mop of prematurely white hair tousled from running his fingers through it nervously. It was well after eleven o'clock at night, and only the janitor, cleaning women, and a few over-zealous men on their way up were in the building. An alien stillness hung over the usually noisy rooms; the fluorescent lights were out, the typewriters muffled by covers. It was like the end of the world.

Outside Fuller's windows the lights of downtown Los Angeles dotted the clear dark sky. It was a sight Fuller never tired of.

Fuller had heard all the California jokes told in the smug wood-paneled rooms of Washington. It never bothered him at all. He never stopped being proud of the great urban sprawl that seemed to grow hourly, spreading along the Pacific, seeping into the desert.

While the rest of America lost hope, Los Angeles hustled on. Naïve, crude, loud, brash, and more alive than any other place in the world. No one had told them down there in that blaze of twinkling lights that America had closed down. They still thought the country worked. They still thought that with a little brains and a lot of nerve the world would open before them. And so it still did.

Though the liberal North was closer to him politically, when he thought of his state it was always of the squat sprawl of neon down South. Perhaps this was because when all was said and done, Los Angeles had no politics, only money. And one thing you learned in government was no matter what you did, no matter if you were liberal, conservative, or middle-of-the-road, it all turned out just about the same.

Not that anybody in Washington talked about that, but they all knew it. The unspoken secret. Policies didn't matter. Only politics. It wasn't what was done, but the doing that mattered.

And Fuller liked the doing a lot.

Being President pro tem of the Senate, representing the crazy patchwork state that lay outside his window, was heady stuff. People waved at him, shouted for him, pointed at him. He'd stand at a podium and see thousands of faces calling his name. He'd stand in front of the camera and know that families all over the country were shoveling down their dinners with their eyes glued on him.

Why it mattered was a question he'd asked himself many times. It was a question without an answer.

Fuller turned from the window and continued his prowl of his office. All around him were mementos, a

211

whole lifetime of pictures, certificates, diplomas. There were snapshots of his family, all grown up now. A portrait of his wife, Gilly, a tall, stately woman with wounded eyes who shared his house but, by unspoken consent, little else.

Next to the portrait of Gilly was an even crueler picture. It was a snapshot of himself, standing arms linked with several of his army buddies from WW II. He looked painfully young, tall, and serious, with a thick crop of black hair that was shaved at the neck so it looked like a thatched roof. He remembered looking as he did in that picture. Sometimes, especially in the morning, he still thought of himself looking like that. Discovering the white-haired, ruddy-skinned old face in the mirror would come as a shock. But then everyone said that about getting old.

What they didn't talk about was the other. For in the end it was more than white hairs that separated him from the solemn boy with the black-thatched hair. It was the sourness, the losses, the wickedness, the regrets accumulated through a lifetime, the corruption of spirit as well as body.

Farther along there was a snaphot of Lacey and Elaine and Fuller and Gilly by the seashore in Connecticut. He turned quickly from the picture. Of all the memories in this room, that one was perhaps the most terrible.

Fuller walked back to his mahogany desk and sat back into his leather armchair. But the last picture, the sight of them, sandy and happy in the bright, fresh ocean breezes, stayed in his mind.

It had been the summer Lacey was making his bid for President, and Fuller was helping with the campaign behind the scenes. It was a summer he'd never forget.

There had been the long nights talking and planning over cold, greasy fried chicken, ordered out long before, then forgotten in the craziness all around them. Fuller and Lacey had never been closer than that summer. They'd been like brothers. More. Sometimes Fuller had thought he could almost feel Lacey's pain, like Siamese twins. Gilly had teased him that he should have married Lacey so he could spend the night with him as well as the entire day. She always said it with a smile, but behind the smile was pain. Because in truth, Fuller loved Gilly as a wife, but it was a whole other thing with Lacey. Fuller would have died for that tall man with the burning eyes. He supposed he had in a way.

He remembered the night it had all begun, the dying for Lacey. They were at the Park Regency in Washington, and Lacey had come into his suite with a look of fear in his eyes unlike any Fuller had seen since the war.

Lacey had gone right for the bar and drunk off a double Scotch. Then he'd made himself another and sat down in a chair, staring straight ahead, his shoulders hunched like an old man.

Fuller hadn't asked him what was the matter; he'd waited. In his mind he'd run through the list of possibilities. It wasn't the campaign. He knew that was going well. It was highly unlikely that Elaine was making any kind of trouble that Lacey didn't know in his heart he could fix.

Lacey got up and poured himself another Scotch.

He stood at the bar, his weight supported by the fake antique veneer, his eyes distant, his face haunted.

"I really fucked up this time," he said finally.

Fuller decided to ignore the fear in his voice. "We'll take care of it. Just tell me what the problem is."

Lacey shook his head and took another gulp of Scotch. "I'm going to have to drop out of the campaign."

Fuller was stunned. "You can't mean that!"

"God, I don't want to." Lacey's voice was choked off. "Jesus, you don't know how I don't want to do that."

"Great. Then we both agree." Fuller walked to the bar. He, too, felt the need of a drink. "Now just tell Uncle Bud what the problem is and I'll take care of it." He smiled reassuringly. "Haven't I taken care of everything else?"

"This is different." Lacey's voice was flat and dull now. The Scotch was doing its work.

"Big deal. I'm a pretty powerful man in case you haven't noticed."

"Sure, I know."

Lacey didn't sound as if he were listening to his own words, and it was then Fuller began to sense the immensity of what was happening.

Lacey turned his haunted eyes on Fuller. "I'd tell you the reason, but I don't want any of this rubbing off on you."

Lacey turned abruptly and headed for the door. Fuller strode after him, grabbed his arm, restrained him. It took all his strength.

"You just don't walk out of here like that!" Fuller

told him angrily. "What if things were reversed and it were me? Would you let me walk out of here?"

Lacey had looked at Fuller with an affection neither of them had even known how to put into words. Then the anguished look returned. "Sometimes I think I might do just that."

For a moment Fuller was stunned by this answer. He looked at Lacey anew, as if he'd never realized that Lacey wasn't as loyal to him as he was to Lacey. In truth, he had always known it. He had felt it in the strong, tough man as they worked long nights side by side. He supposed it was that in Lacey which made him presidential material while Fuller could never hope to rise above senator.

Lacey had walked back into the room and crumpled into a chair. He was rubbing his large hand across his forehead, and Fuller suspected he was doing it to avoid looking into his eyes.

"What about your dreams for America? Was that all a pack of lies?"

Lacey shook his head slowly. "The dreams, the dreams," he repeated softly, almost trancelike. Then he seemed to snap out of it. "Look, Bud, I want that presidency real bad. What would I do to get it? I don't know anymore. I swear to Christ, I just don't know. Maybe that's one of the reasons it's better that I get out now." He looked over at Fuller and tried to smile. "What the hell's the difference what reason I tell myself? I've got to get out."

There was a long silence. Fuller made himself another drink, but he didn't leave the bar. He just stood there drinking, watching Lacey as he slumped in the large easy chair.

Finally Lacey sighed. "I'm being blackmailed."

Fuller downed his drink. He tried to keep his voice calm. "I see. A woman?"

"Worse. Much, much worse. A little girl."

"Jesus Christ!" It was out before Fuller could stop it.

"Bud, I swear I didn't know she was a little girl. If you'd seen her, you would have sworn she was twenty, maybe older." He laughed bitterly. "She was fourteen. Her mother called me the next day to tell me the good news and ask for assistance."

Fuller was astonished. "This all happened in the past. You're telling me something that happened before. Why didn't you say anything to me?" Fuller tried to keep the hurt from his voice. He couldn't imagine keeping anything back from Lacey.

"Shit, man, how do you tell a friend that you're a jackass? Anyway, I thought I had it under control." He slammed his fist violently against the arm of the chair. "Ruined, all ruined. Just because of one stupid mistake. I'm not a bad man, Bud. I'm a good man. How could this have happened?" Lacey stopped; his eyes were frantic and hurt, deeply hurt. "I've been sneaking around, juggling money for close to a year now. Jesus Christ, what the hell am I going to do?"

"Just keep paying."

"Believe me, if that's all there were to it, I'd give that Delano woman and her cunt daughter, Gina, every penny I have. But she's a drunk, and God knows what else she's on, and recently she's been talking crazy. You know the type, crying and screaming. She says she's going to expose me as a child molester." He laughed bitterly. "It'd make a hell of a campaign poster."

"How is she going to prove that?"

"She says the girl was seen going up to my room."

"A setup?"

Lacey shrugged. Long ago he'd realized that it didn't matter. Even if she couldn't prove it, all she had to do was leak a rumor to make it close to impossible for Lacey to get elected.

It didn't take long for Fuller to realize that either. "You just have a feeling that she might talk; she hasn't yet." It was a question.

"Who the fuck knows? Oh, I suppose not. Maybe just to some guy she picked up in a bar, something like that. But she will do it, Bud. I can see her and that little whore, Gina, telling the world. They probably figure Gina'll get a movie contract out of it. Who knows? She probably will!"

"It's your word against theirs. You could fight it, you know."

"Bud, I gave her money. A lot of money. I wouldn't doubt that she's been spending pretty freely this past year. And you can bet there'll be a lot of people who noticed it."

Fuller lowered himself to a chair. "Jesus!"

Lacey's eyes were wild. "I want to kill her. I swear to God, I want her and that daughter of hers dead more than I've ever wanted anything in my whole life."

Lacey's eyes were filled with tears, and he turned from Fuller in shame. Fuller wanted to comfort him, but he stayed where he was, silent, watching Lacey sadly. Finally he made Lacey promise not to drop out of the campaign, at least not until Fuller had tried to talk some sense into the Delano woman.

Fuller had sat up all night, drinking and staring into space. The sight of Lacey crying had torn him apart, and he knew he'd do whatever was necessary to fix things for him. It was strange. Fuller hadn't even considered the state of his own soul as he sat there that long night, wondering how a man got someone killed. He could think only of Lacey.

When Lacey didn't receive any more threatening calls, Fuller had been forced to tell him the Delanos had been killed in a car crash. Lacey had turned on him, eyes fiery, demanding to know if Fuller had something to do with it.

Fuller had lied to Lacey, for the first time ever. He'd told him only that he'd found out about the car crash while trying to set up a meeting with the woman. To Fuller's amazement, this satisfied Lacey. And by the next day he looked ten years younger.

It was only later, as time went by, that Fuller began to suspect that he'd done what Lacey wanted all along.

The rumors began to surface almost three years later. Lacey was already President and the greatest President in almost four decades. Then suddenly the whispers started. In the corridors. At cocktail parties. Some of the press began to pick them up.

Fuller had tried to find out how they started, but he couldn't. Perhaps someone really had seen the Delano girl going up to Lacey's suite. Perhaps the Delano woman had told her story to someone in a bar. In the end it didn't matter.

At first Lacey ignored the rumors, hoping they would go away. They didn't. Then he denied them.

It didn't help. Slowly it became clear that nothing could be done to stop them. Within a month Lacey would be dead politically. Worse. He would probably go to jail, maybe forever.

And then he was killed.

The phone rang, and Fuller snapped it up, activating the scrambler.

"Go on," the man on the other end commanded. It was a cold, mechanical voice, made even colder and more mechanical by the delay of the scrambler.

It took a while for Fuller to answer. "John Thomas Colton is dead. A heart attack. Two days ago."

"I know that already."

"I just had dinner with him and he was fine . . ." Fuller's sentence drifted off.

"He was a wonderful man. His presence in the Trust will be greatly missed." There was a long pause, then finally: "Is that the only reason you called?"

Fuller shivered. "No. Unfortunately it looks like our Mr. Beal has eluded us again. He was lost several hours ago, and we haven't been able to pick him up yet. However, from what Harry can tell, he's shaken the people protecting him, too."

"That's too bad."

Fuller was surprised. "Bad? It makes our job a little easier. Whoever's been protecting that kid is first-rate and damn powerful, too."

"You've been hanging around Chesapeake too long. That's why I said it was too bad."

Fuller winced but said nothing, and the voice continued. "You still don't understand, do you? How much do you figure our Mr. Beal knows?"

"We picked up the notebook he left at the library.

219

He's got the clearing of the ballroom, the large piece of glass, the limousine, the rumors about the Delano girl, the Russian scientists. The parts are all there."

"They've always been there, but everyone was just too stupid to see them. Has he drawn any conclusions?"

"Hardly. The notebook is fairly littered with question marks."

The voice laughed. "Fine. And what would you say is the state of his mind?"

"Scared shitless."

"Excellent. Contact Harry immediately. I don't want anyone harming a hair on Mr. Beal's head."

"A live Mr. Beal can be very dangerous."

"To everyone. Including those protecting him." There was a long pause; then the voice continued, dry and cracked. It was the voice of a man who rarely spoke. "Have you ever noticed people's reaction to a sniper? It's really quite interesting. A nameless, faceless person in hiding, everything veiled. It drives people crazy with terror."

"So?" Fuller hated the lecturing tone of the voice. He wasn't a stupid man, yet it made him doubt himself.

"My instincts tell me that if our Mr. Beal is pushed, he'll try to find out who's protecting him. Nameless, faceless protection is almost as frightening as nameless, faceless enemies."

"You think he'll lead us to the man who's running him?"

"If pushed enough, he will. And we will push him, won't we?"

"We have to keep up the pretense of trying to kill him, or else the others might be suspicious."

"I'll leave all that to you. Just so long as we get it wrapped up in the next two weeks."

"Why two weeks?" Fuller asked, sensing that he didn't want to know the answer.

"In time for the next meeting of the Trust, of course." The voice was mocking and ugly.

"The convention starts in two weeks, doesn't it?" Fuller asked pointedly. There was no answer, and for a moment Fuller thought he hadn't made himself clear. "It's the presidential convention you're after, isn't it?"

The man on the other end laughed coldly. "Just you make sure your men keep up with Mr. Beal. Follow the leads he wrote in his notebook. Plant false clues, visit friends, relatives, anyone he might try to contact and cut them off. Stampede him into our net. Then, after that, everything will be easy. Find the king and kill him. Then the pawn."

The phone went dead. Fuller turned off the scrambler and stared out the window, exhausted. Then, finally, he pulled himself from his chair and turned off the office lights. Fuller had never felt so dried-up and old, as if corruption had sucked everything living from him and just left behind a shell. And in that moment he wondered if he weren't already in that hell which he truly believed existed.

Chapter Twenty-four

Maggie loved to smoke. It wasn't that she was stupid and didn't know what smoking did to a person's health. You had to be living in another galaxy not to know that every drag knocked another couple of hours off your life. But still, she loved to smoke. She loved the smell of it, the feel of it. She loved the way she looked smoking.

When Maggie was a child growing up in New Orleans, she and her three best friends had formed a club called the Pact. There were no laws, bylaws, officers, or even dues for the Pact. They never gave dinner dances or went canning for charities. The basic and only function of the club was to prowl the back streets of New Orleans, smoking Viceroys—even the name had that ring of excitement—bought by Sandy, the only one of the three who looked old enough to buy them. In other words, not only did she wear a brassiere, but she really needed it.

As a child Maggie had been told that only dirty, nasty girls smoked. In fact, this had seemed like a real plus. From what Maggie could see, dirty, nasty girls had big tits, and lots of dates, and ended up living exciting lives on the Keys in Florida, while good, clean girls ended up with three kids, Dodge station wagons, and ring around the collar. With that kind of prompting it was hard to get behind quitting.

Maggie reached for another cigarette, took a sip of coffee, and relaxed into an overstuffed old couch, her long, coltish legs sprawled out in front of her. She was wearing a long turquoise robe with slits on either side, haphazardly thrown on, two buttons doing the work of five, walking the thin line between slut and beauty that most good-looking women do when they are alone.

It was night, long, lonely night, and darkness clung to the heavy secondhand furniture and settled in the corners and doorways. The old rented wood frame bungalow creaked and groaned as it settled. From the kitchen a wall clock ticked irrevocably. Other than that the room was silent. Spunky, Maggie's hoary striped cat with the face of cryptic wisdom, slipped into the living room, saw Maggie sitting alone, and indifferently stretched, then flopped at her feet.

It was going to be one of those nights.

Maggie picked up *Cosmopolitan* magazine and tried to get interested in an article about male orgasms. At present it had little relevance to her life. She read her horoscope and discovered this month was a whirl of romantic activities for that ever-sensible Aries gal.

Slowly Maggie put down the magazine. Even though she hadn't heard a noise, she could tell she wasn't alone in the room. Without turning around, she called out, "Get back to bed, you little creepo."

Maggie whipped around and caught a glimpse of Jason's back as he tried to get back up the stairs and safely into bed before she saw him.

Maggie was off the couch like a shot and captured the little boy halfway up the stairs. She held the back of his pajamas as he tried to scamper upward. He was squealing with laughter just slightly tinged with fear.

"Do you have any idea what time it is?" Maggie asked in her best parental voice.

"Late," yelled Jason proudly. "Very late!"

"You bet it is." Maggie scooped the little boy up with a loud theatrical grunt and carried him up the rest of the stairs.

"I couldn't sleep," Jason whimpered.

"Fine. Then just pretend to sleep."

"I was lonely."

"Where's Big Bear? On the floor as usual?"

"No. But I was still lonely."

Maggie dropped Jason on the bed and stood over him like a menacing angel. The word "lonely" was one that always got to her. She supposed Jason sensed that, which was why he used it. Still, that didn't take out the sting. "What if I sit with you for a while?" she asked, throwing an entire shelf of child-care books to the winds.

Jason hesitated. This wasn't precisely the way he'd seen things working out. He'd been hoping for another hour of television snuggled on the couch, or at least a cup of hot chocolate and some of those fig bars. Nevertheless, it was better than nothing. "Okay," he answered after a while.

Maggie tucked Jason into bed and placed Big Bear in the crook of his arm. Lying in bed with his toy animal, Jason really didn't look all that different from the little baby she'd brought home to an empty house over four years ago. It was only when he spoke and Maggie could feel that will, defiant and strong, pressed tightly against her, that she realized how grown-up he was.

Maggie settled herself in a rocking chair and watched the lined lights of the outside traffic patterning the ceiling. As a child she'd lain in bed and wondered what could be making those patterns. When Jason was two, she'd asked him if he knew what it was. He did. Either kids were getting smarter or Jason was a genius. She preferred to believe the latter but suspected the former.

"I want my kite," Jason said to the darkness.

"Not in the bed. Kites belong in the sky. I'll show you on Saturday."

"Tomorrow," Jason demanded.

"I have to go to work tomorrow, but on Saturday we'll go to the park and fly the kite. Maybe afterward we can go out for ice cream. Now go to sleep."

Bribing Jason was always acceptable behavior to Maggie. Parents needed some weapons.

Jason sat up, clapping his hands together with delight. "Let's fly the kite tonight. You don't have to work tonight."

"Nighttime is for sleeping."

"Then how come you're not asleep?"

"Nighttime is also for spanking."

"Oh-oh," Jason said softly.

"Oh-oh is right. Now close your eyes and go to sleep."

Jason sighed in resignation and stared into the darkness, listening to the creaking of the rocking chair.

Maggie didn't know if it was Jason's strong will or the mention of the kite that she'd bought on Hollywood Boulevard that morning which once again brought back what had happened as she came out of the parking lot.

It was crazy, of course. The man had looked nothing like Beal, and anyway, she had heard he was dead. As she stood in front of the supermarket, juggling a week's worth of cat food and eggs, Beal's mother had told her Beal had been indicted for murder and he'd died in a bus crash. Just like that. All at once. "How is Beal?" "Dead, thanks." She had started shaking.

It seemed impossible. She'd been living her own life only a few hundred miles away, unaware of what was going on. Yet she believed it. Not that Beal had murdered anyone, she knew him too well to believe that, but that he was dead. It had taken twenty-four hours before she could cry, and that was after she punched her hand through a door. Then she cried for two days straight.

It always surprised Maggie just how much bitterness and fondness the memory of Beal brought up in her. Even dead, Beal had power.

The phone rang, and Maggie pulled herself up from the rocking chair. She whispered to Jason, "I'll be back," but there was no reply. Despite himself, he'd fallen asleep.

Maggie made the dash to the bedroom, flopped onto her bed, and lifted the receiver. "Hello." There was a pause, then the click of a phone being hung up. Maggie slammed down the receiver. It gave her the creeps when that happened, though she supposed she should be grateful it wasn't one of the breathers. Unsettled, she rushed down the stairs and turned on the television as at least another voice in the house.

Stretching on the couch, smoking another cigarette, she tried to watch an intensely boring discussion on the economy, but her mind was still locked into the man with the walk and the mannerisms of the past.

She'd been twenty when she met Beal. Twenty and just fresh from New Orleans with five hundred dollars, auburn hair that lit in the sun like spun gold, and pale green eyes. She'd come to be a star, clearly one of the dumber life mistakes, and found herself standing in a huge mob of blondes and redheads combing their hair, checking their lipsticks, fighting tooth and nail for the privilege of saying two words on camera.

She'd taken a job in a doctor's office, registered for night acting courses in a local college, and moved in with an aunt, a sweet, scatterbrained woman who had herself come to Hollywood to be a star and quickly filtered into the large colony of never-weres.

There was no question her aunt presented a case in point to Maggie. Every morning she'd pad to the door and rub her wrinkled eyes as she picked up the milk and her copy of the daily *Variety*. She'd eat, hunched over her bowl of wheat germ and acidophilus milk, *Variety* propped against the honey pot, scouring the pages for an open casting.

For hours she and her cronies would sit on broken deck chairs, swatting flies and discussing how you couldn't ever trust agents and how talent didn't really matter in Hollywood, it was all pull anyway. One moment they'd be bragging about what big shots they'd been and in the next breath railing about how badly they'd been treated. There were several writers among them. All of them had come up with the concept of *Laverne and Shirley* and had been ripped off by the studio.

At first Maggie had enjoyed their stories. By the third time she heard them she thought she'd go nuts. Of course, her parents back in New Orleans had warned her. She could picture them waving good-bye to her at the bus station, gray-haired, smug in their country plaids and tweeds, twitching with a bitterness never expressed.

No, she couldn't go home defeated, that was for sure.

Maybe if Hollywood had demanded something, like starving in a garret, Maggie might have felt some kind of romantic rush. But Hollywood demanded nothing. There were no tragedies, no disappointments, nothing. Hollywood defeated by just boring a person to death.

She'd met Beal while taking a course in theater costuming, which seemed like a possibility for the future to Maggie and an easy pass grade to Beal.

He'd watched her the entire first class. Maggie had rebuked Beal, casting angry looks over at him and finally whispering for him to leave her alone. He'd smiled.

The professor droned on; there was the scratching of pens as the other students took notes, and still those damn eyes had stayed on her. Finally he'd sent her a note. "Can I carry your books back to my apartment?"

She answered, "Piss off."

Again the smile. It was a hell of a smile. Maggie had to admit it was just about the best smile she'd seen in a long time, sly yet cute, knowing yet just the right amount of sadness. It was a killer smile all right. And while Beal hadn't gotten to carry her books back to his apartment that day, it hadn't taken long.

Beal and Maggie had liked each other immediately, though they had nothing in common and probably a good deal because of that. She was an upper-class WASP from a talcum-powder background. He was not just Jewish, but poor Jewish, wisecracking, stubborn poor Jewish, the kind the people back home said wore hats to hide their horns.

Beal always said he'd married Maggie because she was the only girl he knew who wore skirts, a slight exaggeration but in the general direction of what he found so attractive. To Beal she was frilly dressing tables and clean, airy rooms with the murmur of polite conversations. She was everything he had read about and never seen. In short, everything he wasn't.

It always surprised Maggie that her life back home, which seemed to her about as romantic as Spam, was exotic and full of mystery to Beal. On the other hand, she knew that part of his attraction for her was his emotionalism and craziness. She was intrigued. She was terrified. She was hooked.

And underneath everything there was a profound frailty about Beal. She supposed it was that, more than anything, that had kept her beating a dead horse of a marriage for close to two years.

The marriage hadn't failed from lack of trying. Beal had whipped himself into a frenzy of trying, or at least she was sure that was how he saw it. It wasn't even the fact that he had been unfaithful. Although that didn't exactly help things out.

To be coolly rational, as God only knew she hadn't

been at the time, his philanderings had been furtive, childish, and in true Jewish neurotic fashion, he probably hadn't even enjoyed them very much. In retrospect she could see it was much more fear of commitment than the pursuit of lust that had driven him. And fucking to prove a point was never a very satisfying option.

But that was in retrospect. At the time it had been a stabbing wound that tortured her increasingly each time it was reopened.

Even so, she could have stuck. Mostly it was Beal's restlessness that killed the marriage. No job was ever good enough; no apartment, roomy enough. They were always on the move, always in turmoil. There wasn't a dish that wasn't cracked from traveling, a car that wasn't a lemon only thirty days after he bought it. The dream seemed around every corner to Beal, but the minute he reached for it, it turned to ashes, until all that was left were bills, angry landladies, and fear, and Maggie realized what she wanted more than anything else in the world was peace. As much as she'd fought against Dodge station wagons and ring around the collar, this seemed far worse.

The fights grew louder, angrier, full of past bitterness. The things said became more unforgivable. Each time Beal promised to change. Each time he failed. Still, the profound frailty of him held her tight in its viselike grip. Everything was going to hell, and she wanted to protect him from it. She supposed she even wanted to protect him from herself.

They might have gone on like that for years if she hadn't awakened one morning and felt the unmistakable nausea. At first she'd hidden what she suspected from Beal without even knowing why. It wasn't until later, when Beal came home with the news that he'd decided to go back to school and become, of all things, a concert pianist, that Maggie understood why she hadn't said anything.

Beal was handsome. Beal was sexy. Beal was loving. But their marriage was a disaster, and a baby was impossible.

Maggie remembered very little of what happened after that. She could barely recollect packing, then deciding to take nothing with her. She supposed she unpacked. She walked to a bus station and sat on a bench for hours until she realized she couldn't go back to New Orleans. Then, exhausted and scared, she'd gotten a hotel room, watched television, eaten potato chips, and cried all night.

The next day she'd taken a job at another doctor's office and rented the small bungalow she lived in today. The divorce had been quick, cheap, and no-fault. They'd never even seen each other, and Beal never knew he had a son.

Not telling Beal about Jason was undoubtedly the lousiest thing Maggie had ever done in her life, and hearing about Beal's death had done little to alleviate her guilt. Yet deep down she knew if she had it to do over again, she'd make the same choice.

The eleven o'clock news came on the television, dragging Maggie back to today with its long litany of rape, murder, and arson a person living in Los Angeles could look forward to.

Maggie had been right. It was definitely going to be one of those nights. She got up and went into the kitchen, where she ate two of Jason's Ding Dongs and

231

drank a glass of milk, then headed back to the couch to wait for Johnny Carson.

She never made it.

Just as Maggie sat down, a jolt wrenched her head back into the couch. A powerful grip pressed her mouth, covering it sharply and tightly.

She tried to scream. But the scream was cut off.

The hand pressed tighter into her mouth, forcing it open. Maggie tried to bite, but the hand was twisting her jaws open, and the paralysis of fear was making everything far away and unreal. She began to struggle.

There was a cold, hard pressure at her cheek. A voice, sharp with fear, spat out, "Don't move. I have a gun."

Maggie froze, trying to see who held her clamped to the couch. But all she could see was the vague outline of a hand crushing her mouth and the gun pressed to her cheek.

Maggie was motionless, but inside her everything was swirling and jerking around, getting crazy again. Maggie felt herself begin to struggle, and she knew she was doing the wrong thing, but there was nothing she could do to stop herself. She had lost all control.

"I told you I have a gun! Stop struggling, Maggie!"

Maggie stopped, jolted at the sound of her name.

"I'll let go of you in a minute. As soon as I'm sure you won't panic."

She was still, the voice echoing through her head. She was no longer looking to see who held her. She knew.

Beal, too, didn't move. He held Maggie tightly, pushing her back into the couch. The flickering lights of the television were playing on her hair, and he could hear her frightened, shallow breathing. She felt terrifyingly fragile under his hand, so slight and vulnerable, like a captive bird. He wanted more than anything to free her, but the risk was too great.

"I'm sorry, Maggie. I didn't have any other choice. I want to let go of you now. Will you promise not to scream?"

He felt her head nod.

"I still have my gun on you, Maggie. And I'm scared and tired, and I'm not sure what I'm doing. So please don't move fast."

Beal lifted his hand from Maggie's mouth, then walked around to the front of the sofa, holding his revolver loosely, not entirely pointed at her but not pointed away either.

The first sight of a gun is a shock. As you stare into the small black hole like an unseeing eye, the heavy mechanical efficiency of it is stunning.

Maggie didn't move. There was a bright red angry streak across her mouth where Beal had held her, and though she said nothing, her eyes were full of accusation.

Beal walked to an armchair and sat down, trying to avoid her eyes, which held him fixed, struggling like an insect. He couldn't. And his eyes drifted back.

She was still watching him, an angry snap in her green eyes, her auburn hair tangled and tumbled around her small face. "You're still beautiful," Beal said, knowing exactly how lame that had to sound.

"If you're looking for a reconciliation, this is not the way to go about it." It was a killer voice.

"I'm in trouble, Maggie. Desperate trouble."

And still her eyes had him pinned. "I ran into your

233

mother. She told me you were dead. But you don't look very dead to me."

"Yeah, I've been a grave disappointment to a lot of people."

Still the deadly voice. "So, what is it, Beal? Are you, as they say, on the lam? Did you break from the jug? What kind of game are you playing, because I've got news for you: You can't bring it here."

"I can't explain now, but it isn't what you think. I never killed anyone. It was a setup."

Maggie looked at the revolver and then at Beal. Though she'd believed in his innocence before, here was a fairly convincing piece of evidence to the contrary. "I believe they call it a frame, right?"

"Stop it, Maggie! For God's sake, do you think I could kill anyone?" Beal stared down at Sparrow's gun. If he put it away, he'd be taking a chance that Maggie would break and run for the police. Of course, the usefulness of a gun lay only in the willingness to use it. Beal stared down at the gun for only a moment longer, then slipped it into his pocket. "I'm in trouble. Believe me, I wouldn't have come here like this if there were anything else I could do."

The sound of his voice reached Maggie. She looked at Beal's tired face; his frightened eyes glittered as if he had a fever, and all at once she knew that he was innocent and that if Jason hadn't been upstairs asleep, she probably would have helped him.

But Jason was upstairs. She shook her head. "I'm sorry. You'll have to leave."

"I tell you I'm in trouble. I have nowhere else to go. For Christ's sake, I'm asking for a place to stay tonight, maybe a sandwich, a glass of milk. Not too much strain on the old budget, huh?"

"I don't believe it! You're incredible. You break into my house, hold a gun to my head, threaten to shoot me. And now you're angry at me for not falling down at your feet." She was shrill and angry, and she hated herself for it. Finally she shook her head and said softly, "I can't help you, Beal. I guess I never could." Her voice was very sad and there was understanding in it.

Beal didn't speak for a long while, overwhelmed by the past as well as the present. "You didn't even leave me a note," he said at last. "Nothing. I sat around that lousy apartment for days before I finally realized you weren't ever coming back. You could have at least left me a goddamn note, you know."

"There was nothing to say, Beal. At least nothing that hadn't been said *ad nauseam*. I just couldn't go through it again."

Maggie's eyes were soft, and Beal could see the sympathy there. He reached out and touched her hand.

Beal's touch was electric, but Maggie didn't move. Only a few feet above them Jason lay sleeping. She had more important priorities now. Maybe she was lucky she did.

"Look, I feel sorry for you, okay?" she said after a while.

"No. It's not okay."

"Well, it will have to do, Beal. I'm fresh out of any other emotions at this minute. At least ones that you'd like to hear about. So settle for pity."

"There used to be more."

Maggie hesitated, then turned away. "Was there?"

235

Maggie felt Beal's eyes on her and knew she was hurting him, perhaps more than she ever had.

Beal's eyes glittered with anger and shame. "You could have at least left me the past."

He didn't move; disappointment was pounding hard inside him. He wanted to leave and never see Maggie again. But he couldn't leave. Once outside that door the hunt began again. His mind was almost blank with terror; his body ached with tired hopelessness. And out there were only darkness and fear.

Beal pulled out his gun. "I'm afraid you have no choice. Make me something to eat." This voice was sharp and angry.

Again fear rose in Maggie. Beal's face was etched with fatigue, almost distorted with terror. It was a frightening face that stared back at her, the face of a man who might pull the trigger.

Maggie got up from the couch slowly, eyes on Beal, wary and catlike. She was just starting for the kitchen when suddenly she became aware of a noise on the stairs.

Beal had heard it, too. He whirled, gun pointed, body poised for action, aiming at the little figure on the stairs.

"Mommy!" Jason screamed. He was terrified, eyes wide open, caught on the stairs, unsure whether to run back up or toward his mother.

Maggie, too, was frozen. "Stay there, Jason. Don't move. Everything is fine. Just stay there."

"Mommy, Mommy," Jason screamed again, shrill and parched. His eyes were on the gun, and it was clear he knew what it was.

Everything seemed to be slowed, all of them motionless in their own private terror. Then suddenly Jason bolted.

Maggie screamed, "Jason, don't!"

But he was already running, and so was Maggie. She pushed past Beal, no longer aware of anything but the terrified little boy who was crying for her.

Maggie picked Jason up in her arms, holding him tightly, rocking him back and forth, gently making soothing, cooing sounds. Jason buried himself deep into her, as if he could make himself disappear from the danger that was only a few feet away.

But Beal was no threat. He was watching the two of them numbly. The gun was already down by his side, useless metal he didn't even feel in his hand.

Maggie looked up from Jason. "I'm married," she said coldly. "My husband will be back any moment. So you'd better leave."

For a moment Beal wondered if that were true, but the little curly-headed boy who was hiding in terror reached back through the years like an echo and he felt himself and Maggie. Without seeing the features, he could sense Jason was his own. It was just a feeling, but it was a strong one.

"Why didn't you tell me? Why didn't you goddamn tell me, Maggie? I had a right to know." Beal stopped. He knew the answer already. Wasn't his being there, pointing a gun at the two of them, explanation enough?

Maggie had turned back to Jason, touching his head softly and whispering, "Everything's going to be all right. Everything's fine, baby."

Beal saw the two of them locked into one another, tight against him. He was the madman with the gun, the man who'd forced his way into their home and terrified them.

Beal started to the door. He wanted to get out into the darkness of night where no one could see him and where he wouldn't have to see the reproach in Maggie's eyes ever again. He felt very old and tired, like one of those tramps who pace Hollywood Boulevard.

When he reached the door, he stopped. "You were right not to tell me, Maggie. You made the right decision." And then he walked out.

Maggie held Jason tightly and closed her eyes, but Beal's haunted face was still there for her, and so were the tears. Though Maggie knew she was going to regret what she was doing, she lowered Jason to the floor and ran to the door.

Chapter Twenty-five

Berger lifted the H&K semiautomatic assault rifle and held it up for close to five minutes. His arm began to shake from its weight; his finger became stiff. Then suddenly, without even seeming to aim, he pulled the trigger and tore a hole in the heart of a silhouette target attached to a wooden post.

Five hundred yards. He was getting better.

The morning sun was already beating down on the Colorado wastelands, making the rocky land glow with its hot light. Back at the cabin there was cold beer in the refrigerator. Berger could just imagine drinking a case of it without even pausing to catch his breath. Still, he lifted his rifle again and waited five full minutes, motionless, like an animal of prey, zeroing in on the target. Then once again he pulled and ripped apart what was left of the silhouette. He walked back to the target, carefully folded the torn paper, put it in his pocket, and tacked up a fresh one.

Berger paused and looked at the emptiness. He'd been ordered to leave Washington and come to the desert only two days before by the blond man. But already he could feel his body getting used to the angry heat, his mind becoming immune to the quiet aloneness. Berger was a man who knew how to adjust.

He paced back from the target, this time an additional twenty-five yards. Then once again he waited, motionless. It was almost impossible to see him breathing. Suddenly he pulled off another shot. The silhouette took it in the shoulder, then the neck. The next shot blasted its head open.

Berger wiped the sweat from his forehead with his sleeve, walked back to the cabin, and went right for the beer.

Whoever had set up the cabin had known what he was doing. Besides the beer and food, there were some very good guns, plenty of ammunition, and a set of instructions laying out precisely what kind of practicing he was to do.

It was the instructions that gave everything away. For example, Berger's orders were to kill a stationary target of close to six feet tall, 185 pounds within the next two weeks. There were the floor plans of an enormous room with a large platform marked off. His target was just left of the podium.

Given that information, a lot could be deduced. First of all, what would be happening in a large room in the next few weeks? Not much. The UN was closed for the summer; so was Congress. There were probably several hundred conventions going on around the country. A convention made sense; the room was too large to be much else but a convention hall. The grounds were outlined on his instructions. Seventy-five acres with several buildings on it. The one he was concerned with was three floors with a good 400,000 square feet of space. A building that size would have to be in one of America's major cities.

Getaway plans included a river and a cargo ship. Chicago? Could be. Detroit? Could be Detroit. He'd only been there once, but the Joe Louis Convention Arena was new and big. As far as he could remember, Detroit had been figuring in the news a lot recently as the site of a political convention.

So who would be sitting up on the dais? In particular, just left of the center? Well, it wouldn't be the President. He'd be coming out from the wings to make his speech. Probably the Vice President wouldn't be sitting there either. The speaker of the House was from the same party. It could be the speaker of the House.

Berger stopped, shaking his head thoughtfully. Why the hell would anyone want to kill the speaker of the House?

Chapter Twenty-six

Morning light spilled into Maggie's large white kitchen, staining everything a buttery yellow. Spunky, Maggie's wizened old cat, lay in a beam of morning light, fast asleep. Outside, there were the sounds of sprinklers on people's lawns. A dog barked and a next-door neighbor started up his car. Everything felt lazy, like Sunday.

Beal was wearing an old sweat shirt of Maggie's. He was sitting at the breakfast table, surrounded by pungent morning smells of bacon and coffee, while a Bach fugue on the radio made order out of chaos. It was a fugue Beal knew he'd never be able to play well. But he didn't torture himself with that fact. It was the first moment of peace he'd had in weeks, and he knew enough to leave it alone.

Beal looked over at Maggie, trying to read what she was thinking. He wanted more than anything for her to reassure him that last night was real. But her back was to him as she revolved around the kitchen, and silence hung over the room like the smoke of her cigarette, which smoldered in the ashtray.

Jason walked into the kitchen, his eyes cautious and guarded. He paused, caught between the memory of the gun and the fact that his mother seemed to trust the man who had held it. His curly blond hair was slicked back, wet and newly brushed, his clothes clean and ironed, as if he were going to a party. There were traces of Beal in every feature of his face, movements that echoed a father he didn't even know he had.

Beal was in a state of peaceful shock. Only a few hours before, he'd been totally alone, curled into himself with terror. Now the small, serious boy with the curly blond hair and big green eyes instantly opened him out, bathing him with hope and warmth, rooting him to the earth. Beal was astounded and touched more deeply than he would have thought possible. But he was scared, too. Maybe more scared than anything else. It was one thing to want a son and even to daydream about showing him how to throw around the old pigskin; it was one thing to think about what he'd tell his son about the crazy old world and how he'd be able to make it easier for him than it had been for Beal. It was another thing to be staring at the reality.

Jason walked to the table. As he sat down, he threw a suspicious glance at Beal, then quickly turned away. A moment later he glanced back. Beal had his tongue stuck out. Jason turned away, confused and surprised, but almost immediately he shifted his gaze back. Beal had his eyes crossed.

This cinched it for Jason. He started to laugh, then pulled at his eyes and looked up, until all that was ex-

243

posed was the milky white of his eyeballs. A common ground had been found.

Maggie carried the platter of bacon and eggs to the table, and even though she was facing Beal, he still couldn't tell what she was thinking. It occurred to him that perhaps he'd never known; perhaps he'd always been too busy trying to figure out the crazy wheels that were turning inside himself to really know anything about her.

As Maggie filled three plates with breakfast, the old cat dragged itself from the kitchen floor and sleepily sauntered to the table. Placing itself strategically near Jason's ankles, it flopped down, then closed its eyes, nodding off like an old heroin addict.

"You still have cats," Beal said.

Maggie smiled. "It's more like they have me than anything else."

Beal looked over at the sleeping ball of fur. "What's his name?"

Jason answered. "It's a she. And her name is Spunky."

"She sure doesn't look very spunky to me."

"She's old," Jason answered in defense.

"Nonsense," said Maggie. "She just pretends to be old so she doesn't have to do any work around here. The trouble with Spunky is she's lazy. I'm at work all day and Jason's at school, but do you think she's ever once picked up a broom or washed a dish? She won't even answer the phone. Once I left a pad and pencil by her litter box, but she just pretended she didn't know what they were."

"Spunky is dumb," Jason said.

Maggie shook her head. "Like a fox."

For a moment the old cat's whiskers twitched and her eyes opened into slits. But almost immediately they drooped again.

"Maybe if you started easy," Beal suggested. "Like leaving a can of cat food and an opener by her dish."

"Tried it. She's much too clever to fall for that. She just walked over and sniffed, as if she didn't know exactly what we wanted. She pretends like she can't talk, too. Just goes around all day saying 'meow.' Like I said, Spunky is one clever cat."

Jason started meowing happily. Again Spunky opened her eyes, annoyed at being disturbed.

"I tried persuading her to go on welfare, but she refused to sign the forms."

"Too much pride." Beal shook his head knowingly.

"I suppose. Though she certainly doesn't seem to mind sponging off me and Jason."

Spunky slowly unraveled and stretched herself, then walked from the room, a bored look on her venerable face, as if she'd been through that conversation many times and never thought it particularly amusing in the first place.

Spunky's exit caused a long silence. Beal looked over at Maggie, but she was bent toward Jason, urging him to eat his egg yolk. Jason pulled a face. There was a silent battle of wills. Finally Jason sighed and lifted the yolk onto his spoon. Maggie smiled in victory, but she didn't turn back to Beal, and he sensed the reassurance he was looking for would never come.

Maggie broke the silence. "How are your folks?" But her eyes were closed off to Beal.

"My dad's in the hospital."

"Serious?"

Beal shrugged. "I don't know. I haven't seen him. I talked to him on the phone, and he sounded all right. I guess he's just getting old."

"That's serious. I liked your dad, you know."

"Did you feel sorry for him, like you did for me?"

Still Maggie avoided his eyes. "I'm sorry I implied that. I didn't mean it."

Beal sighed. "Yes, you did. I guess I always felt it under everything. I just wouldn't admit it to myself. Oh, well, we did have our laughs, though."

Maggie agreed. "Yes, we did have our laughs." Then she turned back to Jason, coaxing him to eat.

Beal turned away from the two of them. The moment of peace was shattered. It was as if the night before had never happened.

And yet it had happened.

Maggie had put Jason to bed, then brought Beal into the kitchen and made him a sandwich. She'd sat, watching him, her legs crossed, cigarette smoke curling around her head. The slits of her long robe fell open, and Beal could see the smooth pale flesh of her thighs as she rocked her leg back and forth.

Beal had told her everything. She'd listened, occasionally asking questions, mostly sitting in silence. Beal couldn't tell if she believed what he was saying. He couldn't blame her if she didn't. It sounded crazy even to him, and he was living it. But he could see that Maggie believed in his pain. And that was enough for the moment.

Maggie had made a bed for him on the living-room couch and waited until he'd gotten into it. Beal took off his jacket and pants but left on his shirt, embarrassed, not of being nude in front of Maggie but of what it implied. Maggie turned off the lights, softly said good night, then mounted the stairs.

As Beal lay on his lumpy bed, listening to her footsteps receding, the fear and the loneliness came rolling back on him, crushing his chest until he thought he couldn't breathe.

"I still love you," Beal said to the darkened room. "I always loved you."

There was no answer, and he wondered if Maggie had even heard him. In a way he hoped she hadn't. It required an answer that he might not want to hear.

Once again he was aware of her soft footsteps, and he closed his eyes, knowing that rather than answer she had crept away. Black emptiness and silence settled over him. Until suddenly he realized she was back in the room, and the joy was astounding.

There had been no words. Maggie had slipped out of her robe, her pale, slim body just barely visible in the darkness. But Beal didn't need light to see her body. He remembered every line. Her long, elegant legs with their tiny tracings of veins, the soft curving of her breasts, heavy and full, yet tilted upward, like a young girl's.

She knelt to him on the couch and unbuttoned his shirt. When her hands touched his chest, they sent electric sparks through him. The warmth spread as her hands moved down his body. And then suddenly he could feel her breath moist and hot on his skin. She clutched at his hips with her hands and moaned softly. For a moment her lips brushed his stomach, and then the burning liquid heat of her mouth enveloped him. His insides were torn apart with pleasure and need.

Beal reached to Maggie, pulled her to him, crushed

her chest to his. Again she moaned, her mouth opening to his, widening with urgency, and he could feel her trembling as he lowered her to the couch.

Maggie's voice was thick with passion. "Oh, God, I still want you."

Her shuddering body was pressed tightly to his, and as Beal thrust into her dark warmth, a liquid white heat, intense, overpowering, spread outward. He was walking the fragile line between life and death, dangerously balanced on the edge until suddenly they both exploded violently with a scream. . . .

There was the honking of a car outside. Maggie retrieved Jason's lunch box and walked to the door. When she got back to the kitchen, she glanced at the wall clock.

"I'd better hurry or I'll be late for work." They were the first words Maggie had said to Beal in some time, and a million doors seemed to slam shut with them.

Beal pulled himself up from the table. "Okay."

"Where will you go?" she asked, leaning against the doorjamb. Her eyes had softened.

"I'll follow up on those notes I took yesterday. See if they mean anything."

"That isn't what I meant. Where will you stay?"

"I haven't figured that one out yet."

"Maybe you ought to call that man Sparrow." Maggie moved into the kitchen and lit a cigarette.

"You shouldn't smoke so much, you know."

"This is not news." She watched him, catlike.

"You don't believe any of what I told you, do you? You think this is all some elaborate scheme to win you back."

"The truth and you have never been very close friends."

"Oh, well, the hell with you, Maggie." There was no anger in Beal's voice, just tired resignation. "Anyway, I appreciate what you did for me last night."

Maggie laughed. But it was clear she wasn't finding things very funny. "I didn't exactly do it for you, Beal."

"I didn't mean that. I meant giving me a place to sleep, listening to me, not calling the police after I'd gone to sleep."

"I thought about it, but instead, I came back down the stairs and spent the night with you. I certainly haven't learned much in five years." She stopped. "I didn't mean that, Beal. I guess there's still a lot of bitterness. A lot of anger. Last night, when I told you I felt sorry for you, I knew what I was implying. I wanted to hurt you. But I didn't feel sorry for you. At least not in the way you took it. It was something different I felt. I don't think it has a name. Or maybe it does."

She stubbed out her cigarette in decision. "I have a girl friend who can take Jason after school today. I'll call in sick for work and come with you."

Beal shook his head. "No, I can't drag you into this."

"You already have."

"You don't have to worry. I was careful. No one followed me."

Maggie smiled sadly. "That isn't what I meant."

Chapter Twenty-seven

It was a bad day.

Not that it started out that way. It started out well, at least considering that just about everyone in the world was trying to get at Beal.

Not finding the notebook where he'd hidden it was the beginning. Still, as Maggie suggested, everything that wasn't nailed down in Hollywood was usually ripped off within an hour, and since Beal remembered most of the facts and names he'd written down, the day couldn't be classified as bad.

But it got good and bad after that.

Beal called the headquarters of the Secret Service and was able to wheedle out the information that both of the Secret Service men who had surrounded Lacey as he lay dying were now themselves dead. Coincidence. They both had died five years ago. Beal was unsettled, but still, this did not qualify as a major tragedy since Beal hardly needed a reminder that anyone who touched on the Lacey assassination had a chance of not getting through it alive.

What had surprised him even more was that he'd been able to get that much information out of the Secret Service. Anyone who ever had to deal with a government agency knew that getting any kind of definite answer was close to impossible, and an agency like the Secret Service should have been totally impossible. So Beal was starting to feel edgy. But what happened next overshadowed everything.

Beal called his father at the hospital, and instead of his being connected, there was a pause, a long one. Beal could feel his heart pounding in his chest; there was a sick feeling deep in his stomach, and he knew even before he was told that his father was dead.

They called it a heart attack.

After that everything had gone crazy on him. It was as if he were empty inside, not dead, not numb, because that implied feeling, but hollow. No thoughts went through his mind, no memories. If pressed, he probably couldn't even have given a reasonable description of his father. It was as if his body were protecting him, warning him from the dangerous vision of his father's careworn, anxious face as he packed the old Plymouth.

It was an empty shell that sat hunched in the passenger seat of Maggie's VW. Maggie was pressing through rush-hour traffic, running right on the ass of the car in front of her, a beat-up white Chevy lowrider that belched so much smoke it looked like Pittsburgh on wheels. In the back seat, four Mexicans and a dog with a bobbing head watched her, laughing.

Ordinarily Beal would have been shouting at Maggie about her driving. But Beal was silent. He was turned inward, and in fact, he was seeing nothing.

Maggie kept glancing at him anxiously, unsure whether to speak or remain silent. She knew nothing about death, only ancient grandmothers and great-aunts, which wasn't the same thing at all. Even though she had been fond of Beal's father, it hardly qualified as a death to Maggie's world, and oddly enough that made her feel guilty as she watched Beal suffering silently next to her.

Finally Beal spoke. "They killed him."

Maggie knew this was coming. "Beal, don't. People are in the hospital because they're sick."

"He was walking around for fifteen minutes yesterday. He even went to the toilet on his own. Does that sound like a man who's about to die?"

"He was an old man, Beal. Anything could have happened."

But Beal wasn't listening to her. "The worst part is I don't even know which side did it. I wouldn't put it past Sparrow. No, sir. I certainly wouldn't put it past him."

Maggie tried to keep her voice calm. "Now why would Sparrow want to kill your dad?"

"To scare me. To make me so frightened I have to run back to him."

"That's crazy."

"Yeah, well, it's a crazy world. And you see, it doesn't matter who killed him in the end. It was my fault. I should have known better than to call him. I killed him, Maggie. And I could be killing you, too."

"That's ridiculous. So far I haven't seen evidence that anything out of the ordinary has happened."

"That notebook was missing."

"Anyone could have picked it up."

"How about the Secret Service men both being dead?"

"People die."

"Like my father?"

"Exactly. Like your father."

Beal felt sick to his stomach. "I don't want to talk anymore. I want to get out of this car, and I want to leave you alone. Okay? So just stop right here."

Beal's hand went to the door handle, but Maggie didn't even slow down. "I'm taking you home."

"Like hell," Beal shouted. Anger was rising inside him, crazy and dangerous. "You want to be stupid, be stupid on your own conscience. Because people are dying, and they're dying because of me. And I can't stand it anymore." His hand went to the door handle.

"Stop it! You're hysterical, and you're scaring me." Maggie turned onto her street and pulled into the driveway.

It was only when Maggie stopped the car that Beal realized they were already at Maggie's house. And by then it was too late to do anything about it because events were taking over, as they seemed to be doing all the time now.

The back door of Maggie's house was jammed open. And inside, nothing was as it had been.

Clothes, papers, records, toys, even food from the refrigerator were thrown around the living room. Furniture was on its side, drawers pulled from dressers, the contents scattered all over. Huge fluorescent letters were spray-painted on the walls, WHORE! CUNT! PUSSY! Crude, obscene pictures scrawled across the living room.

It looked like the work of a group of sick teen-agers. Or rather it was made to look like their work because Beal knew what it was.

Maggie couldn't move. She couldn't even scream. She stood frozen in the doorway, her eyes riveted to the ceiling.

Hanging by her neck from a piece of cord attached to the light fixture was Spunky. The cat's scrawny, wasted body was hunched in the air like an old, stooped man, head flopped to the side, eyes milky white and staring, mouth wide open, exposing a long, thin, puffy gray tongue.

"Oh, God." Maggie shivered.

Beal took her arm, but he, too, didn't move. The sight of the hanging cat, humpbacked and hideous in death, had evoked another memory for Beal, and he stared at the misshapen body fixed by that memory.

Finally Beal broke from it and tried to urge Maggie away. Maggie turned to him, her eyes wild with fear. He could feel her body trembling. "How could anyone do that? She was just an old cat."

"It was a warning." Beal gently prodded Maggie away from the door and back toward the car. He reached into his pocket and pulled out his wallet. "You better take a hotel room for the night." He pressed several hundred-dollar bills in her hand.

Maggie shook her head but allowed the bills to stay in her hand, aware of very little that was happening around her.

"If you leave me right now, everything is going to be fine. You understand?"

Maggie allowed Beal to lead her to the car, woodenly, as if the legs that moved under her and the hands that clutched to Beal's arm didn't belong to her at all.

Beal opened the car door and waited for Maggie to get into the driver's seat. "If I were you, I'd tell your friend to keep Jason for a while. It's just a precaution, but I think it's better that way. Then you go to a nice big hotel like the Hilton and stay there for a few days, until they realize that we're no longer together."

Maggie was staring at him as if she hadn't understood a word. "Please don't leave me alone," she said, trembling. "I can't stand the thought of them coming after me, and I'm all alone."

Beal took Maggie's trembling body into his arms and held her closely.

"Please don't leave me," Maggie repeated.

Beal held Maggie tightly, closing his eyes against the sight of her fear. But inside his head the cat, hunched in the air, had triggered the memory of another hunched, stooped body. When he'd been up in the mountains, he'd seen a man, a man with a pale, sunless face like death. He'd seen the man for only an instant before he was chased, but there had been something familiar about that face and also something terrible. Whoever that man was, Beal had obviously surprised him in hiding.

And suddenly Beal had a feeling he knew why he'd been chased then and why they were trying to kill him now. Up there in the arid mountains he'd seen a man connected to the Lacey assassination. But he knew it

255

was more than that. Why would a man be so pale and thin? Why would a man be in hiding?

Standing on the pavement, holding tightly to Maggie, he could feel a trembling from deep within his body, and he knew without totally understanding that he had seen the man who had killed President Lacey.

Chapter Twenty-eight

Whenever General Nadler wanted to think, he walked out his back door and took off to the gently rolling Illinois woods with his rifle. There was something about the cleanness of movement, the concentration of fixing a rabbit or deer in the sight, the trembling excitement just before pulling the trigger, the release after you did that made Nadler's mind quick and sharp. Most of all, Nadler enjoyed sitting down for dinner and eating what he'd shot.

Nadler liked to do most things himself. If a person did things himself, he got a feeling of the wholeness. It was true of a job. It was true of life. There was very little that Nadler did in which he wasn't involved right down to the minutia. Back at his house, in his desk drawer, there were twelve checks, each of them for five thousand dollars, made out to three different men. He had drawn them himself, and only he and his assistant, a tall blond man with blank eyes and a professional coolness that never wavered, knew who these men were, where they were, and exactly what they were doing. Delivery of these checks was to be made in two days. His assistant would take a morning plane to Denver, pass out the checks, and be on the evening plane to Detroit. Strictly speaking, these checks were unnecessary. The three men already had their retainers and should by rights expect nothing more until the job was completed. But Nadler knew the value of paying a man handsomely. Especially if there was every likelihood that the checks would never be cashed.

Nadler paced through the fresh-smelling tall grass toward a large oak tree at the back of his land, his rifle held at his side. When he reached the tree, he stopped to stand motionless, his ears alert, his still-youthful body poised as if about to strike. His young baby face with its mustache and cool eyes was tight and hard, wrinkled into total concentration.

There wasn't a sound, no movement in the grass, no shifting of a stone, nothing to tell that life was nearby. But life was nearby. It just took patience to wait it out, and Nadler was a man with patience.

He could see the back of his house from where he was and, just behind it, the wide sweep of lawn with its drooping willows and majestic oaks. There was a good fifteen acres of lawn out there, and it took three privates to keep it up. But the magnificent lawn wasn't for Nadler's pleasure. The large, well-kept lawn was a symbol of power. All generals had their large lawns. It was like medals on their chests or stars on their hats. And Nadler was an expert on power. Perhaps because it meant so little to him.

There was a shift in the grass two hundred yards

away. Nadler fixed his gaze on the spot, his arms lifting the rifle, his hands working into position. He figured it was probably a rabbit, but he knew it could just be a snake. Nadler didn't bother killing snakes as most hunters did. To kill was a waste and should be done only when absolutely necessary.

Again there was a rustling, this time closer, but not close enough. Nadler was motionless. Whatever was approaching would not be scared off by any movement from him.

With the clear, sharp sun beating down on his head, and his body loosening into the feeling of being outside, his mind focused in. On the whole, everything was going well, not perfectly, but how often did things go perfectly? Nadler was quite prepared to settle for well. There were enough backups built into the plan to cover any of the links should they become weak.

The major problem was the rest of the Trust. Nadler had no doubt that they suspected the State of Emergency Plan. Certainly Fuller did. Of course, Colton, too, had suspected and had tried to get his way. Colton had felt that because he supplied money to the Trust, he was indispensable. It was a fatal mistake. His threat of closing off funds from the Trust had been an empty one. He should have realized that diverting money from the military was a relatively simple thing. It was only Colton's mouth that Nadler feared, and his assistant had arranged to shut it forever.

As for the rest of the Trust, Nadler suspected that in the end they'd go along. In truth, they would have little choice. Once the wheels were set in motion, there would be nothing anyone could do. President, Vice President, Speaker of the House. All killed at precisely the same moment. Never in the history of America had there been a crime of that magnitude. There would be no alternative but to proclaim a state of emergency. Then the second phase of the plan would begin.

Suddenly there was a rustling less than fifty yards away. Nadler reacted; quickly shifting, he fixed the place in his sight. His body tensed; his vision sharpened; not even his chest moved with breath.

Again a rustle. Then a brief flash of soft gray fur, lifting off the ground. The rabbit appeared above the line of grass, legs pumping.

There was the crack of Nadler's rifle and the rabbit was caught in midair, shocking upward. A splot of red splattered outward, and the rabbit went limp, tumbling crazily to the ground.

Chapter Twenty-nine

Sparrow entered the elevator at the Holiday Inn and pressed the button for the third floor. As the doors were closing he caught sight of Richards leaving the elevator next to him. While he knew they both were staying at the same hotel, and he was sure Richards also knew, the two men had never seen each other there.

Sparrow wondered briefly if Richards had seen him also. He wouldn't have minded if he had. Richards wasn't about to kill him in a busy hotel lobby. Indeed, Richards wasn't likely to try and kill him at all, knowing that if Sparrow were dead, he would only be replaced.

There was only one time Sparrow had to watch out for Richards, and that was when he was protecting Beal. Richards wouldn't think twice about killing Sparrow in order to get to his primary target. Just as Sparrow wouldn't think twice about killing him to save

Beal. But other than that they would leave each other alone. There were strange rules that they operated under. But there were the rules nonetheless.

Sparrow opened his door. He never bothered with things like hairs or pieces of tissue to warn him if anyone had been in his room. The whole city could come search his room for all he cared. He never left things around. And anyway, he would know if someone had been there. He had a sixth sense about things like that.

The room had been made up, and there was that impersonal look that all hotel rooms have when they're clean, no matter how expensive. Sparrow was used to it. For the past ten years his whole life was filled with rooms that could belong to anyone. In the beginning he had carried with him some mementos of his past life. But it was dangerous, and in the end it didn't help all that much. Now he kept only one picture, and he kept it on him.

Sparrow placed the snapshot on the table next to the bed, a nightly ritual. Then he kicked off his shoes with a long, low sigh of relief, flopped on the bed, and began rubbing the kinks out of his toes, making each of them crack.

Why he kept the picture he couldn't imagine. It was a distorted face of a boy of fifteen that looked back at him. Heavy, drooped features, the ugly grimace of severe mongolism.

It had been taken the year before, when Sparrow made a visit to the hospital in Boston where Roger lived. Roger had been finger-painting; smears of yellow and green paint covered his face. Sparrow remembered holding the camera and calling the little boy's name. He'd looked up with that same blank look he gave the nurses, doctors, and other patients. A look that told he had no idea who they were.

Still, he had looked up and Sparrow had taken the picture. And it was the best one Sparrow ever had of him. In it Roger was grimacing, as if deep in thought. Sparrow supposed he did think, though what of he couldn't imagine. Perhaps he was thinking of the color yellow as he was painting. Maybe he even balanced the color green in there at the same time. But it was a momentary understanding.

Once again Sparrow asked himself why he continued to fly to Boston every chance he had, walking down that long, echoing corridor to the large, drooping boy who was only a shade brighter than an eggplant. Why did he carry his picture around with him, glancing at it every day? Why? Was it because he felt that lump of flesh that stared blankly at him was his fault? Certainly his wife, Sylvia, had thought so. He could see her sitting on the edge of Roger's bed, running her heavy, squat fingers through her ratted brown hair. Her face tormented with anger and guilt.

Maybe Sylvia was right. She had been close to forty when she found herself pregnant and had begged Sparrow to allow her to get an abortion. He had refused. There had been no marriage after that. A year or so later Sylvia had stopped visiting, and Roger hadn't even noticed she was gone.

Sparrow could just as easily do the same, and yet he continued to visit. Out of guilt? Out of love? Sparrow supposed it was probably neither of these reasons and something much more selfish. Roger was the only human being in the world he had to love, and he needed Roger to keep him human.

The phone rang, startling Sparrow back to the world. The sadness on his face vanished, and he was all business as he listened to the hotel operator tell him his answering service at the dance studio was holding a message.

A few minutes later in a phone booth down the street Sparrow picked up his message.

"A Mr. Beal called," the woman at the answering service said indifferently. "He says you're to meet him at Hallie's bar on Santa Monica and Gardner at nine o'clock tonight."

As Sparrow put down the receiver, he grimaced with wonder and did a little soft-shoe two-step out the door. "Well, I'll be a son of a bitch," he said happily.

Hallie's was one of those fashionable gay bars with brick walls, huge gilt mirrors, and enough plants to qualify as a botanical garden. The bar was a hot crush of men in business suits, elegant sport clothes, and jogging shorts, shifting like clouds, passionately greeting a friend, the smile of interest masking that all eyes were turned to the door. After all, California was the land of golden tomorrows and whoever came through that door might be better than what had already been seen.

Sparrow was a man in desperate agony. He pushed to the bar, eyes fixed straight ahead. Already his forehead was dotted with perspiration and his hand was fishing in his pocket for his antacids. Of course, he should have figured what kind of bar it was from the address. Certainly there could be no question that Beal had picked it in order to irritate Sparrow. Any feeling he had begun to develop for Beal vanished, and mentally he inflicted agonies on Beal's person unequaled since Attila the Hun.

Sparrow ordered a mineral water, then began scanning the room, careful that his gaze didn't light for long enough to be misinterpreted. He was not successful.

A voice next to him said, "What's the matter, darling?"

Sparrow froze. Out of the corner of his eye he saw a young man with pale skin, blond hair, and slim, slightly stooped shoulders, wearing only silky jogging shorts and tennis shoes. He was smiling at Sparrow, a dimpled smile that tilted up childishly; his eyes sparkled with mischief, like a naughty elf.

"I'm Andrew." Andrew extended his hand with that baby smile, and Sparrow found himself shaking hands with him.

Andrew leaned confidentially toward Sparrow and sighed. "Isn't this place the pits? Such a meat market." Andrew caught the eye of someone he knew and waved his thin arm in the air, flashing that same devilish smile. "I only come here when I'm really low. But it always ends up making me feel worse. I think this time it really must be suicide."

Again someone tilted his head in recognition to Andrew. He blew him a kiss. "I'm hopelessly depressed. I haven't eaten in days."

Sparrow didn't answer and tried to edge away from the boy. But Andrew didn't seem to notice and continued to chatter happily. "Love, darling. It's the worst. Honestly, if they passed out saltpeter at this bar instead of liquor, I'd be the first in line."

A tall man in a tight-fitting T-shirt and Levi's jeans

bore down on Andrew and grabbed him around the waist, almost lifting him off the floor.

"Oh, darling," Andrew whimpered. "I really think it has to be suicide this time." Andrew had switched his smile to the T-shirt and was moving toward the other side of the room with him, gesticulating wildly as he swore he wouldn't make it through the evening. His small bottom wagged happily under his shiny jogging shorts as he moved through the crowded room.

Sparrow was almost sorry when he was gone. There was something endearing about his childish smile. Dressed differently, he would look like an eastern college boy. It made him think of David.

Sparrow shivered. He'd worked with David for close to a year now and liked him as well as he'd ever liked anyone who worked for him. Was it possible?

He looked around the room. The thought of what all those nice-looking young men did in their darkened bedrooms stunned him. And there were so many of them around today. So many. He just didn't understand anymore. When he was young, they were called fruits and nobody knew one or certainly admitted it anyway. Today they were everywhere. He wondered what the young girls did with all those *fegeles* around. It occurred to him that maybe they did the same, and he shook off the thought immediately.

"Crowded as hell tonight, isn't it?"

Sparrow whipped around, hoping that Beal had finally arrived. It was a tall, serious man in a dark business suit. Sparrow nodded, then turned away.

Sparrow shrank into himself. From across the bar he saw Andrew waving at him. He found himself waving back with a smile.

266

Then slowly he became aware of a heavy cloud of gardenia perfume falling over the bar. He felt two nudges at his back and stiffened. Those nudges felt like breasts, but Sparrow knew whatever they were, they couldn't be breasts. Or if they were, it was one of those weird operations, which was even worse.

He felt hot breath on the back of his bald head, and the smell of perfume was intense. It was the most blatant attempt to pick him up yet, and Sparrow's knees were starting to feel weak and funny.

It was amazing that here he was, a man who had done just about everything there was to be done, a killer, an assassin, and he was scared of a fruit.

"Sorry I'm late, darling," a voice lisped in his ear. "Traffic was simply atrocious. I finally had to take a cab. And you know what it's like getting a cab in this town."

Sparrow turned around slowly. The lisping voice was just too ridiculous to be anyone else.

Beal was wearing a bright red wig that cascaded into a foam of curls at his shoulders. His face was smeared with heavy makeup; his bright red dress was décolleté and tight around his bottom. On his feet he wore four-inch red and green glittery heels.

He was attracting more attention than a bomb threat at Dodger Stadium, and looks of disappointment spread quickly through the room as Beal and Sparrow were seen to be a couple. Out of the corner of Sparrow's eye he saw Andrew flash him the thumbs-up sign, obviously impressed.

Sparrow grabbed Beal's jewelry-clad arm angrily. "You don't have a clue how to take care of yourself, do you? What the hell kind of place is this to set up a

267

meeting? And look at you! If the police don't get you, one of the weirdos in this room will. Now I want you to wash that crap off your face in the bathroom." He stopped. "Forget the bathroom. I know all about what they do in bathrooms in these kinds of places. But we're getting out of here now."

Sparrow had begun to pull Beal from the room when he saw rage darkening his rouged face. "That's right," Sparrow whispered furiously. "Start a fight. That'll make you even more conspicuous than you already are."

"We stay here!" Beal said loudly. He had forgotten the lisp and looked around to see if anyone had noticed. But now that Beal had obviously made his choice, he had become part of the room and most of the eyes were back on the door.

"My father is dead," Beal whispered angrily.

"I know," answered Sparrow, then saw the suspicion in Beal's eyes. "It wasn't us."

"How do I know that?"

"You don't. You take it on trust."

"Sorry, darling, but I'm all out of that." Beal's teeth were clenched, making his simpering lisp sound almost deadly.

Sparrow was wondering why the hell he'd bothered to come. He'd hoped Beal had set up the meeting because he'd become reasonable and wanted Sparrow to hide him. This clearly was not the case.

"Albert tells me you have a woman with you now."

Beal shrugged. He'd long ago stopped being surprised by what everyone seemed to know. "My wife."

"Ex-wife, to be precise. Can you trust her?"

"You'd like to make me think I can't, wouldn't you?"

"I'd like you to be alert to the possibilities."

"Is that why you wrecked her house and killed her cat?"

Sparrow seemed surprised. He tried to cover it. "I don't kill cats. It's not that I like them, because I don't. They always smell of fish and dirty Kitty Litter. But that isn't a reason to kill them. On the other hand, dogs whine too much. I can see murdering a dog."

"They had cans of spray paint and very bad vocabularies."

Sparrow seemed confused. "Where are you staying now?"

"I want to meet the big man," Beal said softly.

"Which big man?"

"The man who runs you."

Sparrow took another sip of his drink and smiled falsely. "Keep your voice down," he whispered.

Beal lowered his voice. "I want you to set up a meeting for us."

"Impossible."

"Not impossible. Necessary."

Sparrow finished his drink with a flourish and put the empty glass on the bar. "Is that why you called me?"

"Right. That's why I called you."

Sparrow shrugged, then looked at his watch. "Well, darling, gotta run." The short, balding little man simpered ridiculously, then turned to leave.

"I know why they're trying to kill me."

Sparrow stopped. He turned back to Beal and saw the smile on his face. "What do you know?"

This time Sparrow's voice was too loud, and Beal wagged an admonishing finger at him. "Keep your voice down, my pet." Beal was smiling broadly. He seemed to be enjoying Sparrow's discomfort a good deal. "I want to see the big man," he repeated.

"Where can I reach you?"

"Call 555-6679 tomorrow at eleven in the morning, darling. Shall I write the number down?"

"I haven't reached senility yet."

Beal leaned over and planted a kiss on Sparrow's livid cheek. "Ta-ta, darling. And don't forget tomorrow." Waving gaily, Beal turned and disappeared into the crowd, leaving behind a cloud of gardenia perfume.

But Sparrow, too, was smiling. Far down the street Albert and Simon would be watching to make sure no one was following Beal, and even if they, too, lost him in the crowds, the number he'd given Sparrow was undoubtedly a phone booth. It would be easy to trace.

By ten o'clock the next morning Sparrow had everything all set up.

There were three men watching the phone booth. A stocky Mexican kid wearing an undershirt leaned over the open hood of a beat-up Chevy. An enormous black man who looked like a wino snoozed on a bench that advertised a mortuary. And an elegant gray-haired man in a three-piece suit lounged in the front seat of a rented Mercedes.

Only two blocks away Simon and Albert, who had indeed misplaced Beal in the night crowds, were keeping well out of sight but readily available in a painted hippie van. A few yards beyond them, in the lot of a

270

large discount house, Sparrow stood waiting, keeping his eye on the length of Santa Monica Boulevard.

It would be simple. Beal would get to the phone booth and wait for Sparrow's call. The phone would ring. Beal would pick it up. And Sparrow's men would close in. Quick, clean, easy.

So why did Sparrow feel so edgy? He felt edgy because it wasn't going to be quick, clean, and easy. He was going to have a hell of a time getting Beal to tell him what he knew, meaning he would have to hurt Beal, perhaps badly and probably a little permanently. Afterward there would still be the problem of keeping Beal in hiding.

Sparrow reached into his pocket and took out an antacid. It was cherry flavor, which was all the store had in stock, and he grimaced at the sweet synthetic taste. He saw it as a bad omen.

Sparrow checked his watch, then looked down the long smoggy expanse of run-down two-story buildings. He could just barely make out the Mexican kid working on his car, the black guy snoozing on the bench, and the guy in the Mercedes parked in a red zone, keeping his engine running.

The painted van with Albert and Simon started up its motor but remained parked by the side of the road.

Two minutes to eleven and everything was in place.

Sparrow took a dime out of his pocket and fingered the smooth, greasy coin, squinting out at the smoggy street. The phone booth still seemed to be empty. But it was hard to tell.

Again Sparrow checked his watch just as the numbers flipped to eleven. He waited another minute for good luck, then slowly walked to the next-door gas

271

station where there was a phone. By the time he got there it was two minutes past eleven, but still Sparrow didn't dial. Waiting for the call would make Beal feel edgy, which was a definite psychological advantage. It would be the first step in proving to him that no matter what he did, no matter how hard he tried, he just couldn't hack it in the real world.

Sparrow deposited the dime, then slowly dialed. The phone went through its mechanical grinding, then rang. Sparrow looked out the glass and thought he saw the Mexican rubbernecking up and down Santa Monica Boulevard. If that were true, it meant Beal hadn't arrived yet. Sparrow drummed his fingers nervously.

Again the phone rang. Then stopped right in the middle of the second ring. Sparrow breathed a sigh of relief.

"Morning, Sparrow."

Beal's voice sounded cheerful. Sparrow doubted it would be so cheerful after his men closed in, as they would be doing in only a few seconds.

"Did you get everything set up for my little meeting with the big man?" Beal asked.

Sparrow stalled. "I had trouble getting hold of him."

"Don't play games with me. I want to meet him or else."

Sparrow laughed nastily. "Or else what?" But already his hand was moving to his pocket for the antacid. His men should be closing in by now, and yet nothing seemed to be happening.

"I've learned enough to go public with it."

"That wouldn't be wise."

"As we both know, I am not a wise man."

Sparrow crunched on his tablet nervously. Where

the hell were his men? He craned his neck but could see nothing.

Beal laughed. "You shouldn't eat so many of those antacids, Sparrow. They plug you up. You know what I mean? Anyway, here's what you do if you want to keep me quiet. You tell your friend I want to meet him on Highway One, three point two miles north of the country store, at exactly three fifteen this afternoon."

Sparrow hesitated, hoping he'd hear a scuffle as his men picked Beal up, but he was beginning to realize that something had gone very wrong. Finally he answered. "He couldn't possibly make it by this afternoon."

"Why?" Beal's voice sounded sharp.

"He lives too far away."

Beal was silent for a long while. "You're probably stalling so you can set up a trap, but I'll take you on. Let's make it ten fifteen in the morning, same place."

"Where can I call you back to let you know if it's okay with him?"

"You don't. He just shows up. If he doesn't, then I take you and him down with me. I mean it, too."

"That's blackmail."

Beal laughed. "Let's not discuss conscience."

Sparrow didn't answer for a long while. He still couldn't see his men. "I'll see what I can do."

Beal started to laugh. "You do that, Sparrow. By the way, aren't you curious how I did it?"

Sparrow tried to sound innocent. "Did what?"

"How many men did you have waiting for me? Ten? Twenty?"

"Don't flatter yourself. Only five, not counting me."

A long pause, then a profound sigh. "All right, how did you do it?"

"Remember my little blue box enterprise? Well, I had to do a little research into the phone company to make it work."

"You bugged it?" Sparrow started to laugh despite himself. "Of course, you spliced into the line and re-routed the call to another booth."

But Beal already had hung up and Sparrow was listening to a dial tone. Automatically his hand went to his pocket, reaching for the antacids. He stopped. Maybe Beal was right about antacids plugging you up.

Chapter Thirty

There is no clean route to power.

Jed watched out the window of his Cessna as the endless sprawl of Los Angeles unfolded, thousands of miniature houses with blue swimming pools glittering savagely in the morning sun like glass eyes.

Jed was sipping coffee out of a styrofoam cup and fighting the urge to jack himself up with a pill. It would be too easy to get hooked on them. As Jed got older, he realized it would be easy to get hooked on a lot of things.

Even power? he asked himself as he lost the fight against pills and downed one with the last of his coffee. The answer wasn't altogether clear, but it wasn't altogether unclear either. Private planes, limousines, instant recognition, people falling silent when you spoke, the accoutrements of power, he could give them all up tomorrow. Not without some regret, but he could give them up. It was the other that held him. The silent power, the molding and shaping of policy, the further-ing of ideas. That was the real power. And in the end it led to corruption just as surely as all the vicuña coats and frost-free refrigerators of the Eisenhower adminis-tration.

There is no clean route to power, he thought. Sure, it could start out clean, but somewhere along the way, and not very far along either, came the slight adjust-ments, the compromises. It didn't matter what the ends; in fact, the more noble the ends, the more seductive the seduction.

You had to be tough today to make it in politics. Maybe centuries ago, when America was starting out, it was different, but now you had to be tough and sinewy. If anyone doubted that, all he had to do was stick around Washington for a while and watch those scrubbed young faces that poured in every year in hot pursuit of a shining ideal. The gentle etching began around their eyes. Catching glimpses of themselves in hotel mirrors, they might surprise the seeping corrup-tion. There would be a moment of horror, but only for a moment. Then the greater good would beckon just over the horizon, and they'd turn from the mirror with a shrug.

Jed sighed. Down below under the red, muffling smog, Sparrow would be waiting. Down below were the lies and half-truths, the corruption he hated. And all because he was sure he was saving the country from destruction. Just how far would he go to save the country? What he was fighting was wrong, so whatever he did was justified. Maybe. But it was better not to think about that. It was better to think about the end, shining brightly just ahead.

As the small plane slipped through the red air and began a wide sweep toward the private landing strip, Jed felt a rush of well-being and knew that the pill was beginning to kick in.

Sparrow was waiting at the edge of the grass, watching the Cessna roll onto the landing strip. He was feeling ragged around the edges, chewing at the sides of his mouth with his teeth. Inside, his stomach acids were having a field day with his guts. Seeing Jed hopping out of the plane, sunglasses glinting in the hazy sunlight, looking confident, only made his stomach acids work double time.

He had warned Jed not to come. It was risky and would undoubtedly prove unproductive. But Jed insisted. He actually thought that, through the power of his personality or some such nonsense, he could convince Beal to act sensibly. It was a quirk of politicians, the greatest innocents this world ever produced; they actually thought their words counted. Sparrow shook his head. Anyone who knew anything about this world knew it just rolled on, inexorably, inevitably. To where? Most likely backward to the primordial slime.

Jed was striding to Sparrow, his long thin Lincoln-esque face softened with his honest, slightly sad smile. He stopped at Sparrow, calculating his mood. "Strong feeling of disapproval and why did I even get tied up with that Jed character, eh?"

Sparrow shook his head, but despite himself, he smiled back. It was hard to stay angry with Jed. "Something like that," he growled, and reached for Jed's briefcase like a servant. It was an instinctive reaction, something to do with the way people felt about power.

Jed gave up his briefcase, instinctively also. They both pretended not to notice.

"All I'm asking is ten minutes to talk to him," Jed said. He put his arm around Sparrow's shoulder, and they walked across the grass to the short, squat brick building that acted as a terminal of sorts. "Besides, I'm rather curious to meet him."

Sparrow grunted in response, and Jed laughed. "I assume you've arranged for a backup plan in case I can't get anywhere."

Sparrow snorted. "To you it might be called backup; to me it's the primary plan." They had reached the terminal building, and Sparrow stopped, looking around quickly to make sure no one was in earshot. "Albert and Simon are organizing things. I've got three limousines, all exactly alike, right down to their license plates. All three will be running on slightly different schedules and in slightly different directions. Only you and I will meet Beal at exactly the right spot on the highway."

Jed was watching Sparrow with a knowing smile. "You told me that's to confuse our friends Richards and Harry. The question is what have you arranged about Beal?"

Sparrow tried to look innocent. "You made me promise to do nothing."

Jed was about to answer when Sparrow cut him off by opening the door. The terminal was one room, barren and dusty, little more than a sheltered area in case it should dare rain on anyone who could afford a private plane. There were only two people in the room, Jed's pilot and a bullet-headed man behind a paper-strewn desk. It smelled of floor wax, diesel fuel, and very good Havanas.

The black limousine was parked directly in front of the building. As Jed came through the door, he thought he caught a glimpse of something brightly colored at the back bumper of the car. He stopped, about to say something, but whatever had been there was gone. Or perhaps it had never been there at all. That was the thing about those damn pills. You ran a thin line; sometimes the feeling of power and strength could become the opposite.

Sparrow motioned Jed back and walked to the limousine alone, scanning the front and back seats, his hand kept close to his revolver. When he was satisfied, he opened the back door.

"And what else have you arranged?" Jed asked again as he slid in.

Sparrow took the driver's seat, started up the car, and pulled out. He handled the car easily, his arm resting out the window like a teen-ager. "What makes you so sure I've arranged anything else?" Sparrow glanced back at Jed slyly. "You made me promise no marksmen, no backup cars, right?"

Jed laughed. "Never for a moment expecting you to listen to me. So you've arranged for a backup car and marksmen. Well, you're probably right." He patted Sparrow's little shoulder. "You do your job thoroughly."

As the limousine whooshed onto the freeway, Jed leaned back in the plush seat and pushed a button on the back of Sparrow's seat. A bar folded down, neat, compact, and very well stocked. The glasses were all cut crystal, and there was even a tiny icebox. "You think nine thirty in the morning is too early for a drink?" Jed laughed, then opened the icebox and pulled out a Coke. "Do you drink?" he asked Sparrow as he opened the top and spilled the Coke into a glass.

"I can't afford to. The risk, not the money."

Jed wasn't drinking his Coke, and he found his eyes on the Scotch bottle. "Lucky man," he said, eyes still on the Scotch. "Drinking is the riskiest vice I have. It's the only one I don't feel badly about." Then he muttered to himself, "Oh, what the hell," and threw a good shot of Scotch into his Coke.

Jed glanced up to see if Sparrow was watching. But the little man's eyes were on the windshield. Jed supposed he had seen. Men like Sparrow made an art of peripheral vision but it didn't matter. He needed the drink to calm him.

"Where is Beal now?" He took a good swallow and leaned back into the seat.

Sparrow shrugged. "He's probably on his way to the meeting place. It's several miles down the coast, a rocky place where a lot of surfers go to break their necks."

"For Christ's sake, Sparrow, I don't want to be seen!"

"Don't worry. It should be quiet today. Even beach bums have to go to work."

Jed was staring at the back of Sparrow's neck in silence. He was still edgy. Sparrow must have felt it because he said, "It was your idea to come."

"I told you so, huh? Sometimes you're like an old woman."

Sparrow glanced back in the rearview mirror icily, his dignity ruffled, and his voice came out all business.

"We picked up a lead on Beal and his wife yesterday. They'd been sleeping in her car, which is why we didn't find them. They dumped her car at UCLA Hospital."

"The hospital? Now what the hell did he hope to learn there?"

Sparrow shrugged. "There was a report of a missing RV in the same neighborhood."

They had reached the ocean. It stretched out before them, vast and gray, pounded smooth and shiny under the hard hazy sun, like sheet metal. The bluffs behind it were burned brown from the long summer, and there were large fire warnings showing a very irritated Smokey the Bear.

Sparrow made a right and started down Highway 1. He was taking it very slowly. "We're a little early," he explained.

"What difference does it make? It'll be a first, a politician actually early for an appointment."

"It makes a difference."

"Ah, yes, of course, that backup arrangement you definitely promised not to make."

Suddenly there was a tinny whine, mechanical and loud, like from a microphone. "You're both wrong," a voice echoed through the car. "It doesn't make a difference. The meeting's been changed."

Sparrow jerked around in his seat. The car swerved to the middle of the road, screeching rubber. He righted the car just in time and slammed on the brakes.

Jed was pressed against the car door, looking around wildly as if he had been cornered by a wild animal.

Again the voice; only this time there was a great deal of laughing, too. "That's right, Sparrow. Pull over to the side. Take it slow and careful. I've still got your gun."

Sparrow skidded to a stop onto the siding of the road, his arm working over the dashboard and upholstery. He pulled up a small microphone from one of the stereo speakers. There was a loud laugh coming from it.

It was echoed by Jed in the back seat. "He's got the car bugged!" He was really laughing now. "Jesus Christ, the kid has the car bugged."

"That's right," came the voice from the microphone. "I want you both to stay right where you are. Don't get out of the car."

"Idiot," Sparrow muttered. He was sitting slumped over the wheel.

"So what do we do?" Jed asked. "Wait for him here?"

"We don't have to wait for nothing." Sparrow jerked around irritably.

Sparrow was right. At the back of the car the trunk was opening, and Beal crawled out, unwinding his legs with a groan. He was wearing a brightly colored Hawaiian shirt, and he had a camera strapped across his chest like a tourist. He was holding a gun.

Beal remained at the back of the limousine, his revolver turned toward Jed. "Throw out your gun, Sparrow."

Sparrow didn't move. His little, watery eyes had the blank, angry look Beal remembered all too well from the first night he saw him.

"There's no percentage in it, Sparrow. Highway One is no place for a shoot-out."

After a while Sparrow's gun spilled out the window.

Beal went for it. He could see the tall, Lincolnesque man in the back seat watching him with an amused expression.

"I've seen his picture in the papers," Beal said.

"Of course you've seen him, jerk. He's the attorney general of the United States."

"Impressive. I want to talk to him alone."

"Big deal," Sparrow grunted. "We all want things, but we don't always get them. That's life."

"Get out of the car, Sparrow, and throw me the keys. Mr. Attorney General and me are going to have a little chat."

"Wanna bet?" Sparrow snapped.

Jed's eyes were sparkling with irony. "I think we should do as he says."

Beal smiled. "There, you see. Mr. Attorney General agrees with me."

"Then Mr. Attorney General is a numbskull."

Sparrow had a black look on his face. Still, he pulled himself out of the car and tossed the keys at Beal's feet. He was shaking his head and muttering.

Beal picked up the car keys, then walked back to the strip of beach. Out on the steel gray water, waves were starting to kick up. There was a lone surfer out there, lying on his surfboard. In his black wet suit he looked like a sea otter resting on a piece of driftwood. A large gunmetal wave began rolling, and the surfer turned, dog-paddling, to shore, trying to get in pace with the wave. For a moment it looked as if he had it. Then the wave broke, and he was tossed up and back into foam.

Jed stood beside the limousine, watching Beal. The strong ocean breeze was ruffling his hair, and there was a sad, thoughtful smile on his face. He looked like one of those long-forgotten pictures of John Kennedy walking along the seashore. Beal had to admit it was a hell of a look, and it made a person trust the man who could manage it.

He resisted the temptation and yelled back to Sparrow, "You call in your two goons, Albert and Simon, and it'll go hard on your friend."

Jed answered for Sparrow. "I'm sure he understands. Don't worry."

Beal laughed bitterly. "Don't worry? I have half this town trying to kill me and the other half wants to imprison me, and I'm not supposed to worry? Well, let me tell you something, Mr. Attorney General, I find myself worrying all the time."

Jed walked to Beal slowly. His face was pensive. "Saying I'm sorry isn't much help, is it?"

"Maybe if you meant it, it might be."

"I do mean it. Not that I would have done it differently. It's too important. But I am sorry."

Jed fell silent. He was looking straight at Beal. Finally he smiled sadly. "What you did back there in the limousine was clever. How did you know where to find us?"

Beal shrugged. "It was the closest private airstrip to our meeting. I figured anyone powerful enough to ruin my life in the big way you have wouldn't have to fly with the common people."

Jed flushed with anger. "I'd hardly say we set out to destroy your life."

Beal didn't answer. His eyes were on the ocean and the lone surfer. Jed followed his line of vision and saw the surfer tossing around on the massive gray ocean. He knew nothing about surfing, but he could tell the kid out there was lousy at it.

Beal was motionless. His pale, sensitive face was haggard; his eyes were hollow and exhausted. Jed could almost feel nervous tension running through every part of his body. It didn't seem fair, and Jed felt angry at himself for thinking he could charm Beal into submission. For a moment he was tempted to tell him everything. Perhaps if he really knew what was happening, he wouldn't take the crazy chances he was taking. But Jed couldn't risk telling him the truth. He couldn't tell anyone everything.

Finally Jed said softly, "I suppose you want to know what's going on. What if I told you it's better for you not to know?"

"I'd believe it."

"But it would make no difference?"

"None at all."

Jed shifted his eyes away from Beal. "I don't know everything. If I did, don't you think I'd be telling it to the nation on television?"

"Then tell me what you know."

The surfer was turning again, watching the wave coming directly at him, splashing around, to join it in its great surge to shore. The wall of water hit him broadside and flipped him over his surfboard. Beal could almost hear the sounds of bones cracking.

Jed smiled slowly. "I came out here to find out what you know."

Beal smiled back. "I'm willing to make an exchange."

"I'll just bet you are." Jed thought for a while. "Okay, an exchange. I suppose you found a lot of things strange about the Lacey assassination."

"Like the clearing of the room?"

Jed agreed. "Someone was cleaning up the evidence."

"That's the way I figured it. Chesapeake would be my number one choice."

Jed was smiling in a way that made Beal suspect he was wrong. "So you don't think it was Chesapeake," Beal said. "Then who? The Lacey Brain Trust?"

"Possibly. They're all in positions of extreme power now. Fuller is president pro tem of the Senate, Keiler's on the Supreme Court, Paisley's in the House, and Nadler's on the Joint Chiefs of Staff. But they're all staying where they are. Odds would have it that at least one of them would make a try for the big job. Certainly a guy like Fuller or Paisley. But the convention's almost on us, and Chesapeake is going to get the nomination virtually unopposed."

"People don't usually kill unless they stand to gain something."

"Exactly. I've been looking into this for almost five years now, and yet still the same question: Who stood to gain?" Jed paused. He was smiling at Beal, that honest, sad smile. "I suppose you found the barrier and the flash of light and the limousine story strange, too. Well, anyway, I did. That's what started it for me. That and, of course, the blackmail."

"What about the blackmail?"

Jed turned away, obviously sorry he'd started on that. "It doesn't matter. I'm pretty sure now it has nothing to do with you."

Beal watched Jed calculatingly. Then finally he said, "I think I saw the man who killed Lacey."

Jed started back. "You what!"

Beal smiled calmly. "Like I said, an exchange."

Jed glared back at Beal; his long, thin face was hard and angry. Then the anger broke, and he smiled, as if he at least were enjoying the game. "A lot of crazy things started happening after the Lacey situation." He paused. "Look, how much do you remember about Lacey?"

"Next to nothing. I wasn't exactly political." He laughed. "I thought it had no relevance to my life."

"Well, Lacey firmly believed that many of the evils of America stemmed from the influence of big business. So did I. When I got in as assistant attorney general, he authorized me to start an investigation of payoffs by industry to the men in government. I reported directly to him. No one but Lacey and I knew exactly what was being dug up. And believe me, it was damned explosive. When Chesapeake became President, he put a stop to the investigation."

"Which makes Chesapeake sound like a good candidate for our assassination theory. Maybe he was scared what you'd dig up on him."

Jed shook his head. "It was penny ante stuff. Besides, what happened next was what was really curious. Blackmail. All over the Congress. How widespread I don't know. But a few of the men who received blackmail notes brought them to me. The information the notes threatened to make public was directly from my files. Believe me, no one but Lacey and I knew about it."

"Or Lacey's Brain Trust?"

"Possibly. But Lacey certainly didn't tell Chesapeake. The only time that guy was let near the Oval Office was for picture taking. And here's the strangest part: What the blackmailers demanded wasn't money. It was a vote, usually for a piece of legislation that was on the whole fairly beneficial to the country."

"Why? It doesn't make sense."

"Tell me about it," Jed said with disgust. He turned back to the sea, but his mind was on blackmail. "Except maybe recently," he said softly.

"Recently?"

"There was a bill passed in Congress last week that extended the power of the military in case of emergency. It was the blackmail again." He shook the nagging fear away. "I don't know. Maybe the bill will work to the country's benefit in the end."

Beal shook his head, confused. "And you think this blackmail for the benefit of the country is linked to the assassination?"

"I think whoever is behind the blackmail organized the assassination, yes." Jed was silent, calculating. "Which brings us to what you saw."

"Just before I was picked up by the police, I was backpacking in the mountains behind Palm Springs. Trying to figure out my life, more or less." He stopped. That all seemed so long ago, almost another lifetime. "Anyway, suddenly these guys came running out at at me with guns and dogs. They were shooting at me, and I ran."

"Why didn't you tell that to Sparrow?"

Beal smiled triumphantly. "I did. But I didn't realize until recently that just before they came for me, I saw a man."

"A man? Which man?"

"I don't know. It was only for a split second. But

288

he was tall and gaunt, very white-skinned, like he'd been hiding out for a long time."

"Is that all?"

"He looked sort of familiar. But I can't figure out where I've seen him before."

"Well, try!"

"Don't you think that's all I've been doing?"

Beal turned back to the ocean. The surfer was resting on his surfboard. Even from far away Beal could tell he was out of breath and scared as hell. Still he was waiting for a wave. It was a minimyth of Sisyphus being reenacted right in front of him.

Jed was watching him. "What makes you so sure he's the man who killed Lacey?"

"Just a guess. The guy was in hiding, looked like he had been for a long time. It makes sense. Whoever hired him, Chesapeake or someone from the Brain Trust, was paying him to keep out of trouble."

"Why?" asked Jed flatly.

Beal shrugged it off. "Anyway, I'm sure whatever I saw was important. If it wasn't, why did they come after me with guns and dogs?"

Jed nodded. "All right. I'll give you that. But if what you think is true, then it's more important than ever that you be kept safe." Jed watched Beal cagily.

"In other words, go into hiding."

"There's nothing else you can do."

"I could tell the newspapers what I know."

"Are you kidding? No one will believe you, and what do you know really? Those people you want to believe you won't. The others, well, they already know."

"I won't go into hiding."

The two men were watching one another, sizing each other up, looking for weaknesses. But none was apparent at the moment for either man.

Jed glanced over at Sparrow and saw him watching the two of them. There was something about the way he was leaning casually against the front bumper, arms crossed, that told Jed Sparrow could feel how things were going and was smiling to himself. It was strange how much people wanted to be right, no matter what the consequences.

Jed sighed wearily. "I took a hell of a chance just meeting you."

"Yeah, you did. Now I know who you are."

It was meant to sound like a threat, and Jed took it in the spirit in which it was intended. His face became gray and drawn. "So it seems we've reached an impasse."

"You know more than you told me, don't you?" Beal asked cagily.

"I've got a wife and kids. If you said anything, they'd kill them. That's the way they'd get at me, you know. Through them." Jed's eyes were going over Beal's face, and for the first time Beal saw just how frightened he was.

"Then help me out. Tell me what is going on."

"You can't tell anyone my name. Not even your wife. And you can't try to reach me ever again."

Jed glanced back to the limousine. His face was cut with deep lines, and suddenly he looked sick and old. "I have no proof of anything. Frankly that's what I hoped you'd give me. But I feel that the country is no longer being run by the Senate or the House or even the executive branch of the government. There's this

290

feeling of an unseen presence in control. I think it all started with the Lacey assassination and is escalating faster and faster until—" He stopped. "I don't know what it's leading to. I've gone forwards and backwards on this thing and come up with nothing. But if what you told me is correct, I've been looking in the wrong place. I've been watching people who are very visible in the government. That's why I was so confused by the upcoming election. All roads led to Chesapeake, yet he already had the power and was doing nothing with it. I had my eyes on the Trust, yet not one of them was making a move. But if you really saw someone in hiding, then maybe everything is backwards."

Beal waited for Jed to continue, but he didn't. "Backwards?" Beal repeated. "I don't understand."

"Perhaps it isn't who stood to gain by Lacey's death. Perhaps it is who stood to lose by Lacey's remaining alive."

"That's the same thing," Beal said. "I don't see the difference."

Jed merely shook his head, then turned abruptly and headed back to the limousine, his shoulders slumped, his eyes dark with the beginnings of understanding.

Sparrow was already inside with the motor running. The moment Jed closed the door, Sparrow pushed into gear and sped away, scattering gravel and dirt, leaving behind only silence.

Beal turned back to the water. The surfer was still there, scrambling for another wave. This time the wave was bigger than the others, and it was bearing down on him like a solid wall. He caught it. The wave surged, and he was a part of it. For a moment he crouched, his fragile legs shaking under him. Then almost instantly the wall of water crashed over him and he was sent tumbling.

Beal didn't watch to see how he came out. He stood at the edge of the highway, scouring the passing traffic anxiously. But no one seemed interested in him, and finally he stuck out his thumb.

Chapter Thirty-one

Albert Perry liked guns. He also liked to use them. Even today he still bought a copy of *Soldier of Fortune* magazine, even after what the crappy rag had done to him. The ad had said, "Wanted: Mercenaries for Kenya. All expenses reimbursed."

Reimbursed like hell. He'd called the number and gotten sent on a wild-goose chase that found him close to a thousand bucks lighter. Within two hours of landing in Kenya he'd been mugged and robbed of everything, including his passport. It had taken him close to three months to get himself back to New York. And after all that he still couldn't get a job for months. Until he met Sparrow.

There was a time when there was plenty of work for a man who liked to kill and liked to get paid for it. It was one of the world's oldest and noblest professions. It really bugged Albert that a lot of people turned up their noses. For centuries it had been the mercenaries who'd done the world's dirty work. Mercenaries were necessary. More than necessary; they were the right hand of God.

But wars were going out of style. At least the small kind that Albert liked to fight. No more Koreas or Vietnams. The revolutions in Africa were becoming more and more scarce. Besides, most of those little wars were over too fast. Even if you got the job and were reasonably sure that you weren't going to get ripped off, you couldn't get there in time.

So Albert was lucky to have a job with Sparrow, and he knew it. Though that didn't mean he didn't have plans for career improvement, which was why he was sitting in the parking lot of Dupar's restaurant in the middle of the night, wearing dark glasses and a black wig to hide his bright red hair.

Albert kept his eyes on the rearview mirror as well as watched out the car windows. Though he'd been careful that no one was following, you could never be positive.

Albert knew there was very little in this life you could be positive of. Death and taxes were what they said. But Albert didn't pay taxes, and as far as death, well, that might be sure, but how it came wasn't.

One thing was certain. Albert knew his death was going to be something quite special. There were two kinds of people in the world. There were the hawks, the strong, crafty ones who knew what was right and didn't mind what they had to do to achieve it. Then there were the sparrows, like Simon, who did what they were told because they didn't know what they wanted out of life.

Ironically Albert had to admit Sparrow was a hawk;

that might have worried him since he was definitely taking a chance by going over to the other side, except that Albert was also a hawk. And a hawk could hardly turn down the opportunity to earn twenty thousand dollars just for passing on a little information.

A green Pontiac pulled into the parking lot and cruised around, looking for an empty space. Albert started up his car, then slipped out of the lot and onto Ventura Boulevard. He took the first right, then a left into the parking lot of a twenty-four-hour supermarket. He turned off the engine and waited.

It was close to a minute before the dark green car pulled into the supermarket lot and the little Englishman with the brush mustache climbed out.

Albert found a parking space and followed.

Chapter Thirty-two

Only the rich can afford silence. While Beal and Maggie rumbled onto a road skirting the ocean in the RV Beal had stolen the day before, the rich were nearby, well hidden behind thick walls, listening to the song of an occasional robin, the whir of a well-built sports car, the muffled footfalls of servants, maybe the soft rustle of thousand-dollar bills.

The road undulated above Santa Barbara, one of the few towns in Southern California that had what would be called gentility by those who had it and snobbiness by those who didn't. Eucalyptus trees, fragrant, yet with the vague remembrance of illness, swept the road, making the sunlight patchy and lined. The road was empty. Not a car or person, horse or even dog could be seen anywhere.

Lining the road on either side were walls, some only iron fences, others brick and stone, all with wrought-iron gates, tipped with gold paint. As the huge RV ground along the road, only the occasional sparkling white portico, overhung by scarlet bougainvillaea, flashed by. In the sweep of the driveway a silvery Rolls-Royce or low-slung sports car glinted richly in the filtered sunlight. Other than that there was nothing to be seen. Only trees and more trees. Live oak, poplar, eucalyptus, pine. The rich sure did like their trees. Perhaps because they helped keep everything hidden, allowing only the barest hint of their lives to show through. A reminder that there were people living behind those walls and that, indeed, they were very different from you and me.

It wasn't necessary to see behind the walls to imagine the French doors, the cool, dim rooms, the roses in cut crystal. Everything was muffled and far away, a drape of silence and perhaps even peace of mind. Certainly it felt that way if you were on the outside. But maybe it wasn't true. Maybe the air back there was filled with the sound of a hundred silent screams.

The compound where Elaine Lacey was supposedly living was off the main road and down a gravel one that lasted less than a mile. Here the houses were even larger, or at least the walls they were hiding behind were higher, longer, and solid brick. When you passed these gates, nothing was to be seen, not even a patch of white or a glimpse of well-polished fender, just the beginning of a wide sweep of driveway and, of course, the trees.

There were no numbers on the gateposts, but from the look of the area, people like them didn't need any. The newspaper reports had said Elaine was living at the old Vernor Estate, which was as old money as America could manage, savagely obtained in moneylending and railroads, then washed clean by bought ambassadorships and enough charity donations to keep a small African nation afloat.

The wall surrounding the Vernor Estate was rugged stone, higher and more impenetrable than the brick ones. There was the usual wrought-iron gate, also tipped in gold, and once again only a prim edge of a sweeping driveway. Beal slowed as much as he dared, trying to see through the forest that lay behind the wall. There were No Trespassing signs every few feet, and something about the whole estate showed that they meant it.

Though there were no guards, the wall was low enough to be climbed, the grounds were wooded enough to hide movement, the feeling was tomblike, ominous.

There was a flash of white against the trees, and a large, bullish woman with a red face and white nurse's uniform paced past the gate. She stopped, hands on hips, watching the RV creep past. It was clear she thought whoever was in it was an intruder and she didn't like that at all.

Beal speeded up, but the gravel road lasted only a few more yards, then ended abruptly at the foot of a mountain. There was no place to turn around, certainly not a space large enough for an RV, where only cars that were the price of a fair-sized house would dare trespass. Beal swung the great lumbering RV around, working in fits and starts. He could imagine the sound of grinding gears bringing a hundred pale, elegant hands to draw back curtains.

Finally he got the RV turned and took it quickly down the gravel road. The nurse was still standing at the gateway, her suspicious eyes screwed against the sun, as if noting every detail for future reference.

It was rumored Elaine Lacey had gone crazy. It was rumored she had twenty-four-hour nursing service and possibly even guards. From the brief glimpse behind the gates it would seem that was true.

Beal drove onto the main road, running the huge elephant of a vehicle as fast as he dared, and he didn't stop until the string of motels, gift shops, and drive-in restaurants began again about a mile up.

Maggie was sitting in the back of the RV at a small ledge which Beal supposed was advertised as a table. Everything in the cabin of the RV was scaled down almost to the point of extinction, a dwarf stove, runt icebox and cabinets, a toy bed. The feeling was like living in a toilet stall. Maggie had made sandwiches, and they were laid out on a plate, the table set with napkins and silverware. She was holding her head in her hand, elbow resting on the table, unearthly sadness in her eyes.

As Beal came in, Maggie looked up and tried for a smile. There was a brief scuffle at the corner of her mouth, but it was a losing cause. Her eyes were red-rimmed and void, as if she'd been crying before and now were beyond even that. "We aren't going to be able to get inside, are we?" Again she tried for a brave smile.

"Yeah, sure we will," Beal answered, avoiding her eyes. He sat down at the table and picked up a sandwich. The ham smell made him sick.

"I was watching out the window," Maggie said. "That nurse saw you. I'm sure of it."

"Leave it to me, okay?" Beal's voice was sharp, and

it surprised him. The sight of Maggie so scared and sad ate into his soul. And suddenly he felt that he couldn't look at her.

"A woman would be less noticeable."

"Absolutely not."

"Beal, it makes sense. If they catch you, we both know what will happen. But I could think of some excuse. And they probably wouldn't even catch me, especially if I go up there just before dinner when everyone is busy."

Beal's heart was beating rapidly, throbbing and painful. "You're not going anywhere. This is my trouble."

"And I want to help."

Beal flared. "No!" It was anger that was pounding through his body, anger at himself and Maggie, anger at everything that was happening to them. He stood up from the table decisively. "I think you should go back home now." It was as if something were taking him over. "That's right," he said, talking to himself. "That's exactly what you should do. You should go home. They want me, not you. They'll leave you alone."

He reached into his pocket, pulled out his money, peeled off two hundred dollars, and slammed it on the table in front of her. "This should be enough to pay for a room for several days. Now I want you to do exactly what I told you to before. I want you to get a hotel room and wait for a while, just until they know we're no longer together."

Maggie left the money where it was. "I'm not going anywhere, Beal. I'm staying here."

The anger was pounding sharply now. Beal snatched back the money and shoved it into her hand. "Oh, yes, you are!" Then he grabbed her by the wrist and pulled her to her feet. "I want you out of here. Now!"

"Stop it! I won't leave you, Beal. You can't make me leave you."

Beal was holding her wrist tightly, and he knew he was hurting her, but he couldn't stop, and he didn't want to stop. It was the powerlessness. They were just two stupid victims, small, unimportant, and there wasn't a thing in the world that he could do about it. It had been four days since he'd returned, and all he'd managed to do was come trampling through Maggie's life, leaving everything broken and ruined. She deserved everything good, and all he'd given her was fear and running. He had a son, and all he could offer him was destruction. The shame was overpowering. And Beal hated himself and Maggie for it.

Maggie was pulling away from Beal, and that made him almost sick with anger. Suddenly he let go of her wrist, throwing her away from him. "Don't you understand? I don't want you here. Get out, damn you! Get the hell out!"

Maggie was jolted back. She could feel her own anger rising and knew Beal was hoping for this to drive her away. She stood where she was, shaking with anger and fear. But this only made Beal's rage even worse, until it was burning white-hot in the center of him, taking him over. He wanted someone to pay for what was happening to him. He wanted to make someone, anyone, suffer the way he was suffering.

Suddenly he wheeled around and brutally tore his arm across the table. The dishes with the carefully laid-out sandwiches crashed to the floor. China shattered into the air. Napkins, silverware, dishes, all of Maggie's

301

little plans smashed in pitiful pieces to the floor. The poignancy only fed Beal's anger.

There were three shelves along the wall, and Beal grabbed hold of one of them, hands clenched tightly, and he pulled it from the wall. Clothes scattered to the ground. But Beal was already at the next shelf, tearing it from the wall, and then the next one. Until pots, pans, plates, silverware were crashing all around him, and the noise added to the burning fury. Everything was going crazy on him, and he wasn't thinking anymore. All he knew was he wanted to destroy. It was a savage world outside, senseless, roaring, and he wanted to obliterate it.

Suddenly he slammed his fist into the wall. Electric pain ripped through his hand, spreading out to his body, in fiery waves. He moaned with the pain and the anger. Then smashed his fist into the wall again. His hand was bleeding, the pain almost unbearable, but still he pounded his fist into the wall, over and over. Until he was no longer moaning; he was holding onto the wall, and he was crying.

Maggie stood watching him. She felt shattered and unstable. She was holding onto the table as if the world were moving too quickly beneath her. Then slowly she walked over to Beal and put her arms around him.

Beal pulled away. "Please leave me alone," he said softly. The anger was gone from his voice, and only the agony was left.

"I'm not going to leave, Beal. I did that once, and I'll never do it again."

Beal turned back to her. His face was ravaged. "Don't you see? I don't want you here. I'm ruining your life. And I just can't stand it anymore."

302

"I love you."

Beal pressed his aching hands to his burning head. He had a terrible headache, and he felt sick to his stomach. "I don't want you loving me. I want you to get out of here while you still can."

"You need me, Beal."

"What the hell are you trying to do? Save me? Well, you can't. So just save yourself."

"I'm not goddamn trying to save you. I love you. Love is crazy. Or maybe I'm crazy. I don't know. But yes, I want to protect you. I want to hold you and make everything better for you. And you call that feeling sorry for you, but it isn't the same thing at all."

"Well, you could've fooled me," Beal said bitterly.

Maggie was motionless. "I want to be with you. I want it to be you and me and Jason from now on."

"God damn it, Maggie. There is no from now on. No futures on this one. Only today. And it's a lousy today, too."

"All right, Beal, then I'll just settle for now."

Beal shook his head. "Don't you see? I look at you and you're so fragile and lovely. You deserve everything in this world. And all I can give you is fear and danger."

Maggie laughed sadly. "You want to know what my life was like before you came back? Don't you wonder at all? Let me tell you something. After I had Jason and kind of licked the wounds, I figured, Okay, world, here I am. So out I went, and I pulled up a barstool next to the rest of the beautiful singles. And then it was all smiling and laughing, one-night stands and cozy weekends, and it stinks, Beal. It's cold and it's lonely and it stinks. Sure, everyone is smiling and laughing, but everything is drying up inside. I was walking through it, not seeing or feeling anything around me. We all looked so young and untouched. Well, we were untouched because we hadn't even begun to live, not really live, not like it's supposed to be. Eventually I realized about the only place I was living was with Jason. Then you came back. And I was scared and angry and bitter and sad, and it hurt, but at least I was alive. And I'm not going to let go of this little bit of living without a fight."

Maggie was crying now and her voice was small and frightened. "I love you, Beal. I really love you. Please let me be with you."

Beal didn't move. He was raw and aching inside and scared of what he was feeling. If he walked to her now, it meant vulnerability and surrender. She saw everything, all his weakness and fear. She saw him shivering and naked. Everything inside himself wanted to run in alarm.

Then slowly Beal was walking to her, putting his arms around her, and holding her.

Maggie looked up at him, her eyes dark and frightened. Beal thought he had never seen anything more beautiful in his life. He ran his finger slowly over her face, tracing her features. "I love you, Maggie." He could feel tears burning inside him, and he was overwhelmed just looking down at her. "God, I love you more than anything in the world." He clasped her tightly to him, feeling her smallness in his arms.

Maggie's lips were searching his out, soft and yielding, her hand touching his and urging it toward the gentle slope of her breast. Her body pressed against his

304

urgently. And when Beal tried to stop, a surge of warmth rushed through him.

It was a dangerous excitement, dark and scary, but Beal was overpowered, and all he could do was yield to the urgent electric waves.

Chapter Thirty-three

Elaine Lacey shifted in bed. There was the numbness mostly. No matter how often she shifted her weight, the numbness would come back quickly. She watched dully as a curtain puffed out with an ocean breeze. Daylight lay in golden shafts across her bed. And in the distance was the soft hush of the ocean pounding against distant rocks. Something between a giggle and a whimper seeped from her mouth. She heard it as some faraway sound, unrelated to her.

There were footsteps outside her door, and she thought briefly that it was probably close to dinnertime. Nurse Folger had promised custard for dessert. Again the painless whimper, strange and disconnected. And after the custard, the long blackness of the night, the rolling on sweat-soaked sheets with nothing to break the eternity except the occasional sound of a night owl and the sharp bark of a dog.

Somewhere, possibly a millennium ago, there was the

memory of another kind of night. The warmth of a strong body holding her and the urgent hardness of a man. The memory brought a stinging of tears to her eyes. But it was like the strange whimper, a vanishing ghost. Only a brief brush with reality.

There was a soft knock at her door. Or at least it seemed like a knock. Elaine was sure of very little. Her brittle, wasted hand made a vague attempt at propping herself up. But almost at the same instant she forgot why. Again the knock. Elaine's face tensed. The thin skin around her eyes drew into millions of wrinkles, like fissures in the surface of the moon. Half-hearted eyes regarded the door listlessly, pupils large and black, deep, empty holes surrounded by almost colorless irises. The kind of eyes one would expect under closed lids at the undertaker.

The door began to open, and Elaine watched passively as a young woman with auburn hair carefully closed the door behind her. She didn't recognize the nurse, but that didn't bother her. Everything was swimming softly by.

Maggie stopped at the door, looking around the large stark white room, barren except for a washstand, bedside table, and hospital bed. She remembered pictures of Elaine Lacey lighting the White House Christmas tree, making the rounds of orphanages and hospitals, pale pink and delicate, a soft kindness in her eyes. It seemed impossible that this was the same woman.

Dwarfed by the bed, the brittle woman seemed shrunken. Her skin, parchment-thin, was etched with a network of fine lines. One arm was lying across the covers. It was wasted and gray, with blue tracings of veins that looked as if they were carrying very little blood.

"Mrs. Lacey," Maggie whispered as she crept to the bed.

The dry little woman was watching her with dark holes that had once been pale blue eyes. A flicker seemed to pass over her face as Maggie called her name, but it was just like a brief breeze fluttering across her features.

Maggie crept closer to the bed, afraid that Elaine would cry out. But she wasn't even watching Maggie. She was staring at the wall with little understanding, as if trying to remember a long-forgotten song.

"Mrs. Lacey," Maggie repeated. Again the strange whimpering noise. "I'm the new nurse," Maggie said, though she could tell explanations weren't necessary. She'd worked at a doctor's office long enough to know the effect of barbiturate addictions. The woman who lay in bed was an empty shell; Elaine Lacey was far away in an impenetrable never-never world. Maggie's coming there had been useless. To bring Elaine Lacey back to reality could take weeks, perhaps months; perhaps she'd never return.

It was close to four-thirty. Within an hour the house would undoubtedly be stirring. An invalid tray would be laid in the kitchen. The large nurse she'd seen pacing the grounds in diligent pursuit of exercise would return, adjusting the nurse's cap she wore jammed onto her head, neatly folding the thick colorless sweater she wore thrown across her wide, muscular shoulders. Once she came back, Maggie would be in danger. It was clear Elaine Lacey was being held prisoner with drugs. If Maggie could see it, any nurse worth her license would know. That meant the nurse had to be in on it. And yet if that were true, why had it been so easy for Maggie to get into this room?

Elaine stirred. Her eyes scanned the room, lighting on Maggie impassively. For a moment a flicker of some kind of understanding crossed her face. "I hope you remembered the custard. Today is the day I get my custard." The words were disconnected and sounded as thin and bloodless as the woman who produced them.

"Mrs. Lacey, who's been drugging you?"

Elaine looked up at Maggie, confused. "Drugging me? No one is drugging me."

"Then they're slipping barbiturates into your food. But someone is giving you drugs. Why are they doing that?"

The little woman's face closed into deep wrinkles. She appeared to be thinking, piecing together forgotten snatches of memory. Then the two empty holes seemed to show some sort of reality. "Who are you?" she asked.

"I want to help you."

Elaine's face was blank.

"Yes," Maggie said softly, "I suppose that's what everyone's been promising you."

"Who are you?" Elaine repeated. Her face was still blank, but this time something else was beginning to creep into it, expression, perhaps even emotion.

It was hard for Maggie to tell just how much Elaine was understanding. Maggie had the feeling that she might be aware of a good bit more than she let on. "You're not as drugged as you make out, are you?" Maggie asked.

This seemed to spring something deep inside the

309

withered shell that once was Elaine Lacey. Her face screwed up tight with perhaps anger, perhaps fear, perhaps a combination of the two. But at least Maggie knew she was getting to her.

"Look," Maggie said anxiously, "you were right not to believe me when I said I wanted to help you. It wasn't the truth. I'm here because I need your help."

Elaine's face pursed into something resembling a laugh.

"My husband is in trouble. He stumbled on information about your husband's assassination. Information he didn't even know he had and still doesn't understand."

A blank stare was coming over Elaine's face, as if everything inside her were slowly collapsing. "Mrs. Lacey, people are trying to kill him." Maggie's voice was desperate. "I have to know why. Your husband's death was a conspiracy, wasn't it?"

Elaine shook her head. "My husband's death? Oh, no, he's alive and well and living in Palm Springs with one of his little chippies." Her face split into a terrible grin. "Yes, my dearly departed husband did love his chippies. The younger, the better." Elaine began to laugh, exposing darkened, rotting teeth. It wasn't a nice laugh.

Maggie pulled back, stunned, but Elaine only grinned at her, exposing those rotten black teeth.

"Wouldn't have thought it to look at him, would you?" Elaine asked with a giggle. "It's always the ones you'd never suspect. Not that I didn't love him anyway."

It took Maggie awhile to pull herself together, and

310

when she did, she was stunned by Elaine's malicious grin.

"Mrs. Lacey, my husband thinks that he wasn't killed by J. J. Foyle. Or at least not by him alone. I need you to tell me what you know about the assassination."

Elaine pulled herself up on one fragile elbow, shaking from the effort. Her vacant eyes sparkled strangely in her bony face. "No one wants me to talk," she whispered softly. "They keep me here to make sure I'm quiet. Nurse Folger, Senator Fuller, all of them."

Maggie moved closer. Her eyes were intense. "Why? What do you know about the assassination?"

"If I tell you, will you bring me my custard?"

Elaine was giggling again, this time more loudly. Maggie put her hand across Elaine's mouth and whispered, "Please, not too loud. You'll get me in trouble."

Elaine didn't seem to mind Maggie's hand over her mouth. From behind it she croaked out, "Custard."

Maggie relented. "Of course I'll get you custard. Just please be quiet."

Elaine nodded, then lowered her frail body back to the bed. "Everyone's trying to keep me quiet. They say I had a nervous breakdown. They say the combination of both my husband and my only son being killed was too much for me." She motioned Maggie closer. "They're all liars, you know. Especially Nurse Folger. In the beginning I was allowed a phone in my room, but she caught me trying to call Jack Anderson, and that was that. Oh, yes, she told me she was protecting me. But let's face it. She knew I'd tell the world about them."

"What about them?"

311

"They have rays, you know. That's how they get what they want."

Maggie pulled back. No wonder it had been so easy to reach Elaine. She was loony tunes all right. Probably Nurse Folger was protecting her. Or at least protecting what was left of her from a cruel and heartless outside world.

"Of course," Elaine continued, "that's how they got my husband. With rays. They made him very ill, poor man. Really put him off his chippies at the end. He even kept Dr. Greenaway, his private doctor, with him all the time that last month." She laughed brittlely. "But his doctor was no help. They wouldn't even let him within a mile of my husband when he died."

Suddenly Elaine stopped, and her empty eyes filled with tears. "I loved Robert, you know. Ever since we were children. I saw the face in the crowd. I saw what was happening. I said, 'Bud, look, please look over there.' And I did nothing. He was everything to me, and I did nothing."

Elaine's eyes were wide and haunted, and again there was that terrible moaning whimper.

A sound came from downstairs, the slam of a door, probably the nurse returning from her walk. Then the dull thud of sensible shoes across the downstairs floor.

Maggie froze, standing at the edge of Elaine's bed, unsure whether to stay where she was or hide. If Elaine told the nurse about her, there was no way of knowing what would happen. Perhaps nothing. Perhaps everything.

The footsteps grew louder and were joined by the creaking of stairs. Elaine was watching Maggie strangely. It was impossible to tell what she was thinking or if she was thinking at all.

Maggie slipped down beside the bed, her heart pounding like the relentless footsteps. Almost immediately there was a loud rap at the door. Elaine opened her eyes and raised herself onto her elbow.

Again a sharp rap on the door. "Mrs. Lacey, are you all right?" The nurse had a booming, intensely healthy voice.

There was a hesitation, then: "Yes, Miss Folger, I'm fine."

"Were you talking to yourself again?" The door swung open, and the large nurse covered the doorway. She had a wide, thick nose, mean little brown eyes set in great meaty sockets, and scant hair the color of a dirty penny. Her face was red, probably from exercise, but also from too much blood, as if she'd got a double portion, both hers and Elaine Lacey's.

"I was talking to myself," Elaine answered, her voice light and bodiless, drifting to the ceiling like a bit of feather.

Nurse Folger laughed gruffly. "Well, as long as you don't start answering yourself, my father used to say."

Again that terrible whimper. "You promised custard for dessert, Miss Folger."

Folger smiled evasively. Perhaps one of her pleasures in being a nurse came from depriving her patients of custard. "Dinner is in five minutes," she resonated, then shut the door.

Maggie listened as the nurse's healthy heels receded down the hall. There was a pause, then the sound of a door being jerked open and closed. Maggie waited a moment longer, then pulled herself up shakily. Elaine

313

was watching her, a strange smile on her face. "She'll bring me it in the end. She always does."

Elaine lay back with a satisfied smile. "In the end I always get my custard." Then her empty eyes drifted around the room in search of Maggie. But Maggie was already gone, slipping down the long flight of darkened stairs and out the door. Elaine let out that terrible whimpering giggle. She was watching the patterns of fading sunlight streaking her bed, and she was smiling. Custard was her favorite dessert.

Chapter Thirty-four

The scrambler tore apart Fuller's syllables, turning them into gibberish, then rescrambling them into sense. "It seems Elaine had a visitor yesterday."

The man on the other end waited for the strange echoing delay, but Fuller said nothing more.

"How very nice for her." The voice snapped with irritation.

"It was our friend Beal."

There was a pause, and this time the voice was very different. "How very unfortunate for her."

The phone went dead, but it took a long time before Fuller replaced the receiver and closed the phone away. He cast his eyes out the window at the smog of Los Angeles.

Representative Paisley and Justice Keiler were sitting slouched on the couch across from Fuller, also looking out the windows of his office at the smoggy haze outside. Only General Nadler was sitting rigid in a chair, his hands clasped on his lap. Though his round baby face was devoid of emotion, Fuller knew he was angry and impatient. He had opposed this impromptu meeting of the Trust as unnecessary and dangerous. Fuller watched Nadler's indifferent eyes staring blankly into space and tried to read some slight trace of emotion, any betrayal that he could have taken for even a primitive kind of humanity. There was none.

It was General Nadler who spoke first. "You know better than to make that phone call in front of us, Bud," he said sharply.

Paisley and Keiler nodded in agreement. Accountability. Except for policies, all transactions were to be kept separate; each man was to be shielded as much as possible. Fuller's job was security for the Trust, and the rest wanted to know nothing about it.

"That's why I did it," Fuller answered tightly. Paisley's and Keiler's eyes switched to Fuller, surprised, but he stared them down. "I think it's about time we discussed exactly what is going on."

"Jeez, Bud," Paisley said amiably. "We just had a meeting last week. Why didn't you bring this up then?"

Fuller avoided his eyes. "You know why as well as I do. You all know why."

"Well, I for one don't," Nadler said. "And I think we're taking a hell of a chance even being in the same city as one another, let alone meeting, just so we can all hold Bud's hand."

Keiler shook his head; his stalklike body had become rigid and alert. "I don't think that's fair, Earl," Keiler drawled. "I've had the feeling that Bud has been dissatisfied for some time, and I for one believe he deserves

access to a forum where he can bring his concerns out
in the open . . ."

General Nadler shut off from the room, blocking out
the droning of Keiler's voice. Keiler was a horse's ass.
Not worth wasting his ears on. Nadler could see
Paisley's eyes were drifting around the room, too. But
mostly they were sizing up Fuller and himself, trying
to decide which side to be on when the smoke cleared.
Fuller posed a threat. How much, Nadler would have
to see. If necessary, Fuller would have to be stopped.
Nadler greeted the thought with equanimity. It wasn't
that he liked killing; he just understood that sometimes
it was useful.

All through Nadler's life he'd been called cruel and
power-hungry. Anyone connected to the military always
ran across that. As a son of a military man as well as
a soldier himself, he'd come to regard it as part of life.
But that was all wrong. He was judicious and impartial.
He had no desire for power. It came to him, but he
never sought it. As to cruelty, Nadler was quite the
opposite. Cruelty implied a pleasure he never felt.
Nadler was an instrument, a finely made weapon of indifference and destruction. It was perhaps only that
knowledge which gave him any pleasure.

Fuller ran his hands through his thick white hair,
making it stand up on end. Even as he started, he could
feel he would be defeated. "The problem is we all
suspect what is happening, every one of us. We all
suspect but are frightened to say anything."

"Suspect what?" Nadler asked with a supercilious
smile.

Fuller smirked back angrily. "What about the state
of emergency vote in Congress?"

"What do you want to know about it, Bud?" Nadler asked coolly.

"Who was behind it?"

"Search me," Nadler answered. "I'm not in Congress."

Paisley reached for a cigarette, lit it, and began to smoke nervously. Keiler's face was serious. He was nodding his head slowly, his eyes on the floor.

Fuller stared over at Nadler. "You know exactly what's going on, don't you?"

Nadler laughed. "Hey, I don't know any more than you guys."

"You're lying," Fuller barked angrily. "You're using the machinery of the Trust without our permission. You sent out the blackmail notes to get that vote, and you know it."

"Now why should I be doing that?"

"Because you plan on creating a state of emergency."

Nadler's face didn't flicker, but he watched Fuller more intently than before. It was easy to underestimate a guy like Fuller.

Keiler, too, was watching Fuller, a look of surprise on his face. "Why on earth should Earl want to create a state of emergency?"

"Come on, Sam," Fuller answered. "We've all suspected." He turned to Paisley. "Haven't we?"

"Hey, this is your meeting." Paisley was smiling. But it was a weasely smile.

"Okay, I'll take it nice and slow for you. Our little blackmail plan wasn't working very well, was it? So we decided the country needed shaking up, remember?"

"We talked about that, Bud, but we voted it down,"

Keiler answered. "There were several plans, one economic, one racial—"

Fuller interrupted. "And one for assassination."

"But we decided not to implement any of them."

"Oh, no, Sam. We decided not to decide. We all agreed something had to be done, but we didn't like it. It was nasty. So we let it slip. We allowed General Nadler to take it over, and we looked the other way."

Keiler leaned forward, concerned. "Do you have any proof?"

Neither Paisley nor Nadler moved. They were sitting this one out.

"I don't need proof, Sam. Use your head. What happens during a state of emergency? You all ought to know by now. Especially our friend the general. Certainly he knows, doesn't he?"

General Nadler sighed wearily. "What I'm sure you're going for is that martial law can be declared and the military can be mobilized."

"Bingo! Great answer. Go to the head of the class."

Keiler's voice was reasonable. "Now, Bud, you know Earl isn't like that. As a matter of fact, he's the least hawkish of all the generals."

"During a state of emergency the Bill of Rights can be suspended, laws can be shoved through Congress, the country can be turned around by force."

Nadler stopped him. "Well now, that's a different story. What you're talking about is something we all agree will be good for the country."

"Am I?"

Keiler's head was bobbing up and down more quickly now, and his accent became more southern. "Relax a moment, Bud. What you're doing is mixing apples and oranges. At first I thought you were trying to tell us Earl here was trying to take over the country by force and create a dictatorship. Now you're talking about a horse of a different color."

"I didn't rule out a dictatorship," Fuller said angrily.

For the first time a smile crossed Nadler's face. But the smile was tight and false. Fuller was dead wrong. Nevertheless, he was closer to understanding than the others, and that could be trouble.

"How would it be if I swore on a Bible that I don't plan on becoming dictator of America?"

"That won't be necessary," Paisley said soothingly. He had obviously decided which side to back and was moving smoothly in that direction.

Fuller sank back into his chair. "You don't deny that you're planning an incident to create a state of emergency, do you?" Fuller didn't wait for an answer. "There's the convention in three days. That would make a hell of an opportunity, wouldn't it? After all, Chesapeake will be open and exposed there."

Keiler took in a breath. For once he was silent, watching.

Nadler laughed tightly. "And then what? I take over? You're forgetting there is a Vice President and a speaker of the House. What about them? Even if something did happen to them, there's a law of succession. As a matter of fact, if I'm not wrong, fourth on the list is president pro tem of the Senate. And that's you, Bud, isn't it?"

It was Keiler who answered. "I think we'd better stop this right here, boys." He turned to Fuller and smiled graciously. "Look, Bud, you're jumping to conclusions. Remember how Colton got toward the end?

320

Running from ghosts and shadows that never were. Yet he was a sound man. Poor Colton. I feel certain had he lived, he would have seen how wrong he was."

Fuller cast his eyes to the windows and looked out at the hazy buildings across the way. If only Keiler were as suspicious of how Colton died as he, perhaps he wouldn't be so sure. Fuller wondered if Nadler knew the truth about Colton's death. He glanced up, but Nadler's impervious mask was in place.

Keiler touched Fuller's arm kindly; his blue eyes sparkled; his stooped, stalklike frame looked infinitely wise. "We can't become divided now. We all know what's important is not the good of any one of us in this room-here. What's important is the good of America. It's for America that we've done everything. We can't lose sight of that now."

The men in the room were watching Fuller, eyes riveted to his face. And suddenly Fuller became scared.

"I suppose you're right," he said softly. "We can't lose sight of the good of the country."

Chapter Thirty-five

The car was an ancient Chevy low-rider, painted a deep velvety black and fairly conservative compared to most of its ilk. Afraid to drive the stolen RV any longer, Beal had bought it for three hundred dollars on the promise that it wasn't hot. Nevertheless, he was driving cautiously. There was nothing the Beverly Hills police liked better than hassling a beat-up Chevy on a slow summer morning.

Dr. Greenaway's office was located in a nondescript building, which, with the strange herding instinct that hits doctors as strongly as Herefords, was given over entirely to things medical.

It had taken Beal almost no time to locate the doctor who had been Lacey's private physician. Finding one man in this great sprawling country might be difficult, but finding a doctor is almost always easy. Between the AMA and the fact that Greenaway was not exactly an everyday name, Beal had easily learned that, except for the few years when he served as Lacey's private physician, Dr. Greenaway had practiced out of Los Angeles. A quick search of the phone book was all that was needed.

If Elaine Lacey had made any sense at all, it would be the fact that Lacey's doctor had not been allowed into the emergency room. Why? What was being hidden from him? Was that a sign that he was in on it? Or did it mean nothing at all?

As Beal pulled his Chevy into the parking lot next to the doctor's building, he felt as if every eye in Beverly Hills was on his car. Even the black parking attendant removed the radio from his ear and looked up as if he were viewing extraterrestrial life.

Dr. Greenaway's office was located on the third floor, down a long gray corridor that smelled of floor wax, disinfectant, and fear. The waiting room was empty except for a grandmother type with swollen ankles and blue hair. She glanced up only briefly as Beal and Maggie entered, then quickly looked back to her lap, where knitting needles were clacking out something long, green, and extremely deformed.

A moment later a small glass sliding window opened, and the receptionist glanced out. She might have had a nice face, slick, shiny skin, almost perfect features, pale blond hair pulled tightly back. But there was something not nice about her face, a brittle hardness that came less from tragedies and disappointment than from the lack of any emotion at all. It was a billboard face, perfect, beautiful, and as thin as paper.

"Do you have an appointment?" she asked. One pale eyebrow arched as she glanced at the doctor's appointment book. It was quite obvious she knew their names would not be there.

Beal leaned into the glassed-in window. "I just want to talk to the doctor a moment."

"Doctor's very busy today. Perhaps I can set up an appointment for another time." She began riffling through the pages of the appointment book, days tumbling quickly under her agile fingers.

Beal interrupted. "I must see the doctor. Now. It's urgent."

Unmoved, the receptionist looked up from her book. "We have several referral numbers." She transferred her shuffling to a little wooden box of telephone cards. "If you'll just tell me what seems to be the matter."

Beal smiled falsely and leaned into the window. "Hey, Dr. Greenaway!" he yelled. "It's an emergency!"

The receptionist shot out her arm and tried to push her window closed, but Beal held it open. The receptionist's face was cracking into a thousand lines; her pale skin was bright red.

The woman with the knitting fluttered to her feet, and, clutching her purse to her wide breasts, backed out of the office, trailing yarn like a long green snake behind her.

The receptionist was just starting to make headway against Beal when the door that led to the inner office opened. A middle-aged woman in a white coat stood in the doorway, arms crossed. She was neat and compact with a thick gray bun that spilled wispy stray hairs down her neck. Her eyes were creased and very blue, startlingly blue. Though few traces were left, Beal could tell as a young woman she must have been a great beauty. It was the way she held her neck and head, the confidence that comes from being very lovely, very young and never leaves no matter what the ravages of time.

The woman watched Beal steadily, taking in everything. She seemed completely unruffled. Beal backed away from the receptionist instinctively, but even so, the steady gaze of the woman made him feel like a naughty child.

"What seems to be the problem here?" the woman asked. She had a middle European accent.

"I'm looking for Dr. Greenaway."

"I'm Dr. Greenaway."

Beal was surprised. "You were President Lacey's private physician?"

"I'm afraid you've made a mistake. My name is Inez Greenaway. You're thinking of my husband, Isaiah."

The receptionist slammed the glass window shut, obviously protesting the doctor's handling of the matter. But Beal could see her watching him through the beveled glass.

"Can you tell me where your husband is?" Beal asked. "It's urgent."

Dr. Greenaway's face was changing. She was still blocking the doorway with her compact frame, motionless, steady, but there was the feeling that her muscles were preparing for movement. "Why do you wish to speak to him?" she asked.

"I was a patient of the doctor's. I've been out of the country for the past couple of years."

"I'm afraid my husband has been dead for some time now."

"Don't tell me. He died five years ago, right?"

"Yes. Exactly five years ago." Dr. Greenaway's

voice was clearly suspicious. The frown lines cut her forehead. And where there had once been confidence in her face, now there was concern, almost fear.

"I've got to speak to you," Beal said. He started walking toward Dr. Greenaway, but already her body was in motion, and she slipped back through the doorway and threw the lock.

Beal rushed to the door and began pounding. "You don't understand. I have to talk to you. It's important."

He could hear the doctor's heels clicking as she ran to the back. The receptionist was right behind her, and there was hurried whispering, the receptionist asking if she should call the police, the doctor answering that it wasn't necessary.

A moment later the little glass window opened a crack, and the receptionist spoke through it. Beal could see her perfect teeth, white, pointed, little, like a cat. "Dr. Greenaway excuses herself, but she'd rather not speak about her husband's death. I'm sure you understand."

"No, I don't understand!" Beal yelled. But the glass window had already been slammed shut.

Maggie was right behind him. "Doctors' offices usually have a back exit," she whispered.

Maggie and Beal rushed down the stairs and into the street. Already the morning crowds of Beverly Hills shoppers had begun to form, tall, tanned men and women wearing fifty-dollar jeans and stiff, angry smiles. There was no one who looked remotely like the doctor.

They found her in the garage, opening the door of a little economy car, a sweater thrown over her whites. Her fingers were shaking enough to make her drop her keys. It was Beal who picked them up.

Dr. Greenaway's confidence seemed shattered, her face a tense mask. "Please leave me alone."

"I have to talk to you."

"I'm an old woman. I can tell you nothing."

"Please, you don't understand. I don't want to hurt you. I'm in trouble. I need help."

Beal was standing there, holding her keys, and Greenaway was looking directly at him, her eyes working over his face. Her gaze shifted over to Maggie, who was standing just behind him, and while the doctor's face still looked scared, there was also sympathy.

She sighed deeply, then said, "It is better we talk out of doors, no?"

Without waiting for an answer, she turned and led them toward a park. The three of them said nothing to one another as they moved quickly through the shimmering heat, but Beal thought he heard Greenaway say under her breath, "So it all starts again."

The park was a long, thin strip of green that separated the business district from the large Beverly Hills houses. There was one bench set in the center, and, running along the perimeter, a miniature garden of cactus and obscenely meaty tropical plants.

Greenaway let out a low sigh as she sat down, but she said nothing. She was staring out into space, and she seemed to be thinking about something that had happened a long time ago.

It was Beal who spoke first. "What did you mean when you said, 'So it all starts again'?"

Dr. Greenaway turned toward him, and he saw a good deal of anger in her stupendously blue eyes. "Don't you read the newspapers, young man? Can't you feel what's beginning to happen to this country?"

Then her voice softened. "Perhaps you don't. Perhaps only us old ones can see the signs. And we're just too weak and scared to do anything about it." Then she waved the subject away with her hand, like an irksome child. The anger was gone from her face, and there was even a small smile, again as if for a child. "But you two want to know about the Lacey assassination," she said.

Beal pulled back, surprised and also suspicious. "How do you know that?"

Again the patronizing smile. "You both look fairly healthy. Scared but healthy. My husband was a remarkable man, but the only reason two healthy young people would want to talk to him would be about Lacey. That's all anyone wanted to talk to him about after the assassination."

"And then soon after he died."

"A heart attack. He was only fifty, overworked, but vigorous. He was a great believer in jogging." She laughed sadly. "So Californian. Every evening he jogged five miles around a track. Around and around. To me it seemed very boring, but he used to say he did his best thinking then." Her face sank into lines. "That was how he died."

"I'm sorry," Maggie said softly, but the doctor wasn't listening.

"It came as a great shock," she said. "I kept up the practice. It was somewhere to go during the day, and also, I suppose, it was a way of keeping him alive."

Greenaway had receded deep inside herself. Beal and Maggie were watching her, their wanting to allow her privacy clashing with the urgency. The urgency won. Beal asked, "What did he say about the Lacey assassination?"

Dr. Greenaway roused herself, but her eyes were closed off, distant. "He said nothing about it beyond what was in the news."

"Then why did you run away before? And why did you think it would be better to talk out here?"

Dr. Greenaway was watching the passing traffic, Rolls-Royces and Mercedeses, huge black limousines with tinted windows swishing silently by. The laugh of a child broke the metallic hum. It came as a surprise.

This time it was Maggie who broke the doctor's silence. She touched her arm gently. "Please. It's very important."

Dr. Greenaway turned her creased eyes on Maggie. "Yes, I can see that."

"We're being hunted."

The doctor nodded sadly. "It shows in the eyes. I would rather you didn't tell me why."

Maggie just sat there. She, too, was looking at the steady stream of cars. "What did you mean by it all starting again?" she asked after a while. "You meant World War Two, didn't you?"

"In a way. Yes. I was in Poland in 1939. Not a very pleasant place to be that year. But I didn't mean Nazism in particular. That's just how I know all the signs." She stopped, shaking her head. "To be frank, I'm not really sure what I meant."

Beal was about to ask a question, then thought better of it. Greenaway was watching Maggie closely. She seemed to feel a bond with Maggie, as if she were viewing her own youth.

"But you feel there's a connection between the Lacey

329

assassination and what you call the signs," Maggie said softly.

"I suppose that's what I meant. For some time now I've felt that the country was being run by an unseen hand. Certainly not the President. Or the political parties. After that last vote in Congress . . ." She hesitated, then shook her head confusedly. "Perhaps the military. Yes. Or someone who wants to use the military."

Beal picked her up immediately. "Someone?"

"I don't know. I just keep feeling it's all leading to something. Something soon."

"Something like Hitler?"

"Never mind. It is probably just the paranoia of old age. We're still all of us looking for boogeymen under the beds, like little children."

"But once the boogeymen were real," Beal said.

"They're always real."

The doctor fell silent for a long while, looking around the park as if in search of her own boogeymen. She seemed to be coming to a decision. After a while she continued. "My husband lived less than a month after the assassination. He had been traveling with Lacey for most of the six months before."

"Was that usual?"

"No. It was very unusual."

"In other words, President Lacey was a sick man before he was killed."

"Perhaps. My husband told me nothing. In fact, he avoided the subject, which wasn't like him at all. Isaiah wasn't a secretive man." Her eyes lit up. "I always used to say he could never have an affair without my knowing. It was a big joke between the two of us." The light vanished from her face. "But during those six months he seemed to be growing increasingly secretive. And I remember thinking . . . well, perhaps he did have a lover." She paused. "Later I found the books. Dozens of them. Books on radiation poisoning."

Beal was shocked. "You mean Lacey was suffering from radiation poisoning?"

"I don't know. Perhaps."

"Well, I can see how he'd want to keep that from the country," Beal said, getting excited. "Suppose there was a radiation leak somewhere and he received a fatal dose of it—" He stopped. None of the rest linked up. Why kill a President if he were already dying?

Dr. Greenaway was watching him. Her creased old eyes seemed to age dramatically; her voice sounded strange, almost ominous. "There were other books also. Books on lasers."

"Books on lasers?" Beal repeated dumbly. "Why would he be reading books on lasers?"

Greenaway was still staring at Maggie and Beal. Then suddenly she seemed to become angry. "That is all I know," she said curtly. "After that he died. And I moved back to Los Angeles." She stood up abruptly.

"Dr. Greenaway, please," Maggie said urgently. "I don't understand what any of this means."

But Dr. Greenaway was closed away, her compact body prepared for movement. "I told you. That is all I know. And I wish I didn't even know that." There was a moment when she stared at Maggie, her eyes very sad, very old. "I wish you good luck," she said. Then she was moving, striding from the park bench, pausing at the corner, and crossing the street without glancing back.

331

Maggie and Beal watched as the doctor joined the Beverly Hills shoppers on the other side of the street. Smart-looking women in expensive clothes, young men exposing great expanses of hairy chest accented by gold chains, the idle rich of Los Angeles, filling up their emptiness at Gucci's. Her sturdy body stood out among the tall, lean, orange-juice-fed shoppers. She was from a different world.

Maggie watched after her a long while without saying anything, a soft sadness over her like a drape, as if she too had seen in Greenaway a shared sorrow, one past, the other future.

"It doesn't make sense," Beal said finally. "Why would her husband be looking at books on lasers?"

"Maybe he was just interested in the subject," Maggie answered. "Everything takes on significance after a person dies."

"No. She told us that for a reason. I'm willing to bet that woman knew more than she said."

Maggie sighed. "I don't know, Beal. That Hitler business sounded a little farfetched. Someone out to take control of the country. There's no one at the top of the administration who would seriously consider doing that. Certainly no one with that kind of power."

Beal agreed. "Not Chesapeake, not any of the other politicians around."

"And the man who's protecting you?"

Jack had decided not to tell her about Jed. The more information she had, the more precarious her position, but he thought about her questions. "He'd have the brains, all right. But if it were him, he wouldn't have stood around talking with me." Beal shook his head slowly. "Besides, I think I saw the man, Maggie. Whoever the hell he is. I think I saw him."

"Dr. Greenaway could have fallen apart after her husband's death," Maggie suggested with little conviction.

"She didn't seem like a basket case to me. She seemed like a sensible woman who was scared, and probably with damn good reason." He paused, trying to work things out. "It just doesn't make sense. Radiation. Lasers. What the hell do they have to do with the assassination of a President?"

"Could he have gotten radiation poisoning from the laser?"

Beal shrugged. "Search me. I don't know the first thing about lasers."

Maggie sighed. "Neither do I. I know they use them in medicine for surgery."

"Yeah. But I don't know where that gets us."

Maggie was silent for a while, thinking, "They use them in rock shows," she said, trying for a smile. "I've got it. Maybe Lacey was killed by the Rolling Stones."

She glanced over at Beal, but he was sitting slouched, his eyes far away, looking at the steady stream of elegant cars, seeing nothing. He was beginning to suspect that, while what they had unearthed might have had something to do with the Lacey assassination, it had nothing to do with that terrible white face in the mountains or the men who were out to kill him.

Maggie tried again. "Maybe he got a fatal dose at Disneyland, and Mickey Mouse had to kill him to keep it from the world."

Beal answered with little interest. "I never saw lasers at Disneyland."

"Sure," Maggie answered. "Don't they use lasers in the Haunted House for those holograms?"

Beal shrugged. "What's a hologram?"

"You know, those three-dimensional pictures that look so real you can walk right up to them."

It was sudden, and it was powerful. Beal froze, a chill running through him. Seemingly unrelated fragments of facts all shuffled together, making a pattern. He was silent, motionless, but a fleeting look of recognition crossed his face, and then something very close to jubilation.

BOOK 3
LATE JULY

Chapter Thirty-six

The Detroit River is the busiest inland port in America. As a Great Lakes connecting link, the river has thirty-one scheduled steamship lines serving more than forty countries. As the home of a multitude of millionaires, the river is always jammed with pleasure boats, regal sailing ships, their masts reaching to the sky, magnificent yachts like the Baglietto so preferred by the Mafia. Just one half mile away on the other side of the river is the Canadian border.

The blond man stood at the wheel of the sixty-five-foot twin-diesel Baglietto, the cool river breezes ruffling his hair. The yacht was one of the best around. It had cost a cool half million, and that was without equipment. With radar and sonar it had come close to $700,000. It would make a hell of an expensive bonfire.

The blond man took out a pair of binoculars and looked out at the Renaissance Center, the huge complex of buildings that were supposed to herald the revival of

Detroit. The skyscrapers and broad plazas sparkled in the hot sun, $500 million worth of steel and concrete that had revived very little except a few men's wallets.

Slowly he shifted his binoculars across the buildings, through the main plaza, to the buildings at the water's edge. In the basement of one of the buildings there was a stairway leading to loading facilities. It would be there that he picked up his men.

The escape route was simple. At 8:05 P.M. the three men would bolt from the Convention Arena, each leaving by a separate exit, each then proceeding to the waterfront by a different route. They were to use public transportation. The police wouldn't expect assassins to be riding the bus.

By the time they reached the Renaissance Center it would be jammed with people. There would be groups huddled around radios, frightened women rushing home. Already the looters and troublemakers would be on the move, hoping to get in some first-rate disorder before the authorities pulled themselves together.

The three men would go unnoticed as they slipped into the basement, then rushed out to the loading dock where the yacht would be waiting.

Yes, it was a good plan. Certainly the three men who would be bolting from the Convention Arena would believe it would work.

But the blond man had no intention of its working. Three men on the loose with a lot of money and a keen memory of his face were not part of the plan.

Chapter Thirty-seven

"See, that's just it. I can't be sure of who or even what I saw that day in the mountains. But whatever it was, it looked like Lacey."

Beal shot a sly look at Maggie as he swung onto the Santa Ana Freeway and almost immediately came to a crawl. It was only noon, but inexplicably the freeway was jammed.

Maggie did not look up. She had a cardboard bucket on her lap and was rummaging through it. "Do you want another piece?" she asked as she held up a brown crinkly object which probably had been a chicken breast before the Colonel got hold of it.

"Is that all you have to say? I drop a bombshell on you, and you ask if I want another piece of chicken."

"Both you and I know that Lacey's been dead for five years." Maggie went back to her rummaging.

Beal turned an irritated eye on her, then looked back out at the steady stream of traffic. "Of course, I saw the man for only a split second, but I remember feeling there was something familiar about him. And now that I think about it, he looked like Lacey. A lot thinner, older, more stooped . . ."

"I wouldn't be surprised. Being dead five years does that kind of thing to a man."

"I get the feeling you aren't taking me seriously."

She pulled out a thigh. "You're sure you don't want some more chicken?"

"Jesus, Maggie. All right, give me a wing." He put out his hand and frowned in concentration. "You see, it's almost as if I knew he looked like Lacey all along, but I just couldn't get at it because I couldn't see how it could be done."

Maggie's face had no expression. "There aren't any more wings."

"That's impossible. I had only one. Not even the Colonel breeds one-armed chickens."

"I had the other one."

Beal grimaced. "There was a time when you used to save all the wings for me." He was only partially joking. "It sure as hell is a lousy time to start liberating yourself."

He looked up sulkily, but Maggie was handing him a chicken wing, smiling. "Okay, I give up," she said, laughing. "How is it possible that you saw Lacey five years after his death?"

"What if I told you what I saw wasn't Lacey himself but a hologram of Lacey?"

"That requires an answer?"

Beal began on the chicken wing, but his mind wasn't much on it. "Listen to this. Say, just say, there was a conspiracy to take over the country. Probably a group of Lacey's top aides. Well, what better way to take over a country than under the leadership of a popular President, a man who was almost a god to America?"

"Lacey was certainly that all right. But he wasn't the kind of man to go in for a dictatorship, not even one of his own."

"Right. But the idea is a good one. It could work. So let's say these guys get together and start kicking some plans around. Well, one of them probably comes up with the idea of using a double. But they veto that because there's the risk of a leak. So then maybe another of them comes up with using a hologram. It'd be simple. All they'd have to do was dispose of Lacey secretly, then trot out their hologram to make public appearances. Meanwhile, behind the scenes, the real powers would be ruling."

"That sounds crazy."

"Yeah, I'm sure they thought it sounded crazy, too. But maybe they talked about it for a while. And pretty soon it started sounding good."

"And you think it was this conspiracy that killed Lacey?"

"No. For the plan to work, they would have to keep Lacey's death a secret."

"Half the world saw Lacey killed on television."

"I know. But you see, someone got there first. Maybe it was a fluke. Or maybe someone else found out about their plan and was trying to stop them."

"Someone like that man who's protecting you?"

"Possibly. I can't tell. But let's leave that aside for the moment. Now Lacey's death must have thrown my conspirators into quite a tizzy. But what if they already

341

had their hologram of Lacey? Eventually they'd see the whole thing could still be done."

"How? A resurrection? Look, Beal, there's a lot of people who have trouble with the Easter story, too."

"I didn't say it would be easy."

Traffic was piling up just ahead. Beal craned his neck out the window. It seemed impossible, but all he could see was a long line of cars and luggage racks filled with surfboards and golf clubs. All around them the cars were packed with hot, tired people and children fighting with each other in the back seat. It was only then Beal realized this was the beginning of the weekend. He was living that far from reality.

"They'd have to wait awhile," Beal continued. "Then there'd be the announcement that Lacey didn't die. You know, like the old Kennedy stories. I can see it all. They'd say he'd been transferred to a hiding place, say, somewhere in Florida or California. For days he'd hovered between life and death. Then the miracle. Suddenly he started to come to. After that it took years of brutally hard work for the valiant Lacey to fight his way back to health. But he refused to appear before America until he was whole again, et cetera, et cetera."

"Five years is a long time."

"They needed it. They had to prepare America first. That's what the blackmail was all about. There's an unseen presence running this country, directing policy, pressuring votes. They rammed the state of emergency bill through Congress. And now everything is ready."

If he was expecting some kind of momentous reaction from Maggie, he was disappointed. She was eating a chicken thigh reflectively, staring out at the traffic

342

jam all around them. "And you think what you saw in the mountains was that hologram of Lacey?"

"That's right. They were probably testing it out."

Finally Maggie turned back to Beal, and she looked concerned. "I didn't realize you'd never been to the Haunted House."

It was only later that Beal understood what she meant.

From far away Disneyland looks like the darnedest place. Suddenly the gray industrial smog is cut by a crazy jumble of strange shapes. Turrets and towers, gables and gingerbread suddenly appear; an icy white papier-mâché mountain reaches to the sky; a futuristic monorail makes wide circles in the air. Looming out of the monotony, the glittering cluster seems to promise magic and fantasy, a world very unlike our own.

But it is only inside the gates that the real magic of Disneyland becomes apparent. For inside the gates there is no garbage, no disorder. Everything is clean and shiny; everything works. Outside, civilization might howl, death and poverty raging like an insistent wind, but inside, everything is candy-cane garbage cans and polite, smiling faces. And for a moment you are tricked into believing that there can be harmony and reason, that the world really can work. Truly it is a fantasyland, echoes of a past that perhaps never was.

Traffic came to a standstill long before Beal and Maggie were even in the parking lot of Disneyland. And after that the car crawled like an insect, inch by inch, until finally they were waved into a space on the other side of the park.

It was no less crowded inside either. There was a

desperation about Disneyland that came from the fact that it was the peak of the summer. It was something like New Year's Eve or the end of the world or the beginning of the end of a marriage. Even in California there was the feeling that the sunshine would one day pass. So people frantically stuffed in the ice cream, laughed, and shouted too loud. The LSD trippers were out full force, their brains sizzling, their eyes black holes of incomprehension.

The line around the Haunted House, a large wedding-cake-like Victorian mansion, was proportionately about the length of an average-sized man's intestines. Even though it was artfully twined around wooden barriers, it was hard to hide the fact that stretched out full, it would probably reach San Diego. Every several feet was a sign indicating the average wait should one be unlucky enough to be standing there. Beal and Maggie checked in at just over an hour and a half.

The sign wasn't lying either. By the time they reached the front of the line Beal's optimism and excitement were a bit frayed at the edges, like an old picture. But once inside, he felt only foolish.

The Haunted House was a legerdemain to delight little children, a clever display of magic and drama that had everyone gasping and laughing. As Maggie and Beal sat in a large easy chair, they were sent spinning into darkness. Suddenly below them there was a magnificently eerie ballroom filled with diners and waltzing dancers, strange three-dimensional figures, yet somehow filmy and insubstantial, leaving traces of themselves spinning after them. It had been clever. It had even been amazing. But it was totally impossible that the display could have fooled a reasonably clever six-year-old, let alone an entire nation.

It had been a crazy idea, full of contradictions and improbabilities. And it had been dead wrong. Beal felt the old dread creeping over him.

As they slumped on the bench just outside the Haunted House, Beal watched Maggie staring at a little boy of about five. He could tell she was thinking about Jason, wanting to telephone him, though she knew that was dangerous, wanting to see him, though she knew it would only bring trouble.

"You can still leave me, you know," Beal said after a while.

"Sometimes I think it's a fault in me that I don't. For your sake, not mine." Maggie's voice was ominous, totally unlike her. It surprised and disturbed Beal. But it seemed to surprise and disturb Maggie even more. "I'm your weak link," she said at last.

Then all at once she was smiling, her face over-animated, perhaps even frantic. As if in the darkness she'd discovered something inside her that was too terrible even to acknowledge. She was pointing at an extremely tall figure wearing overalls that was loping out of one of the back doors of the Haunted House. "Why don't you ask one of the workmen about holograms?"

"Because it won't do any good."

"You'll never know if you don't try."

Beal hated the optimistic smile she was working on so desperately. Nevertheless, he pulled himself up from the bench and started after the workman. It was something to do.

The workman was pressing quickly through the crowd, his head towering above the rest, like those pictures of American GIs in Vietnam. He was cutting a pretty fair pace, and it took some time to catch up to him.

"You work in the Haunted House?" Beal asked as he drew parallel.

"That's right." The workman didn't stop. His face was set tight with a worried, distracted look.

"Do you mind if I ask you a few questions? It'll take only a minute."

The workman stopped, but he didn't look as if he liked the idea much. "Make it thirty seconds and you've got a deal. There's been a breakdown. In Abe Lincoln's jaw." Then suddenly he smiled. It was a nice smile. Full of foolishness and irony.

It was only close up that Beal realized how immense the workman was. He was at least six feet five, perhaps more. And though he couldn't have been more than nineteen or twenty, Beal could imagine all the "Jolly Green Giant" and "How's the weather up there?" jokes he must have gotten already. Probably the only way a person could take being that tall was by playing a lot of basketball. Except he didn't look as if he played basketball; he looked more like a chessplayer. His body was stocky, with the kind of flaccid look that women over forty sometimes get. His face was surrounded by colorless strands of obviously neglected hair. He wore glasses, thick, owlish horn-rims that had slipped halfway down his nose, and behind them his eyes were large, dark, swimming around fast and furious, on a mission to see everything, almost as if his eyes knew they were going blind and had very little time to take in the world. It occurred to Beal that this was probably the case. Everything about the boy seemed impatient

346

and hurried not because of indifference but because life was very short and there was a great deal to do before the darkness.

"I need to know about holograms in the Haunted House," Beal said as he watched the boy's eyes dart from his face, back to the Haunted House, then quickly to the direction he wished he were going.

"They're not holograms. They're mirrored projections, things like that."

Beal got excited. "What's the difference?"

"What's the difference between a whore and a call girl?" Again that smile, but it didn't last long, and already his eyes were darting.

"Well, do you know anyone I can talk to about holograms?"

The boy's face transformed. The distracted look was gone, and he locked his eyes onto Beal. "What do you want to know? I'm an expert." He said this simply, and there was something in his tone that made Beal tend to believe him.

"Could you make a hologram of an object and then pretend it was the real thing?"

The workman was silent, considering the question, watching Beal closely or maybe not; it was hard to tell with those strange swimming eyes. Finally he said, "That would depend on a lot of things. I could make you a tabletop hologram that would fool anyone, that's for sure. And cheap, too. I've done it before to pick up extra money. One time I made these roses for an old lady down the block. One hundred bucks, man. And you could have put it in the garden and fooled the bees."

"I'm talking about something bigger."

The boy leaned closer to Beal. His face was flushed with excitement. "How big?"

"Man size."

He whistled sharply. "You really serious?"

"And one that moves."

"Jesus!" The workman was no longer looking at Beal. His eyes were fixed upward, as if he were getting a glimpse of God and liking what he was seeing a good deal. "You're talking about a real hologram, aren't you? None of that carnival stuff." A beatific smile came over his face, and he shook his head solemnly. "The English do a little of that kind of work. The Russians used to do more, I hear."

Beal stopped him. "The Russians?"

"That's right. Two guys working out of Moscow made a lot of breakthroughs. Guys disappeared five years ago, though. Here no one's interested in holograms. They're just too expensive."

Beal remembered the rumors about the missing Russian laser scientists. It was all beginning to fit.

Then Beal stopped thinking about anything. Because several yards away, in the shadows cast by the Haunted House, he could just barely make out the shape of a small man with a brush mustache. The shadow seemed to move slightly, and Beal thought he saw the little man's hand slip under his jacket to his shoulder.

"You really interested in me making one?" the boy asked excitedly. "I mean. I could do it, man. All it would take is money."

Beal could see Maggie through the crowds. She was on the bench where he'd left her, looking out into space, seeing nothing but the contours of her own mind. Beal looked up. The workman was watching him ex-

348

citedly. "Maybe," he answered, though to what question he wasn't sure.

"It'd cost," the boy said. "Holograms aren't cheap, especially the moving ones. I mean, to do it right, it could cost a lot." The light vanished from his face. He'd become so wrapped up in what he was saying he hadn't been thinking. The man he was talking to didn't look as if he could afford a good meal, let alone a hologram.

Richards was definitely moving. Hand under jacket, he was waiting for the crowds, then slowly inching up to where Beal was standing. Beal glanced over at Maggie, but she was still staring out into space, unaware. It occurred to Beal that perhaps Richards hadn't seen her. But he doubted it. Though the little man's eyes were fixed on a point well beyond Beal, there was something about him that suggested he knew exactly what was going on and was seeing everything.

"I better go," the workman said. He sounded confused and impatient, and he was starting to move.

Beal grabbed his arm and held him. "Please don't leave."

The boy tried to free his arm, but Beal held him tightly. "Hey, man, what's going on?"

"Just stay. Okay? Just stay."

This time the boy jerked his arm free. Within seconds he was striding away, fast.

Beal felt frozen. Everything around him seemed to be happening in slow motion. He could see Maggie stand up and begin walking to him. She was still unaware of what was going on and was smiling at Beal, thinking he was finished talking. Slowly Maggie's face was transformed as she looked over at Beal and began to realize something was wrong. She stopped. Surprise, then confusion, then fear flickered across her face.

Richards was no longer a shadow. He was only a few feet away, sidestepping carefully through the crowd.

Beal looked around desperately, but there was no use running. Maggie was standing only a few feet away. If he ran, Richards would make a grab for her. If he didn't run, Richards would make a grab for both of them. There was no use crying out for help. All that would cause was confusion, and confusion was exactly what Richards needed to hide his movement. Beal felt everything inside himself shriveling. Maggie hadn't moved, and her eyes were fixed on Beal, afraid and unsure.

The little man made his way through the crowd, drawing closer and closer, until he was only a few feet away from Beal. He stopped, and suddenly Beal realized everything was all wrong. The crowd, the daylight, the two of them separated, and Richards totally visible. Something was wrong. Everything was wrong.

Beal turned back to Maggie quickly. "You little bitch!" he screamed angrily. "I told you something like this would happen."

Richards froze, his hand close to his jacket, his eyes working all around the area, nervously.

The crowd had stopped moving, and several people were rubbernecking around, their faces lit with amused smiles.

Maggie pulled back, shock replacing fear. Surrounding her, a group of elderly women with blue hair watched her closely. Beal's face was taut with anger, but she thought she saw him wink. And then she, too, understood.

She whirled on Beal. "Oh, yeah? Well, it's your own fucking fault."

Richards hadn't moved, but his body was poised, and his eyes were unsure. All around him people were turning hungry eyes through the crowd, trying to spot what was going on.

Beal was smiling now. "What the hell would you know about fucking?" It was hard to keep the laughter out of his voice. "The last time you used a bed for anything but sleeping was on our honeymoon."

Maggie turned to the blue-haired ladies, shaking her head angrily as if looking for support. "Sure, of course," she shrieked. "Why should I bother? You know what happens every time we try."

A snicker went through the crowd. A baby started crying, and its mother began rocking it back and forth, but her eyes were riveted to the crazy screaming couple, and she was smiling.

There was the crackle of shortwave and a rustling far back in the crowd. Richards's hand was no longer at his gun, nor were his eyes on Beal and Maggie. He was looking toward the gates of Disneyland and his waiting car. Slowly he began slipping back.

"Come on, hit me!" Maggie taunted. "I dare you to hit me!"

Beal didn't answer. He saw Richards backing away and the rustling in the crowd. Then he heard the short-wave. Maggie was still watching him, hands on hips, her face jeering and superior. Then she heard it, too.

The crowd was parting now, begrudgingly making room for the trail of guards who were closing in. The crackle of shortwave radios had gotten louder, and voices spurted sharp and bulletlike through the air. The guards pressed through the crowd, asking questions and following pointed fingers. But by the time they reached the inner circle there was only the laughing crowd. Maggie and Beal had already disappeared.

Chapter Thirty-eight

There were more than 250 hotels or motels in the city of Detroit, 24,000 rooms, and Berger was positive that he had been given the worst one. If the person who hired him was powerful enough to pull off the plan itself, it seemed impossible he couldn't get him a halfway decent room.

So perhaps he wasn't so powerful.

Berger threw off the thought and began pacing the room. It wasn't much of a pace before he hit the windows. He drew back the dusty curtains and looked out at the street below. There wasn't much to see. Just a city gearing up for the convention that would be starting tomorrow. That and, of course, a lot of big cars. Only Detroit still thought they'd be coming back.

Berger had been out walking the day before and spotted two familiar faces ambling around the convention area. Neither of them seemed all that interested in the layout of the buildings, but Berger knew they were making mental notes, comparing their memory of the blueprints with the actuality. He remembered both of the men from an assassination attempt in Costa Rica. Later they'd all seen each other in the lobby of a Miami hotel, trying to sign up for a Cuba job.

At first seeing the others had shaken and angered Berger. He didn't need backups, and any hint that he might made his usually blank face turn furious.

But the whole operation was too smart to tip off that there were backups even if there were any. So what were the other two ex-mercenaries doing in town? Coincidence? Maybe. Another operation. Possibly. Berger supposed in life anything was possible, which led him to thinking about the idea of three separate assassinations, all for the same company. It was a big operation; he knew that already by the amount of money changing hands. It was a clever operation; he knew that from the blond man's style.

Berger let go of the curtain and paced back to the bed. It smelled faintly of disinfectant and old age.

He had just over a week to wait until the closing night of the convention. In that time he felt fairly sure he'd figure out what was going on. It was something he didn't want to do. The trick in being for hire was knowing as little as possible. That way if things didn't work out, you were okay.

But as he sat on the bed, trying to keep off the inevitable, already the wheels were turning that would lead him inexorably toward danger.

Chapter Thirty-nine

Beal's black Chevy was parked several yards off the road in the tall grass along the mountain curves of Mulholland Drive. Hidden in the weeds and cactus, it appeared as only a blot of darkness in the already dark night. Below, the lights of the valley winked and shimmered like stars, transforming the roads into glittering double strands, fast-food shacks into lustrous pools of light, supermarket parking lots into dazzling milky ways.

Several hundred yards ahead was another parked car, also hidden in the grass. Sparrow kept his eyes on his windshield and the silhouette of Beal's car in the blackness up ahead. He could just barely discern the outlines of Beal's and Maggie's heads as they waited for their meeting with him, completely unaware that it had already begun.

Sparrow reached into the glove compartment and pulled out his dinner, a cheese sandwich and packaged tapioca pudding. He unwrapped the cheese sandwich neatly, then began to eat, chewing slowly, careful to count to twenty before he allowed himself to swallow. He finished off his meal with a carton of lukewarm milk, then sat back and waited, monitoring his stomach for any sign of upset. There was none, though he suspected that would soon change. Sparrow had never had a meeting with Beal that hadn't left his stomach twisted in knots. And this one had all the earmarks of trouble.

Beal had called Sparrow only two hours earlier. He sounded tired and confused, but mostly he sounded scared, very scared. His voice was high-pitched and shrill; his words were fast and slurred. You could almost hear him looking over his shoulder.

Sparrow regarded Beal's fear from afar, inspecting it as if the emotion were unknown to him and he were curious to understand its contours. In fact, Sparrow knew there had been moments of fear in his own life. But that was very long ago. Vague remembrances of himself as a boy came back to him. The shattered tenements of The Bronx, dark streets trembling with the promise of violence. He could see his father, sweating and bull-like, embittered against a country that had promised everything and delivered only anger and poverty, taking out his vengeance on a little boy. His mother long gone, unspoken of. Years ago. Another life. He had been called a crybaby. And he supposed he was. But no one called him a crybaby anymore. Now he was a man who wept for no one. And he supposed no one would weep for him either.

His mind went to Roger, sitting on the edge of the

hospital bed, his dull eyes regarding Sparrow impassively.

Quickly Sparrow folded his sandwich papers, crushed his milk carton, and returned everything to the glove compartment. He climbed out of the car, keeping his eyes on the silhouetted heads farther along the road. Even though he knew Beal didn't pose any threat to him, it wasn't smart to take chances. The beginning of trust was the beginning of the end.

Sparrow kept low, creeping along the night-darkened road, his eyes watching cautiously, his body guarding against even the slightest noise. As he neared the car, he could see the outline of Beal and the shadow of Maggie's head resting on his shoulder. They were sitting in the back seat, which was odd, and they didn't seem to be watching for him, which was stupid. There was an intimacy and unguardedness that touched and angered Sparrow. It seemed impossible two people that inept could make it across the street, let alone stay alive as long as they had.

Sparrow moved noiselessly, his hand raised just above his pocket, poised and ready. Still, they didn't turn. They were faced forward, looking out into the lights below or perhaps at nothing at all. As Sparrow neared the car, the dry grass shifted under him, and he heard the rustling loudly and sharply in his ears. He stopped, crouching motionless, poised like an animal. He waited, but still they didn't turn. Then slowly he rose up and looked around. None of the car doors was locked. He could see the raised buttons. He laughed to himself with a strange kind of anger, then reached out and began moving his hands toward the front door.

Then he realized something was wrong.

It came as a hint of noise, a feeling of air being displaced, everything very muted, but there nonetheless. Yes, he was sure there was something there. He froze instantly, his hand feeling the hardness of his gun. He knew that the noise was someone waiting for him; he could almost feel the heat of the hidden body.

Sparrow didn't move, but his mind was alert, and inside him everything was working, his eyes trying to make out the shadow behind him, judging its size, its shape, and all the while trying to figure out what to do. But it was too late for any of that.

Almost immediately there was a nudge at his back, and it was the softness of the nudge that tipped him off. He turned, hand outstretched, his face hard with anger. "Do you want to give me that gun?"

Maggie was holding the gun awkwardly, as if it might go off at any minute. She thought for a while, then smiled. "No. I don't think I do."

"Look, little girl, guns go off. They aren't something to play with."

"Well, then I guess you better get into the car. We wouldn't want it to go off by mistake."

Beal was rolling down the window, a big smile on his face. He was holding up a rolled shirt, letting Sparrow know it was this he had taken for Maggie's head.

Sparrow's left eye was twitching with irritation, and his stomach was a knot of fire. He muttered, "It's my goddamn gun." But already he could feel Maggie behind him, patting his pockets, removing his gun, and then giving him a brief nudge toward the passenger seat of the car. He obeyed sulkily, opening the door with a jerk, shoving his body in, and slamming the door loudly.

Maggie handed both guns to Beal in the back, then

walked over to the driver's seat and slid in. She was smiling cockily. A smile Sparrow was sure she'd learned from Beal. He'd never seen Maggie close up and noted with irritation that she was very pretty. Instinctively his hand started to his pocket with the antacids, but he stopped. Beal was crazy enough to misinterpret the movement, and Sparrow certainly was not about to ask his permission.

Beal was holding both guns in his lap, watching the back of Sparrow's neck. "You said it yourself. Never underestimate the opposition."

"If you had any sense at all, by now you'd know that I'm not the opposition."

"Well, you aren't exactly a friend either."

Sparrow turned to Maggie with a snide smile. "It's about time your husband learned about life, my dear. There's no such thing as friendship. Friendship is merely a matter of who needs who."

"Is that why you gave Beal your gun that time in the motel room?"

"Exactly. I gave him the gun because as stupid as he is, he's all we had. If a cannon would have helped keep him alive, I would have wheeled one out."

"Aw," Beal said, "and I thought you acted on a humane impulse."

"Sure it was," Maggie answered. "Can't you see he's just angry that we outsmarted him?"

"You mean he really loves me?"

"Absolutely. He just hates anyone knowing about it."

Sparrow gave an irritated wave of his hand, but his eyes were cast out the window, awkward and embarrassed. In fact, he was becoming fond of Beal.

Fondness was a weakness he couldn't afford. Fondness could kill you. Sparrow cleared his throat and tried to sound nonchalant. "If you two are finished discussing my psychological profile, then maybe you'll tell me why you called."

"I ran into Richards at Disneyland this afternoon."

Sparrow jerked his head back toward Beal. "Leaving aside the larger question of why you were stupid enough to go to Disneyland, what happened?"

"Not much. He was there. So was his gun. So were about a million other people."

"Strange."

"I thought so."

"How did you get away?"

"He wanted us to."

Sparrow's face hardened; his voice was sharp. "What do you mean?" It was obvious he had a fairly clear idea what he meant.

"I'm not sure really. But it was just too easy. One man. One gun. Right in the middle of Disneyland."

"You're sure there weren't any backups?"

"If there were, they sure weren't helping him any. Maggie and I staged a fight, you know, calling each other names to draw attention. At first we ran away congratulating ourselves on how damn clever we were. But then we started thinking. If Richards is half as smart as you say he is, he would know something like that would happen."

Sparrow was silent. His hand was already at his pocket, fishing for the antacids; his eyes were on the ceiling of the car, lost in thought.

Maggie broke the quiet. "The only thing we don't understand is why."

360

Sparrow didn't answer for a long while, his eyes blank and staring, his jaws working on the milky tablets. Then abruptly he turned back to Beal. "We have to get to a telephone. Now."

Instinctively Beal's hand tightened on the gun. "Why?"

"I haven't got time for explanations," Sparrow snapped. "Just start the car!"

Beal lifted his gun. He was watching Sparrow carefully, the abrupt tone, the sudden change in the little man's body making him cautious and stubborn.

Sparrow saw Beal's eyes close off and found himself silently cursing, though he knew, in fact, his reaction wouldn't be very different. He forced himself to slow down. "You're right. Richards wouldn't make a try for you at Disneyland unless he wanted you to escape. He wanted to scare you."

"Well, he did that all right," Maggie said. "But why scare us?"

"Because he knew you'd call me." Sparrow looked around anxiously, but all he saw was darkness and the milky lights of the valley below. "They knew eventually that would lead them even higher." He thought for a while, then nodded. "Yes, they must have known for some time that there was a lot of money and power protecting you. To tell you the truth, I couldn't understand why anyone who took the kind of risks you took would still be walking around this planet. But now I know. They didn't want to kill you. They haven't wanted to kill you for some time. They were just tightening the hold, scaring you, in hopes that you'd lead them to him."

Beal's voice was soft. "Which is exactly what I would have done."

A moment passed. The three of them looked at one another in stunned silence. Then Sparrow turned back to Beal, fists clenched, his eyes hard and angry and, underneath it all, almost imploring.

"We've got to get to a telephone. We've got to warn him to break off contact."

Maggie was reaching over to start the car; Beal was lowering his gun, exhaling breath that had been caught in his lungs. Sparrow was turning back jerkily, anxious to get to a telephone, when everything became crazy.

All at once a car was crashing through the darkness of the road a few yards away. Its headlights were off, and only the inside lights were on. They glowed eerily. The windows were down, and there was a glint of red hair, a bony, concentrated face hunched over the blackness of metal.

Beal heard himself scream at Maggie, "Start the car!"

But already there was a strange spitting sound coming from the darkness. Glass shattered, loud, piercing. Again there was a *pfft,* and the shattering sound tore at their ears.

Suddenly there was blood everywhere. Beal was screaming. Maggie was screaming. The heat was tremendous, and it was tinged with the smell of humanity and pain. Sparrow was slumped forward, silent, unmoving.

The other car hurtled out of the darkness, spitting silenced bullets, then thundering past and screeching around the hairpin turn into the black of the night. There was a loud shrieking sound as the car's brakes tore at the road; then, in mechanical fits and starts, it began turning around to come back.

Beal screamed, "Start the car!"

Maggie was pressed against the door, staring wildly at Sparrow and the thick red blood pulsing from his face.

Beal jumped up from the back seat and began making a roll into the front. Suddenly Maggie came to life. She jerked her eyes from Sparrow, tore at the ignition key, and started the engine.

The car roared to life. Everything lurched, and Beal fell forward. As he was sent hurtling into the front seat, he could feel the terrible softness of Sparrow under him and the sickening warmth of Sparrow's blood.

Maggie jabbed at the gas pedal, bursting through the tall grass toward the thin ribbon of mountain road. The fits and starts of the other car had stopped, and it was hiding in the darkness.

Maggie screeched onto the road. As they hit the narrow pavement, the car skidded wildly, tires screaming. The dark chasm of the valley loomed up, then receded as they shimmied over the road.

"No brakes!" Beal yelled.

The car was skidding crazily.

"Maggie, listen to me," Beal screamed. "Take your foot off the brake."

"I can't," Maggie screamed back. But slowly she did take her foot off the brake and the car righted itself. She stepped on the gas. And the winding road began before her, a hole of twisting blackness, blazing at the center from her headlights.

There was a roar, and suddenly the other car started

to move. The spitting sound of a bullet split the night. It ripped at the bumper.

Maggie pressed tighter to the gas pedal. She was just barely aware of Beal and Sparrow next to her. She tried to concentrate on the curving road ahead, but her ears were filled with the sounds of the car behind them and the terrible crack of another bullet as it ricocheted off chrome.

The curves twisted violently. Below, the lights of the valley were very far away, glittering dangerously. Instinctively Maggie's foot lifted from the gas for the brake pedal.

The lights of the valley loomed up, then immediately receded. The car wove the width of the road. There was a terrible screech, and once again the car started shimmying back and forth.

"Don't use the brakes!" Beal screamed.

Maggie lifted her foot from the brake. "You know I can't drive," she said desperately.

Beal pulled himself from Sparrow, pushing him away and toward the door. Sparrow's eyes were wide open, horrified and frozen, and there was a small hole in his hairline where thick blood pulsed in a heavy stream. Beal turned away quickly. He felt as if he were going to be sick.

The other car was still running without lights, less than a hundred feet back. There was a head sticking out the passenger window. Above the metallic shadow of an automatic was the luminous glint of red hair.

The road straightened, and Maggie stepped on the gas. The car behind them screeched loudly as it tore around the last curve; then, just as it was straightening out, the driver hit the brights.

Light flooded their car, bouncing off metal and glass in glaring streaks.

Maggie screamed, "I can't see!"

"Blink your eyes!"

"I can't! I can't!"

"The curves are going to start again, baby. Now be ready for them."

"No! I can't!"

Beal reached toward the steering wheel. "Okay, okay, you want me to take over?"

But already the curves were starting, and Maggie was taking them, her breath leaving her lips in a thin whine. The car behind was also beginning the curves, and the blinding light of its headlights reeled across the darkness.

"Good girl," Beal said. "You're doing great."

Maggie didn't answer. Her eyes were wide and frightened, and she was holding the steering wheel so tightly her hands were white.

All at once there was a choked sound. Sparrow was moving. "My God!" Beal whispered. "Sparrow's alive!" Beal reached over and touched his hand. "Don't worry. We'll get you to a hospital."

There was a terrible choked laugh, then Sparrow's tortured voice. "He tells me I shouldn't worry," Sparrow gasped, and then shuddered violently. His eyes became frenzied, like those of a hunted animal. "Must call," he hissed. Then stopped. Again a gasp, full of horror and pain, but no words.

"Not now," Beal answered. He could feel the wet warmth of Sparrow's blood oozing across his hand, and he wanted more than anything to scream. Sparrow's head was almost touching Beal's shoulder, and it felt frail and brittle, lifeless, like the branch of a tree.

There was a horrible rattling sound; then Sparrow gasped out, "Five-five-five." He stopped, gathering strength. "Four-nine-nine-eight." His lips clicked dry and thick. "Then hang up . . ." His voice trailed off.

Beal twisted back to the rear window. The other car was right behind them, screeching crazily. Again there was a hissing, and the back window shattered explosively.

"They're trying to kill us, Beal!" Maggie's voice sounded like a cry. "You said they weren't, but they're trying to kill us."

"I just don't know anymore," Beal answered. His voice was choked off and very far away.

Sparrow's eyes were closed tight with pain, and his face was twisted into a tight mask. Beal could almost feel Sparrow's jaw tightening against death, trying to postpone the inevitable for a moment of speech. His mouth was moving, and Beal could see he wanted to speak but couldn't. The pain must have been intense, the effort almost inhuman, and Beal knew how much Jed's safety must have meant to the little man who pretended friendship was no more than a convenience.

Sparrow opened his eyes again, and they were shiny with terror. He wasn't going to be able to continue. He was on the edge of silence, and he couldn't come back.

Beal held Sparrow's shoulder tightly, almost as if he were trying to press life back into him. He was no longer feeling the slick, warm blood oozing; all he could feel was Sparrow's urgency. "Sparrow," he called, "tell me. Then what do I do?"

Sparrow's eyelids moved; his mouth hung open. Then slowly he closed it and formed the numbers silently.

"Five-five-five?" Beal asked.

Sparrow tried to nod; then once again his mouth was moving.

"Four-nine-eight-eight? Just like the first number, only the third digit is changed?"

Sparrow didn't nod, but Beal could see his face relaxing, and he knew he was right. He repeated the numbers to himself frantically. It all seemed so easy in the movies.

The black, twisting road ahead jerked to the right. Maggie took the curve fast, tires shrieking. "What's going on?" she asked through clenched teeth.

"Nothing. Just keep up what you're doing. The houses are going to start again real soon. See the lights? They won't try anything after that."

"Is he dead?" Maggie's voice was chilled.

Beal didn't get a chance to answer. The car behind them must have seen the lights, too, because it was pressing forward, and there was the muffled hissing of a bullet and the sound of metal being hit.

Another bullet and glass shattered. The back window collapsed into tiny pieces, spraying the back seat. Evening air rushed in, hot and heavy.

Maggie moaned, and Beal could see she was biting her bottom lip brutally. She hadn't slowed, and she was still taking the hairpin curves down toward the houses too fast.

"Please," Sparrow whispered. He clutched Beal's arm.

"Don't talk. I promise I'll call."

But Sparrow was still looking around wildly and

clutching tightly to Beal's arm. He was forcing himself to speak. There was a windy hissing of air, and Sparrow's eyes were cut with pain and the need to talk. Finally he whispered, "Roger."

Beal turned to him quickly. "Is he one of the men you work with?"

Again the hissing, and the lips began to work. "Who will care for Roger?"

Sparrow's hand tightened on Beal's arm. His eyes were bereft. Then slowly the pain and the fear started to slip from his eyes until only the question was left, and then that, too, was gone.

The tightly packed houses of the valley began and, with them, the light, in soft little pools on the road. The bright headlights behind them suddenly drifted back, and almost immediately they were gone. There was a cross street down below, and traffic glittered on it.

"They're gone," Beal said after a moment.

Maggie didn't answer. She was still sitting forward in her seat, her eyes staring and frenzied, as if she couldn't make herself understand they were no longer in danger.

Beal reached over and touched her shoulder, but it was like stone under his hand.

"He's dead, isn't he?" she asked tonelessly.

"Yes," Beal answered. "Head to Ventura Boulevard. I'd better get to a phone."

Maggie nodded. The strain made her face glitter white in the night lights.

"Do you want me to drive now?"

"I'm fine," Maggie answered mechanically.

The rigidity was beginning to leave Maggie's face, though just under the surface was the panic. And Beal began to realize how close she was to shattering, like the fragmented glass that lay all over the back seat of the car. "There's a gas station just ahead," Beal said, and he could hear his voice shuddering. Then almost to himself he whispered, "Sparrow was right about one thing. There's no such thing as friendship, at least in his business. I caught a glimpse of one of the men in that car. It was Albert, the man who worked for him."

"Is that what he meant when he was talking about Roger?"

"I don't know. I never heard that name mentioned before."

Again the panic crept into Maggie's voice. "What if it's someone important?"

"I think it was someone important. But not to us, to him. Probably a relative or something. I suppose he must have had a wife or kids or parents. As much as he tried to hide it, Sparrow was a human being."

Maggie winced, keeping her eyes away from the bloody figure on the other side of the car.

Beal, too, turned away. He couldn't bear to look at Sparrow. Looking into his eyes those last few minutes, Beal had felt deeply the little man's humanity. He'd never seen the world so clearly before. They were all human beings, every one of them. It came as a sharp, hopeless flash, a vision of terrible loneliness.

Maggie felt shrunken. Though her eyes were fixed on Beal standing in a phone booth on Ventura Boulevard, in her mind she could see the shadow of Sparrow next to her, and she could almost feel the sickening warmth of his shed blood.

The lights of the traffic washed across the windshield, catching at the metal and glass. Warm gas-smelling air was gently moving through the car. Maggie could see Beal dialing a number, waiting a moment, then hanging up. It was all from another world. Everything seemed separate and apart, except for the chill that was deep inside her.

Once again Beal dialed a number, and she could see this time he was talking to someone. The chill grew, spreading through her body in waves. She could feel that she was shivering, but she couldn't move anymore. She remembered dully that there was an unopened pack of cigarettes in her purse. But she didn't even want to smoke.

Finally Beal finished talking and hung up the phone. As he was getting back into the car, Maggie felt a silent scream rising inside her. "What did he say?" she asked. Her voice was almost a whisper.

Beal didn't answer. His eyes were shifted away, but the dark shadows and almost blind look of fear were unmistakable. Deep lines cut his forehead and pinched at his mouth.

"He's broken contact, hasn't he?" Maggie grabbed Beal's arm desperately, digging her fingernails deep into him.

Beal didn't move. He didn't even seem to feel the pain.

Maggie was shivering. "Sparrow is dead. The man who was protecting us has broken contact. And we're all alone."

Beal didn't answer for a long while. He tried for a reassuring smile, but his lips were cold, and he couldn't make them work. He touched the hand that held him and tried to probe Maggie's eyes. But all he saw was panic. "We'll be okay," he said. "We've made it so far, haven't we?"

"We're all alone," Maggie repeated. "Don't you see? It's all part of the plan. They're going to kill off everything around us until there isn't any more protection, until there's nowhere to hide. They got to your father. They got to Sparrow . . ." Her voice choked off.

"Maggie, listen, you heard what Sparrow said. They aren't trying to kill us. You heard that."

Maggie was smiling, but it was a ghastly white smile, like a shrunken head. "You know that's not true. You know what they're doing. They're trying to push us into leading them to the man who was protecting us. But we aren't going to lead them there, are we?"

"No, of course, we won't."

"So they'll just have to push us harder, won't they?" Again the white smile.

Beal sighed, rubbing his forehead with his hand as if he could wipe away the hopelessness. "I'm afraid they've run out of cards. They've pushed us as far as they can."

"No, Beal. They have one more card. They could kill him." Her voice was barely audible. "They could kill Jason."

Beal's head jerked up, but already Maggie's hand was at the door, and she was pushing it open violently.

Beal lunged for her, but she was out of the car, rushing toward the street and the bright, streaking traffic.

She looked back frantically. She was alone. And with the cloud of loneliness, the overpowering need to see Jason redoubled. It came from deep inside her, burning, unreasoning to the point of insanity. She had to see Jason. She had to touch him; she had to reassure herself that he was all right. And also she knew she needed him to reassure her that she, too, was going to survive.

Beal was out of the car and running toward her. There was a moment of indecision; then Maggie turned quickly and rushed into the darkness.

Chapter Forty

Two calls came through at the same moment. Harry Langdon was in the Jacuzzi of his Beverly Hills split-level, sipping a gin and tonic and trying to work the day's anxiety out of his large hairy shoulders. The first call was from his best brassiere cutter, telling him he wouldn't be in the next day. Ordinarily Harry would have raked him over the coals. But tonight he didn't have time, since the second call was from Richards.

Richards's voice was polite and efficient. "They were at a phone booth in the valley. Then suddenly she bolted. He ran after, but he didn't catch her. She managed to get a ride with a large lorry. One of my men tried to follow, but he got cut off."

"You mean she rode off in a truck? Damn you! That could've been the break we've waited for."

Richards stayed calm. "I wouldn't be surprised."

Harry pounded his fist against the hot tiles of the Jacuzzi. "I'm imagining all this. You aren't telling me you lost track of them again. Even the goddamn spiks at my factory wouldn't dare bring me news like that."

Richards kept his voice controlled, but there was a tightness at the back of his throat. "I've been following the two of them for some time now. You begin to know people when you follow them. I reckon we'll find her where she's hiding the child."

This stopped Harry. He clutched the phone tightly. "The kid, huh? You think she'll go for the kid?"

"Maternal instinct."

Harry's voice lightened, and he could feel the tension disappearing from his shoulders. "Yeah. Maybe. Maternal instinct. Very dangerous."

Richards was silent. He doubted the voice on the other end of the phone knew much about maternal instinct. He himself didn't, and he had eight children.

"Naturally he'll follow her," Richards said at last.

"That would be a very stupid thing to do."

"As I said, you begin to know people. I suggest we send all cars to the friend's house immediately."

Harry imitated his accent nastily. "I suggest that would be putting all our eggs in one basket."

Richards cleared his throat but said nothing. And Harry slid down deep into the Jacuzzi, allowing the hot, swirling water to work the kinks out of his neck. He hated to admit that Richards could be right. On the other hand, the pressure he was getting from Fuller was becoming intense.

After enough time to save face, Harry grunted, "Yeah, all right. But wait for me. I'm coming myself."

Harry hung up abruptly; then, smiling angrily, he emerged from the hot, undulating water like a great steaming whale.

Chapter Forty-one

It was dark. Long shadows cast by the dry, rattling palm trees cut the residential street like slats from a venetian blind.

Beal dimmed the headlights of his car and slid over to the curb. Down the block was the small house where Jason was staying. By now Maggie was probably there, too, holding her little boy in her arms, rocking him softly. Or perhaps she hadn't made it that far. Perhaps she'd been picked up already.

Beal didn't get out of the car. He waited, watching the dark street ahead for any sign of movement. It was only logical that they were waiting there, knowing that the tighter they drew the rope, the better were the chances of Maggie's doing exactly what she'd done. Walking to that house down the street was as close to suicide as Beal could imagine. If he had any sense at all, he'd start up the car and leave as quickly as he could.

A few cars slid by, several back doors slammed, the clatter of pots and pans came from the little lighted windows of kitchens, and there were the sounds of hundreds of televisions passing the night away. Separate noises, sounds of another existence, a lifetime away. Beal felt as if he were living in another world.

Still, he didn't move. The thought of Maggie, alone and vulnerable, tore through him. It was her innocence, her basic trust. At least if you knew the world was a dangerous place, you had a chance. But Maggie still wanted to believe that the world was good and fair and other fairy tales her mother had read her with that soft southern drawl from her chintz-covered bedroom. It didn't matter that over the past few years Maggie had seen this wasn't true. Deep down she still believed what she'd learned as a child with an unshakable faith that was both touching and at the same time dangerous.

Beal opened the car door and threw the safety catch on his gun. The street was a tunnel of darkness with splashes of liquid light pooling around the lampposts. Beal started down the street, his eyes rooting in the shadows, alert for any signs of movement, terrified of being alone, yet crowding out all thought, terrified for Maggie.

They picked him up before he even reached the house.

Ten men stood outside a one-room cabin, set far back in the empty ranchlands of Topanga Canyon, surrounded by mountains, grazing land, fences, horses, and cattle, remnants of a past that was all but obliterated by the Los Angeles sprawl. Above, the sky was a wash of stars, and there was the heavy smell of manure and sweet grass in the air.

The men stood looking up at the night sky, smoking cigarettes and talking. One of the men was very large and hairy with small eyes that held a faintly amused look. He said something, and there was a leering laugh from the others as they glanced back at the lighted window of the cabin. Finally everyone except the large man stomped out his cigarette, slipped into his car, and pulled away.

Harry stood watching the stars for a moment longer; then he, too, damped his cigarette and headed inside.

The cabin was Spartan inside, just a few pieces of rough wood furniture, devoid of either charm or comfort. Richards was sitting hunched on a rumpled single bed in the corner. He held a gun loosely in his hands, and his wide green eyes were staring at the floor. He looked like one of those little lemurs, first of the primates, sitting on its perch at the zoo.

Beal was crouched next to Maggie on the floor, two figures huddled together as if from the cold. They were silent, dull hopelessness muffling all thought and feeling.

Beal didn't know how long they'd been there. It could have been five hours; it could have been only a few minutes. It made no difference. Nothing made any difference anymore. They were there, that was all.

From the moment Richards had pushed Beal into the car, then shoved into gear, Beal had known there was nothing he could do. He supposed the fact that they hadn't blindfolded him made him sense the truth. But he would have known it anyway.

Beal felt a shiver go through Maggie as Harry walked through the door and slammed it. He reached over and put his arm around her small shoulders. But Maggie didn't look up. She didn't even seem to feel his arm, as if acknowledging his presence were too painful. Perhaps she knew it was better to remain separate, pulled away from one another in their bodies as they were in their minds.

Harry didn't look at them as he walked to the single bed and joined Richards, but there was a half smile on his lips, and his eyes were sparkling with faint amusement.

Harry began to speak to Richards, and his droning voice reached across the room. Beal couldn't tell exactly what he was saying, but he could tell it had nothing to do with them. He understood what Harry was doing. The longer he didn't let on what was about to happen, the more frightened and malleable they'd become. There was only one thing worse than torture and that was the anticipation of it.

Knowing what Harry was up to didn't help. Beal felt the panic rising in him in crazy racing waves, lighting up his mind with brilliant, terrible flashes. His body felt weak and cold; his flesh trembled with the rush of his own blood.

Beal wondered briefly if Maggie understood what was happening, then looked at her small head staring down at the floor and knew that it didn't matter. The outcome was the same.

Harry stood abruptly. "Sorry to break up this little reunion." He began walking to them slowly. For the first time Beal realized he had a chain in his hand.

Richards, too, was up, holding his gun. Harry glanced back at him, then said, "Keep your gun on the two of them. I'll take the girl."

Maggie shrank back. She could smell the sickening odor of Harry's expensive aftershave. The sight of him standing only inches away tore a scream from her, and she cowered against Beal instinctively, as if she could disappear from the man who was waiting for her.

The sound of Maggie's scream ripped through Beal's hopelessness. Suddenly he was up, moving toward Harry, "Leave her alone!" he screamed.

But Harry's arm was already working. The thick steel chain in his hand jerked back violently, then snapped forward.

A white-hot flash seared Beal's face. Everything seemed to be moving and shifting. Walls, ceiling, even Harry's laughing face lurched upward. Beal rocked backward, grasping the pedestal of a large oak table.

It was some time before Beal realized he was lying on the floor. He could hear Maggie screaming. She was standing in the middle of the room, her terrified eyes locked in on Beal. But her screams sounded very far away. Everything seemed far away. Harry was leaning over him, locking the chain to the pedestal of the huge table. The other end was twisted tightly around his right ankle, holding him chained like a dog. There was just enough play for Beal to move several inches either way, just enough room to emphasize the helplessness.

Beal's face was on fire, and there was the surge of warm blood seeping down his neck. Beal didn't try to fight Harry as he clamped the lock closed and stepped back. He couldn't even get his muscles to move.

Harry turned back to Maggie, his flaccid face immobile, but his eyes sparkling with amusement. "Undress!" he demanded coldly.

"No!" Beal screamed. Suddenly there was no question of his body's moving, and he lurched forward toward Harry. The chain wrenched, and there was a loud shriek as it strained against the wood. Beal felt the chair tear at his leg as he tried to lunge forward. The table shifted slightly, then held, and the chain bit deep into his flesh.

Harry watched dully, his soft, ruddy face unmoved. Then he repeated to Maggie, "I said, undress!"

Maggie didn't move. She stood trembling in the middle of the room, her eyes wide and unseeing.

Harry merely shrugged, then walked over to her, took hold of the collar of her light summer dress and ripped down. Maggie pulled away, looking around wildly for the door. But Richards was standing in front of it, his gun poised, and already Harry was next to her tearing at the soft fabric, his meaty hands working it loose from Maggie's body greedily, though his eyes showed no more than slight interest.

"Leave her alone!" Beal screamed, his body wrenching against the chains, his hands working blindly at the lock. "She knows nothing. Can't you see she knows nothing?"

Maggie wasn't moving anymore. She stood perfectly still, submitting as Harry pulled off her dress, then tore her thin panties. Her eyes were shocked yet dull, staring straight ahead. Only the catch of breath in her throat told she was alive.

"Get over to the bed," Harry said coldly. He grasped her arm and began pulling her over there.

Maggie obeyed. Her arms were clasped around her body as if she could hide her nakedness from Harry. But it was an instinctive reaction, and inside she was feeling and thinking nothing, as if with her clothes her humanity had been stripped from her and she were no longer ashamed or angry or even frightened.

Beal screamed, "Leave her alone!"

Harry motioned to the bed. "Lie down," he grunted.

Beal was tearing at the chain, screaming. But he knew his screams were useless; everything was useless. He couldn't even die, at least not yet. Not until they had gotten the name they wanted from him; then, after that, there would be death.

Harry reached into the dresser beside the bed and pulled out three lengths of rope. Methodically he measured to make sure they were long enough; then he began to bind Maggie's arms together. She submitted, her eyes closed tightly, her face an expressionless mask. Harry tied her wrists tightly, then attached the end to the legs of the dresser. Slowly he moved to her feet and bound her ankles, attaching each end to the legs of the bed.

He stood back, looking down at the naked woman lying in front of him. Shadowy light fell across her body, etching the contours with brilliance, shading and chiseling the sinews with darkness. He didn't move for a long while. It was a pleasant sensation just watching, feeling the terror and hopelessness all around him. It occurred to him that even if Richards were not around, he probably would not rape Maggie. There was something so unclean about the terrible sweating madness, and in the end this was somehow more satisfying.

Richards was turning away. He couldn't bear to look at Harry's eyes. If he had seen lust or even anger in them, Richards could have taken it, but it was the vague amusement that he found so deeply disturbing. Richards knew that Harry had stripped Maggie because the humiliation would add to the fear, making it easier to get Beal to talk. Richards had expected something like this and was steeled against it. He supposed he'd seen worse. But deep down he recoiled from it. A person deserved at least the protection of his dignity to take with him to his death. And in the end there was something about the look in Harry's eyes that told him he hadn't seen worse. He'd seen brutality and anger, he'd seen need, but this was something totally different, and it revolted and terrified him.

Harry allowed himself to look at Maggie for a moment longer. Then he turned back to Beal. "What we're looking for here is the name of the man who's protecting you."

Beal was curled in on himself, his arms encircling his head, as if warding off a blow. "Please," he said softly. "Please leave her alone. She doesn't know his name."

"But you do," Harry returned with that dull half smile.

"No, I don't. I never found it out."

Harry shrugged. "We'll see." He turned back to Maggie and leaned toward her, testing each of the ropes, though this was done more for Beal's benefit than his own. Harry was sure he'd done a good job.

Maggie's eyes were closed tightly, and her lashes glittered with tears. She shivered as she felt Harry's hand brush against her wrists and ankles. Other than that she didn't move.

Harry stood back, watching the naked body beneath him with listless detachment. Then he was moving. His large hand clenched tightly into a fist, pulling backward abruptly. Suddenly he slammed into Maggie's stomach.

She screamed. Fiery pain spread through her body,

radiating outward in electric spasms. She tried to curl into herself, but the ropes tore at her skin. Her eyes were wide open now, and she could see the horrible blank face staring down at her, wide and white. She struggled violently, instinctively, though the ropes held her open and exposed.

Beal was watching, horrified, Maggie's agony burning into his brain. This was how they were going to try to get to him, through Maggie. More than anything Beal wanted to yell out Jed's name and be done with it. He owed him nothing. He owed nobody except Maggie anything, and she was writhing in torture on the bed. Yet he knew the minute he talked, he would be causing her death. And though the possibility of escape seemed very far away, he couldn't give up. He looked around the room frantically for something to help loosen his chains, but there was nothing. He was trapped.

Harry glanced back at Richards. "Now let him know how it feels."

Richards moved to Beal. He was no longer holding his gun in his hand. But then he didn't need to. Beal doubled into himself, pressing back as far as the chain would let him. Richards moved closer, grabbing Beal's wrists tightly. Beal forced his leg up, trying desperately to connect with his foot, but Richards was keeping well away, high over the top of his body, pressing Beal back and down to the floor, forcing him apart.

Richards grunted. His face was tight and flushed from the exertion; his fist was a hard knot of bone and muscle, held in the air, gathering strength. Then suddenly it was crashing down.

Beal cried out in pain, his body trembling and writhing. His eyes were open, but he saw nothing, felt only the blinding pain. He didn't even hear the sound of his own scream in his ears.

Richards let go, and Beal collapsed back into himself. Richards stood back and watched Beal with surprisingly cold detachment. It had been a relief to hit Beal, as if all the anger he'd been feeling since he started the job were centered in his fist, and by his thrusting it, the pain had diminished.

Sanity began to return to Beal, and once again he could see the frightened figure on the bed. "Maggie," he said desperately, "we'll be fine if you just hold on."

The words sounded empty and foolish in his mouth. And Maggie didn't answer. She just lay there, staring up at the terrifying presence of Harry. A soft sound came from her, a moan, a cry, or perhaps something beyond that.

And then Harry was closing in on Maggie again, his fists clenched tightly. Maggie started struggling. The ropes tore at her, and she could feel the hot liquid of her own blood, but she couldn't stop herself. Her eyes were closed tight against the sight of Harry, but she could feel him moving closer, like the chill of a shadow.

The pain broke through her stomach, tearing her apart with a blinding white flash. And then the terror was gone, and only the pain remained, pounding all thought and feeling from her, leaving her nothing that was human.

Beal turned from the sight of Maggie, but her scream of agony burned through everything. And he hated himself as well as the men who tortured her. He wanted to kill blindly. He wanted to feel the shock of flesh tearing and hear the tortured screams.

Harry turned back to Beal and watched him with

384

disgust, a man seeing up close what terrified him most. There had been a time when Harry might have reacted like Beal, weak, alarmed, groveling like an animal, but all that had been burned from him on the battlefields, and he was glad of it.

Harry laughed. It was a tight, brittle laugh, devoid even of anger. Then he shifted his gaze back to Richards. "As my mother used to say, what's sauce for the goose is sauce for the gander."

Richards nodded, then clamped onto Beal's arm, tearing it away from his body. This time Beal couldn't even bring himself to fight. He was motionless. His eyes were turned away, glued to Maggie. And his ears were filled only with her screams.

Once again Richards slammed his fist into Beal's stomach. Beal shuddered back. Electric pain lit up his mind. Then he was plunged into darkness. He thought he was about to pass out, but somewhere far away he could still hear Maggie crying, and he knew that the pain was receding.

"Okay," Harry said. "Now let him watch for a while."

Maggie was still screaming, and as Harry moved back over to her, her cries became louder and more desperate. Beal closed his eyes, trying to keep his mind focused on the fact that once he told them Jed's name, they both would be killed. But Maggie's sharp cry of agony broke through everything, and he knew Harry had struck her again.

Richards was looking down at Beal dispassionately. Beal no longer seemed even human to him. His own anger and fear had replaced all that, and he wanted him to suffer. "He's not watching!" he called to Harry.

"That's all right. He's got ears," Harry answered.

There was a pause, the quiet even worse than Maggie's screams. Then once again Maggie shrieked. It choked off suddenly.

Beal opened his eyes and saw Harry leaning over Maggie. "She's blacked out, damn her!"

Harry walked quickly to a small sink on the other side of the room and filled a plastic glass with water. When he returned to the bed, he watched Maggie for a moment, then threw the water at her face.

Beal was praying that Maggie wouldn't revive, but she did, crying out and struggling, her eyes staring blindly but with more horror than Beal had ever seen in his life. She turned to Beal, trying to form words. Her mouth moved for a while, but no sound came from her lips.

"Remind him how it feels," Harry barked to Richards.

There was a strange feeling of relief as Beal saw Richards move back to him. At least the pain would keep Maggie's agony far from him. But the relief was only momentary, and then the searing pain buckled him as Richards smashed his fist into Beal's face.

There was a loud cracking and a rush of warm blood into Beal's mouth. He started to choke. The sharp edges of a tooth cut the side of his mouth. He shook convulsively, then vomited onto the floor.

Harry stood over Maggie, waiting until he had Beal's attention. "You should thank me for leaving her face alone," he said. "She's got a nice face. It'd be a shame if she had to live the rest of her life as a hag."

Beal pressed his eyes tight, telling himself over and over that if he talked there would be no rest of her life. But the words were losing their meaning.

"Okay," Harry warned. "Whatever you want."

He began moving up the bed. Maggie tried to cover her face, but her arms were torn by the ropes, and all she could do was roll back and forth. She knew it wouldn't do any good. There was nothing that would do any good. There was only the pain, blinding, terrible. She couldn't see Beal anymore. She couldn't even feel his presence. None of that mattered anymore. Not even Jason. All there was was the pain.

"Pity," Harry said to himself, though there was no pity in his voice.

Harry's fist was a thick, hard knot of ruddy flesh. He held it out, looking at it the way a botanist might regard a catalpa leaf; then suddenly he thrust it down.

There was a sharp snapping sound and a shriek of pain. Then silence.

"Jesus," Harry snapped angrily, and walked back to the sink. Again he filled the glass with water and carried it back to the bed.

Richards turned away. The anger was receding, and nausea was coming up. Beal wasn't going to talk, he could feel it now. Beal wasn't going to talk, and Harry was going to become angrier and angrier, and there was no way of knowing what he would do then, except that it would be appalling.

Beal was moaning like an injured animal, and the sound of him wrenched Richards's insides until he wanted more than anything to kill him rather than listen to that sound. It closed off his throat; it made him feel dizzy and alone and shadowed in darkness. It brought up terror, instinctive and primitive.

Harry threw water across Maggie's face, and she came to. There was blood pulsing from her nose and mouth and a large red mark across her face. Coughs racked her, and each time she coughed, blood poured more heavily from her mouth.

Harry was shaking his head. "Too bad your husband doesn't give a damn about you." His big moon face was curled into a smile. Then once again he thrust his fist into her face.

It took close to a minute for Maggie to open her eyes. They were dark and bruised with slashes of red veins in them. She stared up dully, like a sick, tortured animal.

Beal knew he could stand it no longer. At least when they killed them, it might be with a gun. Maggie was no longer crying out. Her face was covered with blood, her pale, delicate body crossed with huge red welts where Harry had beaten her. And Beal knew he would do anything to stop her pain.

Once again Harry was smashing down at Maggie, grunting angrily. There was a loud gasp and then, all at once, silence.

Harry was standing over Maggie, his still-clenched fist red from her blood. "Get over here, Richards," he barked. His voice was tense and frightened.

Beal opened his eyes. Dread was pounding heavily through his body. There was a feeling inside him, a darkness, an emptiness. And even though Harry and Richards were blocking his view, he knew Maggie was no longer moving.

A terrible howl came from Beal. Piercing. Desperate. Hopeless scream. Everything was collapsing inside him. Everything was blackness. He could see or feel nothing but the dark emptiness.

"Shut up!" Harry yelled. Beal's agonized scream was

tearing through Harry's head. He could feel the hysteria starting to pound. He was scared that the girl was dead. They'd never be able to get Beal to talk with the girl dead.

Richards was standing over Maggie, feeling her pulse, leaning toward her heart. There was almost a look of triumph in his eyes.

Harry whirled around, the sound of Beal's scream piercing his ears. "Shut up!" he yelled again, his voice shaking with fury. But Beal heard nothing except his own pain and the empty echo of darkness inside him.

"Stop him!" he hissed to Richards. Before Richards had a chance to move, Harry pushed him aside and walked to Beal. The horrifying wail was tearing his head apart. Never before had he failed, and the scream added to his own confusion and fear. He suspected Richards was laughing at him behind his back, and this infuriated him even more.

Beal was still screaming, a mindless wail of anguish and loss. There was nothing else for him but the scream and the dark. He saw Harry moving toward him as a large shadow even darker than the emptiness all around him.

The shadow moved closer, eclipsing even the darkness, and Beal could feel the horrid chill of death all around him, the stench of decay and corruption under the sickening sweetness of aftershave.

Suddenly Beal was moving, lunging forward with a frenzied scream of hate and fury. The table creaked, then rocked.

Harry stopped. But already Beal was lunging backward. The chain was tearing at his leg, ripping through his skin, but Beal was unaware of anything around him, hatred blocking out all pain and thought. Suddenly he forced his body forward powerfully.

The chain bit deep into his leg, tearing through skin. There was a burning agony and a terrible scraping sound. The chain had sliced his flesh apart, and it cracked against the bone. But still Beal thrust forward, heaving the enormous table until it tilted crazily. Then all at once it tumbled toward Harry.

Harry recoiled. But it was too late. The table glanced off his stomach, sending him sprawling to the floor.

Harry crumpled, his eyes two startled points of shock and pain. The table, carrying Beal with it, buckled, then crushed over, releasing Harry.

Beal's leg was torn, and there was the glittering white of bone. His face was contorted with agony, but he wasn't aware of any of that. Already he was clawing at Harry's chest, wrenching the gun from its holster and turning it on the fat man.

"Unchain me!" Beal hissed. It was a hoarse voice, strange and unlike his own.

Richards whirled, surprised. He could see Beal clutching the gun on Harry, his face distorted with emotions Richards couldn't even begin to imagine. His hand started to his gun, then inexplicably stopped. It was as if he were paralyzed.

"Unchain me!" Beal screamed at Harry.

Harry glanced back at Richards, his dull little eyes lit with terror. "Help me, Richards!" he yelled.

Richards didn't move. Everything seemed distant and unconnected. He could only see Harry, his eyes pleading and terrified. Richards hated his eyes. He hated everything.

Beal saw nothing. Harry was lying in front of him,

his large chest heaving with fear. "Unchain me, or I'll kill you!" Beal screamed.

"Richards!" Harry's voice cut off. He felt a shock, rocking his back, slamming him against the floor. Black coldness spread through his chest. There was a bitter smell all around him. It took several seconds for Harry to know that he was shot, and even then he didn't understand. It was just that everything seemed so cold, and he was shivering violently.

Once again Beal fired, still unaware of what he was doing, working only on instinct. Harry was cracked back, bright red pulsing from his chest, his heavy face contorted by a grimace not of pain but of shock and wonder.

Richards was unmoving. He could see Beal watching him from across the room. Chained to the table, his face scarred from the beating and fury, Beal looked like a ferocious dog. Richards was fascinated by what was happening, detached, and somewhere deep down strangely relieved.

He saw Beal lift the gun; there was a flash and the urgent hiss of a bullet. Richards heard wood splinter next to him, and he knew that the bullet had missed him. He could see Harry lying on the ground, blood seeping across the floor. His eyes were open, and his thick hands were clutching at his chest, as if he could pull the spreading pain from it.

Beal was still pointing the gun in Richards's direction, his hand shaking. He was moaning now, low, angry, like the growl of an animal, and yet Richards couldn't move.

Again Beal fired, dull, burning hatred pushing him. Richards recoiled. Suddenly there was red spreading

391

from his groin, and he was screaming. He hunched over, clutching at himself, his face tight with agony.

Another shot, tearing at Richards's head. He jerked backward and crumpled to his knees. His face was a mass of blood, pulsing in thick liquid waves. He was howling, clutching at his groin; blood coursed down his neck, and his pants were a bright, slippery red. He had never felt such intense pain. It wasn't anything like what they said. It was so much worse. The howl choked off. Richards was still on his knees, lurching; then he slipped to the floor and silence.

Harry's eyes were wide open and staring. He could see Richards only a few feet away, his gun still in his holster. It wouldn't take long to crawl over there and grab his gun. It wouldn't take long, yet Harry knew for him it might take forever. He tried to lurch up, but the dull coldness had become a fire in his chest.

Beal was watching him. "Unchain me," he hissed.

Harry's body shuddered from the effort, arms shaking, legs trembling and liquid. Slowly he pulled himself up and began clawing at the ground. He had to stall for time. Maybe he could still get the drop on Beal. All he had to do was hold it together a little longer. But there was a voice laughing from somewhere. It was a familiar voice, jeering and complacent. He stopped, trying to remember where he'd heard it.

"The key." Beal's angry voice sliced the quiet.

Harry's hand went to his pocket. That's right, he told himself. He was going to stall for time; then, when Beal was busy unfastening his chain, he could make his move.

Harry's hands were cold, and his fingers wouldn't work. It seemed to take hours for him to reach his jacket pocket and fumble for the key. Harry stopped. Somewhere nearby that voice was laughing at him again. Slowly he reached to his other pocket, but the pain made everything shake inside him, and even when he found the key, it kept slipping through his fingers.

Beal watched coldly as Harry held out the key with shaking fingers. Harry was whimpering to himself, his little empty eyes desperate; huge drops of sweat stood out on his thick moon face.

Beal fired. Harry was thrown back, his hands clawing at the air, his eyes widening with shock. A hissing sound came from his lips, and his eyes opened even wider, as if he were seeing something more terrible than could be imagined. And then everything stopped, and all there was was blackness.

Beal didn't move for a long while. Harry was next to him. His arm had splayed out and was touching Beal's leg, the muscles contracting in their death dance. Richards lay in the center of the room, a heap of clothing; a long stream of blood crept along the floorboards.

Quickly Beal reached over for the key that lay next to Harry. His hands were trembling, and it took a long while before he was able to fit it into the lock and snap it free.

Beal pulled himself up. His leg was a screaming agony; his body felt empty. He could barely bring himself to his feet, and when he did, he almost fell down again. Beal grabbed at the table, clutching it tightly. Then slowly, holding onto pieces of furniture, he staggered to the bed.

Her body looked unreal. For a moment Beal wondered if everything were a dream. Maggie's face had been torn apart by Harry's fist; her body, streaked with brutal red marks. It was someone else lying in front of him. It had to be someone else.

Beal reached over and ripped the ropes from Maggie's wrists. There was warmth in her wrists, and as she was released, her arms fell back, rocking her body with the movement. Then everything went limp and lifeless, and she was still. Beal tore at the ropes that bound her legs, and once again, the movement and the stillness.

Beal clutched at her tortured body, leaning toward her heart, his hand grabbing at her wrist, feeling for a pulse.

Maggie was motionless, her savaged face staring and frozen, her battered body limp and inhuman. The room was silent. Only the gentle creaking of the table as it settled into position on the floor broke the quiet. And then, through the echoing stillness, Beal heard the trace of a sound. Urgently he pressed himself closer to Maggie's chest, his hand holding tight to her wrist. From far away, feeble yet perceptible, came the sound of life.

Beal grabbed Maggie up in his arms, a howl of joy and agony deep inside him. But Maggie remained motionless, her tormented body torn apart and useless, her face unrecognizable. And Beal realized that, though Maggie was still alive, there was little chance that she would recover.

Suddenly the phone rang. The sound was as if from another world, a world of sanity and logic, and it stunned Beal. He stood where he was, holding Maggie, confused and unsure.

Again the phone rang, sharp, piercing, and Beal jerked back to reality. He had to know who was on that phone. Hatred was burning inside him, brutal, insistent. Until there was nothing else for him but the hatred and the need for revenge.

Quickly Beal put Maggie back on the bed and stumbled across the room. He lifted the receiver but said nothing, waiting cautiously, silently, like a cat.

Fuller's voice was gruff and edgy. "Harry? Why the hell didn't you call me?"

Beal lowered his voice. "I was just about to—" Beal stopped. His heart was beating crazily, and the words sounded empty and scared.

Fuller didn't seem to notice. He had an anxiety of his own. "You were supposed to call me ten minutes ago, I was getting worried."

Beal remained silent, listening intently to the voice on the other end of the phone. He had to remember the sound of the man's voice. That voice held a clue to all his pain and suffering. That voice held a clue to Maggie's torment. If it belonged to someone important, he would find out who. He didn't care how long it took.

"What's going on?" Fuller was becoming tense and urgent.

"Nothing, I told you . . ."

"Jesus, shit, this isn't Harry! Who is this?"

Beal didn't answer. He just stood rigid, listening to the tones of the man's voice, letting them burn into his mind forever.

"I asked who is this!" Fuller was yelling. Then there was a fumbling sound, and a second later the phone went dead.

Beal replaced the receiver, then quickly scanned the room. Whoever that was, he would now know that something had gone wrong. Soon he would send someone to check up on the cabin. He was probably calling right now.

Beal left Maggie on the bed and went to the sink. They must not know that Maggie was injured. Once they knew that, they would check all the hospitals; once they knew that, they would be able to get to Maggie. He must make it look as if they both had escaped unharmed. Beal dampened a rag and rushed back to the bed, cleaning up the blood from the floor with frenzied strokes.

Just above him Maggie lay motionless. There was nothing about her that seemed alive. Beal ignored the doubt that pounded through him and finished cleaning. Then he gathered up Maggie's clothes and gently lifted her into his arms. He didn't lean toward her heart or touch his hand to her wrist. He dreaded the thought that the sound he'd heard before was only his own blood rushing through his body. If Maggie were dead, he couldn't bear to know.

Beal limped painfully to the doorway. The moon was high, and the ground was streaked with silvery light. There was the sound of an approaching car, and suddenly headlights veered across the sky. A car started down the private road to the cabin, bumping and skidding on the gravel. But Beal didn't wait any longer. Silently he slipped out the doorway and disappeared into the darkness.

Chapter Forty-two

The room was dark; only a thin line of light filtered under the door. From down the hall he could hear several of the Dobermans barking and racing around their cage. He supposed they were being fed.

His lunch would be ready now, too. A steak, salad, perhaps a baked potato. Hunger was rising in his stomach; still, he didn't move. He remained slouched in his chair, cloaked in darkness. He was thinking.

Robert Lacey had learned to love his own mind. At first the self-imposed isolation and the solitude had almost driven him crazy. He had thought of his wife, his friends, every aspect of his life constantly, dwelling on mistakes and pleasures, turning them over and over in his mind, feeling the jagged contours.

He laughed as he remembered himself then. The Lacey who had sneaked into the bunker deep in the California mountains, terrified of the rumors that were threatening to surface at any moment, had been a distracted man, unfocused, a man of the world. Slowly, painfully, he had shed that Lacey like a snake its skin, and the Lacey of today was clear and sharp, a man of purpose. The isolation had burned him clean. The isolation had changed him.

He even looked different. Though he worked out every day, ate sparingly but well, his once-strong body had become stooped and thin. Flaccid skin hung from his bones. He supposed it was partially because he'd suffered for close to six months from the aftereffects of radiation. He supposed it was due to the isolation. Lacey hardly went outside anymore, and after having been spotted outside his bunker in the mountains, he'd become almost terrified of the open air. His already pale skin was now horrifyingly white. At first he'd tried a sunlamp, but that only gave him a masklike look. It hardly mattered. Lacey saw very few people anyway.

It occurred to him how long it had been since he'd asked for a woman to be smuggled in. The last time he had, he'd found himself becoming extremely violent, too violent. The thread of sanity had come dangerously close to snapping and Lacey felt that murder was not just possible but perhaps inevitable. He stopped just in time. The woman had been returned to the world far richer than she'd left, and there'd been no repercussions. Still, it served as a warning. He couldn't afford any mistakes now that he was so close.

Long ago he figured out his sudden enjoyment of violence. It was all connected to that stupid Delano girl in Chicago. Though she was long dead, the anger in him wasn't. If President Lacey hadn't "died" when he had, the rumors would have killed him. The girl had

.almost ruined his life forever. Now it gave him pleasure to ruin hers, *in absentia*.

Lacey felt himself hardening at the thought, and his hand moved toward the intercom. Perhaps he should get a girl. He stopped himself. The convention had started. The end was only a few days away. After that he could do as he pleased. Now he must be cautious.

Slowly his hand shifted to his genitals, and a heat swelled through his body. The throbbing grew, as in his mind a faceless woman lay nearby in the darkness. He imagined her red-smeared, silly mouth opening with fear. He imagined glittering machines of enormous proportions surrounding the woman. And him in the shadows watching.

Then he stopped, allowing the image to sink back into the darkness. These things had to be done slowly. He wanted to think quietly now. He wanted the image to lie there in the darkness, a future pleasure, while he spent some time with himself in the companionship of his own mind.

Lacey reached into a desk drawer, pulled out a bottle of Scotch, and poured himself a stiff one. He sipped it slowly but with little pleasure. It was strange how being alone changed a man, how what was once pleasure became mundane, how what was once mundane suddenly became pleasure. It had been years since he'd felt anything like the grief and torture of life. He remembered the stabbing pain of learning that his son had been killed in an auto accident. Breath had stopped. Life had stopped. He remembered the torture when he realized that everything he'd worked toward was going to be ended and he was going to be blackmailed by that Delano woman forever. Living was harsh, sharp, cruel. Living was mindless. No wonder government was corrupt and weak, the world debased and limited. The world wore a man down. It was only when a person lost his stake in living that he was equipped to be alive.

Lacey smiled to himself. The past five years had purged him, burning him clean of everything, including the ridiculous vacillations that men called considerations. There were no such things as considerations. There was only power. And though by necessity his power was secret, known only to the Trust, it was no less important for it.

Lacey enjoyed reading the newspapers with their childish speculations as to why the country was going sour. It gave him a surge to watch as the whole of America was sent plunging toward a disaster that only he could avert.

But he couldn't talk to anyone about that. Only Nadler knew most of his plans. He was glad that the State of Emergency Plan was up to Nadler. Nadler was solid. The rest of the Trust suspected, of course. Fuller in particular was becoming a problem. But it didn't matter. They'd all go along with it in the end. They were in too deeply to do anything else. They had helped him plan his assassination; they had helped him set up his invisible power structure, though at the time its purpose had been somewhat different. They'd made their own beds.

It seemed strange when he thought of the progression of events. He had been so naïve. They all had been so naïve. And so scared.

Lacey didn't remember who had suggested the hologram first, but he remembered how foolish the idea had seemed.

Then the whispers and rumors about the Delanos had become worse, and Lacey knew he was very close to being ruined, probably even jailed for life. It hadn't seemed fair. He was the best American president of the century, and he was going to be condemned to ignominy because of one stupid mistake.

Again the idea of a false assassination had been brought up. This time it sounded less crazy. A hologram had been settled on. As dangerous as the plan was, it was less risky than using a double, a bulletproof vest, or blanks in Foyle's gun. Accountability. If things went wrong, Lacey could plead innocence of the whole thing. He could be shocked and horrified at what was undoubtedly a cruel prank.

But nothing had gone wrong. President Lacey had "died" that night, his reputation and good work intact.

The first meeting of the Trust had taken place three months later. It had all seemed so sound. Five men who were high up in the power structure, presided over by a man who was no longer a part of the world and its intense pleasures and pains. The Trust, a body of powerful and judicious men to help the country toward sanity.

Lacey had known all along that industry had a stranglehold on the government of America. In fact, it could be said that industry ruled the careers of most of the major figures in the country, using their vast money resources to finance campaigns, stymie opposition, and even control the media when necessary. One of his first acts as President had been to authorize Jed McKuen to

401

start a secret investigation of government payoffs. And the information he'd gathered had been staggering.

Though Lacey would never have planned things that way, his "death" gave him an excellent opportunity to change all that. He'd had the information in the McKuen report duplicated, then stored in the computer in the bunker. It would be through that information that Lacey and the rest of the Trust would rule. Blackmail was a corruption, of course. But, Lacey had reasoned, it was a necessary corruption. What they were fighting was far worse.

General Nadler had organized the messengers; Senator Fuller, with the aid of Harry Langdon, the network of men who were to protect the Trust, should protection become necessary. The private planes had been hired, a large helicopter bought, the bunker built and equipped, thanks to Colton's money. And that first meeting had been full of anticipation and hope.

In the end the Trust was a failure. The whole system worked against it. And though Lacey had always considered himself sophisticated politically, it was only then that he truly understood how deeply corruption went into the center of government. He should have realized it before. It was only logical. A senator from Texas who voted against the oil interests or a legislator from Michigan who disregarded the concerns of the auto industry found his funds quickly diminishing. Savaged in the press, unable to finance the necessary television time, rarely asked to speak at important meetings, a man who complied, quickly lost the power he had. And almost immediately a new man would miraculously appear, a man with all the financing and support the legislator had so foolishly rejected.

At first Lacey had burned with cynicism and doubt. What had started out as an unselfish, idealistic plan to help the country seemed childish, weak, the work of simpletons. Eventually Lacey realized it was impossible to fight the corruption of America with the simple and feeble tools that the Trust had at hand. Only major surgery could cure it.

That was when the State of Emergency Plan had come into his mind. America needed a shock, a jolt that would shake the country to its very foundations. Then, with a strong and total grip on the government and the people, a new order could be imposed.

Once Lacey realized this, it amazed him how easily the whole thing could be arranged. America was vulnerable to a shock on many fronts. Economically the country had been steadily weakening for decades. Anyone who read the newspaper knew that something as simple as a well-executed evacuation of funds could crumple the nation's economy. Something pretty close to that had been tried already by the Arabs. It served as a warning, a warning which absolutely no one heeded. Racially the country was extremely vulnerable. Once again there had been a great deal of warning, also unheeded. And while there might be a peace at present, it was less a peace than an armed truce. Lacey knew that primitive and deep inside man was always the fear of someone different. Hitler had known. All through the ages leaders had known.

Unfortunately the problem with either of these courses was that they would work too well. The country could so easily be plunged into chaos that it was unlikely it would recover for a long while.

There was one other course of action that could be

taken, and that was political assassination. It was quick, sure, and only temporarily debilitating.

It had been a mistake to have Nadler bring this up at the meeting of the Trust, and Lacey had felt that immediately. Colton had protested, as had Fuller. Paisley was holding to the fence, watching cautiously as the tension mounted in the room. And while Keiler had seemed to be on Lacey and Nadler's side, they both were aware that, once outside that room, he could be convinced to go the other way.

It had been a nonverbal communication. Lacey had simply lit a cigar and stared out into space coldly. But Nadler had understood.

After that the meetings had been private, just between the two of them. The State of Emergency Plan was to go into effect. But the rest of the Trust was to be kept in the dark.

It would be simple. At exactly 8:00 P.M., closing night of the convention, at precisely the same moment the President, Vice President, and Speaker of the House would be killed.

That would leave Fuller, the president pro tem of the Senate, as the new President of the United States. It would be Fuller who would declare the state of emergency. No one would balk at it. The killing of the three top officials of the American government would necessitate it. And that was where Nadler would come in. He would make sure the rest of it would go like clockwork. After an appropriate amount of time had passed, Fuller would be persuaded to make the startling announcement that Robert M. Lacey had not died on that night in Los Angeles. He'd been badly wounded and presumed to be incapacitated for life. But a miracle had occurred, and slowly, painfully, Lacey had recovered. Later he'd elected to remain in hiding rather than disrupt the country.

After that Fuller would appoint Lacey Vice President and, in an act of self-sacrifice, step down. Lacey would then be in place. Clean, neat, effective. And if Fuller balked, Nadler would be around to change his mind. But Lacey knew that Fuller wouldn't balk; he'd go along by choice. He always had.

Lacey finished off his drink and felt the warmth of the whiskey rising in his body. Again his hand moved to his genitals, and he stroked himself, his mind alight with soft flesh held tightly open by steel clamps.

He smiled tightly. The only snag in the whole plan was some little creep from Los Angeles who had stumbled onto the most explosive secret of the century. He had seen President Lacey five years after he had died. And he was on the loose with that knowledge. Yet in the end there was nothing he could do about it. In the end there was nothing anyone could do about it.

And with that thought Lacey's mind shifted from the dark, twisting future that lay ahead, and once again his hand moved to his body and the quickening heat.

Chapter Forty-three

David Burns was sitting on the patio of the Beverly Hills Hotel in a soft beam of sunlight, cracking crab and sipping a good Chablis. His Moroccan suntan was still intact; his clothes were the latest on Rodeo Drive. Nevertheless, he stood out among the crowds of eager Hollywood deal makers, hustlers, beauties, and has-beens who rush daily to the Polo Lounge of the Beverly Hills. Perhaps this was partially because he was eating alone. In a place where one went to see and be seen, eating alone implied failure. But mostly it was because of his eyes, expressionless, bored eyes, eyes that needed nothing.

At the table next to David, a young, bearded screen-writer, obviously out of work, was trying to whip up enthusiasm for his idea in a grossly outsized producer. The writer was laughing too loudly, eating too fast. How he would hate himself as he once again opened the door to his musty apartment and sat down to while away the day watching soap operas.

David sympathized with him. In effect, he was in the same position. He had learned early that there was nothing more pathetic than an out-of-work spook, constantly checking with his answering service, calling up old acquaintances on the pretext of a friendship everyone knew was impossible in their business. There was the smell of dead flesh and desperation about them. That's why he always made it a rule that he had to spend at least two hundred dollars a day when he wasn't working. New clothes, large extravagant meals; at all costs he had to keep up appearances, to himself as well as others.

David was glad he had made the effort. Deep in the shadows of the restaurant he could see Sparrow's Simon drinking at the dimly lit bar. Simon's eyes seemed to drift all around the room, lightly landing everywhere but where David sat. Coincidence or not? Simon could be on a job and therefore not want to see David, or he could be out of a job and therefore not want to see David. Or Simon could be watching him. The dark little man finished his drink quickly, threw money on the table, and left.

Within five minutes the question was answered. The maître d' placed a flamingo pink telephone on David's table as if it were a delicately cooked entrée, and all around him heads whirled in his direction, trying to figure out who he was. David smiled to himself as he lifted the receiver and received the address of a phone booth.

The call came through an hour later. David had expected to hear Sparrow's voice on the other end and was surprised when it was a younger, less ironic voice that went through the wrong number ritual.

David gave his answer, then waited. It took several seconds before the voice said, "Sparrow is dead."

David was stunned. He stood, clutching the receiver, staring out into the glaring midday light of Beverly Hills. It wasn't the idea of death that threw him. In the two years he'd been in the business he'd seen five men die, and it had affected him far less than he would have imagined. But Sparrow was a different story. He felt terribly alone standing on the sun-streaked pavement, the heavy pounding of traffic all around him.

"Are you there?" the voice asked after a while.

"Yes, sure," David answered. "Who is this?"

There was a sigh. Jed was trying to decide whether to trust David. He came to the conclusion he had no choice. "You saw Simon earlier, I assume. I'm the man who pays the bills."

"I see," David answered slowly. He, too, was trying to decide whether to trust the voice on the other end. "Why are you calling me?"

Again the hesitation with the same decision. "Sparrow had come to the conclusion that the men were no longer trying to kill Beal. Instead, they were smoking him out. Trying to get him to lead them to the man who was protecting him."

"You?"

"That's right. Me. I told Beal to break contact. But I have my doubts that he will. He sounded close to cracking."

"It would be reasonable to conclude that he is."

"Yes. He's out there all alone now. As much as he

disliked Sparrow, he relied on him. It was Sparrow who gave him courage, though I don't think he realized it."

"Sparrow was that kind of man," David answered sadly.

Jed's voice held a sadness of his own, and underneath it lurked fear. "Yes, I felt it, too. He goaded you into acting better than you would. Somehow disappointing him always seemed worse than anything."

David stared out at the baking streets. Two long-legged girls in shorts and halter tops roller-skated by. They looked about twenty years old. Only their open giggles betrayed that they were closer to fourteen.

David remained silent. He didn't want to talk about Sparrow anymore. He wanted to take it somewhere quiet; he wanted to mull it over in solitude. Finally he said, "You still haven't told me why you called me. You have Albert and Simon."

"Albert went to the other side." Jed's voice was sharp and angry; then it cracked. "Beal's been missing since yesterday evening, and Simon can't get a lead on him. Everything's falling apart. I relied on Sparrow. I left everything up to him. It was a mistake. I know that now. But that's past." He paused, then continued softly. "I know that Sparrow trusted you above the others. Can I trust you?"

It was the question of a politician, manipulative, full of flattery and dependence, yet one that gave you no chance of refusal. "What do you want me to do?" David asked finally.

"I want you to pick up Beal. It's not going to be as easy as Morocco. Even Sparrow was beginning to have trouble finding him."

"Life is a good teacher."

"Exactly." Jed paused, and this time his voice sounded deathly. "There are rumors that he was taken last night and that he and his wife escaped. He killed two men. They say the whole thing was savage, very savage. He sounded crazy before, and now—"

"Which is why you want me to pick him up immediately."

"If the others find him first, I'm afraid he'll blow everything sky-high." There was an embarrassed silence. "He knows who I am."

"That wasn't very wise."

"Sparrow warned me, but I didn't listen. I fucked up royally. But there's nothing I can do about that now."

"Except kill him."

Jed was silent, a man fighting an internal battle, a man who knew in the end what the outcome would be and hated himself for it. Then finally he answered. "Yes. Except kill him."

Chapter Forty-four

Mike Randle had to stoop low to the time clock to see the numbers. He waited impatiently, his thick glasses slipping way down his nose, while the numbers slowly crawled to five o'clock. His card was ready. He slammed it in, threw it back into the rack, and loped out into the crowds of Disneyland. He was moving quickly, seeing and hearing very little around him, his whole body concentrated on returning to his apartment, shoving some food in his mouth, then getting back down to work on his laser.

As he passed the candy shop, someone slipped from behind one of the buildings and started down the sidewalk behind him. Mike didn't notice it. His mind was racing with thoughts of the used laser he'd picked up several months before. It was fairly small as lasers went, but for him it was like going to the moon, a real breakthrough. Because this one was a pulsed laser, able to capture objects in motion, putting out as much energy in its momentary beam as an entire power station. Originally the laser had cost over $400,000. It had been sold and resold to various universities until it was no more than a pile of metal waiting to be sold for spare parts. Mike, through the aid of Sheila, a friend who worked at one of the labs, was able to relieve the university of responsibility for selling the laser by lifting it late one night. Mike had felt some guilt about that but consoled himself with the knowledge it was in the interest of science. Besides, it had taken close to three months for Mike and Sheila to get the old laser in something resembling working order, so it wasn't as if they hadn't suffered. But all that was over now. Tonight they were going to test it out.

As Mike walked through the gates, the man following him dropped back, carefully obscuring himself in the crowd. The caution was unnecessary. Mike's mind was concentrated on the sparkling beam of light he was going home to, and in fact he was only vaguely aware there was life on earth.

He had promised to delay the testing until Sheila could leave work and get over to his house. He doubted it was a promise he would keep. Nor would Sheila expect him to keep it.

In Mike's strange separate world, Sheila was about as close to a friend as he could get. She was tall and blond and attractive in a large-boned orange-juice-fed way, product of the Hollywood streets where children were allowed to roam freely, smoking grass and discovering each other, while their mothers drank away their disappointments and brought home the long string of night uncles. At eighteen there was very little Sheila hadn't tried and nothing she didn't know.

Why she remained friendly with Mike was always a mystery both to him and to her. She supposed he represented some kind of sanity to her, at least a sanity she could understand. Or maybe it was the fact that he was able to get on alone. She couldn't do anything alone. It even terrified her to spend too long in the bathroom.

But all Mike needed in life was his science, the strange sparkling light, the cold gray metal of machinery. In truth, Sheila found holograms only vaguely interesting. But hour after hour she worked by his side and listened to his plans with the patient devotion of a stray.

Mike knew Sheila was interested in more than his mind, but he chose to ignore it. She was too valuable as a friend to mess things up. Besides, Mike had never been with a woman. He found the prospect of being with one terrifying. He found the prospect of not being with one appalling. All in all, it was not a very comfortable subject for Mike, so he confined his thoughts to the subject of holography, which was always comfortable.

His Studebaker was a moldering pile of rusty metal at the far end of the parking lot. Among the shiny Chevrolets and Fords it looked like a humpbacked dinosaur, relic of another era.

Mike reached into his pocket for the keys. He came up with several gum wrappers, two batteries, a small roll of electric tape, fifty-three cents, and a good-sized roach of Acapulco Gold. He tried the other pocket, shuffling through his palm for the key impatiently.

Behind him the shadow slipped from car to car, then

stopped. There was a click, heavy, metallic. And then the shadow started forward again.

Mike was reaching into his back pocket when there was a sudden nudge at his back.

"Don't move."

Mike froze, his right hand still in his back pocket, the other in midair, filled with clutter.

"I've only got five bucks." His voice was tight and quivering. "Here, you can have everything."

Mike was moving his outstretched hand to the shadow behind him when he felt another hard shove in his back.

"I said, don't move!"

Mike stopped, terror gripping him. "What do you want?"

"Get into your car." Again the nudge, hard, urgent.

"Okay, okay, relax. I've got to move to get into the car." He paused. "So I'm going to move now."

Slowly Mike's hand came out of his back pocket, holding his keys. Without turning, he moved the key to his car door and began opening the lock.

"Quickly, damn you!"

Mike instinctively turned to the voice, then stopped, terrified, as he realized that just one quick movement might be enough to send him blasting to that great laboratory in the sky. But already he had caught a glimpse of the man behind him. The man's face was bruised and raw, but Mike recognized him immediately. "Jesus Christ!" he said, surprised. "You're the guy who stopped me before."

"That's right." Beal's voice was hoarse and very tense. "Now get into the car."

"Where are we going?"

Beal laughed. It was a hard, angry laugh, tinged with craziness. "Can you make a hologram out of films? Like newsreels?"

Shock and fear were vying for control of Mike, and it took some time before he choked out, "Only a multiplex. It's a cheap imitation of a hologram. Why?"

"How about the tapes? Do you know how to doctor tapes?"

"You've got some strange way of commissioning a project, man."

Beal's hand tightened on the gun. "Can you?" he rasped.

Mike nodded slowly. The intense face with the ripped and bruised skin was staring at him ghostlike. Deep lines cut Beal's forehead and mouth, and his eyes were circled with dark swollen flesh. It didn't seem like the face of a killer. It seemed much more the face of a victim.

"Put the gun away," Mike said soothingly. "You don't look like the type to use it."

"I have already," Beal hissed.

A look at Beal's hard, angry expression told Mike it was the truth. Quickly he turned back to the car and, with shaking hands, opened the door.

Mike's messy one-roomer seemed different to him as he opened the door and flicked on the lights. He stopped in the doorway, adjusting his glasses, his eyes darting around the piles of dirty laundry, papers and bits of old food that were scattered around the only piece of furniture in the room, a large worktable, dominated by a hunched dustcloth.

Nothing had changed. Mike supposed it was the gun

in his back which made things different. He guessed guns had a way of doing that kind of thing. In truth, Mike was a stranger to violence. He'd never even seen anything like it. And so it frightened him, but not nearly enough.

"In," Beal barked.

Mike nodded and started into the doorway. Just as he was moving across the threshold, he heard a noise. Instinctively he knew what it was and that it would be trouble.

Beal heard the noise, too. He whirled around, clutching his gun. His heart was beating frantically, and his body was tense and alert.

"Sheila, stop!" Mike yelled loudly.

But it was too late. Sheila was rounding the first-floor landing, her feet moving faster than her brain. Suddenly she saw the gun and stopped.

Beal was hunched low, his finger on the trigger, his eyes finding the sight and fixing it on her. "Get up here."

Sheila didn't move. The fear was making everything weird and murky. She knew the man with the gun was yelling at her, but she couldn't tell what he was saying.

"It's okay," Mike yelled to Beal. "She's a friend."

"I said, get up here!"

Sheila stared blankly for a moment. Slowly she mounted the stairs, holding on to the banister for support. She was shaking crazily, and her legs felt as if they wouldn't hold her up. It reminded her of the time she'd been hauled into the principal's office on LSD. Only worse. Much, much worse.

After Sheila had walked into Mike's apartment, Beal slammed the door shut and stood in front of it. His eyes were scanning the room, frantically looking for any sign of a trap. Finally he pointed his gun at the worktable. "What's under the cloth?" he barked suspiciously.

Mike walked to the table and pushed the dirty underwear and bills away, then carefully removed the cloth.

A long metal cylinder stretched four feet across the table, its gray metal gleaming in the failing evening light. It looked like a futuristic weapon, a nuclear warhead, a ray gun of enormous proportions.

"What's that?" Beal jabbed the gun in the direction of the cylinder.

"It's called a pulsed laser," Mike answered. He stopped and tried for a brave smile. "How's this? You put the gun away and then we talk."

"How's this? I don't put the gun away and you talk."

Sheila glanced at the gun and shivered. "The guy's got a point, Mike."

Beal looked over at Mike and Sheila. They were huddled together like two frightened jungle animals, tall young animals unable even to bolt. Sheila was wearing one of those long, formless peasant dresses that are always ripped at the hem from being dragged on the street. It made her look like a naughty child, and it was that which reached Beal. He lowered the gun to his side, though he still held it loosely. Slowly he walked over to a mattress shoved in the corner of the room and sat down.

He kept the gun visible, resting his hand on his knees. "Tell me about lasers."

Mike sighed, then leaned toward the sleek gray machine. He flicked a switch, and suddenly a thin shaft of dancing electric light shot through the laser to a glass screen across the room.

Beal's body shocked, but the beam had already stopped. He looked quickly from Mike to Sheila. They were merely staring at the laser. "How the hell did you do that?" Beal asked shakily.

Again Mike flicked the switch, and the blinding light shot its dancing beam across the room. Mike didn't turn from the light, though he knew its power made his already weak eyes dance with phosphorescent dots. Looking at that beam of light, he forgot the hard, intense face across the room and even the gun. Looking at that beam of light, he forgot everything but the science.

"What you're seeing is an intense beam of laser light. It lasts for only a millisecond."

"How does it work?"

"You serious?"

"Deadly."

Mike nodded solemnly. "Well, it's all based on atoms. Inside the body of the laser is a synthetic ruby, which, as you probably know, is composed of atoms. Right now those atoms are asleep. What the laser does is sort of wake them up. We call it raising the atoms to an excited state."

Mike looked up. Beal was watching him, his pale white face knotted in concentration. It was hard to tell what he was thinking. It was hard to tell if he was thinking at all. Sheila, too, was watching Mike. She looked scared, but some of the tension had gone, and he could tell she was relying on him to save her.

"All right," Mike continued. "Now, if you fire a unit of energy—we call this unit a photon—at an unexcited atom, you excite it. And if you fire a photon at an already excited atom, it emits two photons. Two for one, you see? And if you start that kind of chain in a tube with reflective ends, everything keeps bouncing back and forth, exciting new atoms. Put a little hole at one of the ends, and you let some of the energy out. That's the light you just saw. The rest returns back to the chamber to excite new atoms."

Mike's eyes darted to Beal. And again he remembered the urgent face and the gun. It was hard for Mike to remember anything when he was talking about holograms. Talking about holograms was almost as good as making them. And making them was better than anything else.

"Do you understand any of that?" Mike asked after a moment.

"I don't see how that makes a picture."

"Ah!" Mike exclaimed, and again the tight face and the gun receded and there was only the science. "Basically, to make a hologram, a ray of laser light is split in two by a beam splitter. One beam is sent directly to a photographic plate. It's called a reference beam because in essence it is telling the photographic plate what light is like without any object interfering. For example, say you wanted a hologram of me. You split the laser beam in two and send one beam directly to the plate. What you're saying is this is what it's like when Mike's not around."

"And the second beam?"

Mike was lost in the science now. He was pacing back and forth in front of the laser in huge strides, his eyes darting. "The second beam is sent to the subject. In this case that's me. Suddenly I'm bathed in laser light. And when that happens, I start reflecting all over the place. But here's the thing. The light waves I send out vary in intensity, depending on my shape and size. And when these waves are reflected back toward the holographic plate, they bump into our old friend the reference beam—in other words, light waves without Mike. This sets up an interference pattern. The holographic plate simply records the difference between these two beams. And after it's processed and then projected, you have a hologram."

Beal didn't move. As he sat on the mattress, his gun held lightly in his hands, his eyes wide and staring, the urgent anger of his face seemed to disappear, and the terrible sadness beneath came through. "But that's just one picture," Beal said after a while. "I want to know about moving holograms."

"Same principle," Mike answered excitedly. "Only that's where a pulsed laser comes in. You set it to strobe at thirty times a second, and instead of a holographic plate, you use film set to move at the same speed." Mike stopped, and a deep frown cut his face. "Of course, the complications are staggering."

"Would it be possible to make a hologram that lasted five minutes?"

"Maybe the Russians can do it. But I've never heard of one." Mike's swimming eyes turned to the ceiling. "At thirty times per second . . ." He turned back to Beal with amazing rapidity. "That would make nine thousand separate pictures."

But Beal was lost in his own thoughts. "Even at five minutes it would be cutting it close. They'd have to use the hologram for state visits, news conferences,

They could keep it short for a while, but pretty soon the press would begin to catch on."

Sheila shot a look at Mike. But Mike merely shrugged. They didn't have much choice but to go along with Beal. If he were crazy, he'd be more likely to be reasonable if they went along with his craziness. And if he weren't crazy? Somehow that seemed more frightening.

Mike turned back to Beal. "If you want me to tell you whether a hologram is possible, you're going to have to tell me what you're looking for."

Beal watched Mike in silence. Finally he nodded. "Let's say a person wanted to make a hologram of a President of the United States, for instance, and then trot it out for special occasions. Could it be done?"

Mike let out a low whistle. "Let me think about that." He paused, shaking his head. There was something about Beal's eyes, perhaps the sadness, perhaps the intensity, but all at once Mike had a feeling that Beal wasn't crazy after all. Just scared, very scared. "As I said before," he answered after a while, "there'd be staggering complications."

"Color, for one," Sheila told him.

Mike picked her up. "You bet. You could use trichromatic film, but let's face it, I don't know anyone who's been able to duplicate color perfectly."

"You said a guy at Harvard has done some good work."

"Adequate. I could do as good. And it would have to be perfect. There'd be news conferences. And newsmen are pretty damn observant." He fell silent again, thinking. "And that's just a small part of the problem. In order to display the hologram, you'd need life-size

421

film. I'm assuming the hologram would have to be kept secret, and you can't exactly hide life-size film."

Sheila interrupted. "Maybe someone came up with a magnifying lens of some kind."

"If they had, I'd know about it."

Beal interrupted. "Let's just say, these are the kind of people who can keep things secret."

Sheila looked at him cagily. "Like, say, the government of the United States?"

"For example." Beal looked away evasively.

"I guess those kinds of guys can keep anything secret if they want to," Mike said. "Okay, let's say they had this lens, probably from the Russians. All they'd have to do was project the magnified film onto a sheet of Plexiglas."

This stopped Beal. He remembered the report of a large sheet of glass behind the barrier in the Hilton ballroom, and it jarred him. "How large would the sheet of Plexiglas have to be?"

"Very large. But that would be relatively simple. You could set up the glass beforehand; the real problem would be in the shooting of the hologram. You'd have to use an incredibly powerful pulsed laser. There's no telling what the results would be bombarding a human being with that kind of power."

"Radiation poisoning?"

Sheila nodded. "Blindness, radiation poisoning, cancer, impotence, warts, piles. At the very least he'd get pretty sick."

"That's one of the reasons we can't do that kind of work in America," Mike added. "We just don't really know. Of course, in Russia they can afford to be a little more slipshod on restrictions. I mean, who's to question?"

"Mike's right," Sheila said. "The chances of something happening during and especially afterward would be too high. Hardly worth the risk."

"Yes. But my guys wouldn't care. They planned on getting rid of him afterward anyway." Beal stood up; his mind was going fast. So it was all possible. As crazy as it sounded, it was possible. They had gotten the Russians and their knowledge of holograms; then they'd shot pictures of Lacey secretly. He stopped, looking over at the large laser across the room. Finally he turned back to Mike. "How could you set it up to make a hologram without letting the subject know?"

Mike laughed. "You couldn't."

"No, listen," Beal said, "there has to be a way."

"You've seen the size of the laser and the light it puts out. It'd be like trying to hide the Empire State Building."

"Well, maybe you could trick him," Beal suggested.

"Guy'd have to be pretty dumb, man."

But Beal wasn't listening anymore. "It's impossible," he said softly. Then once again he stopped. He remembered Jed standing at the ocean, the wind ruffling his hair. "Maybe you should flip things," he had said. "See who stood to lose most by Lacey's living." Suddenly everything was turning upside down, flipping around and then coming out full and whole. All at once everything made sense. The Plexiglas at the ballroom, the barrier, the clearing of the room, the two Russians, the man in the mountains, even Dr. Greenaway's warning about the future. It had been Lacey himself Beal had seen in the mountains. He had seen the President of the United States, five years after he had been assassinated.

Beal had been sitting, staring into space, for a long while. How long he didn't know. It was as if he were living in a different world now, as if space and dimension and time no longer existed, and it was only the desperate, reckless hate that had any meaning.

"I want to use your phone," Beal said abruptly. Then, without waiting for Mike and Sheila to answer, he stood, looking around the room.

He found the phone under a pile of T-shirts and began dialing quickly, clumsily, his revolver clutched in his hand, his eyes on Mike and Sheila. It took three tries for him to get the right number, and a long time before the hospital answered.

"Good evening, L.A. Memorial." The voice was plastic cheerfulness.

"I want some information on a woman who was brought into emergency late last night."

"Name?"

Beal hesitated. "There was no name given. But she was sick, very sick. I think she was in coma or shock. The doctors will know who she is."

"Are you a relative?"

"No."

"I'm sorry. We're not allowed to release information about patients except to relatives."

"All right, yes, I'm a relative, okay? Just switch me through to emergency."

The operator's voice was mocking. "Then, if you're a relative, you must know her name."

"Look, I want to know if she's alive. For God's sake, that's all I want to know."

"I'm sorry, unless you're a relative . . ."

Beal had forgotten all about Mike and Sheila. He clutched tightly to the phone, his gun crushed against the dial. "Please, please, I've got to know. I've got to know."

Once again the voice was plastic. "I'm truly sorry. But it's hospital policy. Perhaps you'd like to come in here. Our visiting hours are between three and eight—"

Beal slammed down the receiver. His head was burning, and he couldn't breathe. He could feel Maggie was dead. He could feel it as he had with his father. Yet he knew there was a chance that she was alive. Perhaps it was better that he didn't know; perhaps it was better to keep her alive in his mind.

Suddenly Beal remembered that Mike and Sheila were in the room. He whirled around, his hand tensed on the gun. But they hadn't moved. They were still standing across the room, watching him, confused and scared.

"I want you to make me a multiplex and doctor some tapes," Beal said tightly.

Mike was watching Beal closely, those strange swimming eyes working over his face. "Why?" he asked after a while.

"Never mind. Just do as I say." Beal reached into his pocket, pulled out two hundred dollars, and shoved it toward him.

Mike shook his head. His legs felt weak, and he was terrified that he was going to keel over, but slowly he began walking toward Beal. "Not till you tell us why."

Beal didn't answer. He just held tightly to the gun,

425

feeling his hand shaking, as the tall, loping boy slowly approached him. Beal knew he could never shoot him. And he had a feeling that Mike knew it, too.

When Mike was close to Beal, he stopped and put out his hand. "You might as well give me that gun."

Beal laughed hollowly, angrily.

Mike forced himself to keep his hand out. "You know if I help you, at some point you're going to have to trust me. You'll fall asleep. Your attention will be diverted. It's inevitable."

Beal looked cagey. "Then you promise to help me?"

"That depends," Mike answered, stalling for time. "Is it dangerous?"

Beal wanted more than anything to lie. If he couldn't kill them, at least he should be able to lie. But he couldn't do either. All he could do was stand there, holding his useless gun, dumb, weak, and afraid. He supposed the reason was he'd caused enough hurt to people as it was.

"Yes," he answered softly. "I guess even talking to me is pretty dangerous."

Sheila was watching Beal; her eyes had softened, and there was sadness and understanding in them. "Who's in the hospital?"

"No one. A friend." Beal's voice was angry and sharp. Then the anger receded, and he wanted to tell someone, anyone, how he felt. Even if they kicked him out and called the police, he had to tell it. Maybe for the last time.

Beal's voice was shattered. "My wife's in the hospital. I think she's dying. Maybe she's dead. I told you before, even talking to me is dangerous. I meant it." Beal stopped. Then quickly he clicked the safety on

426

his gun and handed it to Mike. "It's up to you," he said sadly. "I wouldn't blame you if you just threw me out."

Mike nodded and put the gun in his pocket. Then suddenly he turned away; his strange swimming eyes were darting around, but in truth, he was trying to keep them from Beal's haunted face. If he looked at Beal's face, it was impossible to desert him. If he did, he knew he wouldn't ever be able to feel at peace with himself. He supposed that was how men going off to war had felt. He supposed after all the reasoning and second thoughts that in the end they'd had no choice but to help.

Slowly Mike turned back to Beal. His darting eyes were at rest. "Yeah, I'll do it," he said softly.

BOOK 4
EARLY AUGUST

Chapter Forty-five

Detroit was packed. There wasn't a spare room to be had at any price; there wasn't even a seat at a restaurant or bar that wasn't hotly contested from six o'clock on. In particular the brightly lit Renaissance Center with its skyscrapers and huge vistas was a mob scene. It looked like feeding time at the zoo; it looked like the last scene of a sci-fi thriller when the monster attacked.

Nevertheless, Berger pressed his way through the wall-to-wall white socks and polyester, whiskey breath, and beer bellies. As much as he hated crowds, he couldn't spend another minute in his tiny hotel room. On his arrival he had started a collection of dead flies from his windowsill. He was now up to thirty-five, and he'd filled eight matchboxes with their corpses. Five days down. Two more to go.

As Berger pushed through the crowds of conventioneers, he thought he saw someone slipping up be-

hind him. It looked like the blond man. Quickly he
ducked into a doorway and waited. The crowds pressed
by, but the blond man was not one of them. Finally
Berger started into the stream of people again.

Berger had been having the feeling he was being
followed all day, and each time he turned around, he
saw nothing. He supposed it was the boredom that was
making him jumpy. Certainly it wasn't the job he was
on.

Berger had run through the plan several times since
he came to Detroit, and it was sound. There was a
narrow space between the decorative false wall of the
Convention Arena and the real wall. In the basement,
at the back of a janitor's closet, there was a break in
the false wall big enough for a man to crawl through.
Berger would cram himself between the two walls and
shimmy one hundred yards to the right. At that point
there were wooden support beams that he could use to
climb upward. When he came to several large pipes, he
would know that he had reached the main floor. Just
above the pipes there was a space where the assault
rifle was hidden, and just above that there was another
break in the false wall. This one, just large enough to
clear the barrel and sight. Inside the Convention Arena
the break would be hidden from view by an American
flag.

After that he would have to wait. The wooden beam
under his feet would be thick enough to support his
weight, but he would have to be careful not to lean
too heavily on the false wall. There would just barely
be enough room for him to check his watch, waiting
through the endless speeches and demonstrations until
it was 8:00 P.M.

At 8:00 P.M. the empty chair to the left of the podium would be filled. And he would jam his finger back on the trigger. He expected it would take only one shot.

Getting out would be somewhat harder. He would leave the rifle behind, then once again begin his crawl. But this time, only inches away on the other side of the wall, the convention would be going berserk, and the entire police force of Detroit would be rushing in.

Berger had been given convention badges and identification cards; he even had his own polyester double knit and white socks to wear, but if anyone were in the janitor's closet when he exited, he'd be in big trouble. Nevertheless, it seemed unlikely that a janitor would be picking up toilet paper or sweeping compound while the whole Convention Arena was in chaos. So Berger felt relatively safe. And anyway, he had a handgun hidden under the towel shelf, just in case. In truth, the hard exit added an extra thrill to the job. So while he was worried about it, he had to admit he kind of liked the worrying, too.

Berger slipped into a hotel and stood blinking in the brightly lit lobby. Couples were streaming out into the night, old men with plaid trousers that barely reached their ankles, blondes tottering on pencil-thin heels. The smell of sour mash and tobacco was overpowering.

He headed to the bar, a wood-paneled dim room well hidden away. The room was packed with men, laughing, calling to one another heartily, poking fingers into flabby shoulders and stomachs.

Berger pushed to the bar sulkily. He felt trapped in that sea of humanity. He knew that had any of them

SHELLEY KATZ

realized why he was there, they would have run from him, screaming in horror. But in fact, Berger found the pressing crowd all around him far more horrifying than any murderer like him.

He ordered a double Dewar's and downed it quickly. Standing at the bar, he mentally tried to figure out how many of the drinkers around him he could belly-up before he was finally wrestled to the ground.

With a good rifle he could take out the first row around him in less than ten seconds. He'd have to be sure to whirl on the bartender next while the second row was moving up.

He smiled to himself, shaking his head. There'd be no second row moving up. Just one man and an assault rifle could scatter that room like an open anthill.

Chapter Forty-six

Bud Fuller was pacing his office nervously, revolving past the autographed pictures and plaques, lifting paperweights and letter openers. Lights were flashing on his telephone, but he didn't answer the calls. Outside, his waiting room was jammed, but he didn't even open the door. He supposed his secretary and aides were running interference for him, making lame excuses. It wouldn't be right to tell everybody that E. Bud Fuller, the president pro tem of the Senate, was having a nervous breakdown. But he suspected that was exactly what he was having. Or maybe it was something worse. Maybe it was the final breakdown, damnation.

Fuller's eyes fell on the snapshot of himself and Lacey with their wives. Quickly he looked away. He was glad that tomorrow was the last day of the convention, and he'd be leaving for Detroit to make the closing-day speech. At least Detroit held few memories that were good, and it was the good memories that seemed to hurt most.

He felt this most strongly every time he looked at his wife. Once she'd been the laughing woman with sand in her hair, mugging for the camera. Now she hardly looked at him, nor could he bring himself to look at her. They each walked around their house like embarrassed strangers, every noise seeming louder than it was, the silence growing and growing until they were encased in it. When occasionally their eyes did meet, it was like a shock of pain. For in that moment they saw each other's sorrow and, by reflection, their own. Suicide had occurred to him, but in the end he knew he was too weak and frightened to do anything but revolve around his office, trying not to think, yet feeling the wheels turning inside him, with no end in sight.

It had been three days since Beal had disappeared from that cabin in the woods, and Lacey was calling him all the time now, his voice furious, crazy with anxiety, then suddenly overly optimistic, euphoric. He was talking about the convention all the time now, hinting that something important would be happening there but refusing to answer anything specific. Fuller knew that Lacey had plans for the convention, plans that didn't include him. He wondered briefly if it was because Lacey figured that he wouldn't go along with them. But in the end Fuller knew he would go along with anything. It was too late to dig himself out of the corruption he'd buried himself in. As painful as it was, the act of actually trying to pull himself out took more strength than he had.

For days he'd been trying to reach Paisley and Keiler, but they weren't answering his calls anymore.

436

It was impossible to tell what they were up to. Perhaps it was through them that Lacey hoped to implement his plan. Probably it was Nadler. The irony that Fuller felt jealous of this hit him for a moment, and then it, too, was gone. Fuller wasn't able to hold on to any thought very long. Only one. And that was that he was scared.

Yesterday's paper had carried a small article about a burglary at KNT Television Film Library. Film reels of Lacey were missing as well as several taped speeches. Fuller had asked Lacey about it but he'd denied knowing anything. There was something about Lacey's voice that made him believe it.

Fuller fell into his desk chair, exhausted from pacing. He thought he heard noises coming from his outer office, but it was all the same to him. Everything seemed far away and unimportant. It was only the revolving wheels inside him that had any meaning. And all that led him to was darkness.

Again he thought he heard noises, and this time there was a loud yell from his secretary. Suddenly the buzzer sounded, and his door clicked open.

A young man pushed in, wearing a suit and tie, wing-tipped shoes, and a large "Save the Whales" button. He stopped just inside the door, hands on hips, watching Fuller with a strange, almost detached expression of anger on his bruised face.

Fuller's middle-aged bluenosed secretary burst in just behind him, looking around wildly. "He sneaked in with a group of environmentalists. I've alerted security."

It was almost like a dream for Fuller. He couldn't

move; he just stared at the young man with the blond hair and the angry eyes.

"Hi, I'm Beal. I hear you've been looking for me." Beal smiled angrily.

Fuller said nothing. He was just watching Beal stupidly, as if he didn't understand what was happening or as if he didn't care.

"I don't suppose you'll remember, but we spoke to each other on the phone the other night. You have a very distinctive voice. Or maybe it's my musical training. I knew I'd put it to some use." Again Beal smiled. It was a terrible, angry smile.

A moment later two security guards burst into the room, their elbows crooked, hands on guns. They were over to Beal in seconds and holding him by the arms with machinelike efficiency.

Fuller remained motionless, trapped behind the great expanse of mahogany, staring at them numbly, as if he were no longer even trying to understand.

"I wouldn't do it if I were you," Beal said sharply. Implicit in his tone was a threat.

This pulled Fuller back to reality. He sighed, long, low, but oddly devoid of feeling. "Leave him alone. He's all right."

The crooked arms still hovered over their guns, but the men loosened their hold on Beal's arms. "You sure?"

"I told him to come here," Fuller answered. His voice was mechanical, and Beal thought he almost heard relief in it.

The secretary and security guards waited for a moment, eyebrows raised, eyes ironical; then, after exchanging looks, they left.

Beal remained where he was, looking around the office. It was immense, made to look even larger by the great expanse of windows. Outside, a brutal sun pounded Los Angeles, but inside it was transformed into buttery-soft rays, highlighting the polished furniture.

Slowly Beal walked around the office, stopping at the mementos and trinkets of a lifetime, picking them up with an interest he did not feel.

Fuller was slumped in his large leather desk chair, terrified that Beal had come to kill him; terrified that he hadn't.

Finally Beal stopped and turned back to Fuller. "I want you to call Lacey. I want to speak to him."

Fuller laughed hollowly. "Lacey's dead."

"Certainly. Well, resurrect him then. Because I promise you he'll want to hear what I have to say."

Fuller was looking out the window at the pounding, harsh sun. "And if I don't call?"

"I won't kill you, if that's what you mean. But I have a feeling that Lacey might. Of course, by that time it will be too late for him, too. You might just as well call him. You have nothing to lose if you do. And everything if you don't."

Fuller rubbed his thick mop of white hair with smooth, manicured hands. "What if I told you none of this means a damn to me anymore?"

"But it does to him."

"What if I told you I don't give a damn what matters to him either?"

"It's a little late for second thoughts."

Fuller stared blankly at Beal, then opened the locked

439

drawer in his desk. He lifted the receiver and dialed several numbers.

Beal walked over to the large mahogany desk and held out his hand for the receiver impatiently. Fuller stiffened; then everything seemed to go out of his body, and he handed it over to Beal, slipped from behind his desk, and retreated to the other side of the office.

Beal was smirking, but his eyes were without pleasure. While still holding the receiver, he walked over to the other side of the desk, took Fuller's chair, and sat well back, his feet on the shiny wood.

At his ear there were a series of mechanical clicks, then suddenly a voice, hard, demanding: "Yes?"

The moment Beal heard Lacey's voice, his feet were down on the floor. He leaned forward furiously, his eyes sparkling, his lips pressed tightly together. He looked like a man desperately trying to keep his sanity. It took Beal awhile to be sure of his voice. "It's Beal," he said at last. "Surprised?"

There was a silence as Lacey gathered his thoughts. "I don't believe I know anyone by that name. You have the wrong—"

Beal interrupted. "Save it. I'm over here with your friend Fuller. He thought you might be interested in what I have to say."

Lacey snarled, "That fool!"

"Yeah, well, I'll agree with you there, though for different reasons. But anyway, that's not what I called for. You see, I know everything now. How you managed your assassination. Why. I even think I have an idea of what your plans are for the future. It wasn't easy. I'll give you that. It took a lot of digging around and some pretty fancy thinking, too." He laughed angrily. "But you don't care about that, do you?"

"You're right there!"

"I'll bet you want to know why I called."

"It's safe to assume."

Beal shot a look at Fuller, but he wasn't watching Beal anymore. He was across the room, crumpled on the couch, his hands covering his face.

"I think you and I ought to meet," Beal said. "Alone. You know, sort of man to man."

Lacey merely laughed.

"I'll bet after I tell you why, you'll change your mind." Beal stopped. He could hear his voice begin to shake, and his hands were cold and wet. He'd been able to keep the thought of failing far away during the past three days as he'd frantically made preparations. But now, as he sat in Fuller's immense office, talking to the deadly cool voice on the other end of the phone, failure presented itself to him as a probability.

Beal's insides began to tighten painfully, and he felt very small behind the large desk. He clutched the phone tightly, trying to stay calm, but he could feel everything weakening, and he was afraid.

Beal's voice was quiet. "When your friend Harry was beating up on us, he repeated a very interesting maxim, 'What's sauce for the goose is sauce for the gander.' Ever hear it? Well, despite a mistake in gender, I think he was on to something there."

Lacey cut in impatiently. "That is getting us no-where."

Beal ignored him. "You know that convention going on in Detroit? You'll never guess who's going to it tomorrow night." Beal paused. He could hear Lacey breathing expectantly on the other end of the phone, and that made him feel better.

Beal smiled tightly. "You are, Lacey. You see, I've made a hologram of my own. Well, actually it's a multiplex. Inferior things, those multiplexes, cheap as hell and not nearly as good as the hologram you made. But good enough for my purposes. I made it from old newsreels. Call KNT Television and find out if a lot of footage isn't missing."

"I know about the missing film."

"Good. Well, tapes are missing, too. Of course, I had to play with the tapes a little. You know, sort of doctor them. And once again I didn't have time to do a very good job. But you should hear what you have to say! You tell how you rigged the assassination. And why. You even mention names. And you're going to tell it all at the convention tomorrow night."

Lacey was silent for a long while. "What made you choose closing day of the convention for your little display?"

Something in Lacey's voice made Beal realize he'd hit pay dirt. "Blind good luck, I'd say."

"Not because a little white-headed bird told you, eh?"

Beal glanced over at Fuller. But he was sitting crumpled on his couch, seemingly unaware of what was going on. "No. Your stooge is well in place."

"I see." Again Lacey was silent for some time, but when he spoke, he sounded calm. "Let's just say you can pull off this little display, though seriously I doubt it. You can't possibly expect anyone to believe you. They'll just think it's a practical joke, one in very bad taste, by the way."

442

"Maybe they will. But you're forgetting one thing. You aren't planning on staying where you are forever."

"What makes you think that?" Lacey's voice was tight.

"It's history. How's this? America's in trouble. What happens? Well, people start looking around for someone to tell them what to do. Who better than a dead god? The next part would be hard to pull off, but you were a big hero once, maybe you could swing it. I can see the headlines. 'President Lacey Is Not Dead.' No. He was seriously injured. Hidden away by friends. Then, slowly, miraculously, he began to make a recovery. How does that sound?"

"Very accurate indeed." Lacey laughed coldly. "I'll give you better marks than Fuller. He prefers to delude himself that everything has remained the same as five years ago." Again he laughed acidly. "Back then I saw my job as helping out from behind the scenes. I would be the invisible, benevolent presence, a kindly, watchful eye that could advise and influence through powerful friends."

Lacey's voice was full of teasing nastiness, and the sound made everything tighten inside Beal.

"When did all that change?" Beal asked angrily.

"As you said. It was inevitable. It was history."

"Unfortunately my little display at the convention is going to raise some serious questions when you suddenly try your reappearance act. Remember, I'll tell the exact way you did it and why you did it. They won't believe the display, but later they may."

Lacey thought about that. "How do I know this isn't a bluff?"

"That's why I want to meet with you. There's a nice

deserted stretch of highway between Malibu and Trancas. Go one point two miles north of the country store and stop on the ocean side of the highway at exactly five o'clock in the morning. Then you can see for yourself. If you like my little display, get out of your car and walk to it. But make sure you come alone. I'll have people watching. Believe me, just one sign of someone else and we'll pack up our display and head straight for the convention."

"Unless you find yourself dead before then."

"It's too late for that now," Beal said coldly. "You see, the thing about a multiplex is that only the first one is hard to make; duplicating isn't all that difficult. You get my drift? I have another one hidden away, waiting. Only I know where. But the instructions I left with my friends are quite explicit."

Lacey was silent. Beal couldn't even hear him breathing.

"So I can assume I'll be seeing you on the beach tomorrow morning?" Beal asked. He was no longer expecting an answer. "Oh, by the way, be sure to bring a gun. I'll have one, too."

Lacey burst into laughter. "A showdown, eh?"

"That's right. A showdown."

Again Lacey didn't say anything. Beal could hear a wall clock humming from across the room. The sun had moved and struck the room so that the furniture cast long shadows. Fuller was still on the couch on the other side of the room, his head in his hands. Beal wondered if he was listening to the conversation or if he was just buried in himself.

When Lacey finally spoke, Beal could hear the false calmness, and he knew he'd rattled him.

"Why not just go ahead with the convention display? You'd be ruining me politically anyway. Why bother with this infantile showdown?"

Beal's voice was like a knife. "Because I want to watch you die."

Lacey laughed acidly. "And what if it's the other way around?"

"That's the chance I'll have to take."

"I see." He thought for a while. "Of course, there are no guarantees that you have this display. It might just be a trap. But I suspect that you'll just tell me that's the chance I'll have to take."

Again Lacey laughed, but Beal wasn't listening anymore. His heart was pounding loudly, and the scared feeling was starting again. And then the line went dead.

Beal replaced the receiver. Slowly he pulled himself from Fuller's desk and walked to the doorway. He paused as he opened the door and turned back, but Fuller didn't even look up. He just sat on the couch, his hands covering his face.

Less than an hour later Beal was walking on Hollywood Boulevard. He moved quickly up one block, then shifted down a side street, waiting in a doorway for close to a minute before reversing direction and heading back to Hollywood. He stopped at a bookstore, pretending to check out the window display, but his eyes were on the brilliant boulevard around him and the shoppers passing by.

Finally he slipped into a phone booth, spilled a handful of change onto the wooden ledge, and dialed Washington. He told the secretary his name, then waited.

It didn't take long.

"Jesus Christ," Jed said excitedly. "Where in the hell have you been?" It was as if Jed had never told him to break contact.

"To hell and back." Beal stopped. Then suddenly his voice became frantic. "Look, I know you told me to break contact, but I've got to meet with you. Lacey's alive."

"He's what?"

"Same place as we met before. Highway One. At five thirty tomorrow morning. Only this time you come alone and unarmed. I've got something to show you."

Jed broke in. "Listen to me, Beal—"

"I haven't got time. Come alone and unarmed. I'll be watching."

Beal slammed down the phone before Jed had a chance to answer. He left the phone booth quickly, slipping down a side street, then suddenly changing his direction, beginning the feints and pauses, trying to smoke out the invisible men who were always just a step behind him.

Evening light spilled into Mike's apartment, staining everything a hellish red. Beal was lying on the floor in a sleeping bag, unmoving, curled in the darkness of sleep.

Mike and Sheila were sitting on the mattress across from him, drinking beer and watching the exhausted figure on the floor as last light made patchy red streaks across his body.

Neither of them had spoken for a long while. They were thinking of the long night ahead and what would happen tomorrow.

446

Finally Sheila broke the silence. "You're worried it isn't going to work, aren't you?"

"Something like that."

"You did a great job, Mike. Considering what you had to work with, you did a brilliant job."

Mike looked down at Sheila's encouraging face and tried for a smile. "Considering doesn't count. The stakes are too high."

"You think Beal'll get hurt?"

"I think he'll get killed, man."

Sheila recoiled. "You don't really think that?" But his face told her that he did. "And us?" she asked. "What do you think'll happen to us?"

Mike avoided her eyes. "We'll be sheltered. We don't have anything to worry about."

Sheila didn't press him. She supposed she'd suspected all along that it would be dangerous for them, too. Still, it seemed very far away and unreal. It was impossible to believe that anything could really happen to her. "Do you think Beal realizes he might get killed?" she asked softly.

"I'd bet on it. But I don't think he cares. He isn't extra-fond of living anymore. Even if by some miracle his plan succeeds, I think he'd end up committing suicide. Everyone's got to have something to live for. And all he's got is hate. Once that's gone . . ."

Sheila shook her head. "He'd find something else. He's that kind. He's been trying to stay alive too long to give it all up now."

"I hope you're right."

"I'm sure I'm right," Sheila answered, but she didn't sound sure. "People are trippy. They'll do just about anything to survive."

"That's because no one took their dreams and bashed its head in."

"But you went to the hospital. You said she's still alive."

"Big deal," Mike said softly. "I saw her, man. All covered in white. In the place where the vegetables grow."

Sheila shivered violently, and Mike moved closer to her on the bed. She could feel that he was shivering, too.

They sat there for a long while in silence, neither of them speaking or moving, staring down at the figure asleep on the floor.

Beal's sunken cheeks and black-rimmed eyes looked terrifying as he lay unmoving in the bright red evening light. As if the fate they foresaw for him had already taken place and he were a corpse.

448

Chapter Forty-seven

The hazy sun rose over Washington, D.C., sparkling into the wide boulevards and iron dome of the Capitol, glinting off the Aquia Creek, Virginia, sandstone of the White House.

At exactly 7:00 A.M. President Chesapeake awakened without an alarm clock, jumped out of bed, and began his customary quota of fifty sit-ups and twenty-five stretches. Already by that time his Vice President, Skip Connella, was breakfasting on cornflakes and bananas, skimming *The Washington Post* propped against the sugar bowl. While Jack Spiro, speaker of the House, was taking a shower and singing "But Not for Me," much to the amusement of his housekeeping staff.

At seven thirty the President left the family dining room and, just as he did every morning, headed for the Oval Office, his heavy frame striding purposefully, his dark face set seriously. Aides nearly half his age would stop in wonder at the energy of the sixty-five-year-old man from Oklahoma, whose great-great-grandfather had been on the wrong side of the Indian wars.

Today President Chesapeake was moving even more purposefully than usual. It would be a very busy day. Yesterday he had been renominated at the Detroit convention, and after the morning meetings with the NAACP, League of Women Voters, and the head of the steel union, he would return to Detroit to put the name of Skip Connella, his Vice President, before the convention.

As President Chesapeake settled into his chair and began his customary reading of the news summaries, he could feel his mind splitting off. For under the relief and excitement of once again being his party's nominee for President, there was the ever-present deepening shadow. It had been there for years, that strange feeling that everything was becoming uncontrollable, that America was somehow slipping through his fingers.

Berger awakened with a scream. It was only six thirty in the morning, but he jumped out of bed and started to dress. He couldn't remember what he'd been dreaming, though the sensation sat heavily on him. It felt as if he'd been running, and there was that desperateness, as if he'd been crying in his sleep.

Usually dreams and premonitions meant absolutely nothing to Berger. But he couldn't laugh at this feeling, and he dressed and slipped out of the hotel in less than ten minutes in response to it.

He supposed it was all connected to the suspicion that he was being followed. Everywhere he went, he sensed the presence of the blond man. Part of him doubted there was anyone following him and suggested that probably it was all nerves. But the other part felt sure that the blond man was indeed just behind him, and with anxiety tightening his chest, Berger began a series of feints and doubling backs to try to shake him.

Chapter Forty-eight

By five thirty a misty faraway sun was rising from behind the skyscrapers of Los Angeles, casting a milky
white light on the little strip of beach running parallel
with the highway. Thick fog swirled and shifted ghostlike in the early-morning breeze, making the huge red
bluffs surrounding the highway look primitive as they
appeared and disappeared in the fog. Beyond the perimeter of vision, waves crashed toward the shore.
Their rhythmic pounding was like drums.

As the mists lifted, a little dog could be seen. It was
obviously lost, confused, and frightened. It sniffed the
sand forlornly, hoping to catch a clue to its owner's
whereabouts. Finally it seemed to give up and settle for
a good pee against a nice-smelling rock.

There was the sound of a car, some distance away
but coming closer. Then quickly a large black car
loomed out of the fog.

Far up in the bluffs there was an electric crackle,

mechanical and out of place. Then Sheila's voice broke through. "I think I see him."

Mike's voice returned the message, crackling through the empty hills. "How many cars?"

"It looks like just one."

"Yeah, well, the others are probably keeping back a bit. Has it stopped?"

"It's slowed to a crawl. I can only see one man in the car, and it doesn't look like Lacey. But I've got a feeling there are others in the car with him."

"Surprise."

Sheila paused a moment, looking down at the winding oceanside road below and the black car sliding onto the shoulder next to Mike's beat-up old car. "He's stopping now," Sheila said softly.

"Good," Mike answered. "Turn on the loudspeaker."

Once again there was quiet. The black car was parked along the beach, its motor still running, its windows down. The driver was looking around cautiously. His lips were moving slightly, as if he were talking to himself or to others well hidden in the car.

Suddenly a voice echoed from the loudspeaker high in the hills.

"Good morning, gentlemen! I'm glad you could come."

The driver was looking around wildly, and this time he didn't even try to hide speech.

"I'm afraid the meeting's been changed," Beal's voice announced. "So you can forget about using your back-up cars. As you can tell, you're being watched carefully. I wouldn't try to fool us again."

The driver had lifted an automatic to the window,

but it was pointed into the emptiness. There was nothing to shoot.

"Lacey!" Beal's voice echoed. "Do you hear me?"

There was no answer from the car.

"I'll assume that you can. Now, if you want to stop my display, you're going to have to do as I say. Do you see the old car parked near you? Well, I want you to get into it, Lacey. You and you alone. Like I said, you're being watched. Get into the car, and you'll find the new meeting place on a slip of paper in the glove compartment. The choice is yours. You can drive to the meeting and take your chances. Or you can wait for the convention." Again Beal laughed.

There was a rustle from the back seat of the car, and two armed men sat up, clutching their weapons. Then a third man appeared next to the driver.

"This is madness," Lacey hissed out.

There was a laugh from the loudspeaker. "I'll give you that, Lacey. But for once it's my madness. You've got no other choice but to go along with it."

Against the lightening sky the image of a lone man looking at the water stood out on the sand. He was a tall man, broad and strong, with a determined, slightly ironical face. It was the figure of a man of importance, a man to be reckoned with.

Mike was standing in the bluffs, looking out at the three-dimensional image on the sand when Sheila's voice crackled over the shortwave from several miles back. "He bought it!" Her voice sounded amazed.

Mike slipped back down into the rocky hills. There was a click as he shut off the shortwave; then once again there was the sound of crashing waves and the image of a lone figure standing on the sand, looking out at the horizon, as if it could see all the way to China.

A few seconds later the sound of a car cut the quiet as Mike's beat-up old car rumbled through the fog. This time there was only one man inside.

Lacey slowed as he closed in on the figure on the sand. When he was parallel, he pulled off the highway onto the shoulder and bumped to a halt. He switched off the motor, and once again there were only the crashing waves.

After a while Lacey rolled down the car window, then sat unmoving, watching the figure on the sand, his face an expressionless mask.

The figure turned slowly to face the car, but its eyes were on the bluffs beyond, the determined, ironical face captured in a moment of smiling.

Lacey couldn't take his eyes off the image. It was like running across an old faded picture of oneself taken long before consciousness, a little boy in baby clothes, a mother with the enormous rolling belly of pregnancy. It had been only five years since Lacey had looked like that image on the sand. Yet it seemed a lifetime.

Captured in the image, Lacey could see exactly what had happened to himself. All the appetites and emotions were etched on the ruddy, unseeing face that stared out from the sand. Tall and vigorous, the image seemed almost more alive than the real man. For a moment that thought penetrated through Lacey's emptiness, but the moment passed almost immediately. What had happened was for the best. The Lacey of today had purged himself with fire, and he was a new man.

The figure on the sand began to move, its mouth

opening and closing, as if it were speaking. And with the movement the distortions became apparent. No longer was it lifelike. Lacey laughed at himself. How could he be frightened by what was no more than a rather impressive home movie shown on an invisible screen?

A moment later the figure began to speak. "I had arranged for a limousine to be waiting behind the hotel . . ."

The voice was Lacey's, but it sounded tinny and unreal, and there were mechanical clicks and jumps.

"One of my greatest problems was finding a body to replace mine. I don't think I have to tell you how that was done . . ."

Lacey remained where he was, watching, listening. Could this distorted image truly be able to disrupt his plan? It seemed impossible. Yet could he risk it? The thought that the warped, flimsy figure on the sand could ruin everything held him tightly, and he stared out of the window, transfixed with anger.

"Everything was projected onto a large Plexiglas screen. The one everyone was trying to figure out after the assassination . . ."

Lacey pulled a revolver out of the glove compartment and thumbed the safety.

"Everyone who was with me when I was 'dying' is now dead or has disappeared. Dr. Greenaway, the Secret Service men. Check the records on the dates. You'll find it quite illuminating . . ."

Slowly Lacey opened the car door and slid out.

"It also explains the famous dilemma of the cleared room, doesn't it? . . ."

Anger was pounding in Lacey's head, and for the

first time in years a shadow closed quietly in on him. The shadow of fear. Lacey held the gun in his hand. It felt heavy and clumsy.

He tried not to think about the fact that he hadn't shot a gun since he was in the army, but it pressed in on him, vivid and startling. He cursed himself for coming. The supreme egotism of it. He should have remained in hiding and taken his chances. But he knew that was impossible. The convention was going on right now. Everything was so close.

Lacey closed the car door behind him, but still he stayed where he was, caught between two fears, the fear of proceeding, the fear of the consequences if he did not.

But with the fear also came anger, molten and strong, and he gripped the gun and started to move. He looked neither right nor left. It would do no good to look for a sniper. If there was one, it was too late to do anything about it. And the thought of showing anything like the momentary fear he had just felt so repulsed him that it seemed even worse than death by a sniper.

As he began to walk, his mind sharpened. Men like Beal were stupid enough to make this a real showdown. Had he been Beal, he would have been a sprawled corpse long ago. Only lunatics still believed in empty words like "honor," while he knew it was only results that counted; the means could always be justified later by a good speech writer.

Lacey walked onto the sand. Everything was becoming clear again. As he neared the image on the sand, he saw the watery sun glinting off the Plexiglas screen. Suddenly the distortions became huge flaws, the colors bled like rainbows, the vertical bars became apparent.

The image captured in glass faded and dimmed. And with the dimming Lacey's fear also disappeared.

He stopped. The image was silent, a transparent ghost reflecting milky morning light. A truck rumbled by on the highway, but Lacey didn't even turn around. He was waiting for what would happen next. He wanted to be prepared for it.

There was a rustle several feet ahead on the beach. The sound of movement from behind a boulder. Beal stood up, holding a revolver. Lacey's grip tightened on his gun, but he didn't raise it. There was no need to move for the moment. Beal was too far away to present a threat.

Beal looked frail and crazy standing on the sand, his body tensed like an animal. "Not bad, huh?" he yelled to Lacey. His voice was wild and reckless; his face, taut with the need to destroy.

"Amateurish," Lacey called back. There was irony in his tone, but his face revealed nothing. Even the anger, burning inside him, was hidden out of sight, and Beal was confronted with a deathly blank stare.

"Still good enough to ruin your chances," Beal yelled. But a stab of fear went through him. The face across from him was as cold and indifferent as the bluffs surrounding them. It was the face of a man who could watch death and destruction with equanimity. Beal tried to hold down the fear, but he could feel it rising urgently inside him, as frenzied as his need for revenge.

"Perhaps you're right." Lacey's gaunt face broke into something resembling a smile, but it was so devoid of humor or even humanity it chilled Beal far worse than anything he could imagine.

Beal's heart twisted, and his hands began to numb. He had wanted to ask so many questions, but now they seemed empty, as hollow as the face across the sand. Finally he managed to yell back, "Why?" But he didn't continue. It was impossible even to think with that taut, expressionless face staring blankly at him.

Lacey's face split with a cold smile. "Why what?" he called back. "Why did I do it?" He laughed tightly. "I think you know the answer to that question already. Or perhaps you're talking about the cosmic why. Are you waxing philosophical on us? Why all those lives for mine? I haven't exactly been keeping a body count, but I suppose, counting those poor prisoners, it would reach to over thirty men in the past five years. Thirty men's lives for mine. Is that what you want to know?"

"Yes." Beal's voice was starting to crack and tremble.

Lacey laughed, and the sound snapped through the air hollowly. "Why not?" He paused, his impassive eyes lit with sarcasm. "You think I'm toying with you. But indeed, I'm not. You ask me why. Why preserve myself at the expense of others? Why do I feel my life justifies all those deaths? I was never a man who believed in heaven, hell, and damnation. Do you?"

He stopped, waiting for an answer, but there was none. Beal was motionless, the fear pounding brutally through his body.

"Have you ever thought how many living creatures a man kills in his lifetime?" Lacey's face looked like little more than a collection of bones in the misty white light. "All those little ants and gnats, slugs, microbes, not to mention vegetables and animals. With every step a man takes, he kills. Certainly you don't believe we shouldn't walk, do you?" Lacey's laugh cracked through the silence. "I don't know why you think of yourself as more humane because you draw the line at human beings. Personally I would prefer to save the cow and dine on fillet of man."

Again Lacey laughed, looking at Beal with his void eyes, waiting for a response that never came. "I think a more important question is: Why do anything when in the end it will all be the same? After all, given another twenty years, I'll be just as dead as if I had died five years ago. So why bother? But again, the real question is: Why not? And to that, Mr. Beal, I do not have an answer."

Beal stood silent, Lacey's harsh voice echoing through his entire body. He had wanted desperately to ask Lacey that last question, expecting he didn't know what, but almost anything other than the answer he received. Looking at that gaunt face, Beal suddenly saw himself as Lacey must have seen him, nothing more than a clumsy fool who was in the way, an ant or slug. Perhaps he was right. It was men like Lacey who succeeded, not men like Beal. The fact that he could never have done what Lacey had was a failure in him. Humanity was a weakness, a vulnerability. Humanity led to defeat. And suddenly the need for revenge that had been burning inside Beal felt like the foolish dreams of a very small man, a man who would fail.

Lacey glanced at his watch pointedly. "Today is a big day for me, and it's getting late."

Beal tightened his grip on his revolver, but his fingers felt stiff, and he could barely get them to work. Everything was cold and murky, as if the mists that swirled all around them had entered Beal's soul, obscuring the anger and purpose, leaving only fear.

Lacey began to move, his gun held before him, his bony face devoid of fear or rage or anything but determination.

Beal saw Lacey begin toward him, but there was nothing he could do. Everything was far away and unreal. All he could feel was the fear swelling inside him, swirling and trembling like the mists. His legs were weak, and his whole body was shaking. He told himself to raise his gun, but the command came from somewhere far off, soft and unimportant. He had been pushed too far. There was an emptiness in the center of him, and while outside, everything seemed blurry and distant, inside, there was only darkness.

Lacey kept moving. His mind was now a concentrated beam of light, like the laser that had cut through the air toward him all those years ago. He could read every expression in Beal's face. He could read the indecision and doubt. But there was no joy or even triumph on his bony face, only cold appraisal.

Beal was frozen to the sand. His arm felt weak, flesh without muscle or bone, insubstantial and ineffective. Again he commanded it to raise, but his brain was as frozen as his body, as if all the weeks of suffering had eaten away at him, and now there was nothing left to fight.

Lacey walked deliberately, closing in on his target, his finger tense and ready, his cold eyes prying into Beal's and unearthing failure. He felt a vague stab of disappointment. It was going to be so easy. He quickened his pace, his gun held out before him, watching the distance lessen and the pale figure waiting to be killed. It felt good to be on the outside again. His body seemed like a machine. Everything was working inside him, his eyes measuring and judging distance, his brain calculating the steps. Until suddenly his body told him he was close enough and screamed for him to stop.

Lacey's legs tightened; his feet clenched the ground, shifting and centering his weight. His arm moved up steadily, yet quickly. And he was aiming.

Beal tried to make his body move, but he was frozen to the sand. The specter of failure was vivid in front of him. He had watched, helpless, as Maggie was tortured. He had done nothing until it was almost too late. Soon it would be the same for him. In one brilliant, torturous flash he could see his own body sprawled on the sand. He could see Lacey smiling coldly at his victory.

Then suddenly everything inside Beal began to work again. It was as if, having seen his own terrible failure, he was released from it. The rage was back, burning sharply. His grip tightened, and his arm moved up, quick and sure.

But it was too late. Lacey saw the movement and pulled the trigger.

Beal rocked backwards. A stab of cold shot through his body, swelling and quickening. Everything seemed strange and slow. Beal's head was turning toward his arm. He saw the blood spreading across his sleeve. But in the same split second that he took in the knowledge he was hit, he also realized that he wasn't hit badly.

Lacey grasped instantly that he hadn't killed Beal and that he must pull off another shot. There was a hesitation, a moment of fear and indecision, as if failure had never occurred to him and he needed time to adjust to the idea.

Already Beal's body was steadying itself, his gun raising, his eye finding the sight.

Everything was thrown off. Lacey's legs felt weak, awkward, and unsure; his timing seemed wrong, his finger less steady. He was fighting for recovery, but there was a tightening deep in the center of him, and suddenly he was afraid.

Beal fired.

There was a flash of white light, exploding outward. Lacey jolted backward, molten pain tearing through him. His body was on fire. Everything was slipping under him, but he couldn't tell if he was standing or sitting or lying on the ground. The white light was growing larger and hotter until the whole world was alight. And then Lacey realized that he'd been shot and that he was dying.

At the same moment Beal fired again.

Suddenly there was a new pain tearing through Lacey's body, throwing him backward or downward, he couldn't tell which, because once again there was another jolt and then another, and Lacey was sinking to the ground without even understanding what was happening. There was only the light and the tumbling and the terrible white pain, bursting outward, spreading across the universe, obliterating everything with its intensity. And then suddenly a sharp crack in the light, and everything crashed into darkness.

Beal stood rigid, pulling the trigger, feeling the recoil shocking him back, the smell of cordite biting at his nostrils. He fired again and again, until the gun was empty and the shock and the smell faded. Still he pulled the trigger, aiming at the already shattered body that lay spilling blood in soft, warm waves on the sand.

There were no sounds except the empty clicking of the revolver and his own crying, desperate, hopeless, and very unreal.

It took almost a minute before Beal stopped. Slowly he became aware of the distorted shape lying on the sand in front of him.

Lacey lay, limbs splinting outward. His clothes were red and oozing, with dark holes where the bullets had pierced flesh and shattered his bones. The flesh had been torn from the top of his head. Only his face remained whole, and there was a look of unearthly shock burned on it.

Suddenly a violent tremor swept through Lacey's body, and for a moment he seemed alive. But almost immediately the torn muscles went limp again, and Lacey was once more only a shadow on the sand.

Beal didn't move. He was standing, staring down at the lifeless, sprawled body. Lacey looked so insignificant lying on the sand. All at once Lacey's death meant nothing to Beal. How could he have thought that it would make up for the weeks of running and torture? None of it meant anything. There was no revenge.

The *Goldberg Variations* echoed crazily through his head, distorted, cracked. Where there was once harmony, there was now dissonance; where there was once beauty, now there was only ugliness.

Nausea clutched at Beal's throat. Salt began to flow into his mouth, and his stomach spasmed. The pain in his arm was burning, but he no longer felt it. He felt nothing but emptiness and sickness.

Beal turned from the sight of the body, his legs weakened, and he allowed himself to sink to his knees. A convulsion swept his body, and he was vomiting. It was as if all the poisonous hatred were being torn from his body, and he knew he never wanted to kill anything ever again.

Jed drummed nervously on the car door as he looked out at the foggy gray sea that whipped past his car window. David was driving slowly, scanning the highway for the meeting place. Jed glanced over at him and wondered briefly what he was thinking, but it was impossible to tell from his face. It didn't really matter anyway. Jed supposed he was just trying to find a way to forget what he was feeling. The truth was he hated what he was feeling; he hated what he had to do. The young man who had started out as merely a link in the chain of political intrigue had become a human being to him, a damn nice human being, too. Jed shook his head, as if he could shake off his thoughts. "Life can sure be lousy," he said out loud.

David smiled thinly. "The alternative ain't a bowl of cherries either."

"No, I suppose not." Somehow David's detachment helped a bit, and Jed relaxed back into his seat. In the end it didn't matter. He had no choice.

As they rounded a curve, Jed spotted an old Studebaker parked on the other side of the road, pressed tight against the red bluffs of Malibu. "Over there," he said, pointing.

But David was already slowing the car, pulling over to the shoulder of the road, and stopping just across the highway from Beal. "I'd better stay here," David said. "He'll probably be jumpy enough that you didn't come alone. We don't want to chance him bolting now."

Jed nodded, but his eyes were on the car across the road and the shadow of Beal's head, watching from the driver's seat.

"Are you sure you can get him from here?" Jed's eyes were locked on the shadowy figure in the car across the highway.

"I'm sure I can't get him from here. I'll need you to distract him. Get out of the car and start walking across the highway. Then, when he's watching you, I can jump from the car."

Jed whirled on him. "You're kidding!"

"Relax. I told you I was a good shot."

"Jesus!" Jed turned back to the window. He could hear David loading his gun, the cold metallic click of the heavy gray steel, the thud of well-made equipment.

Jed sighed. "I want to talk to him first. Don't start shooting until I raise my arm."

"Fine with me. Just make sure you hit the pavement after you signal."

"Don't worry about that!" Jed tried for a smile, but everything felt frigid, a plastic world with plastic people walking around in it.

Jed stared out the window for a moment longer; then, steeling himself, he opened the car door and climbed out. He stopped at the side of the car and turned to Beal. Once again a wave of sadness swept over him. For a moment he was tempted not to go through with it. But he knew he couldn't do that. He had to do what was right.

Beal's voice broke the quiet. "Hey, Jed! Look over there. On the sand next to the boulder."

Jed turned cautiously and started onto the sand, careful to move slowly. Beal was edgy and suspicious; he had been pushed as far as he could go, and any sudden movement could be dangerous.

At first all Jed saw was the Plexiglas screen, and he wondered how it got there, why it got there. But then his eyes caught sight of a twisted heap on the ground.

He stopped, stunned. Lacey lay distorted and immobile on the sand. He looked unreal in the strange misty half-light. And in the end he looked insignificant.

Jed recoiled. This was the object of a chase that had lasted close to five years. Every day Jed had tortured himself with visions of what would happen to the country, all because of that small, twisted pile of flesh. It seemed impossible. All the fear, all the death, all the torture of the past five years had come to this.

Beal hadn't moved. He remained in the car, a little figure against the red bluffs. "He was planning to be President again," Beal yelled. "Only this time with none of the legal niceties of election."

Jed couldn't speak for some time. Beal hadn't lied. The body on the sand was Lacey. And now he was dead. He stared over at Beal, shocked and awed. Finally Jed held his hands to his mouth and yelled, "Un-fuck-ing-believable! How in the hell did you do it?"

"It doesn't matter," Beal called back. "Come over here."

"I need to know how. I need to know why."

"When you get into my car," Beal answered. "Then we'll talk."

Jed was motionless, unsure of what to do. But inside

him regret was pounding heavily. In the end nothing had changed. He knew what he must do.

"What's the matter, Jed?" Beal yelled. "I asked you to come over here." He sounded edgy and angry. Every word was an accusation.

Jed forced himself to start moving. He walked back off the sand, his eyes on the little figure in the car across the highway. When he got to the pavement, he stopped. Again he yelled, "How did you do it, Beal?"

"What does it matter? I did it. Isn't that enough?"

"Yes. I suppose."

"Then why aren't you coming over here?"

Jed glanced back at David nervously. He was no longer looking down at the gun in his lap. His arms were moving, and Jed thought he could see the gray metal of the automatic being raised. He quickly turned back to Beal, wondering if he'd seen it, too. But Beal sat motionless in the driver's seat.

Jed started into the road, keeping his eyes focused on Beal's car, trying to block out the regrets, trying to keep only the purpose and resolve he'd felt before.

"That's better," Beal yelled. "When you get into my car, then we'll have our little talk."

Jed kept his eyes on Beal, but his mind was back with David and the gray automatic he was holding. He found himself praying that Beal would die instantly. He found himself praying that it was all over.

As Jed approached the yellow divider, he could see Beal's face. It was sunken and haggard, filled with torment. Even from far away Jed could see the agony he'd suffered.

"I'm so sorry," Jed said sadly. He wanted to say more but couldn't. The sight of Beal was burning through everything, and he couldn't bear looking at him.

"What are you sorry about? Lacey's dead. You and I are alive. What's there to be sorry about?"

"You've got to understand—" Again Jed broke off.

"Understand what, Jed?"

"This country is in enough trouble as it is."

"Fuck this country! What has this country done for me?"

"If people found out, it would cause a panic." Jed paused, then continued softly. "Don't you see? No one must know about this. No one!"

All of a sudden Jed stopped. His arm went up, and he ducked to the pavement.

David flung the car door open and leaped out onto the road, the automatic raised. There was a moment of silence and then pandemonium.

Suddenly the air was filled with the terrible sound of shattering glass, bullets rebounding against metal, tires hissing. Glass was smashing everywhere. Huge pieces of metal flew through the air, then clattered to the road. The boulders made the sounds echo, redoubling on themselves until the noise was deafening. The radiator was pierced, and steam spewed from the car.

Jed was crushed to the ground, the sounds of destruction echoing all around him. He had covered his head with his hands, and his eyes were closed. But nothing could block out the sounds.

The shooting stopped a moment later. And only the echoes remained, dimming and softening until they, too, disappeared and it was silent.

Jed remained where he was. He was trembling from deep inside. He couldn't move. He just lay there, crushed to the pavement, his eyes closed, looking into darkness. Then all at once he felt something touch him, and a scream tore from his lips.

"Hey, relax. It's me." David's voice held the beginnings of a laugh.

Jed opened his eyes and saw David leaning over him, holding out his hand to help him up. Jed ignored it and pulled himself from the ground. There was something repulsive about David's hand. As if David alone bore the taint of the killer.

Jed turned back to Beal's car. Glittering glass and pieces of metal were all over the road, glinting strangely in the morning half-light. He could just barely make out the top of Beal's head, slumped against the steering wheel, and a shiver tore through him.

"We'd better check to make sure," David said.

Jed didn't answer. He was breathing deeply, trying to regain the purpose and sureness that he'd felt so strongly before. "It was necessary," he said softly. Then, aware that David was watching him, he turned and nodded. "Let's go."

Sunlight was sparkling all around the car. Even Beal's slumped head was covered with pieces of sparkling glass. Jed forced himself to look. There was no blood as Jed had feared. Nor was there any movement. Everything seemed unreal in the bright, glittering light, and he felt relieved and, once again, justified.

As they neared the car, there was a shifting in the bluffs. But neither of them saw it. Their eyes were on the shattered car. There was something wrong. As they closed in on the car, Beal's head faded and dimmed. There was an eerie glittering. Slowly they began to realize that they weren't seeing Beal's head at all. Just a shattered screen with a three-dimensional image of Beal encased in it.

A rifle thrust forward. Still Jed and David looked at the smashed Plexiglas screen, confused and uncertain.

A quick rustle. Then the shadow of Beal, standing, rifle up and aimed. There was a sudden angry yell.

Jed and David jerked back, their heads moving up the bluffs to Beal, who stood above.

"You see, Jed. Now you know how I did it."

But already Beal was pulling the trigger. Bullets tore through the air, brutal, fast, spitting outward.

First David. Then Jed. Mouths open, eyes staring in disbelief, the ultimate surprise, death. And then another bullet. And another. And they were just two senseless, dancing lumps of flesh and broken bone.

Chapter Forty-nine

Berger glanced at his watch. It was 7:45. It must have been close to 100 degrees behind the false wall, and Berger could feel the sweat trickling down his armpits. His fingers felt swollen and slippery, and once again he rubbed his hands against his shirt to dry them. He should have brought a rag or rosin. It was a stupid mistake, and Berger cursed himself silently.

On the other side of the wall he could hear the cheering and shouting of the convention. It had been going on for close to ten minutes now. And though he couldn't see much through the break in the false wall, he'd seen enough convention coverage on television to know what was going on. Undoubtedly the President and Vice President had arrived, and all the leisure-suited farmers were going nuts with intense devotion.

Again Berger looked at his watch. It was 7:55. Slowly he raised the assault rifle to the break in the false wall. When the rifle was even with the break, he inched the barrel forward until it was resting lightly on the wall. Then he looked through the sight. There was a man sitting in the chair just left of the podium now. And he'd been right. It was the speaker of the House.

Berger shifted the gun, aiming carefully; then he stopped. He'd been in place for over eight hours now, and his body felt numb and far away. It was an act of will to get anything to work anymore. Still, he flexed his fingers ten times, forcing the stiffness out, then fixed his eyes on the five-foot-nine 150-pound target sitting on the dais.

Berger's mind shifted to the blond man. Berger had spent close to four hours trying to draw him out, slipping into buildings and waiting, changing directions abruptly, but every time he turned around he'd seen nothing. Though Berger had never been the kind of man who had attacks of nerves, he was beginning to believe his fear of being followed was just that. He wasn't sure whether that made him feel better or worse.

At exactly 7:59 Berger began the countdown. The cheering and shouting were beginning to calm down, but Berger was no longer listening. In his mind there was a stopwatch, ticking off the seconds. His muscles tensed, alert, ready. His eyes zeroed in on the target.

The man on the dais was scratching his knee and looking around as if he were very bored. The seconds ticked slowly, hushed, full of potential.

Berger's toes tightened; his mouth stretched, tight, eager. He counted down from ten; then suddenly his finger was moving, pulling back, steady and sure.

EPILOGUE

It was raining. Los Angeleans, spoiled by their eternal summer, fussed and muttered to themselves, cursing damp shoes, wet-smelling clothes, and frizzy hair.

Beal drove through the wet sullen streets nervously. It had been almost a week since the incident on Highway 1. In that week he'd done little more than eat and sleep and try not to think. He'd gained back some weight, and in his dark suit and tie he looked handsome again. But his eyes hadn't changed much; the haunted agony was still there.

Maggie was the same. Though the cuts and bruises on her face had receded and she looked beautiful once more, she still lay in the hospital, cold and distant, as if existing in another world. The doctors had said there was little hope. And Beal knew enough to believe them.

Beal glanced around at Mike and Sheila in the back seat. They were sitting close to one another, Sheila's hand planted firmly on Mike's knee. An act of owner-ship that Mike didn't protest. Beal supposed it was the close brush with mortality that had changed things for them. He supposed it had changed things for a lot of people.

The repercussions of the week before had been startling. The three most important leaders in govern-ment were dead, all by assassination, all at the Detroit convention. The assassins had not been caught. But a luxury yacht on the Detroit River had gone up in flames less than an hour later, and it was believed there might be a connection.

Within minutes of the assassinations, the president pro tem of the Senate, E. Bud Fuller, had been sworn in, and contrary to expectations, he had not called a state of emergency.

Almost immediately President Fuller had announced that he would not serve beyond the late President's term. And the next day, in a surprise move, Represen-tative Paisley, Justice Keiler, and General Nadler all resigned. Beal supposed Fuller had applied pressure, probably even threatened blackmail. But ultimately Beal just didn't care.

Beal pulled off the freeway and onto a treelined street. The rain was slowing, and the sweet smell of green lawns and fresh air was carried into the car in damp, soft gusts.

What happened to the rest of them, Beal didn't know. He supposed the lines at the local unemployment office must have swelled as all the out-of-work spooks hit the pavement, looking for new jobs.

Surprisingly enough all the upheaval in the govern-ment seemed to have a calming effect on the country.

People were scared, and at least for the moment they seemed to realize they needed one another.

In the end Beal didn't care about that either. There was nothing he cared about anymore. There was an emptiness inside him, a deep wide blackness, devoid of love, hope, joy, peace, kindness, humanity. The void was only occasionally broken, and that was by sharp, painful flashes—memories of Maggie. He doubted he could go on much longer.

Jason was wearing a suit. He stood at the curb of his house, his face was confused, and just under the surface there was terror. His mother's friend, Bernice, was holding his hand. Perhaps to comfort him. Perhaps to keep him from running away.

Bernice had tried to explain to Jason that his mother was very sick and might be ill for a long time, but he hadn't seemed to understand. Every day Jason pretended that Maggie was coming back, steadfastly, stubbornly, with the hopefulness of a child. Bernice said he was beginning to make her believe it, too.

Beal drew up to the frame house and stopped. He didn't turn off the motor or open the door; he just sat in the car, looking at the little boy standing only a few feet away.

Jason, too, didn't move. He was frozen, wary, and afraid, watching Beal like a threatened animal.

The sight of Jason standing there, so confused and scared, tore through Beal. He was like a haunting memory, aching with echoes of Maggie and himself. Just looking at him made everything come rolling back on Beal in great agonizing waves, and all he knew was he wanted to run. He couldn't bear looking at Jason.

Jason made him feel again. And Beal didn't want to feel anything ever again.

Still, Beal didn't move. He just sat in the car, trying to keep his eyes from the little boy. Then suddenly Beal turned away. Savagely he smashed his fist against the dashboard of the car. Electric pain shot through his hand, and he cried out from it. But still, the image of the little boy was there, sharp and painful in his mind. And Beal knew that it would never leave him.

He waited for a moment longer, then turned off the motor and climbed out of the car. Slowly he reached out his hand.

Jason hesitated. Fear and hope, love and despair all vying inside him, making everything crazy and fast and very scary. He watched Beal for a long while, his body alert and ready to run. Then suddenly everything relaxed. Jason reached out and took Beal's hand.

And somewhere in the dim corridors of Maggie's mind, something stirred.